FATHER'S SUN
THE NORTHWOMEN SAGAS

SUSAN FANETTI

THE FREAK CIRCLE PRESS

Father's Sun © 2017 Susan Fanetti
All rights reserved

This is a work of fiction. Names, characters, places, and incidents are a product of the author's imagination. Any resemblance to actual persons, living or dead, events, or locales are entirely coincidental.

ISBN-13: 978-1546742067

ISBN-10: 1546742069

ALSO BY SUSAN FANETTI

The Northwomen Sagas
God's Eye
Heart's Ease
Soul's Fire

The Brazen Bulls MC
Crash, Book 1
Twist, Book 2

THE NIGHT HORDE MC SAGA

The Signal Bend Series
Move the Sun, Book 1
Behold the Stars, Book 2
Into the Storm, Book 3
Alone on Earth, Book 4
In Dark Woods, Book 4.5
All the Sky, Book 5
Show the Fire, Book 6
Leave a Trail, Book 7

The Night Horde SoCal
Strength & Courage, Book 1
Shadow & Soul, Book 2
Today & Tomorrow, Book 2.5
Fire & Dark, Book 3
Dream & Dare, Book 3.5
Knife & Flesh, Book 4
Rest & Trust, Book 5
Calm & Storm, Book 6

Nolan: Return to Signal Bend
Love & Friendship

The Pagano Family
Footsteps, Book 1
Touch, Book 2
Rooted, Book 3
Deep, Book 4
Prayer, Book 5
Miracle, Book 6

The Pagano Family: The Complete Series

PRONUNCIATIONS AND DEFINITIONS

To build this world, I did a great deal of research, and I mean to be respectful of the historical reality of the Norse cultures. But I have also allowed myself some creative license to draw from the full body of Norse history, culture, and geography in order to enrich my fictional representation. True Viking culture was not monolithic but instead a various collection of largely similar but often distinct languages, traditions, and practices. In The Northwomen Sagas, however, I have merged the cultural touchstones.

My characters have names drawn from that full body of history and tradition. Otherwise, I use Norse words sparingly and use the Anglicized spelling and pronunciation where I can. Below is a list of some of the Norse names and terms used in this story, with pronunciations and/or definitions provided as I thought might be helpful.

NAMES:
- Åke (*AW-kyuh*)
- Bjarke (*BYAR-kyuh*)
- Håkon (*HAW-kun*)
- Leif (*LAFE*)
- Solveig (*SOL-vay*)
- Vali (*VAH-lee*)
- Ylva (*IL-vah*)

TERMS:
- Æsir—(*ICE-eer*) the pantheon of Norse gods.
- Ångermanälven—(*OHWNG-yer-mahn-AY-lev-en*) a river in mid-Sweden.
- Bifröst—(*BEE-froost*) the rainbow bridge leading from Midgard (Earth) to Asgard in Norse mythology.
- Hangerock—an apron-like overdress worn by Viking women.

- Húsvættir—(*HOOS-vai-tir*) nature spirits who kept the household, like the English "brownie." Singular: húsvættr.
- Jötunn—(*YOH-tun*) one of a race of giants.
- Norðrljós—(*NOR-dhee-ohs*) the Northern Lights.
- Sjaund—(*SHOUNd*) a funeral feast, after which the deceased's heirs claim their legacy.
- Skald—a poet or storyteller.
- Skause—a meat stew, made variously, depending on available ingredients.
- Skeid—(*SHIED*) the largest Viking ship, with more than thirty rowing benches.
- Thing—the English spelling and pronunciation of the Norse *þing*. An assembly of freemen for political and social business.
- Úlfhéðnar (*OOLF-hyeh-nar*)—a special class of berserkers who took the wolf as their symbol. They were known to be especially ferocious and in some sagas are identified as Odin's elite warriors. Singular: Úlfhéðinn.

In memory of my father.

PROLOGUE
DAUGHTER

THE GIRL SHE WAS

Six Years

As the ships sailed into the harbor, Solveig ran to the fore of the crowd and pushed in between her grandmother and Håkon, her brother.

"Usch, child," her grandmother said, combing back a loose blonde tress and tucking it into Solveig's braid. "Always you are elsewhere than you should be. And where was that this time?"

"Helga's cat had kittens!" She loved kittens. And puppies. And goatlings. And all baby animals. But kittens best of all.

Her grandmother shook her head. "And are kittens such a rare thing that you would miss the return of your father and mother from their great raid? Two of your mother's cats littered while they were away. We are overrun with kittens."

"Dagmar. Something's amiss." Bjarke, at her grandmother's opposite side, spoke, his voice low and dark, like night thunder. There was such foreboding in his tone that even Solveig understood it—even Håkon, more than a year younger, seemed to understand it; his hand grasped Solveig's and squeezed.

She looked out at the nearing longships, which had come close enough to drop their sails and go to oar, and tried to see what Bjarke could see. Their mother and father had been gone for a long time, Solveig thought, but not too long;

summer was still warm and bright. They had gone off to raid in a faraway place called Anglia.

Her father was the Jarl of Karlsa. He'd left Bjarke, his good friend, in charge of Karlsa, and their mother had left her mother in charge of their children.

Their father raided every year, sometimes more than once, but this was the first time in Solveig's life that their mother had gone as well. She was Brenna God's-Eye, a great shieldmaiden, and the skalds told many stories about her— and about Solveig's father, Vali Storm-Wolf, as well. Both were legends.

But to Solveig, they were simply her mother and her father. She missed them when they were away, and she was glad they were back. But something was wrong. She didn't understand what it was, except that usually when the raiders came home, everyone was loud and happy. They had been that way when she'd run from Helga's house to wait at the pier. But now everyone was quiet. There was a low mumble rolling through the gathered crowd; she tried to open her ears wide and hear what people were saying. Behind her, two women spoke, and she turned her head so she could focus her ears on them.

"Where is he?"

"He always stands at the prow, but I don't see him. Where is *she?*"

"Would the gods take them both at once?"

"That is how it should be, the two lovers hand in hand, though I hope not yet. They are too young. Their children—"

"Öhm! Enough!" Solveig's grandmother wheeled on the women, whose mouths snapped shut, and then turned to Solveig and forced her head forward again. "Pay them no mind, child." Her hand shook against Solveig's cheek, like she was chilled. Or frightened.

Solveig didn't know who they'd been talking about. So she did what her grandmother said and stopped thinking about them. She looked for her mother and father on the ships. Her father was usually standing up front, just behind the dragon's head, when he came home, but there was no one there this time.

The people on the ships were quiet, too. Usually, people on the shore called out to the raiders, and the raiders called back. Usually, there was much more noise.

Solveig began to understand that the wrong thing was about her father, who was not standing where he should be. Raiders were warriors, going off to fight for and win treasure and honor and glory, and to have their stories told in the sagas. Many, many times, she had watched her mother and father and all the other warriors in Karlsa practice fighting, with swords and axes and spears and shields, so they could make war on the weak people of other worlds.

She couldn't see her father or her mother. The ships were pulling up to the piers now, and she couldn't see them at all. She let go of her grandmother's hand, and her brother's hand, and she walked forward.

"Solveig!" her grandmother called, but she moved forward, drawn by a terrible curiosity.

Her mother was there; she had been sitting, and now she made her way to her feet. Solveig saw her fair hair in braids she knew, and, relieved, she broke into a run just as men jumped out to tie up the first ship.

Her mother's arm and neck were wrapped up in dirty bandages, her arm bound to her side and across her middle. She'd gotten hurt in the raid. She had many scars, but Solveig had never seen her hurt before.

"Mamma!"

Her mother looked up. Weary anger had pulled her face tight, and Solveig felt real fear, though she didn't understand yet why.

Solveig's grandmother reached her just then and clamped her hand around her wrist, keeping her in place. As she drew Solveig into a stifling hold, she called down to the ship. "Brenna. Daughter, are you well? What do you need?"

Her mother gave her a small, tired smile, but she didn't come out of the ship. She turned and looked down again, and Solveig finally saw what was really wrong. Not her mother in bandages.

Her father, her mighty father, bound to a litter, being lifted out of the ship by six men, carried up to the pier. He wasn't moving. His eyes were closed. His chest was bare except for bloody, dirty bandages. His skin was shiny and grey.

A strange *whoosh* went through the crowd as the men carrying him climbed onto the pier, and the people on the shore saw the litter. And then all sound seemed to die.

Solveig stood in the silence and watched the men carry her father toward the great hall. Her belly felt funny, like something small and frail inside her had curled up at the bottom and died.

"Come, daughter."

She felt her mother's hand on her head, and she looked up into the beautiful face she loved above all others but one. "Did Pappa go to Valhalla?"

The weariness in her mother's eyes twisted into something like hurt, but then she smiled and brushed an errant lock of hair from Solveig's eyes. "No, Solveig. He is the mightiest of men, and he lives. It is up to Frida and the gods to make him well now. Hello, Håkon. I have missed you all so very much."

She patted Solveig's brother on the head, then bent down and lifted little Ylva, the youngest of them, into her unhurt arm. To her mother, she said, "We need Frida, Mother. There is so much fever, and he hasn't woken for days."

"She was at the pier, waiting for Jaan. She is already in the hall."

Solveig's mother nodded and headed up the berm toward the hall, Ylva in her arms. Her grandmother and brother went after them. Solveig stood and stared at the emptying ship. Everyone had been happy when they'd sailed away. Everyone in Karlsa had been happy when they'd seen the ships on the horizon. Now everyone was sad.

Her father was the Storm-Wolf. The stories said that he'd fought Ægir, the lord of the sea, and won. He'd challenged Thor himself to combat and remained standing. He'd been split in twain in battle and put his parts back together to fight on.

He denied all these things, said they were stories, not truths, but Solveig believed them all. Never had she known her father even to be ill. He was big and strong and fierce. He was kind and warm. He was the mightiest of men, and her mother was the mightiest of women. Everyone agreed they were favored by the gods. How could they have been hurt?

She didn't understand. Her head filled with noise, like Thor's thunder, and her chest seemed to shrink and squeeze her heart.

"Solveig! Come!" Her grandmother stood with her hand stretched out, beckoning.

Solveig ran the other way.

Geitland was a much bigger place than Karlsa, and Solveig always felt smaller and less brave in the wild bustle of the town. On this visit especially, when they had grand guests from afar, her parents' good friend, Astrid, and her husband, Leofric. He was a prince, which made Astrid a princess. They would be King and Queen of Mercuria someday.

Mercuria. A kingdom of Anglia. Solveig remembered that her father had almost been killed in a raid on Mercuria, and her mother had been badly hurt. She remembered the grief of the failed raid; Karlsa had lost many warriors. They'd thought Astrid dead for a long time, too. She didn't remember many of the details, only enough to be confused by the celebration of their visit. They were friends, even after all that had been suffered and lost.

Her father and Jarl Leif of Geitland had once taken a massive fleet back to Mercuria to start a war and had returned instead allied with the people who'd almost taken her parents away.

She'd seen it many times in Karlsa's great hall. Her father wanted people to be friendly when their conflicts had been settled. He believed that there was greater strength in friendship than in war.

Her mother didn't always agree. Many times, Solveig had lain quietly in her bed, feigning sleep and listening to her parents talk out their own disagreements on matters of the hall. She listened because she wanted to understand. She was the daughter of the Storm-Wolf and the God's-Eye, her life was filled with great heroes of the sagas, people touched by the gods, and she wanted to know all she could of everything, so that when it was time, she could take her place among them.

"Their ship is so grand," Magni, said, stretching out on his belly beside her. "I want one like it when I grow up."

Solveig rolled her eyes. Magni was the only living son of Jarl Leif and his wife, Olga. He was almost a year younger than she and still a child with much to learn. He needed to listen better. "Our ships are much grander than his. His is too big and too deep and can sail only in open water. Our ships can go anywhere."

"But his has *rooms*. With *beds*."

"Comfort is for soft people, not warriors. It's why we're better than they are at everything. Where's Håkon?" She looked around; she was supposed to mind her brother, but he'd gotten bored with watching the hall, and she hadn't. She liked to listen in when the adults didn't know. She learned far more from the things they tried to keep from her than from the things they tried to teach her.

She'd heard him leave, but she hadn't thought long about it. Only they two had sailed with their parents for this visit. Ylva, Agnar, and little Tova had stayed home with their grandmother. Håkon was next oldest. He had eight years and was old enough to mind himself, even if their mother didn't think so.

"Gulla found him and sent him to bed. She's looking for us, too, but I went through the goat pen and she didn't see me."

"She'll not find us here." Solveig had discovered this gap under a grain bin, against a wall of the great hall, a few years earlier. She'd kept it a secret unto herself until Magni had demanded to know where she disappeared to so often. When he'd claimed that Geitland was his home, not hers, and it was wrong to keep secret places from him in his own home, she'd made him swear an unbreakable oath never to reveal it. They'd cut their thumbs and mingled blood.

And then, the very next summer, he'd let Håkon follow him, and she'd had to make her little brother swear on blood as well. Magni hadn't meant for Håkon to follow; he simply hadn't noticed—which was just as bad, and perhaps worse.

Boys were fools.

She wasn't sure how dolts like Magni and Håkon might someday grow into great men like their fathers. It seemed a tall mountain for them to climb. Nearly as tall as her climb to her mother's greatness.

Solveig appraised the boy beside her now. She knew, from listening, that his parents and hers wished them someday to be wed. Since she'd heard that, during their last visit to Geitland, she'd tried to imagine mating with Magni. She'd known him all her life, and she liked him well. He couldn't help that he was a boy and boys were fools.

He was pleasant to look at—as tall as she, though he was younger, with long blond hair and dark blue eyes like his father. For all that, he was not so bad. But she couldn't imagine doing with him the things men and women did together—the grunting and groaning and sweating.

Truthfully, she couldn't imagine doing those things with anyone. She turned from Magni and resumed her watching. It seemed strange and unpleasant, even though men and women all seemed to seek it out as much as they could. Her parents certainly did. In the great hall right now, most people had wandered back to their own homes, and those that remained—Astrid and her husband, Magni's parents, her own, a few others—had stopped talking amongst the group and started murmuring in mated pairs. While she watched through the gap under the wall, her father pulled her mother onto his lap and put his hand between her legs with a loud grunt like a bear.

She didn't want that. What she wanted was the other thing—the way her father looked at her mother across the hall, when her mother didn't know. Solveig didn't know what that look was, but it was…replete. And utterly bare. She wanted a boy

16

to look at her like that. Even if she never actually saw it directed at her, she wanted a boy to feel for her so deeply and truly that he looked at her that way when her back was turned.

Or the way her mother smiled when she heard Solveig's father laugh. That smile was akin with her father's secret look. It made Solveig's chest feel warm and full to see them both.

In those moments, not in their wild wrestling, Solveig saw her parents' love for each other. That was what she wanted. Someday. When she was worthy of such love.

"Usch," Magni groaned quietly beside her. "I don't want to watch that. Let's go to the water. I want to look at the ship."

"Why do you suppose they do it so much?" Solveig asked, ignoring his suggestion and his foolish obsession with the Mercurian ship.

"Erik says it's like when you scratch an itch. He says you can do it to yourself, too."

"Who's Erik?"

"He has twelve years," Magni answered, as if that were enough. She supposed it was. Twelve years was grown. Some boys got their arm rings and became men when they had twelve years. Sometimes, they took wives as well.

"Have you ever done it?"

He pulled a face and shook his head. "You?"

"No." She considered Magni again and wondered if they should try.

"Do you want to?" he asked before she had decided.

"Do you?"

His shoulders came nearly up to his ears. "Perhaps it's nice."

Solveig doubted that. But she nodded. "All right." She leaned toward him and pursed her lips.

Magni leaned toward her, and their lips touched.

He smelled pleasant, like wood fire and the goat pen. His lips were warm and dry, tense and puckered against hers. His breath, coming through his nose, tickled her cheek. It wasn't unpleasant. Or pleasant. Or really anything at all. Their blood vow had had more feeling than this.

Solveig didn't know what to do next, so she pulled back. She rubbed at her lips; they tingled.

Magni rubbed at his lips, too. "Can we go look at the ship now?"

Relieved that the experiment was over, and more sure than ever that whatever it was their parents liked so much about rutting, it wasn't for her, Solveig sighed and scooted back from the wall. "It's not as good as our ships. Let's go and I'll show you."

Thirteen Years

Solveig stared up at the sky, a cloudless canvas of brilliant blue, no variation in its color at all, from horizon to horizon. Below them, Karlsa was quiet. The revels after the raiders had departed had gone on long, and those who remained behind were slow to begin the next day.

Time changed when the raiders were gone, and not only when the people were weary and ill from drink. The pace of the town slowed to languor, and only essential business was conducted. Everyone seemed to hover, waiting.

For her part, since the time her father had come home strapped to a litter, Solveig had never been able to put worry from her mind when he sailed away. On that day, when she'd been only small, she'd lost the belief that he was strong as a god. He was only a man. A great man, the best man, but only a man, and he could be taken from her.

Her worry was greater when her mother stayed home, as this time she had. Her father told many stories about the times her mother had saved him. He said often that his wife was fully half of him. He needed her at his side. But Solveig's youngest sister, Hella, barely more than a babe, and small and frail, had taken ill, so her mother was in the hall tending her, and her father was alone in the wide world.

"When we are wed, will you live in Geitland, or will I live here?"

Solveig rolled her head on the soft grass on which they lay, at the edge of the Wood of Verðandi, and studied Magni's profile. His cheeks were yet smooth, but his face had changed since she'd last seen him. It had become more angular, more manly. He looked much like his father.

"Who says we're to be wed?" Honestly, everyone said it. Even she herself thought about it. It wasn't an unpleasant thought, and sometimes, she entertained it for quite a while. Sometimes, things inside her stirred and ached, and all she could think of was him.

He turned and met her eyes. His were a blue darker than her own, more like the sea than the sky. "Everyone. Do you say we won't?"

She shrugged and turned back to the sky. An eagle flew across the smooth blue and then dived, and she didn't need to lift her head and look over the cliff to know he'd plucked a fish from the water below. "I say that when we wed, and whom, and *if*, is not for anyone but ourselves."

His hand went over hers where it lay on the grass, and he squeezed. She felt his new arm ring, bestowed only weeks before, when he'd declared his loyalty to his father. She hated that twisting band of gold and silver, not for what it said about him, but for what the lack of such a thing said about her.

In Karlsa, as in Geitland, women were not given arm rings. They swore their fealty, and they fought alongside the men as equals, but they were not gifted a token of their allegiance. Solveig enjoyed trinkets and baubles, but it was not for its sparkle that she envied Magni his arm ring. She cared not to be excluded. Magni wore that arm ring, and now all he met would know he was a man and had been deemed a worthy one. Solveig would have to prove her worthiness every day.

She tried to pull her hand from his, but he held fast. He'd grown taller than she since they'd last seen each other as well, and stronger, too.

Magni shifted to his side, still holding her hand, and looked down at her. His long hair fell forward from his shoulders and shaded his face. Its ends brushed her neck. "I would wed you, Solveig. Not for our parents' wish. For my own."

That stirring she sometimes felt became a spasm, and her chest ached. But she wanted more than him. She had only just begun to train to fight, still with wooden swords. She wanted to find her honor and make her parents proud. When girls her age wed, they soon swelled with babes and spent their lives chasing children and chickens.

Her mother had wed much later, after she had made her name. Her father had been even older. She would wait for love until she had honor of her own.

"My mother and father are legends. I'm made from them. If I'm anything less than a legend myself, I diminish them. That's all that matters—I must do them honor. I'll wed no man until I have made my story and it shines with theirs."

Her voice trembled, and she cleared her throat to rid it of its weakness. She felt strangely exposed, and that made her feel defensive. She'd given something away just then, though she wasn't quite sure what.

His expression changed, and Solveig saw pity in it—and with that, she was sure that she'd exposed something raw and weak in herself. She yanked hard and freed her hand, pushing him away. She sat up and turned, making distance between them and facing him directly.

"If you share a word I've said with anyone, I'll kill you."

Magni put up his hands, as if warding off a blow. "I keep your secrets, Solveig. Always."

He did, but her vulnerability wasn't calmed. "Swear."

"I swear." He pulled his short blade from his belt. "I'll swear on blood, if you need it."

They'd made many such oaths, and both carried scars from most of them. Most had been childish vows, only requiring the solemnity of blood because they'd been too young to know any risk greater or to keep deeper secrets. But this one felt especially important, even if Solveig wasn't sure why. "Yes. Blood."

Without a blink, Magni drew the tip of the blade across his palm. She took the blade from him and made a cut on her own palm. The sting was mild and familiar. They clasped hands.

"I, Magni Leifsson"—his voice always deepened when he said words he thought important—"swear to you, Solveig

Valisdottir, never to speak the words we've spoken here on this day to any other soul, or to share their import with any other soul. On my blood, and on my honor."

"Swear on your arm ring, too," she added as an afterthought, studying the sunlit glint of his new trinket.

"I swear on my arm ring as well."

Satisfied, she tried to release his hand, but, again, he held on. "I will wait, Solveig. I would wed you, when you wish."

Fifteen Years

"Pick it up." Solveig's mother brought her sword up and held it before her, pointing it straight up to the gods.

It wasn't really her sword. Her true sword was a storied thing. She'd wielded it through many great raids and slain hundreds of men and women. She'd never named it, but everyone Solveig knew called it the God's-Eye Blade.

Her mother's eyes were unlike any other eyes in the world. They didn't match. One was blue, a paler shade than Solveig's, who had her father's eyes. The other, though, was every color in the world, and through it ran brown lines that made the image of a rooted tree. Yggdrasil, the world tree. People said that that eye was Odin's own, the one he'd sacrificed so that he might gain all the world's wisdom. Thus, she was known and revered all through their world as the God's-Eye.

She said that it was a story, not a truth, like all the stories about her, and the stories about Solveig's father as well. But Solveig listened hard everywhere she went. She watched and saw, too. And she thought deeply about the things that she heard and the things that she saw.

She thought that stories were truths, no matter how many facts they stretched. The story of a thing was what really mattered.

There was truth in the belief in them, and there was magic in the telling. She didn't know if her mother's marvelous right eye was Odin's very one. Neither did she know why it couldn't be. But she did know that her mother was a great warrior. Her mother wanted that awe and fear for herself, not for her eye, but Solveig thought that one was the same as the other. People knew her as a mighty shieldmaiden, and they also believed that her eye had its own power. However they came to it, the awe and admiration they felt for her were true.

The same was true for her father. He said that the great stories of him were really times when he'd been saved. He hadn't fought Ægir, but the jötunn had simply spat him out of the sea and saved him. He'd been badly hurt in battle, nearly split in twain—and he had a long, wide scar down his back to prove it—but he'd only fallen to the ground to fight no more that day, and he would have died right there had not Solveig's mother saved him. In grief for the loss of his firstborn child, her older brother, who'd died on the day of his birth, he'd challenged Thor to kill him, not to fight him, but Thor had had mercy and let him live.

She believed that her father's versions of events might be more factual, but not that they were any more true. People made their truth in the telling. What had happened wasn't as important as what was made of it.

They also said, now, that his heart had been run through with a spear but he had not fallen, and that his heart had pushed the spear out on its own. She knew the facts—she vividly remembered seeing him carried off the skeid in a litter, his soul only inches from the door of Valhalla. It was one of her most complete early memories. Most of the people who now told the story of his mighty heart had been there the day he'd been carried off the ship. Many had been present on the day he'd been wounded. They knew the facts and told the story anyway. The facts were different, but the story was true.

He'd been shot with three thick arrows. One had struck near his heart, and all of the wounds had putrefied before they'd gotten him home. He'd nearly died. Often, in the weeks that he lay insensible, they'd thought that he would.

But he'd survived and recovered completely, but for the new scars on his broad chest. And that was the real story. Again and again, Vali Storm-Wolf had taken injuries that would kill any mortal man, and again and again he'd recovered and reclaimed all of his strength. Those were facts of things that happened.

His heart *was* mighty enough to push a spear from its chambers. His body *was* strong enough to hold itself together. His will *was* powerful enough to take on the gods. That was the truth the stories told.

"Pick it up, daughter. We go again."

The God's-Eye Blade hung in its scabbard in the great hall, beside her mother's shield. But the dull iron of the practice sword her mother wielded now seemed legendary in her hands.

Solveig glared down at the hunk of iron her mother had knocked from her hands. A true blade awaited her, one that her father had given her mother upon their wedding. A day would come when she would be worthy to wield that gleaming thing. But not now. Now even worthless iron was more than she could hold. Her palms and fingers still ached and quaked with the force of her mother's strike. It took all her concentration not to allow herself to shake the pain away.

She was the daughter of legends, and she wanted nothing in the world so much as she wanted one thing: to be worthy of their truths.

Standing before her mother, pain singing through her hands, she didn't feel worthy of anything.

"Pick it up, my sun." Her father's shadow fell over her and the dull blade she had not yet recovered. He must have come from the hall to watch her humiliation.

She did as he'd said. When she stood straight and wrapped her hand around the hilt of the practice sword, he stepped behind her and put his arms around her, closing her sword hand in his, and gripping the elbow of her shield arm. His weapons were axes, not a sword, and he didn't fight with either shield or armor, but he knew well how to wield all the tools of the warrior. He was a berserker of the Úlfhéðnar— the fiercest and boldest of all warriors.

Seeing her father's intent, her mother relaxed her stance and let her dull sword point downward.

In her father's arms, dwarfed by his body, Solveig felt stronger, like some of his storied might had moved into her through his touch.

"Always know the field around you. Front, back, and sides. Never expose your tender center. Protect yourself neck to thighs. Keep your shield facing your opponent, always, and brace it well"—he lifted her shield arm and set it where he wanted it, pushing her shoulder down and in—"and use your blade from the side. You cannot be disarmed if your blade is not where his blade is. Step to the side and push in." He moved her body sideways and then forward, bringing her sword arm down and across to slash the air. Three more times, he made the same move.

Above her head, she felt him nod, and then her mother lifted the sword again and brought her shield up as well. Her mother attacked, and her father moved Solveig's arm so that her shield took the blow. He pushed her inward, moving her sword arm, and she connected with her mother's body for the first time, slashing with her harmless blade across her mother's midsection.

Her mother smiled, her magical eyes landing first on Solveig and then lifting to linger on her father. Moving like water, her mother stepped back and came in again, and Solveig's father helped her block the blow.

It was all slow and graceful, like a dance rather than a fight, but Solveig better understood what she was supposed to see and feel and do.

She relaxed and enjoyed the dance, letting her parents, the Storm-Wolf and the God's-Eye, show her the steps of love and war, and she felt, for the first time, that she might someday be a shieldmaiden worthy of her lineage.

PART ONE

SEEKER

1

Solveig shrieked and leapt forward, over the body of the Frankish soldier who'd just fallen to her sword. The ground all around her was littered with bodies. The liquid heat that always filled her joints and muscles in a fight throbbed and surged. Her mother described the feeling as bloodlust. Battle rage.

Power.

The Franks wore shiny suits of armor from head to toe, so that they scarcely looked like men. It was difficult to strike a killing blow on such a metal man, one had to aim one's strikes precisely, but the same metal that protected them made them slow and blind. In her three years of raiding, Solveig had learned well how to exploit the faults of armor until she could find her chance to aim her sword for its joints and gaps.

Some of her fellows had taken to wearing some form of the armor themselves. It was made of links, called mail, and the smiths of Geitland had crafted it so that it didn't encumber quite so much. Solveig preferred the freedom of boiled leather, but her mother wore mail now, on her father's insistence. She had taken a blade to the stomach the year before and nearly died.

Solveig had five siblings, three of whom were yet young enough to need their mother, so now their mother wore mail.

The oldest of her siblings, Håkon and Ylva, fought with Solveig and their parents here in Frankia.

"SHIELD WALL!"

Awash in battle rage, Solveig heard her father's shout as if at a great distance—too great a distance to be understood. She sought out another fight, but none was close by. All the soldiers were dead.

"Solveig! Now! To me, my sun!"

At her father's use of the endearment, she spun toward him and saw another wave of Franks rattling across the field at them, and her memory finally heard the call for a shield wall. Hurtling over the bodies of the fallen, she went to her father. Her mother, brother, and sister, and Magni, and all the raiders ran toward her father and Leif.

They all knew what to do and were ready and in position when Leif echoed her father and shouted, "SHIELD WALL!" All their shields went up, closing the raiders into a massive oaken barrier. Unshielded berserkers, like her father, took position, ready to leap out.

As the force of Franks neared, their armored feet rattling the earth, Solveig's father shouted "BRACE!" and, as one, the raiders pushed their feet into the ground and their shoulders to their shields and stood ready to resist the impact.

The soldiers seemed nearly to bounce back against the united strength of shields and will, but they pressed again, their metal shields against the locked oak of the raiders. Solveig's father leapt up from the center with a great roar and cut down soldiers who tried to go over the top. His axes swung in massive arcs and made blood rain over the raiders.

When the pressure against the shield wall took all their power to resist, Leif yelled, "OPEN!" and they let a break form at the center. Soldiers fell into the midst of the raiders, pushed to their doom by the crush of their own people. When Leif yelled "CLOSE!" and the wall sealed up, those trapped among them had no chance at all of fighting. Solveig drove her sword up, under a mail shirt, and watched the man's shock when he understood that a woman had killed him.

Always, the Christian soldiers attacked like this, in their shiny armor, all alike, in rows and lines and orderly waves, and always, the raiders cut them down. Solveig had heard the stories of the failed raid, the one that had scarred both her parents and nearly taken her father to Valhalla, the one that had ended, eventually, in their continuing alliance with the Anglian kingdom of Mercuria, and she had heard many times that the Mercurian soldiers had fought differently, more like raiders.

But she had only raided in Frankia, and these soldiers always lined up in pretty rows to die. She had never known a failed raid.

The soldiers began to flank the shield wall, and the pile of bodies in their midst was taking up too much room to maintain the brace, so Solveig wasn't surprised to hear her father shout "RELEASE!" and break the wall. She was glad; a shield wall was effective, but there was no dance in that fight. She preferred to be free to move as she would and find the fight she wanted.

She did so now, ducking the blade of a soldier and slashing her sword under his arm. It wasn't a killing blow, but it disabled his weapon arm, so that she could aim her next blow to end him.

A roar at her side caught her attention, and Magni was there, slashing her soldier across the face and then across his hips, disemboweling him. He stood as his insides cascaded in a heap onto the ground, and then he folded to his knees, and then fell on his face at Solveig's feet.

"That kill was mine!"

Magni grinned and shook his head, and Solveig might have bashed him with her shield if another soldier hadn't charged them right then. She shoved Magni out of the way and rammed forward, knocking the soldier back with her shield before he could swing his sword true. He stumbled and tripped over his heavy, metal-shod feet, landing in the bloody mud. Lest Magni steal this kill as well, Solveig drove her sword into the Frank's face.

She freed her blade and wheeled on Leif's son with a growl. "Find your own Franks!"

Magni laughed. "A dead Frank is a dead Frank. It need not always be a competition."

Solveig opened her mouth to retort that *he* was the one who always made it so, but her first words were drowned out by her mother's battle cry, and they both turned toward the sound as the God's-Eye cleaved the head from a soldier whose sword was mid-swing, aimed at Solveig. He'd been coming up on her back, and neither she nor Magni had noticed.

The man's helmeted head struck Solveig in the chest with such force that she coughed out half her body's air.

Solveig's mother turned her legendary stare on her and Magni both. "Enough! Now is not the time for squabbling!"

She turned abruptly, seeking more fight, but right then a shout went up among the Franks, and there was an odd moment of broken rhythm. Soldiers who could do so began to run, and Solveig understood that a retreat had been called.

The raiders lowered their weapons and let them run; neither Leif Olavsson nor Vali Storm-Wolf led raiders who killed for the sake of it. There was no honor in killing a fleeing man. They stood and watched the retreat.

One soldier, as he ran, thought to take a last raider on the way and bellowed as he attacked Magni. Magni threw up his shield to block the blow aimed at his head. The soldier's high aim exposed most of his middle, and Magni jabbed. A raider's sword was forged to slash rather than stab, but with enough force, it could run a man through and end him. Solveig had done as much when she'd driven her blade into a soldier's cheek; now, Magni's sword went through the gap of armor at this man's side. His blade went in through his ribs and, if Solveig might guess, sliced his heart open.

He hung on the sword, gasping and shocked, blood running from his mouth as well as down the blade of the sword, both at a rush. Magni knocked the soldier's helmet off and grabbed his face, holding the dying man with one hand as he freed his sword. He let go, and the final Frank collapsed to the sloppy ground, dead.

Håkon ran up, grinning and dripping blood from head to toe. His cheek flapped loosely, which was clearly the cause of some, but hardly all, of the blood. Their mother dropped her shield and grabbed him by the neck. "Let me see."

Solvieg's brother squirmed and pushed her back. "It's not so bad. Are we pushing on? There must be a village!"

Leif and their father came up to their cluster. Their father grabbed Håkon's chin in his meaty hand and gave his cheek an appraising look. "Go to the healer."

"But Father, the village!"

"No." It was Leif who answered. "We are deep up the river now. There is a city not far. Christian cities mean rich men. Perhaps the Frankish king. We will wait and see what they do."

"Where is Ylva?" Solveig's mother asked. "Vali—was she not near you?"

Solveig's father nodded. "She fought well. But she was not at my side when the retreat was called."

Ylva was their third child; she had sixteen years, and this was her first raid. Everyone in the cluster turned in different directions to scan the battlefield.

"YLVA!" they all shouted. The other raiders heard the call and began to seek and call as well.

If she was on the battlefield, and if she had been capable of calling back, she would have. But she did not.

The search grew more frantic. Those who were capable, and not helping other wounded raiders, turned over every body, seeking the jarl's daughter.

It was the shield Solveig saw first, lying on the ground at the edge of a pile of bodies.

All of Karlsa's raiders carried the shield of Vali Storm-Wolf: a red eye on a blue field. Ylva's shield was no different from the others—except that it had been brand new and unblemished as she'd set out on her first raid, and she was the only novice among them. The wood had been smooth and the colors rich, not yet exposed to blade or blood or stormy seas.

It was spattered with blood now and scattered with the dents these soldiers' swords made, but its colors were yet fresh and rich. Solveig grabbed it and found that it was still attached to her sister's hand, sticking from the bottom of the pile of the dead.

"HERE!" she yelled and dropped to her knees. "SHE IS HERE!" She tried to shove at the bodies crushing her sister, but her leverage was wrong, and the ground was soft with the leavings of death, and she could do little more than shake them.

Then her father was there, looming over her, He threw the bodies away like so much driftwood, roaring as he let each one fly.

Ylva lay at the bottom of the pile, her boiled leather chestpiece—modeled, like Solveig's, after that which her mother had long worn, in a heavily patterned weave—cut open across the front. Her insides glistened, red, and wet. And moving. She was alive. But Solveig could tell from the stench that rose up from her sister, overpowering even on that field of death and dismemberment, that Ylva could hardly live much longer. Too much of her had been cut open.

But she, too, was the daughter of legends. Their father's story said that he could not be killed. Perhaps the same was true for his children.

Their father went to his knees at Ylva's head. He lifted it gently and laid it on his thighs, and her eyes fluttered and opened.

"Pappa?" She had not called their father by that name for years. It was a child's word, and Ylva had not wanted to be a child since Agnar had been born after her. She'd hated being third in line, always lagging behind her older sister and brother, never able to do all they could do, and she'd hated being set aside for Agnar, Tova, and Hella, younger and needier than she.

But the tiny voice that had made the child's word had no more strength than that of a dying infant.

"I am here, little wolf. I am here. Be at ease."

Their mother landed on her knees beside Solveig and shouldered her out of the way as she picked up Ylva's hand. "We must get her to the healer!"

"Brenna." Their father's voice rasped with grief, and he nodded toward the chasm that had opened in their daughter's

35

chest. The purplish pink of her lungs showed inside their bone cage, fluttering with each stunted breath, and the wet rope of her entrails swelled from the wound and spilled their contents. "Look. There is noth—"

"There is! There must be! She is a daughter of the Storm-Wolf!"

More than the horror of Ylva's wound, it was that, their mother's naked fear and grief, that made Solveig sure her sister would die. Brenna God's-Eye was a warm and loving mother, but her love was fierce. She had no patience, even in the children she loved so dearly, for weakness of any kind. Not for fear, or self-doubt, or surrender. Solveig had never seen her mother afraid before, but she was terrified now.

"Will I…Valhalla?" Ylva asked in that tiny, leaving voice.

"No! It is not your time! Your story has not yet been made!"

"Brenna!" their father barked, and their mother went silent. He bent low, and his greying braid, as long as his whole back and as thick as Solveig's forearm, fell over his naked shoulder. He kissed Ylva's brow, brushing his grey beard back and forth over her face, as he had often done when they were small, to make them giggle. Ylva's pale lips turned up in a ghostly smile.

"You are the God's-Eye's daughter and a shieldmaiden in your own right. You fought like your mother today, and the Valkyries stand here, waiting to honor you. You will be in Valhalla with the gods, and with your grandmother, the great Dagmar Wildheart, and with your grandfather, Gunnar Redbeard. And you will meet Thorvaldr, your eldest brother, loved so well by the gods that they took him at his first breath. You will feast and fight and love and play, and we will join you when we may. You are loved in every world, Ylva. My little wolf."

Ylva's eyes closed, and her chest lifted, her lungs shuddering as they filled with bloody air. When the breath came out again, it was loud and wet and rough. A death rale.

She took two more breaths just alike, and then no others.

"No!" the great Brenna God's-Eye screamed. "No!" She snatched Ylva from their father and clutched her to her chest. "No! Vali, no!"

Vali Storm-Wolf pulled his wife and their dead child into his arms.

Solveig knelt where she was, her heart racing and her mind a great riot of senseless noise, churning toward a crescendo. And then, when she thought she might scream, it all stopped. Every part of her went silent. She was as numb as if she, too, had died.

A heavy hand squeezed her shoulder, and she turned, her neck seeming to creak like a rusty wheel. Magni crouched beside her. He, too, like them all, wore the blood of his enemies across his face, in his hair, on his hands, but his expression was gentle. In his dark blue eyes, she saw the sorrow she should have had in her own heart.

She wanted to feel it; she *needed* to feel it. She loved her sister. But it wouldn't come. No feeling at all would come. Inside, she was cold and empty.

Above them, Hâkon stood at Leif's side, making a long shadow over the scene. "Mother, Father," he said. Their father looked up, and so did Solveig. "Look."

He tipped his head to the side, and they turned their attention to the scatter of bodies their father had pulled from Ylva. They were all Frankish soldiers. Ylva's short axe was still embedded in one's skull, and her sword was buried in the side of another man, whose mail had broken away.

"She killed at least those two. I think she killed them all."

Their father studied the scene. Their mother looked up, her face soaked in salty tears, and did the same. Then she nodded, once, and turned to her husband.

"Yes," their father said. "She killed them all even as she was rent open. She was a great shieldmaiden, if only for this brief time."

Ylva had been buried under four men. Solveig didn't know how she could have killed all four and still have been buried under them. But it didn't matter. The facts were unimportant.

The truth was in the story, and Håkon had just made the first telling.

Solveig turned to her father and waited to catch his attention. "Ylva Little Wolf."

Their father had a special endearment for each of his children. Solveig, born on the summer solstice, with the mark of the sun on her shoulder, was his sun. Håkon was his bear, though it was not a name he'd often used since Håkon had been a man grown.

Ylva had been his little wolf.

He smiled sadly and looked down at his dead daughter's body, clutched in her mother's arms. Her fair hair was dyed red with the blood of war. "Yes. Ylva Little Wolf."

~oOo~

The sun rested on the western horizon before Solveig's father—Ylva's father—collected his second daughter from their mother and stood. He was the first among them to move, and they all sheathed their weapons, hung their shields on their backs, and followed him toward the site they'd marked for their camp.

Raiders had already begun to stake the camp, setting the spear fence and the frames of their tents. Women were at work on fire and food. A cluster of wounded waited at the healer's tent, which had, as always, gone up first. Some men were gathering the bodies of their dead—only a few besides Ylva. They would bury them here, where the Valkyries had claimed them, and lay their swords and shields and axes with them.

Their swords and axes. Solveig turned back, remembering her sister's weapons, but saw Håkon walking behind her, cradling them both in his arms. He had not forgotten.

Her turning made her realize that Magni had hold of her, his hand wrapped around her arm, just above the elbow. Staring down at his hand, she drew on her arm, but he held fast.

She lifted her regard to his face and found him watching her with those sad eyes.

"You need not hold me. My legs are steady."

"I know."

"Then let go."

As he did so, a smile played at his cheeks. There was something in his expression she thought she should understand, something she didn't think she liked, but her head and heart were busy seeking sorrow for her sister's death and couldn't be bothered to wonder about Magni Leifsson's odd looks.

She looked away from him and saw that all of the raiders had stopped their work to stand and watch Vali Storm-Wolf and Brenna God's-Eye bring their dead daughter into the camp. No other fallen raider had been accorded such attention.

And still, Solveig felt nothing.

Suddenly, everything around her seemed more than she could understand—her mother's ragged grief, her father's quiet sorrow, Magni's sad eyes, Håkon's stoic watchfulness. Even Leif's shocked silence seemed to press down on her.

She broke away from her family and ran toward the forest.

2

Magni watched Solveig go, running toward the trees as if Hel herself had ascended from below, climbing the skulls of the ignoble dead, to chase her down and carry her off.

She ran off alone, before there had been any parley with the Franks. The woods might hold any number of dangers.

He turned back to his father, and her parents, and her brother. No one else had noticed her departure; Vali and Brenna were wholly focused on the body of their younger daughter, and Magni's father and Håkon were wholly focused on Vali and Brenna.

The camp had come to a standstill as Vali carried Ylva's body in.

The thought that the Storm-Wolf and the God's-Eye might lose two daughters on this day, if Solveig found trouble in the woods, drove Magni to speak into the funereal quiet. "I'll go for Solveig."

Håkon shook his head. "She'll not thank you for it."

Her brother was right; when Solveig ran, she meant not to be followed. Magni knew her well—at least as well as Håkon or any of her blood kin. Probably better than her blood kin. He and she had been keeping each other's secrets all their lives; the faint scars of their many oaths crisscrossed their fingers and palms.

He knew the things she would tell no other, and he knew things she had told no one. He could see in her even those things she would not say. She was not quite a year older than he, their parents were the dearest of friends, and there had been no time in his life when Solveig had not, in turn, been his closest friend. Eight hundred miles separated their homes, but not even an inch separated their souls.

Once, she'd known that as well as he, but she'd forgotten it as she'd chased her parents' renown.

All her life Solveig had felt the burden of her parents' legacy. She was beloved of them and had never known doubt of it, but she feared always that she could not meet the challenge of their story. She was fierce like her mother and strong like her father, but inside her, a tempest stormed. The only fight from which she would ever run was the one that occurred inside her own mind and heart.

Magni's father considered the silent, still line of trees marking a wood growing gloomy in twilight. "Go for her. There will be no moon tonight. Bring her back to the circle of the camp."

With his father's approval, Magni threw his shield onto his back and ran after his friend.

~oOo~

By the time he found her, the sun had fully set, and twilight lowered into night. Though summer night was not deep dark here, it was far darker than home, and the woods were dense. Shadows had merged into near blackness. Only the torches at the camp offered any light—and precious little at that, since she had gone so far into the wood. All that faint glow offered was orientation.

He found her when she swung out from behind a tree and put a dagger to his chest.

He jumped back, out of range of her blade. "Hold! It's me!"

"You tromp through the woods like a boar." She sheathed her blade; in the dark, the movement was more of an impression than a certainty, but he heard the short slide of metal into leather.

"I wasn't trying for stealth. I was looking for you. Come back to the camp. We've had no parley yet with the Franks. It's not wise to be out so far on your own."

"It's too dark without the moon. They won't mount an attack tonight."

"That's what they said, remember, in Mercuria, the night that they burned the camp and took Astrid."

"I know the story. I was there when my parents returned and we thought my father would die."

"So you know that you're a fool to be out here on your own." He used the word to provoke her, and he succeeded.

She hit him in the chest with her open hands. "Never am I a fool."

He grabbed her hands and held on when she tried to pull free. "Solveig. You must come back. Don't give your kin more worry tonight."

Her arms relaxed, and she stopped trying to free herself. "I cannot."

Rather than ask why, Magni simply waited. She would explain.

A wide span of silence passed before she did. "Do you know the thought that is loudest in my head?"

The question wasn't meant to elicit an answer, he knew, so he continued to wait.

"My dead sister already has a greater story than I do."

This time, when she tried to break free, Magni let her go. She made her way in the dark as if she knew exactly where she was headed, so he followed the moving shadow that was her form.

He wasn't at all shocked, or even surprised, by her admission—he'd suspected something like it. When she sat, he made his way to the same place, discovered a large, flat rock, took his shield from his back, and sat beside her.

"Will you sit there like a shadow and say nothing?"

"What would you like me to say?"

Rather than answer his question, she said, "All I can think of is her story. She will be the great Ylva Little Wolf, who took down an army even after a soldier killed her, and I'm but a blank face in the background. I can't mourn. I'm empty inside of anything but envy. My heart is a stone." Magni felt her turn and face him. "And I will kill you if you speak of this."

He chuckled and found her hand in the dark. "You know I will not, even without the threat of doom." Turning his hand over so she could feel his palm, he added, "Would you have me swear on blood?"

She didn't answer, but she turned his hand over again and pushed her fingers between his. She needed no blood to know that he would keep her trust.

Solveig was made up of the greatness of her parents, and Magni was made up of the greatness of his. He was a capable

44

and brave warrior himself, but he knew his story wouldn't be made on the battlefield. His strength was in his seeing.

His parents were wise above all other traits. His father, Jarl Leif, was renowned as a leader in war and in peace. He was strong and brave in battle, and he was fair and thoughtful as a jarl. In both, he was a keen strategist. The sagas told of a man who led, in battle and in the great hall, with his heart first and his mind close behind.

His mother, Olga, wasn't physically strong at all. She was small of stature but mighty of heart. All Magni's life, the people of Karlsa had come to her for solace and understanding, and she had offered it freely, from her bottomless reserve of kindness and insight.

Magni had always felt their two great hearts beating inside his own. Their strengths gave him strength and made him feel right with his place in the world. Someday, he hoped Solveig would feel something alike and understand that her parents' legacy was a boon, not a curse. They had made her what she was, and she was magnificent.

For now, though, he knew his friend's turmoil, and he knew what would ease it. It was his time to speak.

"No one could doubt the love you bore your sister. No one would question it, no matter what your mind says now. Mourning will come when and how it will. And, Solveig, your story is only beginning."

"Brenna God's-Eye had fifteen years when she saved the jarl's children. Vali Storm-Wolf cut a man in half before his beard was full on his cheeks. I have nearly twenty years, Magni. What yet is there of me to tell?"

Magni wished he could see her clearly, so that she could see him, but he didn't need light to know the face before him. She was beautiful, with her mother's fair coloring and her father's intensely blue eyes. Blonde and blue-eyed was nothing remarkable among their people; dark or flame were more unusual, and yet Solveig's beauty was extraordinary. She was the tallest woman he knew, taller than her mother and only a few scant inches shorter than he, who had his father's height, and she had a visibly powerful body. But her features were delicate, almost elfin—a pointed chin, an elegant nose, and a mouth with lips just as plump and sweet as they should be.

His lips had touched those perfect fruits on three occasions, none of which had been enough.

Their parents wished them wed. They'd known this since they'd been small, though neither Magni's parents nor Solveig's had ever spoken of it to them. A childhood spent spying on their elders had opened their ears to many secrets; that one was among the most benign.

When they'd first learned of it, they'd both accepted it as a fate already determined and then set it aside as unimportant. When they'd neared the age of adulthood and begun training for battle, Solveig declared that she would wed no man until she had made her story.

Magni loved her, then and still, as more than a friend, and he would happily have wed her, but he knew better than to make any pointless protest of her declaration.

"How many Franks did you kill today?" he asked now, before his memories made too long a silence.

"Eleven," was her answer. "Twelve, if you hadn't taken my last."

Always, she competed with him. "That kill was my seventh. You had no need of it to best me. Solveig, you are a great warrior. Your story is already being made. Ylva's story is ended. Yours is just beginning. As is mine. Who's to say what our legends will be?"

She sighed. "Her story is ended on her very first raid. I should have watched out for her."

And now they were to the heart of the thing. "She was a shieldmaiden and well trained. You're blameless here. We all risk a death like hers when our ships land on foreign ground. A good death, so she can live on. That's what her story is."

Another sigh, this one thick and wet, and Magni reached his arm out in the dark and drew her to him. She let her head rest on his shoulder. She didn't weep, but her hand tightened with his, and Magni knew she was comforted.

He laid his cheek on her head. Her braids were stiff and smelled of blood and earth—as, he knew, did his own.

"We must go back," he murmured. "Your parents need no more worry tonight."

~oOo~

When they returned, the camp was well staked, and Magni left Solveig with her parents.

Men and women ringed the main fire, feeding their bellies and resting their bones after their hard fight. Magni stepped in to collect a portion of meat and a horn of mead and then stepped away, in no mood for the heat or the company. But when he saw Håkon sitting off on his own, just inside the light of the fire, he went to him.

"May I sit?"

Solveig's brother nodded. His cheek had been stitched closed but left unbandaged. Swollen and dark, puckered around each stitch, it looked far worse than it had when the flap of his skin had been loose. He would have a majestic scar.

Magni's face was as yet unscarred; he felt a ripple of envy.

When he sat, he saw a covered body lying on a bier beside Jarl Vali's tent. Ylva lay apart from the other fallen raiders, who would be buried at dawn.

"Do they mean to burn her?"

"Not here," Håkon answered around a swallow of mead. "They want her to sleep beside them tonight. My mother…" He sighed and let that sentence die. "She is not herself."

There was condemnation, something nearly like contempt, in Håkon's tone, and Magni didn't know what to say. He stared at the body, silhouetted by the glow from inside the jarl's tent. Shadows moved behind the gaps in the hides—Solveig and her parents.

"To lose a child is the hardest pain." Magni's father walked up as he spoke and crouched before them. "You've neither yet mated, so this you cannot know. But there are two wounds that will bring down even the mightiest warrior: the loss of a child, and the loss of a mate. It is no weakness to show the pain of either wound. Don't keep a hard heart for your mother now, Håkon. She's been brought low by a sword just the same as if it had pierced her own heart. More, perhaps. She needs your love and care, not your impatience."

Håkon dropped his head, abashed. Without another word, he drank down the mead in his horn and stood. When he walked toward his family's tent, Magni's father took his place.

No one knew the pain of loss like his father did. Magni was his eighth child, and the only one to live to see nineteen years. All seven of his siblings had died long before he'd been born. His father had lost children to illness and misadventure and violence. To violence, he had lost his first wife and a son not yet born, and he had lost a son wearing a new arm ring, on his first raid. He'd lost children in every way it was possible to lose them.

Magni saw well, into people and around them, and he gleaned the knowledge he could from that seeing, but he knew he would never know the pain his father had felt in his life.
They sat together now in silence, while the camp settled into quiet around them.

The fire was low when his father spoke again. "I think we'll not press on from here. If the Franks bring us good treasure, we should go."

According to the map, they were not far from Paris, the true treasure of Frankia. It had been their intention to reach it. "Many will be unhappy to turn back."

His father nodded. "True. But they would be more unhappy to be defeated, would they not?"

They'd gone through the Franks like a hot blade, on this raid and those before it. "Why would you think we would be?"

"In that tent is the Storm-Wolf and the God's-Eye, both in grief. Their heart and fire lead us all. That's always been the truth of our strength. They are known to be favorites of the gods, and warriors seek to be worthy to fight on the same field, so they fight with all they have. Brenna…Håkon is right. I've seen her lose much, but I've never seen her this way. It reminds me of Toril, my first wife. A mother's grief is a maddening, weakening thing. She'll not be strong again until she can set aside this loss. It does us harm to try to fight when our legends are weak—greater harm than a lost raid. The Franks fear us now because they cannot beat us. If we are driven back from the city, then we lose the advantage of their fear."

Magni had seen warriors fight with the rage of grief and the fire of revenge. They fought wildly and without restraint. "Will she not want vengeance? Will Vali not? Wouldn't they be even more fierce?"

"Of course they want vengeance, but not all ferocity is useful. They are leaders with me, and we must do more than simply fight. We must see the field and execute a plan, and blinded by rage they will see nothing but the need to kill. Vali especially will be reckless, and he is not immortal, no matter what his story tells us. To lose the Storm-Wolf would break more than this raid. But Vali will care for Brenna first and do what she needs. I can make him see that we need to go home now and regroup. When we return, we'll take Paris, and that will be a great vengeance."

"How will you convince the others?"

Magni's father looked him straight in the eyes. The embers of the low fire made glowing lines across his irises. "Heed me well, son. The work of a jarl is, above all else, to speak and to listen, and to do both well and clear. Tell the truth, and tell it plain, but tell the truth that is enough and no more. Listen and be open to new ideas, but don't be too easily swayed. Know your mind and know the why of it. These are all things you excel at naturally. You have your mother's insight. So tell me how you would convince the others not to push on toward Paris."

Magni looked around the dark, quiet camp. Few beside those on watch were yet moving. The only sounds were of settling people—sighs and snores, a few moans and grunts from some who'd found a partner to warm the night.

Vali's tent had gone dark. Without the glow of their candles, Ylva's body was nothing more than the faintest impression, a slightly less dark spot in the black.

He remembered how the entire camp had stopped to watch Vali carry her in, and the way people had scrambled to make the bier on which she now lay. None of the eight other dead had been accorded such reverence, though they were esteemed warriors themselves and far more seasoned than Ylva had been. But everyone understood that the daughter of

50

legends was a legend as well and due a greater portion of their respect.

It was the burden that Solveig felt so keenly—to be worthy of the respect she was already shown.

"We should take Ylva home. People will understand that we must carry her back to be released among her people, from her home, so her way to Valhalla is straight. The gods will thank us for our good care of the child of the Storm-Wolf and the God's-Eye."

It was unusual, to carry the dead back home. Bodies beyond life that lingered too long in the world began to rot. But there were ways to keep a body long enough for the sail back to Karlsa. Gudmund, their battle healer, would know what to do.

What was left of the fire shone too scantly to light his father's face, but Magni could sense his smile. A heavy hand clamped onto his shoulder, and he felt the praise in that touch.

"Yes. That's the right truth. No one here would deny the rightness of it. When the Franks come to parley, and if they bring treasure to urge us to go, we will go, and we'll be as one in the choice."

"And if they don't bring treasure?"

Just as he'd been able to sense his father's smile, he knew that his question had made it vanish. His father's tone was grim when he answered.

"Then we will have no choice but to fight."

3

Solveig woke with the sun, but already her father and brother were out of the tent, and her mother was fully dressed again, lacing up her chestpiece. She hadn't washed since the fight; her braids were hard and matted, and smears of blood arced across her cheek and forehead, and over her throat. The patterns of the blood, made not by spray but by rub, told that it was Ylva's, brushed across their mother's skin as she clung to the body in anguish.

Solveig looked down at her hands. She hadn't washed, either, and she, too, wore her sister's blood mingled with the Frankish spray of their enemies.

Her insides roiled. The battle had gone nearly to the end of the sun, and the rest of the night was little more than a blur. She hadn't eaten since she'd broken her fast with salt cod and water on the ship the morning before. Her stomach woke to that knowledge and cramped into an empty fist, but she had no appetite.

Ylva was dead. The pestering child who'd clung to Solveig's shadow all her life, who'd howled and stormed whenever she'd been left behind, who'd been a near-constant vexation in her need to do as Solveig did, was dead.

When that recollection finally, fully hit, it did so like a charging ram, and Solveig pressed her hand to her chest with a gasp. The sorrow she'd sought before found her, and its tears drowned the awful, burning envy that had tormented her the night before.

Her mother turned an impassive face to her and watched as she wept. "When you leave the tent, be composed, Solveig. A shieldmaiden's tears are for no one's eyes but her own."

Solveig stared up at her, seeking the right retort. Her mother had displayed none of her renowned strength the night before. She'd keened over Ylva's body, and she'd lain limp in their father's arms through the night.

But it was true that she hadn't wept, not that Solveig had seen. And now, she was the God's Eye again. In the face of that stony power, Solveig could think of no words to say.

Her mother watched until she wiped her eyes, and then, with a sharp nod, she left the tent, and Solveig was alone.

~oOo~

With no appetite, and itching with the need to be clean, when Solveig left the tent, she turned away from the fire and headed toward the water. She wanted the blood away.

She passed Magni on the way, and sensed him spin and trot to catch up with her. "Again you go off alone? I think not."

"I'm only going to the river. I need to wash." She turned toward him as she spoke and saw that he was clean.

He was a handsome man, much like his father, with the same thick fall of golden hair and the same night-blue eyes. His beard already had a man's fullness. He was as tall as Leif but not quite as broad. Neither was as big as her father or Håkon, however, so she didn't think of Leif or Magni as tall. She herself was only a few inches shorter—then again, she was a head or more taller than most women.

Remembering that he'd been exactly what she'd needed the night before, offering soft words and good sense to quiet the noise in her head, Solveig found a smile for him. "Join me if you like."

He returned her smile with a broader one of his own and grabbed her hand. "Come. There's a quiet place, a stream that feeds into the river."

She let him lead her toward the river. He turned to the east, which surprised her, as it took them toward the Franks. They entered the woods, and she tensed, listening and watching. "Last night you said the woods were dangerous before the parley."

"Last night, you went off alone. Now, we're together. Look."

The sound of gently rolling water bubbled up around them, and Magni waved his hand like he was presenting her with a gift. "I'll keep watch."

The stream was lovely, with a gentle, mossy bank and a small pool at the base of a waterfall, its water a dark, bluish green.

What she had seen of Frankia was lush and verdant. Soft, rounded hills rose up from the banks of the river and faded into woods thick with foliage. The earth was the rich dark that supported teeming life within and above it, and the air was replete with the scents of that life.

Solveig ran to the woods when her mind howled because there she could be alone without feeling alone. She could sit on the dark earth and dig her hands into the ground and feel part of something great. In the woods, even here in Frankia, she could feel the presence of all the nine worlds and find her place within them.

She began to disrobe, setting her sword and shield aside. Magni turned his back to her and walked off, standing watch near a cluster of smooth, pale boulders.

She smiled to herself. He'd seen her naked body dozens of times, from when they were still babes in arms. It had been a while, to be sure, but he seemed shy to see her skin now.

As she undressed, some of his shyness caught in her, and she found herself turning her back to him as well.

When she was bare, she unwound all her braids, and then she stepped over the soft, springy moss and put her foot into the water. The spray of the cascade sprinkled her skin with icy kisses, so she wasn't surprised at the cold of the deep pool.

Solveig liked the cold, the way it made her skin taut and tingly. She sank into the water and put her head under, staying below the surface as she combed through her stiff hair, working out the blood and grime until her fingers slid smoothly through her floating locks.

Her chest was tight with the need to breathe, and her heart pounded, but she lingered beneath the surface a few seconds more, pushing herself, finding her limit. When she could stay under no longer, she found the streambed and set her feet down. She pushed up with all the power of her strong legs, leaping clear of the water with a great gasp.

More than blood had been washed away. She felt strong again, and clear, inside and out.

"Gods, woman!" Magni was crouched at the edge of the pool, and as Solveig blinked the water from her eyelashes, she saw deep worry carving lines in his brow. "I thought you…"

He didn't finish. When Solveig understood what he thought—that she'd meant to drown herself—she used both hands to send a great splash of water at him, dousing him completely. "I would never! I am no coward!"

With a shake of his gold mane, he bowed his head. "Forgive me."

"You know me. Always you have, and none knows me better. You wound me to think I would do such a craven thing."

In truth, alone in the woods the night before, the thought to end her life had entered her mind, when she was trapped in a maelstrom of envy and guilt and throttled grief. It hadn't been despair provoking the thought, but disgust in herself. She dishonored herself and her sister to feel envy for the story of her death. But she dishonored them more to wish herself dead.

The thought had been fleeting and was now gone, as was the disgust. Magni had helped her vanquish them both. Now, it was as if he could see the echo of that weakness in her, the way he saw everything, and she felt naked and abashed. She stayed in the pool, keeping the waterline dancing over her collarbones.

He watched her quietly, beads of water making his beard glitter in the tree-dappled sunlight. She watched him in turn, waiting for him to speak. Her belly fluttered and rolled uncomfortably, and the beat of her heart quivered in her throat.

The horn blew—one blow, announcing a single rider. A messenger, no doubt, bringing a petition for parley. Solveig came out of the water at once and stood before Magni, who held out her tunic. But when she tried to take it, he didn't let it go.

"Solveig…"

All at once, she understood that contemplative stillness with which he'd watched her, and the fluttering of her own body. For most of their life, they'd danced near the edge of it, the idea that they would someday be mated. It sometimes seemed a foregone conclusion—a true forging of their parents' long alliance, and of their own friendship. Her own heart and mind often reached for him, even when they were hundreds of miles apart and always when he was near. Magni felt like a part of her, a crucial part.

But Solveig had ambition beyond a mate, and she had told Magni exactly that. More than once.

She shook her head. "No, Magni. I've told you."

She would soon have twenty years of life. Many women of her age, even shieldmaidens, were wed and had children—two or three or even four. Women of their people married at a like age that men got their arm rings—as young as twelve years, and most often by fifteen or sixteen years. People with more than thirty years were elders. To live fifty years, an age her father and Magni's neared, was unusual enough to be remarkable.

For a woman to have twenty years and not be a mother was certainly remarkable, unless she was a legend. Even Brenna God's-Eye had been wed and delivered of a daughter before she'd had twenty-two years.

Solveig was old enough, and alone enough, and ordinary enough, to be the cause of talk in Karlsa.

She wanted the mate, the children, the warm home. She wanted the love her parents had; just the night before, lying nearby as her father and mother grieved together, she'd ached to feel that love, even in mourning. But she wanted one thing more. When she had made her story as a warrior worthy to be known as the first of the line of Storm-Wolf and God's-Eye, then she would turn her eye toward a mate.

If that mate were Magni Leifsson, she wouldn't be disappointed. Neither would their parents be. Neither would Magni; the look he gave her now said it silently but plainly. He wanted her.

She loved him like a brother of her blood. He knew all of her secrets and held them dear. With such trust and love between them, it would not be so great a task to grow something deeper. Perhaps it already had grown, though she refused to entertain those thoughts or immerse herself in those feelings.

Because then she would be his, and she couldn't allow that until she was first her own.

"No," she said again. "I cannot."

As he released her tunic, he cocked his head, and his eyes sparked. "But would you?"

Magni found his pleasure amongst the many willing women of Geitland, she knew. On the other hand, she had rebuffed all advances men made on her, and she'd made none of her own. But it was different for an unmated woman than for an unmated man. Women carried a greater burden of risk in seeking their pleasure, and it wasn't a burden Solveig wished to heft.

She would have no love of body before she had love of heart, and she would not have that yet.

Though he sought his pleasure liberally, the question Magni had now asked was the first gesture toward her that he'd made since he'd kissed her on the night of the summer solstice, a few years before. He'd been drunk on celebratory mead, and she wasn't sure he remembered it happening. She remembered clearly.

The three words he'd just uttered were more direct and intense than his drunken tongue in her mouth had been.

"I would," she answered, hurrying into her clothes. "But not now."

"Would you have me wait?"

She stopped in the midst of belting her tunic. If she said yes, would he avoid other women until she was ready? What if that were years?

"I would make no demands on you, Magni."

He reached out and grabbed her arms. "Would you have me wait?"

If she said yes, she would feel the burden of his expectation, his anticipation, while she made her name. But she would be glad if there were less chance that another woman might draw him away in the meanwhile.

"Solveig." He shook her lightly. "What is your wish?"

A wish was easier to say than a demand. "I wish you would wait for me."

"Then I shall."

He pulled her against his chest and kissed her.

This was not a kiss like the night of the solstice. This was not a kiss like their first, under the grain bin in Geitland. It wasn't even a kiss like their second, when they'd tried to mimic Leif and Olga and had pushed their open mouths together.

Those three kisses had been the total of Solveig's experience, but since them, Magni had mastered what they had only mimicked and played at before. Though he was younger than she, he was more experienced. He was also wiser.

That was true in all things, of the flesh and of the mind. Magni saw, and thought, and then he felt. Sometimes, Solveig seemed able to do none of those things, in any order.

At first, his lips simply rested on hers, supple and warm, his beard soft against her skin. Neither open nor closed, simply relaxed, and still, it hardly seemed a kiss at all.

But then he moved, just slightly, brushing over her lips. Without an intent to do so, Solveig opened her mouth, and a kind of a sigh slipped past her lips. It must have been an invitation, because Magni released her arms and coiled her body into a fervent embrace, and then she understood what a kiss really was.

His tongue pushed into her mouth, but not in the fat, flailing way it had done years before. He seemed to be caressing the inside of her mouth, especially her tongue, and it had the effect on her body that cold did—making her tight and tingly—but she wasn't cold. Far from it. Her cheeks burned, her muscles seemed almost to melt, and there was a fire in her belly she'd never felt flare so hot before.

Again her body moved without her intent—her arms wound around his neck, and her hips surged forward, pressing against his. She felt his sex, a solid rod across her belly, and she pressed more closely to it, until Magni groaned into her mouth.

Solveig was perhaps inexperienced in these matters, but she wasn't stupid. She'd touched herself and found pleasure. She knew how coupling worked, and she'd seen her share of unclothed people, in the full variety of shapes, sizes, and dispositions. She'd seen her parents many times, and not merely undressed but making good use of it. Their beds were all in the same room, after all.

She'd seen Magni bare often enough…but it occurred to her then that it had been just as long since she'd seen him bare as it had been since he'd seen her. They'd been children then, she with breasts barely sprouted, and he much narrower of frame and smoother of cheek.

Oh, she wanted to see him again. Suddenly, with that fire inside her making her sex throb, she wanted that more than anything.

Overwhelmed, noise rising up in her mind, Solveig broke away. Magni let her go at once, though he was as flushed and breathless as she felt. They faced each other, wordlessly, the only sounds their laboring breaths and the waking woods around them.

"The horn," she said, when words made sense again.

She moved in the direction of the camp, stepping around him, but Magni caught her hand.

"I will wait, Solveig."

She squeezed his hand. "I'm glad."

~oOo~

The rider had gone by the time Solveig and Magni made it back to camp, and the raiders were clustered at the fore. Solveig saw her father in their midst, his head above the crowd.

As she and Magni approached, their fathers watched them come. The two men wore the same expression, one that Solveig found puzzling.

"They're surprised," Magni muttered at her side, answering the question in her mind. That was something he did often— answer a question she hadn't asked aloud. "I think they'd given up on their hopes for us. Now they're wondering if we went off to the forest for a rut. That's my guess."

Her cheeks went warm as she met her father's intense regard. But there was no condemnation in his expression. Nor any gentleness. She couldn't make sense of it, not even with Magni's insight.

No matter. They arrived at the fore, and Leif grabbed Magni's tunic and drew him forward in a shock of aggression. "Heed the horn. You both know that. We thought the messenger might have been a diversion."

Ah. Magni had only gotten part of their feelings right. First, they'd thought they'd been killed or taken. Not until they'd seen them return had they thought they'd been in the woods for a rut and had ignored the horn. That was the look—surprise, perhaps with pleasure, mixed with worry and relief, and a thin edge of censure.

"Forgive me, Father," Magni said to Leif

At the same time, Solveig's father drew her near. "You are well, my sun?"

She nodded. "I was washing. That was the delay. I had to dress." Too late, she understood the implication of her words, and her face flamed as her father looked over her head and narrowed his eyes at Magni, who was nearly as wet as she was. She hadn't made the situation better.

But she had nearly twenty years, and Magni had nineteen. They were grown, with the will to do what they would. What was more, all their lives, their parents had wanted exactly this—a thing which had not yet even happened.

Confused and angry, her mind beginning to bang loudly against her skull, Solveig jerked away from her father's grip, which had been gentle and thus easily broken. "Will there be a parley? And where is Mother?"

"Your mother is with the healer, preparing your sister to come home with us. We leave on the next dawn. The messenger asked for our terms. We gave them. Now we wait for our treasure."

"Not to Paris?" Oh, how she wanted to breach that city. That was where her story was, she was certain.

But her father shook his head. "We'll raid here again, and the city will be ours. Now, we take your sister home."

His eyes lifted above her and held on something behind her. She turned and saw her mother standing in the middle of the camp. Everyone moved around her, giving her a wide berth. She stood motionless, and stared at her husband.

This was a different look from the secret one she had, but it was no less vulnerable, no less raw, no less a look of love. Solveig didn't need to turn back to her father to know how much love was in his eyes, returned to his wife.

Instead, she turned to where Magni stood and found his eyes on her.

~oOo~

The next morning, the raiders laded their ships with three large chests of gold and silver.

Solveig stood on a hill overlooking the river and watched as her fellows settled the chests, one each in three of their four skeids, then laded all four ships with their supplies and provender. Farther inland, a row of dark forms spiked a bare hilltop—the king or duke or earl or whatever noble name they called their ruler here and his top men (it would be all men; Christians didn't allow their women to have power or strength) arrayed on horseback, in a row, making certain that the raiders took their gold and silver left.

The elder raiders told that it was the richest ransom any people had ever paid at once, on any land. That the Franks could spare it so easily, and offer it so freely, could only mean that farther up this river was a city full of treasure beyond imagining.

Paris. The raiders who claimed it would be legends, all of them.

This river had a name that sounded like the raiders' word for *late*. Solveig found that apt; she was late, overdue, delayed. Twenty years, a full score, and her story had not yet begun. She felt more impatient than ever, with Magni's promise to wait for her still echoing in her ears, and the touch of his body still tingling on her skin.

A subtle hush moved over the struck camp below, and she looked down again. Her father, her brother, Magni, and Leif carried the wrapped form of Ylva on a litter. Her mother walked behind it, carrying Ylva's shield, sword and axe across her arms. They carried Ylva onto the fourth skeid and settled the litter at the stern, where the treasure rested on the others.

A treasure in each ship, three of gold and one of blood. Three gained, and one lost.

A story made, and a story left behind.

Solveig walked down the hill to join her family.

4

Vali stood near the prow of the ship and watched the sun sparkle over the water, all the way to the horizon. From his vantage, he could see the other three ships, each at a safe distance, but close enough to be of use. Håkon was on the other of the Karlsa skeids; he'd wanted some independence from his parents on this sail, as he continued to learn the ways of a longship.

The voyage had so far been ideal, with enough breeze in the right direction to fill the sails and hurry them home. They were bringing more treasure home than ever before. Karlsa and Geitland would know wealth beyond their imagining.

On another day, his spirits would have been high and his heart full.

But on this day, behind him, at the stern, lay his second daughter, wrapped for burial. Gudmund, Leif's battle healer, had prepared her body, in some way Vali didn't want to understand, so that they could bring her back to Karlsa to be buried beside her grandmother.

Ylva, the fiercest of his children. His little wolf. She'd been so hungry to raid, long before she'd been nearly old enough, and so furious to be made to wait until she had sixteen years. But Brenna had been stalwart on that point, for all of their children. All three who'd made that age had hated being held off so long, but Brenna had wanted them strong and full grown before they faced battle.

Ylva had tried every kind of way around it, including, the season before, cutting her hair and trying to pretend she was a boy from another family. The ruse had fooled no one, but Vali had enjoyed her persistence. He'd expected her to be a great shieldmaiden, like her mother and her older sister. And she'd fought well here in Frankia.

But she had been brought down on her first raid.

Vali well knew grief and pain. He well knew rage and desperation. There had been times in his life full of it all. He'd known joy and contentment, too, and his life had long been far more full of joy than pain. Yet his sorrow for Ylva settled into a familiar hole in his heart.

Still, she had died in battle, fighting with honor, and he had no worry for her any longer. His grief eased in his knowledge that she would be in Valhalla, with Thorvaldr, and Dagmar, and the gods.

His real worry now was for Brenna.

He turned from the water and looked down the long line of the ship, to where his wife sat beside their daughter's body. She was quiet but not at rest.

Brenna had been the fulcrum of his life for more than twenty years. Together, they had known life's greatest sorrows and its greatest joys. They'd held each other up through trials and failures, and they'd celebrated thrills and successes together. Fear, trust, pride, doubt, loss, gain—everything he'd lived in most of the latter half of his long life, he'd experienced through his love for his wife, and for the children they'd made together.

Never in all those years had Vali known her to falter as she did now. Her mourning for Ylva seemed to consume her. The first day, he'd been shocked at the wildness of her grief; his stoic shieldmaiden had been frantic in her sorrowful fury. But since, she worried him even more, though she seemed more her usual self. She was stoic again, and she had engaged in the work of the raid as she normally did, participating in the parley and in the talks before and after it, doing her part to strike the camp. Perhaps those who knew her less well thought she had regained her footing.

But Vali knew better. No one knew her as he did, and there was a wrongness in her quiet now. A chill. Brenna had often been thought to be cold, but she never had been. She was strong, and impatient, but never unfeeling. Quite the opposite; his wife often felt too much, and sometimes shied away from the torrent.

When she was younger and unwed, she'd kept a little hut in the woods, just for that purpose—to flee the tumult of the world. Since Brenna had come to Karlsa with him and started a family, she no longer fled quite so literally, but she hid quite a lot of emotion behind her marvelous eyes.

That was what was different, and what had Vali so concerned: he'd always been able to see her emotions playing out in her eyes, no matter how still and silent all the rest of her might have been. Now, though, the light behind those orbs had died. She was dull and withdrawn, as if she were empty. He sent up a plea to the gods that she would be restored once they were home and could give Ylva the burial rituals she deserved.

Their eldest daughter worried him as well. She'd bolted after Ylva's death, and she'd been distant and enigmatic since. He wasn't as concerned about her running to the woods; like her mother, Solveig fled to seclusion when she was overwhelmed, and, like her mother, great waves of emotion often overwhelmed her.

Brenna and Solveig were alike in nearly every way. They were even nearly identical in their looks, except that Solveig had eyes like his own, both the same bright blue. The God's-Eye was Brenna's solitary burden and gift.

When Solveig had been small, that sameness between them had been a boon, forging between mother and daughter a bond as strong as any steel. But in the early years of her adulthood, something had changed between them, and Solveig seemed to see her mother as a rival more than anything, to challenge and compete with her, and to set the bar of her own success above her mother's head. Vali didn't understand what had happened, or why, but he hated the chill that had rooted in the heart of their love, and Brenna did, too.

His gaze wandered from his wife to his daughter; Solveig sat between two empty oarlocks, resting on the wale of the ship. With the winds so favorable, most of the raiders were at leisure, so there was nothing especially unusual about his daughter enjoying the view. He'd been doing the same thing himself—but his thoughts were dark, and he knew that hers were, as well.

Perhaps it was merely grief numbing his wife and daughter in this worrisome way; Ylva's death was the first loss of such magnitude they'd known since Thorvaldr, and the pain was all the keener for the years they'd had with her.

No. Thorvaldr's death was the worst. Their first son had been taken moments after his birth, stolen from them before he could forge a life. Ylva had died young, but she'd had a good life and a good death.

They all chased that death, and his little wolf had caught it. She hadn't cowered in the back of the fight, she had stood at his side and taken all comers. That was something to celebrate. Too much sorrow for the valiant dead was selfish. Rather than weep for their loss, they should cheer for her gain.

Yet there his wife and daughter sat, morose and mute, apart from each other, and from him.

~oOo~

Geitland being far more southward than Karlsa, the raiders docked there first. As always, they would split the spoils in Geitland's great hall. Normally, the Karlsa raiders would feast and rest before they continued the journey home, another two days' sail when heading north, but this time, with Ylva to bury, already several days after her death, they could not spare the time. They would split the spoils, and they would feed, but they meant to sail again after only that much rest. None of the Karlsa raiders grumbled, weary though they were. Few had complained about leaving Frankia behind so close to Paris. They understood that Ylva's death had weakened them beyond the loss of one brave but inexperienced raider.

The people of Geitland were there to greet them all, and there was a general resound of celebration as the ships approached and docked. That good cheer quieted when people began noticing Ylva's body. Håkon leapt from the other Karlsa skeid and helped Vali carry her to the shore. Brenna and Solveig followed behind them.

Seeing them approach with the litter, people hurried to erect a makeshift bier to hold her while the ships were unladed and then replenished.

When the litter was secure, Vali laid his hand on his daughter's wrapped head. He was glad he couldn't see her; he wanted to remember her as she'd been in life, as she would be in Valhalla, not in whatever state the elements were making of the flesh she'd left behind.

Brenna stood at her feet, looking down at her with those quiet, dull eyes. He tried to remember when last she'd spoken; he didn't think she had at all on this day.

"Brenna." He went to her and lifted her hand, where it hung slack at her side. "Come. Olga is here." Their friend stood back a few paces, holding hands with Leif and with Håkon.

71

Solveig stood with Magni. They weren't touching, but there was something protective in Magni's posture. Vali recognized that stance and the feeling that drove it, and he knew that, for the boy, at least, there was something more than friendship finally between the two.

To love his Solveig would be as hot and wild, as beautiful and intense, as if to embrace the bright orb for which she'd been named.

As it was to love her mother. "Brenna. Come."

She shook her head, her eyes never leaving their daughter's body. "I'll stay with her. I don't want her to be alone."

He pulled on her hand. When she wouldn't come, he stepped closer and hooked his arm around her shoulders. "Brenna, please."

She shrugged him off. He couldn't remember the last time she'd rejected his embrace. "I'll stay here."

Olga came forward as well and slid her hand into Brenna's. "You have business, Vali. Go to the hall and do what you must. Leif will send a girl down with food and drink, and I will keep watch with Brenna. None alone today."

Her voice was strong and clear and full of compassion. Her eyes showed her sympathy for them and a sorrow of her own. Vali nodded. He kissed his wife's head and followed Leif up the berm toward Geitland's expansive great hall.

As he passed them, he saw Solveig's hand catch Magni's and hold.

Maybe there was something more between them for Solveig as well.

By the time the treasure was divided, between the jarls and among the raiders, the servants of the hall had a meal ready. It was good to eat warm, rich food, prepared in a kitchen, after many days of salt cod and leiv bread—or, at best, what foreign woods and a campfire had to offer. Vali kept an eye on his men and women, not wanting them to enjoy their food and drink so much that they would be unable to sail in an hour's time.

"The sun will set in a few hours, Vali," Leif said, sitting beside him. "If you wait until dawn, you'll have only one night sail in your journey."

Vali shook his head. "I must get my people home. Too long has Ylva waited to be freed. I feel an ill wind around me. Brenna…" His sentence faltered and died. He didn't know how to express his concerns.

"I saw this with Toril as well, Vali. A mother's loss…I think no man can know it, even should he love his children with all his heart. She is doing well, with that in mind." He clapped a hand on Vali's shoulder. "When the burial is done, Brenna will have to look on other things, and she'll be as she should be."

"I hope you're right, my friend. All the more reason not to delay."

"Then let's see you off, before your crewmen are too full of mead and drunk with gold to be of use."

~oOo~

In Karlsa, in the way of their clan, before the hall and in view of the sea, they built a funeral pyre. Women of the town strew flowers over Ylva's still-wrapped body, and the people of Karlsa chanted their petition to the gods to ease her path through the doors of Valhalla. A goat was sacrificed, and its blood poured over her body.

As the smoke of Ylva's spirit, released at last, rose into the blue sky, Åsa, a seer who lived deep in the woods, sang to the gods in a high, crystalline voice to let them know that a worthy shieldmaiden would be at their door.

This was why they'd ended the raid and come home. So that their daughter would be sent on her way surrounded by all the people who loved her. So that she would take the same path to Valhalla that her grandmother had taken not so long before.

Vali stood at the pyre and remembered the day he'd laid a tiny bundle of blankets in the middle of a smaller but similar mound of firewood. They'd been in Estland, far from home. It had been deep winter, and Brenna had lain in a bed above him, insensible and near death. He'd been alone, even with friends at his side. Never more alone in his life than on that day.

Vali believed—he had to believe—that Thor had claimed Thorvaldr for his own. A great storm had crashed down on the castle at the time of his birth and death, full of violent winter thunder. That had been Thor, coming down to claim the child for a grander life than this world could hold.

Perhaps that was why Ylva had been taken at her first raid. Perhaps she had impressed the gods. It eased a father's heart to think so.

The fire burned long and hot. Vali stood with his wife and children in a silent row, while the town chanted around them. As he had in Estland, years before, he watched until the fire ate all it could and died, until there was nothing left of his child but ash and bone.

When the bone and ash were cool enough, Vali and Brenna collected it all into a carved wooden drum. Their children and the town followed them on foot to the hill just outside the town, where the people of Karlsa buried their dead.

Vali laid the drum in the grave, and Brenna set her sword and shield beside it. Each of their other children—Solveig, Håkon, Agnar, Tova, and Hella—set items of Ylva's life that she had been especially fond of or that might be useful. As the oldest, Solveig might have gone first, but she deferred to her siblings and waited until the end. Then, atop Ylva's shield, and the brooches Dagmar had given her, her lapis earrings, a carved horn cup, and a ragged woolen blanket she'd favored since she was small, Solveig laid Ylva's axe.

After she set the axe, she remained crouched at the graveside. When time stretched and she didn't move, Vali took a step, meaning to go to her. But Brenna held him back with a hand on his arm and took the steps he'd intended. She crouched beside their eldest daughter. Standing behind them, Vali marveled anew at their sameness. In hangerocks of similar hue, pale blue, the shared gold of their hair braided nearly alike, they seemed mirror images of each other.

Brenna didn't touch Solveig, and Solveig didn't seek it. They simply crouched together beside the grave and stared down at the last sight of a girl they'd both loved and protected as well as they could—far more than that girl had wanted.

Regarding that moment of simple quiet, mother and daughter so alike, Vali knew some ease. Brenna would come out of her grief. She and Solveig would be strong together. This was why they'd ended the raid early. To heal his family. To heal Karlsa. Paris would be there when they raided again, and they would be strong and whole and ready for the fight.

Håkon went to pick up a shovel, and, taking that as a cue, Brenna and Solveig stood in unison. They turned back to town. Brenna took Agnar and Tova's hands, Solveig took

Hella's, and they walked back. Those who'd joined them at the hill joined them now on their return.

Vali stayed back with Håkon. He picked up the other shovel, and together, alone, they buried Ylva Little Wolf under the earth.

~oOo~

That night, he came into the private quarters, to the corner that was their room. The three youngest of their children were asleep. Håkon and Solveig were still out—Håkon probably with a girl, Solveig most likely off on her own.

Neither of their oldest children, grown though they were, seemed inclined to leave the hall and make families of their own. Håkon enjoyed variety, and were he not careful he might find himself with a family whether he wished it or no. Solveig…like her mother before Vali had claimed her, she seemed uninterested.

But she was getting old—more to the point, he and Brenna were getting old, and he wanted his children well settled before age slowed his reflexes in battle, and the Valkyries finally took him. Magni would make a good match for her, for many reasons, and he'd seen a spark between them lately. Long had he and Brenna, and Leif and Olga—especially Brenna and Olga—enjoyed imagining that their children might someday be wed.

He laughed at himself. He was like an old woman, making matches.

"What makes you laugh?"

Brenna sat on their bed, unbraiding her hair. Encouraged both by her conversational question and by the light tone with which she'd uttered it, he joined her and took her hands

76

away, so that he could do her braids instead. Few pleasures in his life surpassed this simple one—to feel the silk of her hair wrap around his fingers as he unwound her braids.

Though she had more than forty years, Brenna was yet a beautiful woman. Her long, fair hair showed little grey, and her soft skin showed many scars but few creases. Her body was a bit larger and softer than it had been, but in ways Vali found alluring. The carrying of their many children had marked her belly and breasts, but each mark showed how she'd nurtured their children well and given him strong, good, beautiful sons and daughters. He worshipped every mark on her body, those of nurturing, of battle, and of suffering. Each one told the story of a great, full life. He worshipped her.

She sighed and relaxed to his touch. Now that they'd sent their daughter on, her grief was abating and would allow her to heal. "What was funny?" she asked again.

Vali was glad to see her express any interest in anything. He smiled and laughed again, just a quiet chuckle. "I was thinking of Solveig and Magni, and laughing at myself for my interest in them."

Brenna shook her head. "Magni would be better off to find a woman in Geitland."

He stopped his fingers and leaned over her shoulder to see her eyes. "Why do you think so? I thought you wanted the match."

"It would be a good match, but Solveig is too..." She gave up her thought with a sigh.

"Too what, my love?" He dropped her hair and turned her on the bed so that they faced each other.

"Restless. Impatient. She wants too much and she wants it all at once. She holds everything off because she doesn't know how to take a little, save it, and wait for more. She's afraid to settle, so she'll have nothing."

Another sigh, and Brenna moved away, standing and releasing the clasps of her hangerock. "She's too much like me, and Magni is too little like you. He won't press the point. He'll wait and wait, and he'll grow old, or he won't wait, and he'll give up, and she'll still be seeking everything all at once, seeing nothing where there is plenty, and standing empty-handed in the midst of it all."

Vali stood and went to his wife. He helped her shed her gown, and then he took her hands in his. "That's a dire pronouncement. Perhaps we should intervene?"

"She'll not be happy to be meddled with."

He disagreed, though he didn't say so aloud. He thought Solveig wouldn't protest a bit of parental meddling. Brenna tended to step far back from her mothering role when her children were old enough to raid—too far back, he thought. Though they were grown, they were not without need of guidance and care. Again, he knew it was a surfeit of love and concern that held her back, not a lack of it, but it wouldn't surprise him if Solveig and Håkon were unable to see that for themselves.

Rather than say that and dig at a wound in his wife's already sore heart, he closed her in his arms and bent his head to hers. "I think we're in our rights to meddle a bit. She's still sleeping under our roof, after all. She's not so grown quite yet, no matter her age."

His wife smiled then, for the first time since Ylva's death. It was a soft, hesitant thing, swollen with sadness, but beautiful and hopeful nonetheless.

5

Magni felt a bead of perspiration trickle though his hair, down his temple, and into his tunic. Once he noticed that one, he felt several others, moving over his scalp, down his back, under his arms. Unwinding a leather thong from his wrist, he wound his thick mass of hair into a quick braid and tied it off.

He hopped off the cart and headed to the well for a drink and a splash of cool on his face. The solstice was near, and summer sun beamed down over the dusty little village, making the world seem slow. Though most people in this tiny community were outdoors, getting what breeze they could, still the place was quiet, and people moved at half pace.

Cool wafted up from the deep well, and Magni let his head hang over the edge while the damp chill soaked his face. Then he dropped the bucket and pulled up fresh water, as icy as winter. Winters here were long and summers short; the deep earth stayed cool all the year round, no matter how the sun shone during the weeks of summer.

He caught the ladle and took a long draught of water that sent a pleasant shock of cold through his summer-heated body. Then, on a whim, he pulled his tunic over his head and soaked it in the bucket. Better soaked with cold well water than with his own hot sweat.

As he wrung the shirt out over the ground, he felt soft fingers touch his back. "This is new," said a voice as velvety as the touch.

"Sassa." He turned and smiled down at the pretty village girl. She stood with one hand, the one that had touched his shoulder, still raised, and the other hand empty. She'd been remarking on the tattoo across his back. It was new since they'd returned from the last raid to Frankia.

She dropped her hand and smiled prettily up at him—the kind of expression that was an invitation. Magni had accepted Sassa's invitations before and been glad of it. There were parts of him, particular parts, that wanted to accept this invitation as well. But he'd made a promise.

"Did you come to see me?"

He pulled his tunic on, covering his bare chest and sucking in a sharp breath as the cold wet lay on his skin. "I'm here with my mother. She's attending Geirlaug."

As if to vouch for the truth of his statement, a scream erupted from the longhouse their cart was stopped before.

Sassa turned toward the sound, then back, her beckoning smile yet intact. "Yes. Of course. Mother said that she was near her time. I didn't know that your mother had been called already."

Magni's mother had been a healer in her world, and in Karlsa, before he was born. When she'd married his father and come to Geitland, which had already had a healer and a midwife, she'd set aside that work and focused on helping his father lead.

But two winters ago, an illness had gripped Geitland, and both the healer, Birte, and her apprentice had been taken from them. Since then, with no one in Geitland trained in healing except Gudmund, their raid healer—who was proficient at treating battle wounds but had no patience for other ailments or the people who had them—Olga had taken up her healing work again.

She treated mainly the people of the town of Geitland; most outlying villages had healers of their own, or shared one among a few hamlets. But the nearest villages, like this one, relied on many of the services Geitland provided. When she went calling, or was called, beyond the edges of the town that was their home, Magni's father insisted that she be attended by a guard. Often, that guard was Magni. He kept an ear and an eye to his task, but the truth was, there wasn't much guarding to do. His parents were beloved and revered in Geitland.

He'd spent a few afternoons, and one late night, with Sassa, keeping himself occupied while his mother did her work. Sassa clearly expected him to do so again now.

But he'd made a promise, and it was one he meant to keep. Finally, Solveig had allowed herself to see a future beyond the name she meant to make for herself, and that future included him. So he would wait, and he would help her achieve what she so fiercely desired.

In the meantime, he was a young, virile man, and the ripe fruits of Sassa's impressive bosom swelled her hangerock. She pushed her hands up under his wet tunic and stroked his belly. No matter the intent of his mind, his body felt her soft touch, and smelled her sweet, earthy scent, and pined for the delights she offered. He was sorely tempted. How long would Solveig make him wait?

Maybe only until they raided again. If they took Paris, she would be satisfied, he thought.

He groaned and caught Sassa's wrists, pushing her a step back. She frowned, and he knew that frown. Nothing good came from a woman who had the thoughts that shaped an expression like that.

"Forgive me, Sassa," he tried. "I cannot."

"You think I'm no longer good enough even for a rut under a tree?"

Another scream pierced the walls of the longhouse nearby. Magni was often praised for his skill in soothing harsh feelings, so he called up all the skill he could now. He took her hand and held it loosely, gently. "You are beautiful and sweet, and a joy to be with, Sassa. You are better than a rut under a tree. But you know I'm promised to another, and the time has come to be true to that."

He was capitalizing on the old rumor, that he and Solveig had been shaped for each other by the gods themselves. He'd never spoken of it before, to anyone, and he was sure Solveig hadn't, either, but it seemed prudent now—and now that he'd said it aloud, he knew that he'd have to repeat it to the other girls he'd enjoyed. He also realized that the rumor would become a story now, no longer something that was muttered, but something that was told.

He'd just told the beginning of their story. Unable to stop it, a smile broke across his face and swelled his cheeks. Solveig thought that they couldn't be together until her story had been made. But she was wrong. Her story could be, would be, made *because* they were together. And his would be made as well.

Sassa didn't like that grin. She squinted up at him suspiciously. Before she could speak, he bent his head and kissed her cheek, lingering there just long enough.

"You are a treasure, Sassa Olegsdottir. But you're not mine." He added a wistful note to the last sentence, and he felt her soften and sigh.

~oOo~

When his mother came from the longhouse quite a while later, the sun had moved deep into the trees, and the air had cooled to a subtle chill. Magni had helped a farmer repair a wall, he'd been well fed by Sassa's mother, and was now stretched out in the back of the cart, carving a figure from a likely piece of deadfall he'd found. The light was getting too poor to do much more.

He sat up when the door creaked open, and his mother stepped out. Her head was wrapped in a linen scarf, and he could just see the edge of the wide streak of pale grey that swept from her forehead and cascaded down the full length of her long, dark hair. The braid she'd woven and rolled was still tucked beneath the wrapping. Despite the hours of hard work she'd put in, she was tidy. There was just a little spot of red at the edge of one sleeve, and her cheeks were flushed, but otherwise, one wouldn't know to look at her that she'd spent the best part of a day bringing life into the world.

Magni hopped down. "All is well?" He'd heard the cries of an infant sometime earlier, but no word had come from the longhouse. Geirlaug was a widow; her man had been one they'd lost in the last raid on Frankia.

His mother smiled. "All is well. It's a hard thing, to find happiness while in mourning, even for so great a gift as a child. But the child is a son, and she will call him Kalle, for his father. He will help his mother find her way again."

She turned toward the cart as she finished speaking. Magni was about to take hold of her arm, to suggest that they'd lost too much light to make the trip back to the great hall, when his mother's legs failed her, and she nearly fell to the ground. Rather than take her arm, he lunged forward and caught her around her waist. "Mother!"

"I'm well, Magni, I'm well."

"You are not!" When she tried to stand on her own, he instead swept her into his arms. Then he stood there, stunned. She was a tiny woman, barely as high as his chest. He'd never picked her up before, and she weighed little more than a child. She was so calm and quiet, so serene and gently strong, that he thought of her as mighty, despite her small frame. In his arms, though, she seemed frail, and it frightened him. No wonder his father never let her beyond the town limit without a strong fighter at her side.

Holding her, he wasn't sure what to do. The shadows wavering against the side of the cart gave him his answer, and he carried his mother to the fire at the village's center.

The village was only ten families grouped together to share work and resources, with no great hall or even a leader of note, and no name of its own. Like all similar communities, on warm nights like this, with no hall in which to gather, people came out to the center and supped together at a cheery fire. This one had spits of small game stretched across it and several pots of stewed vegetables heating along the side. There was leiv bread and hard cheese and strong mead.

Geitland hadn't known privation for a long time; even tiny places like this could put on a feast as hearty as any laid by servants in the great hall.

As Magni carried his mother to the circle of the fire, two young men stood, freeing up one of the thick logs that made up the seating around the pit. Nodding his thanks to them, he set his mother down and crouched beside her. "What can I do?"

She patted his cheek. "Stop fretting, *kullake*. I'm only tired." He narrowed his eyes and studied her, and she laughed. "Magni. I am well. I'm hungry, however. Would you bring me some food?"

He stood and turned to do just that, but Sassa was already coming toward them with two plates, mounded with food, in her hands. Behind her, a young boy held two small, flat-bottomed horn cups, carrying them in such a way that Magni figured them to be full of mead.

"Thank you, Sassa," Magni's mother said as she took a plate, and then a cup. "And Bjørn. Thank you."

Magni took the other plate and cup, offering Sassa a nod and a smile, and he sat on the log at his mother's side.

"We'll have to stay the night," he said before they began to eat. "There won't be enough moon to light our way home."

"Sadly, yes. Your father will worry, so we'll need to leave with the dawn. But we can stay with Geirlaug tonight."

As they ate, Magni watched his mother pick at her food, taking dainty bites. He was struck for the first time by her age. Perhaps it was simply weariness drawing her features, but he saw creases at the corners of her eyes, and in the tender skin beneath. Lines framed her mouth as well. His beautiful mother was growing old.

But she did seem somewhat restored by rest and food. She caught him staring, and she huffed at him. "Magni, enough. Usually, when you join me here, your attention is elsewhere." She nodded toward the fire, where Sassa was stirring a pot.

Magni watched the girl for a while.

"Magni?"

He turned back to his mother and decided to add another bit to the story. "I've had my arm ring seven years."

"Yes, you have."

"I've raided four summers."

"Yes." She reached out and squeezed his arm. "My heart weeps each time you sail and sings with each return."

"I'm a man. There's more I want than play."

His mother shifted her attention to the fire and Sassa, and then came back to him. "Not Sassa, then."

"No, not Sassa." He waited, his eyes steady, knowing he wouldn't have to say.

"Ah. At last. But she's restless. A seeker on a long path. There's much yet she fights about herself and the world. Is she ready?"

His mother saw always into the deepest part of people, so it was no surprise that she would see the turmoil in Solveig. "She will be. I've told her I'll wait."

She smiled and cupped a hand over his cheek. "I think Solveig is fortunate, then, to have so true and strong a mate standing at the end of her journey."

~oOo~

"The season grows old, Leif. When do we sail again for Frankia?" A rumble of agreement carried the question around the hall.

Magni's father sat in the jarl's seat, beside his wife. "We await word from Karlsa, Torsten. As you know. When they are ready, so shall we be."

Another rumble, this one more restive, greeted that statement.

Magni stood near the base of the raised platform that held his parents. The rest of the men and women of Geitland stood or crouched or sat inside the hall, ringed around the platform. His father called a thing regularly; he had no interest in ruling by edict and instead sought his people's counsel in most things. Since Astrid had left them, years ago, Ulv was his most trusted advisor. Magni sat in on most of their meetings, but to listen, not to speak. His father expected him to take his seat one day.

Magni wasn't sure he wanted it, but he would take it, when the time came, and he would fight for it, if he had to, because to do anything less would dishonor his father and the great legacy he'd built.

His father's story was not so filled with magic and mystery as the God's Eye and her Úlfhéðninn wolf, but it was an epic saga nonetheless, a tale of a beloved and mighty leader, who'd bested a powerful jarl and his warrior sons, and whose heart was so strong it beat free of its cage. A jarl who'd brought a generation of wealth and prosperity to the people of Geitland and had taken them to far lands to conquer and claim.

But now, at this thing, the warriors in the hall were unhappy, and Magni was glad he bore his sword. They'd been persuaded to leave Frankia for Vali and Brenna, but now that the God's-Eye and the Storm-Wolf were in Karlsa, out of sight, the Geitland raiders had forgotten how powerful and convincing their grief had been. Now, here in Geitland, raiders wondered why they'd agreed to turn away so close to the goal, and why one family's grief had been deemed so much more important than any other.

"Why wait for Karlsa? We are stronger. If we raid without them, all the treasure will be ours. We've let them suck on our teat long enough!" Whoever had said that had not been brave enough to step forward, but his words earned a murmur of approval nonetheless.

As the discontented grumbling became louder, Magni's father stood. He held out his hands. "Friends!" The hall quieted. "Long have I led Geitland. Have I ever mistreated your trust or given you cause to doubt my wisdom?"

The hall remained silent. Magni understood that thick absence to be the sound of men and women who were still unhappy yet knew they could not answer his questions with any word but *no*.

Into the quiet, Jarl Leif continued, "You say we are strong enough, but we are only as strong as our alliances. We are mighty because we are more than ourselves. Who here hasn't seen Vali Storm-Wolf fight? Who here would doubt that he fights with the gods at his back?"

No hand went up.

"Who here needs more than he already has? Who here goes hungry, or cold, or weak?"

No hand went up.

"None of us. For a generation, we've raided with Karlsa, and we are all stronger for it. We are rich. Our families are safe. The gods approve of our unity. More than the strength of the Storm-Wolf, more than the God's-Eye's power, we fight with Karlsa because we are friends, and that steadies our swords and steels our backs. You know this. Not many of us remember the time in Estland, but everyone here has heard the stories. The bond between Karlsa and Geitland was forged in fire. We might be separated by earth and air and water, but not by spirit. We fight together because we are *one!*"

He'd raised his voice as he'd spoken, shouting the last word, and it seemed to ring in the air after he'd closed his mouth. Magni could feel that the room had changed completely and all the discontent had been eased. His father noticed it, too. He nodded. "Let me hear your voices if you wish to wait and take Paris with Karlsa at our side!"

The walls of the hall shook as the warriors shouted.

Yes. His father's shadow was long indeed.

6

At the summer solstice, Solveig stood beside her father in the prow of a Karlsa skeid and watched Geitland swell as they neared the port.

She had been born on the solstice, now a full score years before, with the mark of the sun on her shoulder. All the people of Karlsa believed she had been touched by Sunna. Everyone had expected great things from her, a girl so fortunate to be born of two legends beloved of the gods, and to be kissed by the sun herself.

Yet she had achieved nothing of note in twenty years of life, no feat that would cause anyone to name her in a story. She was a blank face in the background. An observer.

But now they would return to Frankia. They would take Paris, and there she would find her story. Or know that she would live and die in obscurity, a dim shadow under her parents' light.

Her father's arm went around her, and his hand settled on her shoulder. "You look fierce, my sun."

She blinked and looked up at his strong, smiling face. Her whole life, that face had given her strength and comfort. It had changed as she'd grown; a long warrior's life had woven grey heavily through the dark strands of his hair and beard, had drawn lines on his brow and around his eyes, but one thing had not changed: she had only to look on him and know his love for her.

"I'm ready to return to Frankia. I'm thinking about the raid." That was true enough. The rest of her thoughts were not for her father's ears or any other. Except Magni. He knew. But, then, he knew everything.

Thinking of him, Solveig returned her attention to the nearing port. They were close enough now that she could see the people moving on the shore, gathering to welcome the ships. As it was the solstice as well, there would be even more reveling and feasting than usual on the departure of a raiding party.

The ship wasn't close enough for her to make out individual features and be sure whether Magni was on the shore already or not.

"When we take Paris, the gods will cheer and the world will quake," her father said.

Solveig nodded. "Yes. I feel as though I was born for that alone." The tone of her own words, and their meaning, surprised her—she'd exposed more need than she cared to. To a father as mighty as hers, she wished never to appear weak.

"You were not, Solveig." She could hear that he'd turned to her again, and his head was closer, his mouth almost at her ear. When his arm flexed and drew her into an embrace, she let herself be comforted. "You were born for many things. Not only that. You are more than your sword."

She shook her head against his chest, feeling young and small.

"Yes, you are, and someday you will see it. Ah, you are so like your mother."

Not wanting to hear that, knowing it wasn't true, Solveig pushed free of his arms, but he wrapped his hand around her wrist and kept her close.

"Yes, my sun. Like her, always you fight against the burden of what others see in you. For Brenna, it was her eye and the power people believe it has that she struggled against. For you, it is your parents, and the stories people tell of us."

Shocked, Solveig finally returned her eyes to her father. His eyes were alight with kindness and patience, and his smile deepened the creases in their corners.

"You think we didn't know? That we don't see? You and your siblings are everything to us. We watch you. We *see* you." He looked out ahead. "The one you were looking for is there now," he said with a nod.

Solveig followed his line of sight and saw that Leif was now on the shore, standing taller than most others around him, especially his wife, at his side. Magni stood beside her. Two golden towers framing a tiny, sable queen.

"There is nothing…" She didn't finish, because she didn't know what she'd meant to say. To deny that she was looking for Magni on the shore? To deny the reason she might be? To pretend that it was only friendly interest? Or to push her father's insight out of her head?

He squeezed her close again. "So like your mother."

If only that were true.

~oOo~

After a loud, boisterous thing in a great hall crowded with raiders from Geitland and Karlsa, where final discussions were had and plans made for the voyage to Frankia, everyone spilled out into the bright twilight of the solstice night. While the men and shieldmaidens had been cramped inside the hot hall, the women and children of Geitland had been preparing for the celebration. The exterior walls of the hall, the longhouses, the huts, and every other vertical surface were festooned with fragrant greens and blossoms. Tall spires of woven greens awaited strong men to erect them. In the town circle, the frame of what would be a magnificent bonfire awaited its spark.

As Solveig stood and took in the festive sights, a small girl skipped up to her and held up a floral wreath from the collection that hung from her little arm. "Well, thank you, pretty," she said and let the girl set it in her hands before she scampered off to find another woman to gift with solstice flowers.

Solveig set the wreath on her head.

"Wait." Magni stood behind her and lifted the wreath, then set it back in a slightly different position. He turned her around and smiled at his work. "There. Now it's perfect."

She wore boiled leathers, and her hair was in braids. Hardly a look to complement a wreath of flowers. "Perfect?"

His smile became a grin. "Perfect." He tucked a wisp of hair behind her ear.

"Magni!" his mother called. Solveig and he both turned. Olga was waving him over to help erect one of the verdant spires around the circle.

"Don't go far. I'll be right back." With a quick squeeze of her hand, he trotted off.

Again, Solveig stood and watched. Håkon and their father, and Magni and Leif, were all at work erecting the spires. Her mother and Olga stood nearby, with other women, decorating and sending little girls off to drape flowers and scatter wreaths.

Everyone was laughing and joyful. Even the men who'd been arguing in the hall minutes before laughed now as they worked and drank.

The celebration of the summer solstice began in joy and ended in solemnity. The longest day meant that the next one would be shorter, and the next, and the next, until they were shrouded in darkness.

On this day, they celebrated what good fortune they'd had, and they fortified themselves against harsh luck in the deep winter.

And, like every celebration, they feasted. And drank. And then drank more.

Solveig could have gone to help, she should have, but her feet wouldn't move. She didn't feel part of what was happening.

Then she saw a Geitland girl, a pretty one with fiery red hair, lift up on her toes and raise her arms high to drape a garland over Magni's shoulders. Solveig knew that girl, though she didn't know her name. That hair—the color of setting sun on a hot day, and wild with waves that escaped her braids—few others had hair like it. Or the blush-colored spots sprinkled over her nose.

She knew that girl. Last summer, on more than one occasion, Solveig had watched Magni go off with that girl. Go off with her to kiss her the way he'd kissed Solveig in Frankia. Go off with her to do far more than that.

Solveig had followed, once. She knew exactly what they'd gone off to do. Now, that girl had adorned him with flowers, right in the town circle, where everyone could see. And he didn't take them off. She went on her way, and he went back to work with flowers over his shoulders.

He'd told Solveig he'd wait, but it was foolish of her to expect him to wait as long as she'd need him to. More than foolish;

it was selfish and unfair. He was a man, young and strong. It would be unkind to demand he'd wait so long, to deny himself the needs of his body. So she shouldn't feel hurt and angry now. Just like she shouldn't have felt hurt and angry last summer.

She knew how he felt. She knew what he wanted. It was she who would deny them both. So there was no good cause to ache now.

No one was paying her any mind; she could slip away into the woods, and not even her parents would notice. No one would.

She took the wreath off her head and tossed it to the dirt as she skulked away toward the forest.

~oOo~

"Solveig! Stop!"

She'd gotten only a few strides into the trees before she heard Magni's breathless voice behind her. She didn't stop, or quicken her pace. Not until he overtook her and blocked her way did she pause.

He still wore the garland over his shoulders.

"What?" Even she heard the canine snarl in her word.

"You're angry. What could I have done to make you angry since we last spoke?"

Rather than answer, she crossed her arms. But her treacherous eyes dropped to the garland, and he saw.

He laughed, and if she'd had a blade, she might well have finished him right then. "You're jealous? Of Torunn?" He pulled the garland off and let it fall to the forest floor. "You needn't be."

"You've been with her. You've mated."

"I have not."

Solveig knew that was a lie. Her hand became a fist, and she swung it at his face. He blocked it, catching her fist in his grip—and then laughed again. So she kicked him. That one, he didn't block.

"Öhm! Gods!" He let her go and rubbed his sore shin against his other leg. "Solveig, I'm glad you're jealous. It heartens me to know you feel so much for me. But I don't want to fight you over such a thing. Torunn means nothing."

"I know you've been with her. I've seen you."

That surprised him, but he showed it only in his eyes. "I have, yes. But she's not my mate. She's a girl who enjoys a rut. As do I." He stepped close and lifted her hands in his. "I seek nothing more from any other woman. I would that you would be my wife, Solveig Valisdottir. This has always been my wish, and you know the truth of it."

She did. She'd been thinking the same thing while she'd watched him toy with that girl. "Why did you accept the garland? It's the solstice." The celebration on this night was about more than flowers and bonfires and mead. It was about fecundity. A woman offering a man flowers meant something.

"You would have had me shame her in the circle?"

Yes, in fact, Solveig would have preferred exactly that. But she shook her head, realizing that her sentiment was petty and unkind.

Magni stepped even closer and drew her arm around his waist. "You saw me take her garland, but you didn't hear me tell her no. I did, you know. I told her she should find another man to take her flowers."

He bent his head to hers, but she turned her face away. "Everyone saw you."

"Then let them see me with you." His fingers caught her chin, and he turned her face to his. "Solveig. My heart is yours. I would take your flower and treasure it always."

She hadn't missed the silent meaning weaving around his words. "You said you'd wait."

"And I will. I am waiting. I've been waiting for you for years. How long will *you* wait?"

He was so close; she could feel his beard, just a feather's touch over her cheek. His breath was warm. His chest was broad and firm. She breathed in his scent—leather and linen, wood fire and sea air, mead, and just a scant hint of summer flowers.

With him all around her like this, she couldn't think. He'd said words and seemed to be waiting for her to say words back. Marshaling her will, she remembered what he'd said. How long would *she* wait? "I don't understand…"

"You deny yourself, Solveig, as much as you deny me. More, even. Would you not wish to know what it is you're jealous of?" He bent his head, and she felt his lips on her neck. Then his tongue, swirling tiny circles over her skin.

Her heart seemed to be clambering for freedom, gripping the bars of her ribs and trying the climb through. To keep herself steady, Solveig clutched at the closest thing—his back, it was. She coiled her fingers into the linen of his summer tunic.

She wanted him to stop, so her heart would settle, but then he did, and she missed the touch. It was all she could do not to cry out for the loss.

When they were small, she'd always felt their age difference. She was the older, and she'd been bigger than he and stronger, smarter and wiser. He'd followed her lead, and she'd counseled him and offered sage pronouncements about people and the world. But Magni had eclipsed her. Not only was he bigger and stronger, but he was wiser. Perhaps he was even smarter. He was the one who understood things best now. Certainly he had more experience in most things that didn't happen on a battleground—and he had as much experience on the battleground. His parents hadn't made him wait to raid until he'd had sixteen years.

They'd gone on their first raid together. And every one since.

In some ways, they were already mated. In some ways, they'd always been.

But that was the very reason he would eclipse her completely if she attached herself to him now—he was *more* than she was. In everything. Bigger, stronger, wiser, kinder, better. Less than a year of longer life hardly mattered, and that was all she could claim.

Before he could kiss her again as in Frankia, and steal her sense and her will, Solveig pushed back and freed herself from his embrace.

"You needn't wait for me. I don't know when or if I'll want what you want." She wanted it now, but she used the word to make distance between them.

And she could see that it had worked. He winced, as if she'd pinched him. "You say you don't know if you *want* it? Me?"

As before, she answered by crossing her arms. This time, it was because she didn't trust her voice.

"Very well."

Before he left her, he picked up the garland and draped it over his shoulders.

~oOo~

The sun never set on the solstice, but the light dimmed to a soft evening glimmer. Solveig stayed in the forest, just close enough to the center of Geitland that she could see the glow of the bonfire, hear the music and the laughter. Just close enough to know how very far away she was.

Perhaps she was wrong. Perhaps she should run into town and find Magni, tear that girl off him if she had to, and tell him to show her the things she didn't know. Perhaps she could be happy as his woman. She wasn't happy like this. If she couldn't be a great shieldmaiden, perhaps she could be a great wife. Someday, Magni would likely be jarl of this place. He would need a great woman at his side.

But that wasn't her, either. She wasn't warm and caring, like Olga, any more than she was mighty and fierce like her mother. Her father had said she and her mother were alike, but his eyes were clouded by fatherly love.

In truth, nothing about her was remarkable.

A shadow moved in the fireglow. No—not a shadow, a silhouette. Someone was walking toward her. Solveig eased backward, into cover. Though she was unarmed, she wasn't afraid. She simply didn't wish for company and wanted not to be seen.

But the shadow continued straight toward her, and as it neared, it became a person. A woman. Her mother.

Fighting off the temptation to continue hiding, Solveig instead came out of cover and went to her. They met near the tree line.

"You're missed, daughter. Your father will gather a search soon. Now is not the time to disappear from us."

Ylva had been in Valhalla several weeks, and as far as Solveig could tell, everyone in her family had felt their grief and found its end. Her sister was missed and always would be, but life was back to its normal way again.

Except that her mother was…duller. There was only a shade less of her fire, but it was noticeable.

"Forgive me. I didn't mean to worry you. I only wanted to be away from the crowd."

Her mother smiled and took Solveig's hand. "I know that feeling well. Come. Let's sit and be away from it together."

She led her back into the woods, to the very tree whose gnarled roots she'd been resting on, watching the celebration.

Her mother wore leathers as well. She didn't have a wreath, but a few stems had been woven inexpertly into her braids. Solveig imagined her father's large hands doing that work, and she smiled at the tender image and the ache in her chest that it made.

"I met your father on a day when I ran to the woods to be away from people."

Solveig knew the story well. The little girl who'd saved the boy from his father's blade. It was one of her father's favorites. He'd gesture and storm and snarl, telling about how his own father had dragged him into the woods and forced him to his knees, meaning to render him mute for the offense of asking a question. He'd tell of his fear and powerlessness—and he'd tell of a little girl who spoke with the booming voice of a god and struck his father down with only that.

Then he'd stick out his tongue and show them the notch in it, where the blade had started its work. All the children would gasp and reach out to feel it.

All her life, her father had regaled her and her siblings with the stories of their parents, stories in which Brenna God's-Eye was always the hero. Solveig knew them all by heart. But she didn't stop her mother from telling this one now.

In fact, she couldn't recall if her mother had ever told the story herself. Through the eyes of her memory, Solveig could see their mother sitting with them while their father told it. She could see the patient half-smile she always wore when their father told stories. But she couldn't hear her tell it herself.

With that realization, Solveig became keenly interested.

"Your father's told you the story many times. What he saw of it. For me it was different. I didn't think about being brave or righteous. I certainly didn't think of my eye. I saw someone being cruel, and it made me angry. I stood up because I was so angry. I spoke up because I was angry. It was the first time I felt battle rage in my heart. His father ran because everyone ran from my eye in those days, when I was small and no one knew anything else about me. It wasn't my power but his superstition that saved your father. And he, your father, feared me just as much. He would have run if he hadn't been injured. When I knew that, I walked away from him, and I didn't see him again for many years."

Solveig felt a stone of disappointment settle in her belly. There was no magic in this story, and no hero. In fact, in this story, her mighty father was less than simply young and weak. He was cowardly. She shook her head, as if that would clear the memory of it from her mind.

Her mother chuckled softly and patted her thigh. "Real life is never so exciting or inspiring as a good story, my heart. You know that. I've heard you say as much. I had a story forced upon me, so I prefer reality. Your father would have run that day, but he was never a coward. He was a young boy, and he believed the story about me. Any young boy would quake if he thought the Allfather himself stood before him, even in the guise of a little girl. But because of our meeting in the woods, he never went back to his father, and he grew to become the Storm-Wolf—a great warrior and a great jarl. Those are facts as well. So his story is as true as mine, in a way."

Solveig would never be able to think of her father's story the same way again, however. "Why did you tell me?"

Her mother sighed and looked out toward the town. "Because there is a young man who came from the woods earlier with a storm over his head and now sits glowering at the fire, drinking too much mead. Because you sit here in the woods when there is a celebration afoot, and there are people everywhere in it who love you and miss you joining them. Because I remember a night of midnight sun just like this one, when I held my perfect child in my arms and knew happiness greater than my heart could hold. Because you seek a life that is made of stories and not realities, Solveig, and while you look into the clouds to find your destiny, here on the earth there are delights you're missing. I ran to the woods when I was young to get away from a story. You run from a *life*. You will never know the happiness I wish for you until you look around and see what awaits you here on earth."

Solveig didn't know what to feel or what to think. So much of what she'd thought she'd kept locked away inside was *known*, by her father and her mother both. Had Magni told them? No—when would he have? And why would he have? She turned her hand and examined her palm, crossed with the scars of their blood oaths. No. Magni wouldn't have betrayed that trust.

So then she was not as stoic as she'd thought. Even at that she'd failed.

Most confusing was the anger. She was angry at her mother, and she didn't understand quite why. Her mother's words had been loving and open. She'd meant to be encouraging, Solveig knew that. But she sat beside her and grew angrier and angrier. Why?

Because the import of those loving, encouraging words was that Solveig's destiny, her whole purpose, her quest, the thing she wanted, needed, above all else, was mere fantasy. Because her mother didn't believe she would be a great shieldmaiden.

No, that wasn't what her mother meant. Was it? Solveig's anger said that it was.

Her mother didn't believe in her.

She stood up and walked deeper into the woods.

Her mother let her go.

7

Olga tied the lacing and fastened the tabs on her husband's chestpiece. Thick leather oiled to nearly black, boiled to the hardness of armor, and heavily woven with steel rings front and back.

She moved from his side as he lowered his powerful arm. Standing before him, she traced the pattern that took up the center of his chest: an encircled five-pointed star. A tribute to her and her belief in the power of the elements: earth, air, water, fire, spirit. The red jewel at the center of the star, at its heart, was his tribute to her spirit.

He had worn a chestpiece like this one, remade whenever necessary, as long as he'd been Jarl of Geitland. But the red jewel was more recent, added when Geitland's wealth had become so great and so constant that he'd grown accustomed to it, when he'd felt he could afford the vanity of a rare gem embedded in armor.

Almost twenty years had she been Leif's wife. Longer than that had she loved him, and she loved him more every day. For nearly twenty years, every summer, at least once and often more, she had watched him sail away in a ship lined with shields, bearing his sword on his back.

One day, he would not come back. Or he would come as Ylva had come; a wrapped body ready for burial.

Or their son, who now raided always with his father, would not come back.

Or she would lose them both at once. Every new raid was a chance that she would lose everything. In twenty years, she had accepted that truth, but she had not grown accustomed to it.

This raid, only short weeks after their return from Frankia, worried her more than all the others before it. There was no particular reason that she should fret more now than elsewise, and yet she did. Perhaps it was Ylva's death that had her so afraid. Brenna and Vali's grief had throbbed around them. Olga had lost much in her life already. If she lost Leif or Magni…

She leaned forward and pressed her lips to the red jewel in the heart of the star. "I long for the day that you stay home when the ships sail. And Magni as well. I long for the day when Geitland's plenty will be enough."

"Olga." His warm, strong hands cupped her cheeks and lifted her face. He smiled down at her. "It's more than wealth and plenty. You know this."

She did. Despite her years in this world, it was something she didn't fully understand. Something she would never wish to fully understand. They raided not only for treasure but for war. That was the true prize—not this life but the one that followed it. Death was their greatest treasure. "Such a waste to chase a death and forfeit a life."

He smiled and kissed her nose. "I've forfeited no life. I've lived long and well, and I've as much happiness as any man. I have you and our son. When I die, it will be my time, and I will have you always in Valhalla, because I've lived a life of honor, and so have you. Hiding in the hall will not give me that certainty. We are a people of war and valor, as well you know."

She reached up and stroked his beard. He was fairer than she, and his hair and beard were golden, but white threads glittered in amongst the strands, and the hair on his chin had gone entirely white. She'd hoped that, when he grew older, he would rest more, but he showed no signs of it yet. Nearly fifty years of life he'd had. Few warriors of their people lived so long without setting their swords aside.

"I love you with my whole heart," she whispered and rose onto her toes so he would bend his head again and meet her lips with his own.

"You are my heart's ease," he murmured into their kiss.

~oOo~

"Magni, come." She held out her hands, and her son stepped into them. He was tall like his father and dwarfed her just the same, but still he laid his head on her shoulder, bending his frame nearly in half to do it. She brushed her hand over his golden mane, exactly like his father's had been in his youth. In appearance, he was like Leif in nearly every way. It was in his heart and his mind that she could find herself.

They stood on the pier. The great longships were laded and nearly full with raiders. The time had come for Olga to bid her loved ones farewell yet again.

Magni stood straight and smiled down at her. He seemed this morning a bit worse for the night before. He'd drunk heavily, and morosely, during the solstice celebration. Olga had seen Solveig scowling along the edges of the group this morning as well, keeping herself distant from family and friends alike, so she suspected that she knew the reason for her son's dour mood. Ah, the wild heart that beat inside that girl. So much turmoil for one so blessed.

But blessings might be curses, too.

Magni kissed her cheek. "Be well, Mother."

"And you. Come home to me, *kullake*. And bring your father with you. Safely, the both of you."

"We shall. We'll come home in great honor and glory, with Frankia as our own."

All Olga wanted was for them to come home whole and well, no matter what happened in Frankia, but she knew better than to say so. Though he didn't crave the fight the way Leif did, Magni was his father's son. He'd been trained and tutored by him, and he sought the same honor. He would no sooner stay home than cut off his own arm.

So she hugged him one last time and sent him on his way.

While she watched her son, her one and only living child, board the ship, she felt a well-loved presence at her back, and familiar strong arms encircle her waist.

"It is time, my love," Leif murmured at her ear.

She acknowledged his words with a tip of her head. "Come back to me." She'd said nearly the same thing to Magni, but that had been an instruction. An order. For her husband, it was a plea.

"I will never be parted from you." He turned her to face him. "Never again. When I die, I will be waiting for you. I will stand at the door of Valhalla until you cross its threshold."

Olga had not been born of these people, and she hadn't shared their belief in Valhalla and the wild gods that stormed its halls. But over the many years of her life in Karlsa and Geitland, she'd gained a certain affinity for such beliefs and found them coloring her own thinking.

In the way of her own people, death was an end of one's knowing. One person did not move on to another life, but went into the earth to become part of the cycle and feed another's beginning. There was no life after, no other world. There was only this one.

Now, though, she fervently hoped that Valhalla was a real place, and that Leif was right.

~oOo~

While she stood and watched the ships shrink toward the horizon, their great sails—two the black and white that were Geitland's colors and two the red and blue that were Karlsa's—swollen with wind, she heard the distinctive rhythm of Ulv's steps on the wooden dock.

He'd been badly injured in a long-ago raid. Birte, Geitland's healer until her death, had managed to save his leg, but only just. Now he walked with a stick, and that leg was rigid as a post.

Ulv had been a friend to Leif for all the younger man's life. He was the son of the former jarl, Åke, whom Leif had overthrown, but Ulv had sworn his fealty to him without hesitation, even after Leif had killed his older brothers and banished his stepmothers and younger siblings.

There were few people in the world whom Olga hated, but Åke was one of them. Even years after his death, she despised him. He'd been a heartless, vile man who had taken much from her and had nearly taken everything. He'd taken from everyone she loved.

But Ulv, his third son, was a dear and trusted friend. In the many years since Astrid had gone to Mercuria and not returned, he'd been Leif's right hand. Unable to raid, he took over the leadership of Geitland when Leif sailed, and he kept the people in good stead in their jarl's absence.

Olga did her part as well. In name, she was in charge during Leif's absence, but there were things about this world she hadn't understood well enough in the early days to manage on her own, so Ulv had helped her. Over the years, they'd developed a strong partnership, not unlike the cooperation she had with Leif. Ulv handled matters of practicality and business, and Olga handled personal concerns. Even knowing the ways of this world, even after this world had become her own, she preferred to work in partnership with Leif, and when he was gone, with Ulv.

Ulv stood with her now as the ships finally disappeared over a horizon that seemed to her shadowed in gloom. He didn't speak until they were gone, and Olga hadn't yet moved.

"Olga? Will you come into the hall?"

Another feast would be going on in the hall. The stag they'd sacrificed before the raiders had boarded would be cooked and eaten while the townspeople drank to the raiders and sent word to the gods to keep them well.

Olga was tired of feasting. Lately, she was always tired. She was sad whenever her husband and son went away from her, but what she felt today was more than that. She felt a foreboding. Something ill that loomed on that shadowy horizon. She sent her mind back, over the morning, as the raiders had prepared to embark. Perhaps it was only Magni and Solveig and their glowering that had darkened the mood. Solveig's lurking on the edges, boarding a ship away from her parents and from Magni. Brenna and Vali sending curious, concerned glances toward their daughter. Perhaps it was only that.

She shook herself, trying to cast the ill feeling away. "Yes." She made herself smile. "Let's go in and do proper honor to the raiders."

~oOo~

Early on, Olga had learned that if she counted days or spent too long studying the horizon, if she spent too many of her waking hours waiting for the raiders' return, time stretched endlessly, and her worry increased twofold each day. None of her worry could speed their return, but it could certainly make time reach out to madness. So she allowed herself to be sad on the day of their departure, and no longer. After that, she rose every morning and proceeded with her life. Even with that extra shadow of foreboding this time, Olga set her worry aside.

These days, her life was taken up by work she'd given over years before. Geitland had already had a healer when she'd wed Leif, and a midwife, so Olga had turned her attention to other work. But then Birte and her apprentice had died of an illness that had spread through Geitland, and there was no one else near enough to take their place but Olga. Her skills had grown stiff with disuse and her knowledge dusty, but as she'd haltingly helped a few minor cases, her talent had returned to her.

With no likely apprentice yet found, it seemed that Olga might be Geitland's healer for some time. She was glad for the busyness of the work, though she did worry about another illness sweeping the land. A plague had almost killed her, long ago. And Magni, while he grew inside her. A healer who feared contagion should find a replacement as quickly as she could.

The week after the raiders' departure, Olga went to a near village to tend to the broken arm of a little girl who was much braver than she was big or wise. Later, she rode back to town on the sturdy little mare Leif had given her, with Sigrid, a hall guard, at her side. They both pulled up when two boys came running up the path, toward their horses.

They weren't in sight of the town yet, and the boys were flushed and breathless. Olga felt alarm building in her chest.

If she'd been sent for, it was most likely because there was trouble.

"What is it, Lars?" She leaned over the pommel of her saddle. "Take a deep breath so your words will come."

The bigger of the boys did as he'd been told. He gulped a great swallow of air. "A ship! A merchant ship! Ulv says you should come!"

A merchant ship! Her brother!

Olga kicked her mare into a gallop and charged ahead.

"Olga!" Sigrid called from behind her, but she could catch up. Olga would not slow down.

~oOo~

"I'm sorry to have missed your man again," Mihkel said, leaning back against a table.

They had the hall to themselves; all the rest of Geitland was at the harbor, enjoying the wares he'd brought, and those being carted in from the countryside by farmers and craftsmen eager to have a hand in replenishing his great ship—and a stake in the buying mood of the people of Geitland.

It wasn't unusual for Leif and Mihkel to miss each other. The raiders sailed in the summer, and traders only came this far north in the warmest weeks. Lately, it seemed more normal for her husband to be away when her brother arrived.

Other traders than her brother docked in Geitland during the summer, of course, but Mihkel was the most regular. He docked his ship here about once every other year, sometimes a bit more often. For a streak of seven years, right after he and Olga had been reunited after a long separation, he'd sailed to town every year.

Olga was happy to have as much of him as she could have. He was all that remained of her blood family, and he was precious to her. He'd gone off long ago, as a young man, to find adventure and fortune, and he'd found both. And then he'd found her again.

"Leif will be sorry to have missed you. And Magni as well. You charm him with your stories of strange lands."

"How is the boy?"

"No longer a boy. He has nineteen years, and is a warrior like his father. A man grown and chasing his destiny."

Mihkel chuckled. "You sound like a raider yourself, Olya. Another cup of mead, and you'll be telling me stories of gods who rut in the skies."

As if his words had summoned her, Birgit, one of the hall servants, came up to fill their cups. "Would you have more to eat?" she asked.

Olga saw her brother's eyes devour the girl's nubile body, which was curvaceous enough to shape her hangerock. Mihkel was older than Olga, about Leif's age. Sun, sea, and salty wind had carved their names on his tanned face and hands, yet he was handsome all the same. His long hair and short beard were the color of night—white moon and black sky—and deep creases made charming rays from his eyes when he smiled.

He'd never married. For all Olga knew, he'd never loved. If he had, he'd never told her of it. He said that a life like his was meant for solitary men. Though his ship teemed with life, and privacy was a rarity, all the men on it were loners and misfits. They were men who could dwell on the sea, far away from any society but their own.

So no, she didn't think he'd ever known love. But that didn't mean he didn't know lust—or sate it.

When she saw that Birgit appreciated her brother's naked interest, Olga laughed and patted his shoulder. "Go, if she'll have you."

Mihkel caught the girl's hand. "Will you have me, lovely girl?"

The girl's eyes went to Olga, as if for permission. "If you'd like. The choice is yours, *kullake*."

"I would like," she said to Mihkel, with a coy dip of her head. "Very much."

Mihkel took the pitcher from her hands and set it on the table. "Then come. I've been long at sea." He stood and hooked his arm around Birgit's waist, then turned back to Olga. "I'll find you later, Olya."

"You needn't search far, Mika. This is my home, after all."

~oOo~

Olga stood up from Leif's seat. She stepped down from the platform and put herself between the couple who'd come before her. The man had just lifted his fist at his wife, who was swollen with his child. Turning to the man, she put her hands on his chest and made him take a step back. She could feel Ulv behind her, stirring in readiness, lest the man take her handling of him poorly.

"Erik," she said. "Don't compound Arva's grievance. A wedded man who sows his seed outside his home has a wife to answer to. A man who strikes a woman with child has a clan to answer to."

"This is my clan, not hers," Erik grumbled. But he calmed, and Olga stepped back.

Arva had been brought to Geitland inside her mother's body, on a raiding ship, as slaves. When Leif had freed the Geitland slaves, her mother had continued the work she'd been conscripted to do: weaving. She'd been accepted into the community, as had her daughter, as freewomen.

They were different, though, from the people of Geitland. Most of them had seen others like Arva and her kin only when the traders came to port. Her skin was a ruddy bronze, and her eyes were black, as was her hair, which was thick and heavy and gleamed like finely polished wood.

Olga had watched as Arva had grown into a young woman, and she'd seen the young men pulled to her foreign beauty. Only Erik, though, had taken her seriously as a possible mate, after the death of his first wife.

Now they were wed and expecting their first child. And Erik had strayed.

Arva had barely looked up as she'd spoken, seeking redress, and Olga was sure that the blow Erik had nearly dealt her here in the hall, before the jarl's seat, would not have been the first time his wife had felt his knuckles on her body. Olga knew it with the same conviction that she knew her own name. She knew it as well as she knew how such blows felt, how the skin burned and the muscles ached, how the bruise grew more tender in the first healing, as blood rushed up to the surface.

She'd been married once before Leif, and that man had taught her many harsh lessons about the weakness of men.

Olga had known Erik most of his life. He'd been friends with Magni, for a while, until their interests had diverged too far. She'd been glad to see the separation. Erik had been the kind of boy to cause trouble and lay the blame elsewhere, dodging consequences at any cost.

When he'd mated with Arva, she'd thought perhaps he'd grown past his pettiness. Clearly, he had not. To answer his grouse, she said, "Arva is as much your clan as I am, Erik Eriksson. I, too, was not born of this world. I, too, was once held in thrall to another—to Leif, in fact. Would you claim that I am not of the clan of my husband? Of your jarl?"

His face turned crimson, and he looked down at his boots—but not before he sent an icy blink of a glare at her.

Olga turned to his beleaguered wife. "You are brave for bringing your grievance here and making it known, Arva."

Interesting that she'd brought the infidelity, and not the violence, to the hall for redress. Olga thought she understood. If Arva claimed that he'd beaten her, especially while she was with child, the consequences for Erik would be harsh. For all their warlike ways and brutalities, for all their rough pleasures and harsh penalties, Olga's adopted people treated their families with gentle hands. They had great care for mothers, great affection for children, and great respect for women, be they wives or mothers or shieldmaidens, or some part of them all.

Arva loved Erik. She wanted him to be better, but she didn't want him hurt. So she'd brought the lesser offense to bear. Olga thought she was naïve, and played a dangerous game. A man who would beat a woman once would do so again. When such a man was shamed in public, there was little hope that he would be temperate in private while the shame burned.

It behooved Olga, then, to dampen the fire. "Do you deny your wife's claim, Erik?"

"I do not. A man has needs, and she won't meet them."

Now Arva looked up, seeking and finding Olga's eyes. "It is not right, to bring him into me, where our babe grows. This is not right."

"See?" Erik's tone was belligerent, almost petulant. "If she were of my clan, she would not believe such a thing."

Though Arva had lived her whole life in Geitland, her mother had obviously kept some of her old ways. Geitland people didn't believe that harm or shame would come to mother or child if she coupled during a carrying. Olga knew that it wasn't unsafe. Indeed, Leif and she had coupled until she'd grown too big and sore to enjoy it. This belief was a vestige of a life Arva had barely lived.

But she didn't owe her husband the use of her body on any terms but her own.

Seeing the path to a solution, at least of the problem that had been raised here, Olga took Arva by the elbow and led her off a few paces, for a bit of privacy. "Do you desire Erik, Arva?"

Her lovely dark skin reddened. "I do."

"Would you couple with him if it were safe and good?"

She didn't answer, but her black eyes were steady, as if she were waiting for a chance, so Olga went on. "Do you trust me? Do you believe in my wisdom and counsel?"

"Oh, yes. You are good and wise, Olga."

"Then heed me. You'll do no harm to your child or yourself, body or soul, if you take your husband into you at this time. If he is gentle and loving and causes you no pain, then it will be good and safe to love each other as husband and wife should."

"Truly?"

"Truly, *kullake*."

Arva smiled, and Olga led her back to her husband. Before she concluded the matter, she stepped again to Erik and looked straight up at him. "A man who beats a woman has no home in Geitland, Erik Eriksson. A man who beats a woman while she carries his child has no home in the world."

He blinked, and his cold look wavered. "I am accused of no such thing," he protested.

"No, you are not. Consider it a warning." She went back and stood near the platform. Ulv came to stand at her side. "Erik doesn't dispute the accusation of infidelity. Arva will set the terms of her redress."

Arva's eyes and mouth widened with surprise. But she drew herself together and turned to her husband, laying her hands over the mound of her belly. "I only want you to swear to me. Here. Make a vow to be gentle always, with me and the babe, and to be true to us. Here, in the hall, make that vow."

Erik sent a guilty, embarrassed glance around the hall. There wasn't much of a crowd; this wasn't a thing. The real business of Geitland happened when their jarl was in his seat and the strongest men and women were present. Olga and Ulv handled the small problems that arose, and Ulv managed the town's defenses. They'd been in peace for a long time, friendly and allied with the most powerful jarls, so town defense consisted of a few outposts and patrols.

Finally, Arva's errant husband went down to one knee. He took her hands from her belly and held them. "I swear, Arva. I will be gentle and true, to you and to our child. Forgive me for my weaknesses."

Olga wasn't sure he was sincere, but she couldn't fault the words, and they'd made Arva happy. She grinned and nodded, and Erik stood and kissed her. Then she whispered something at his ear, and he flinched. He turned and looked at Olga.

His nod might have been gratitude, and it might have been sincere. She nodded back.

~oOo~

That night, as Olga unwound her braid and combed her hair, the door to the private quarters burst open, slamming against the wall like thunder. Olga squealed in shock and stood up from the bed, her heart pounding.

With the heavy door open, she could hear commotion beyond the hall. Screams—she heard screams. And shouts. The clang of metal.

They were under attack.

Ulv stood at the threshold, sweating and disheveled, his sword drawn and his face creased with rage. "We're overrun! Gather what you can. I must get you away from here now!"

That dark foreboding she'd felt as the ships had sailed two weeks before, and had been shunting to the side ever since, filled her head now with a shriek like a flock of crazed birds.

It wasn't the raiders who'd borne the ill shadow. It was Geitland, bereft of its strongest guardians and vulnerable to attack.

With her head trapped in that cacophonous terror, Olga didn't resist. She didn't ask a single question; no such thing could find purchase in her head. She simply snatched up the clothes she'd just shed and let Ulv grab her and drag her away, out through the back of the hall.

PART TWO

WARRIOR

8

"It's no good to set your sights there," Håkon sneered, his teeth tearing into a piece of salt cod. "She'll not have you. She'll have no man. Old as she is, she'd have had one by now if she wanted one. She loves herself more than she could love anyone else."

Håkon sailed with them because Solveig had blocked him from boarding the second Karlsa skeid with her, and their parents had already shoved off. He'd been in a dudgeon for the whole voyage, carping to Magni about his sister at every opportunity, like a bee buzzing in his ear.

"I'm not talking about your sister with you. Not like that." Magni took the water skin from him and tipped the spout into his mouth as he leaned back against the wale. The wind had been strong and fair for two days. All four skeids sailed nearly abreast, and most of the crews were taking their leisure.

They took it while they could. For all the fair weather they'd had, the sun had risen red that morning, and the horizon was dark. The sails had begun to ruffle in the way that bespoke changing skies. A storm brewed, not far off.

Håkon took the skin back and pressed on. "All the girls swoon when you're about. You don't need my sister."

Losing his appetite, Magni tossed his strip of cod back into the barrel. "Why concern yourself with who I need? What care is it of yours?"

"I care for my sister."

Magni lifted his eyebrow at that. Solveig and Håkon had been close when they were young—they all three had been a merry band, when they were together—but for the past few years, since Håkon had started raiding, brother and sister had been tense and cool with each other. Solveig was the superior warrior, and it galled him.

"I do. She's my sister, and I love her. I'll kill anyone who hurts her. Anyone. Even though she thinks she's better than the world."

That was the farthest thing from true; Magni knew it, if her brother did not. Solveig didn't think she was better than anyone. She thought she *should* be better than almost everyone. She thought that anything less than perfect about herself was failure. She thought greatness was the legacy her parents had handed down to her, and she thought she was unequal to it.

The irony was that she *was* great. She was strong and fearless. Her sword struck true, and her eyes saw the whole of any battlefield. Perhaps she wasn't the wonder that her father was, but she was every bit the warrior her mother was. In fact, Magni thought she was better than the God's-Eye. She was faster and more agile—perhaps like her mother had been in her youth. But Brenna was growing old, and her fire for the fight had cooled.

Those thoughts were for himself, and possibly, someday, for Solveig. For no one else. He wouldn't talk to her brother about her. Not like that. More than simple discretion held his tongue. It was also protection. As much as he loved Håkon like a brother, as good as their friendship was, a thread of caution wove around his feelings for him where Solveig was concerned. Håkon throbbed with envy for his sister.

Moreover, Håkon didn't like the idea of Solveig with Magni, and Magni had an idea about why.

He thought Håkon meant to challenge his sister for Karlsa, when their father died. That might be years off, or it might be days. But it was known that Brenna would not take the seat of the jarl in the event of her husband's death. The seat would pass to Solveig, for her to keep unless she was challenged and lost.

Håkon wanted to be jarl himself, and he didn't like that his sister would have first claim, when he was the oldest living son. More than once, he'd mentioned that in other jarldoms, sons had first claim.

If he challenged her, Solveig would beat him. Håkon was a brave and able warrior, but he wasn't as good as his sister. He had a deft mind, but not one as agile as his sister's. Most importantly, he was rash and arrogant. He believed he deserved greatness. Solveig strove to earn it, even when she already had it. She would win, whether she was alone or not.

Magni didn't know whether she would kill him in the effort, but regardless, it would do her critical harm to face and best her brother like that. She would consider the challenge a betrayal, and she'd be correct. There'd be no victory in that.

But if she were wed to Magni and have all the power of Geitland at her side, without reservation, Håkon likely wouldn't even try. The balance of power would be too much for him to tip, and he'd know it. He was ambitious and arrogant, but he was far from stupid.

Another reason for Magni to try to bring down the wall she kept building between them: to preserve her relationship with her brother.

She'd said she wasn't sure she'd want him, and that had cut him to the bone. But she hadn't meant it. Magni knew her heart. He always had. She loved him like he loved her. What she feared wouldn't come to pass; he wouldn't hold her back. He would stand at her side, not in her way.

So he would wait, and she would see. He would find a way to show her.

~oOo~

The winds lashed the skeids, and rain like sharpened blades slashed the raiders' faces as they struggled to bring the sails down and secure them. Three times, the wind grabbed hold of the rope as if with a fist and yanked it from Magni's hand. The third time, the harsh hemp sliced into his palm. Even through the tumult of the storm, that pain made itself known.

"AAGGGHH!"

At Håkon's shout, Magni saw the wildly whipping sail wrap around his friend and drag him overboard, knocking him on the wale as he went. He hung suspended over the roiling sea for a heartbeat, and then the wind caught the sail a new way, and tossed Håkon into the water as an afterthought, at some distance from the ship.

Thinking of nothing but his friend, Magni dived in after him. Before he hit the surging waves, he heard his father shout his name.

He came up with a great breath full of rain and searched the surface. At first, he saw nothing but the storm—monstrous foaming waves, thick curtains of stabbing rain. Then a boil of foam became a fur, and he saw Håkon's back. He swam to him. His body seemed to have turned to stone, and every stroke wanted to pull him downward, but he fought on until he had his friend and turned him over.

Håkon was still—whether senseless or dead, Magni didn't know. Blood ran from an open wound on his forehead. If Brenna and Vali were to lose Håkon as well…No.

124

Like whispers under the bellowing storm, he could hear the shouts of his father and others on the ship. Magni tried to determine where the ship was, through the rain and fog and spray. "HERE! WE'RE HERE!" he shouted and fought off the need to swim. Better they find him; his senses were too confused. "HERE!"

A dark mass loomed suddenly beside him, and he felt hands grabbing at him. He fought them off and handed Håkon to them instead.

When Håkon was back on board, Magni's father leaned down and dragged him into the skeid. Before anything else, his father embraced him, holding him so tightly Magni felt his back crack.

His father shoved him back and stared hard at him, pushing his wet hair from his eyes. "Are you well?"

"Yes. I'm not hurt. Håkon—is Håkon alive?"

When his father turned to check, Magni looked around him. Gudmund had turned Håkon on his side and now pounded him on the back.

In the midst of this storm, raiders still worked. The sail was secure, and another large canvas was battened down across the wale, to offer them some protection. But anyone who could take the time watched Gudmund, and an eerie quiet filled the storm while the healer tried to revive Brenna and Vali's son.

Finally, Håkon coughed and spluttered, and he vomited up a rush of sea water. His eyes fluttered and squinted against the rain. He was alive. He was well.

Magni's father turned back to him. He grabbed his face in both hands and slammed a kiss to the top of his head. "You are a great man, my son. To do such a thing without hesitation, with no thought for yourself, is to be brave beyond measure." Squinting against the pelts of rain, he gave him a wan smile. "And I am thankful I didn't lose you to the effort."

They crawled under the shelter to wait out the storm.

~oOo~

When calm returned, past dawn the following day, they crept out from under cover to see what the storm had wrought. The sun broke through grey clouds, and the sea yet surged crankily, but the wind was fair and in the proper direction. Though the sky was clearing, fog had settled on the surface of the water, so they could not see whether they were still on course. Dazzling strips of colored light danced and glittered in the fog, where sunbeams sliced through.

Magni had the sense of being in a world beyond the one he knew. Perhaps they had sunk after all, and they were no longer in Midgard. It wasn't Valhalla. Was this Vanaheim, or Alfheim? He stared at the colors hanging in the sky, more vivid than the norðrljós that danced in the night sky. Was this the Bifröst?

He shook off his wayward thoughts; the storm and the sea had knocked his sense loose.

At his side, he father turned to him. "Son?"

He shook away the paternal concern with nearly the same movement with which he'd cleared his head. "I'm well. Only the world feels odd just now."

"Yes. Fog and sun together are unusual. It's as if we were hurled to the top of Yggdrasil, above the clouds."

Magni smiled; they'd been thinking similar thoughts.

126

Håkon stepped between Magni and his father. Other than a lump under the cut on his head, and a cough from the seawater, he was well.

"Do you see the other ships?" he asked Magni's father. "My parents? My sister?" There was real concern in his voice, for Solveig as much as for their parents.

"The fog is too thick yet," was Magni's father's answer. He cupped his hands around his mouth. "HELLO! ALL SHIPS HAIL!"

"HELLO! LEIF!" Came a reply almost at once, and not far off. That was Brenna's voice.

Håkon laughed and clapped Magni on the back. "MOTHER!" he shouted, then was beset with coughing.

"HÅKON!" Vali shouted. "ALL IS WELL?"

Håkon nodded and took a breath to shout his answer, but Magni held him back with a hand on his arm. He turned to his father. "The other ships aren't hailing."

The other ships—one from Karlsa, and one their own. On the other ship from Karlsa was Solveig. She'd been in a temper when they'd pushed off from Geitland and had boarded apart from her family and from Magni.

He hadn't protested it—in fact, he'd told himself he didn't care—because he'd been in a temper of his own, his feelings still bloody from their talk in the woods.

If she'd been lost in the storm—he cut that thought off.

Brenna and Vali must have realized the same thing at the same time, because Vali's deep voice shook the sea. "SOLVEIG! HELLO! SOLVEIG!"

Magni ran to the stern of the ship, needing to try a different direction, and shouted as well. "SOLVEIG! SOLVEIG! ARE YOU THERE?"

Leif turned toward the center of the ship. In the biggest voice Magni had ever heard from his father, he shouted, "HOLD SAILS! WE STAY UNTIL THE FOG LIFTS. KEEP CALLING!"

~oOo~

By the time the fog lifted, the sun was nearing its highest point, and Magni's voice was gone. Others had taken up the shouting, but he still stood at the wale, searching an opaque sea.

Vali and Brenna's ship emerged from the fog first, and Håkon greeted his parents' waving arms with his own. Then they got back to searching and calling for the other ships.

When it was clear, they saw the trouble. The ships were far flung, too far to hear or be heard.

But they were afloat, near each other. A cheer went up, and Vali and Leif sent their ships toward those they'd feared lost.

Magni, thinking about Håkon floating face-down in the sea, grabbed hold of an oar and kept his eyes locked on the ships, hoping to see Solveig standing at the wale.

As the ships approached each other, hers was the first face he made out. She was as rumpled by the storm as the rest of them, but the sun shone down on her and turned her fair hair to pale fire.

When she saw him, she smiled, and the sun dimmed in comparison.

Yes, he would wait.

~oOo~

Only a matter of weeks had passed since last the raiders had seen the mouth of Frankia's great river, the Seine. The damage they'd inflicted on the little hamlet and its god house had not yet been repaired, and little effort seemed yet to have been made toward that end.

The people of the village, guard and peasant alike, had seen the skeids approaching, still under full sail and carried swiftly by good wind. They flurried about, preparing to be attacked. Magni squinted, trying to understand if they had a plan of defense, but he could discern none.

"They thought we were gone for good," Håkon said, standing at his shoulder.

"Or at least for the season. Look"—Magni pointed to the god house. He had seen a common pattern of movement. "They gather around their god to guard it." They had taken good treasure from that house, with barely a drop lost of their own blood.

He turned to his father, who stood high on the prow, his arm hooked around the dragon's throat. "Father, do you see?"

"I do. Beware. That is how we were taken sidelong at Mercuria, long ago. They baited us with an empty church. A smart Christian would not have replenished treasure in a place that had been so easily sacked." He twisted his body and raised his voice to address the raiders. "Let us not be lured by the dream of easy pillage. This place is not where our bounty lies. We fight here to thin their ranks, and nothing more. Paris is the prize. Drop sail! We fight as we land!"

129

A group of Frankish soldiers had formed lines on the village side of the river, and arrows flew at the ships while the men still rowed them inland. Karlsa and Geitland had raided as one for a generation, and their strategies were honed to innateness. Leif and Vali called out almost in one voice, and shields went up all at once, protecting the rowers. As arrows rained down on the solid wood, archers rose up and fired back.

At the fore of the ship, at his father's side, Magni watched from under the cover of his shield. Frankish archers fell, and the swordsmen behind them as well, but he also heard each cry and splash that signaled the loss of a raider. Two of theirs had been lost. Three. A small number, but still too many for so early in the fight.

But this was when they were most vulnerable, when they could not fight with their true weapons of war. When their blades were quiet.

His hand pulsed around his drawn sword, tightening and loosening, tightening and loosening, until he could no longer determine where his body ended and his weapon began.

Finally, they made the shore. Most of the first Frankish defense lay dead or dying, turning the river's edge to bloody mush. Those who were left fled inward, sending arrows back as they ran. Magni and his clanspeople leapt from their ships, roaring and splashing through the shallows.

"Leave no armed survivors!" Vali bellowed as he charged ahead of the rest, his thick braid swinging across his broad, bare back.

They didn't find a real fight in the village, either. Two score men, soldiers and village men, probably fishermen, alike stood at the town entrance and stretched back toward the god house. The *church*. That was a Mercurian word, though. Franks had a different word for it. Something like *leglees*. Whatever they called it, it was the house of their god. One god. A dead god. Killed by his own people, as Astrid had once explained it.

No wonder he didn't protect them from attack.

Vali and Leif led the charge, as always. Brenna and Solveig, and Håkon and Magni, were right behind them, as always. All the raiders ran in, shouting together, making thunder with their shared voice.

That singular spirit held even after the fight engaged, though the sounds filling the air became a cacophony. Metal on metal. Metal on wood. Flesh and bone beaten and rent. Blood spilled.

Magni fought as he always did: like he was no longer human. Not that he was stronger than his human body or felt the work of the gods on his weapons, but simply that he and his body no longer had human concerns or pains. He was pure fight, and his mind split into two parts and yet remained whole.

One part, the higher part, kept its sense of the battle itself— where the fight was, where it came from, how the field shaped and shifted, where the people he cared most for were and how they were. That part knew but didn't distract the other part. The lower part was in the fight, letting his muscles do what they were best at. That second part of his mind focused on his opponent and anticipated his movements so that his own body could adjust.

It was a state of being completely aware of everything around him and yet entirely quiet and particularly focused.

Some called it battle rage or bloodlust. But Magni felt neither rage nor lust when he fought. He had no craving for the kill.

He only craved that feeling—that he was one with the world. Everything made perfect sense, because it was all one thing.

Unlike most, Magni tended to fight defensively. There was a knowing that came when one's opponent attacked first—the arc and power of their swing, their preferred stance, any number of details might be learned if one waited to make the second attack and not the first. So he was patient, and he waited, and it had stood him in good stead. He'd never been badly hurt in a raid. Or even moderately hurt. A few bruises. A light cut or two. Nothing yet that had left more than the faintest scar.

His worst scars were on his palms, from swearing blood oaths with Solveig.

Scars were revered among their people, so he had occasionally thought to let himself be struck, just so he could look more like a warrior. Håkon's cheek, the wound only recently closed from their previous raid on Frankia, would be an impressive scar, and the injury had been minor.

Magni pulled his sword from the belly of a farmer bearing a scythe. Sensing movement at his back, he spun, and, seeing the glint of metal even before his eyes had settled on the blade, he sent his shield up and out, interrupting the blow and knocking the blade to the side. This soldier was old, far older than his father; his face was sagging and fleshy, and red as a banked fire under his heavy helm. Were the Franks already so beaten that they had no better soldiers than this lot?

Entertaining pity for a combatant was folly, however, so Magni fought him as if he were a worthy opponent—and the Frank proved himself to have once been a warrior of some note. He blocked Magni's first blow and sent one right back, forcing him to duck and scramble backward, barely getting his shield in place. The blow struck the wood with moderate power.

This would be a contest of strength, then, because this Frank knew the dance—in fact, he fought not unlike a raider. Magni put his shoulder behind his shield and leaned in. He charged and swung at the same time, knocking the Frank back and slashing at his sword arm.

He drew blood, but didn't disarm the man, or take him from his feet. When he swung again, the Frank blocked that blow and slashed, nearly striking Magni across the chest. Like many of their raiders, Magni didn't wear metal armor. Range of movement kept him safer than metal could. But that strike, which left a furrow across his leather, would have opened him wide if he'd been an inch closer.

His higher mind left off its study of the battle at large, and Magni focused his full attention on the fight before him. The old Frank he'd been so ready to pity was putting up the hardest fight of his life. Magni roared and charged forward, meaning to bash him with his shield and full body, but the man stepped aside at just the right moment, and Magni went past him. He spun before his vulnerable back could be struck and changed his approach, pulling his shield and jabbing with his blade.

Their swords weren't made for stabbing. They could and would pierce a body, even an armored body, but as a killing blow. In mid-fight, the rounded point was as likely to glance off a strong opponent as impale him. But Magni's move forced the Frank to block it, and that shifted his body enough that he exposed what Magni really wanted: his tender belly.

He moved his sword with the motion forced by the Frank's block and turned it into a slashing arc, cutting across the man's torso, just under the edge of his armor. The cut was lower than Magni had intended, across his hips and the base of his belly. A few inches higher would have been mortal, but it was enough to bring the old man finally to his knees, and then down to the ground.

Magni kicked him over. He wanted to see the man's face when he dealt him his killing blow.

The peaked Frankish helm rolled off as his body flipped over. His hair was fair and thick, white at his temples but pale yellow otherwise.

Magni lifted his sword high, intending to drive it through the broken mail and into the man's heart.

"Hold! In the Allfather's name, hold! I am you! Like you!"

He'd spoken in words Magni knew. The accent was different, far different, but the words were the same or near enough. Magni lowered his sword, but he kept his hand firm around it.

The old man was from Scandinavia. One of their own, fighting for the Franks.

Magni lifted his sword again. He had no patience for a traitor.

"Hold! You come for Paris, *oui*—yes? I know Paris!"

Throwing his shield on his back, keeping his sword drawn, Magni grabbed the man by his mail armor and dragged him back to his feet. This was for greater men than he to decide.

He would take the traitor to his father.

9

Solveig crouched with her parents, Leif, Magni, and a few of the more seasoned raiders, grouped around their prisoner. Their father had sent Håkon to aid in staking the camp. He'd gone off in bad humor, angry to have been excluded when Solveig hadn't been.

She had little to say or offer, but she watched and listened with keen interest as her father and Leif questioned the old man who was from both worlds. His name had been Ogmundr, but he was called Amaury now.

He was badly injured, and his grasp of their language had rusted, but they'd learned that, as a younger man, he'd been pulled from the sea after his ship had sunk. He'd been taken prisoner and released when he'd abjured the gods of Asgard and taken the Christian god as his own. Then he'd been conscripted into the Frankish army.

In Solveig's mind, where he'd been born didn't matter. He'd betrayed the gods, and he'd fought against his own kind. For years, he had. He was a Frank like every other Frank, and he couldn't be trusted.

But her father and Leif shot question after question at him, like a barrage of arrows.

"It cannot be unbreachable," Leif said. "Or they would be locked in as others were locked out. There must be a break in this monstrous wall."

Amaury gasped and tried to shift his legs, clutching his bleeding belly. "Please…I answer what you ask, *mais je*…but I die soon. Have you no…*guérisseur?* No…healer?"

Solveig's father leaned close and pushed his hand into the man's wound, making him cry out like a young girl. "You answer, and then you will be seen to." He pulled his hand away. It was coated with thick, dark blood. "Where is the breach?"

"There is a gate!" the old man cried. "A gate. Thickest oak…and strongest iron. Guarded by the best of the king's men. It can be opened…but never…broken." He swooned, sagging forward against his bindings.

"I'll go for Gudmund," Magni offered.

"No." Solveig's mother stood up, and the others stood with her. "We need nothing more from him. He's a traitor and cannot be trusted. Whether he speaks true or false, we must see the city before we attack it." She turned to Magni. "Would you finish your kill, Magni?"

Solveig watched as Magni considered the insensible traitor surrounded by them all. He seemed to hesitate, and she thought she understood why. Magni fought those who fought him. In her knowing, he'd never killed anyone helpless, as the traitor now was. There might come a day when he would have to kill as punishment, when he took his father's seat, but he'd not been in that position before now.

But the old man was a traitor, and a Frank. An enemy. He deserved a death. What was more, Magni had already dealt him a wound that would become mortal if left untended. Killing him now would be a mercy.

Solveig felt as though she could see those thoughts move through Magni's golden head. Finally, he nodded and drew his knife from his belt. He went to the old man, twisted his fist into his hair, yanked his insensible head up, and sliced his throat open.

~oOo~

"If he was true about the wall, we aren't strong enough to take defenses like that. We need to ally with Gunnar and Tollak and return in force."

"No." Leif and Vali answered Magni at the same time.

Magni dragged his hand through his hair. He still wore the blood of his kills from the fight, and he drew new streaks through his blonde locks. "But why? We are but hundreds. If Paris is as protected as he described, we can only take it if we can come in from many points."

Solveig's father cocked his head and gave Magni an admiring nod. "Your thinking is sound, Magni Leifsson. But I would not ally with Gunnar or Tollak for a raid so great."

"But they are our friends! They settled Norshire with us!"

Magni was angry and tense, and Solveig had to clutch her hands around her middle so she didn't reach out to him. They'd barely spoken since the last night in Geitland, and they'd spent no time alone. She was to blame, she knew. She'd wounded him. She'd done it purposefully, to force distance between them, but now that she had it, she was bereft. He was her friend, and she'd lose that if she wouldn't be more, as he wished them to be.

She wished it as well, but she feared so much what she would lose, should she gain him.

Leif set his hand on his son's shoulder. "Our alliances were strong with Ivar and Finn, but now the friendships are of tradition more than trust. Their sons have ambitions that cannot be trusted. It is said that Tollak killed his father."

"Said, not proved," Håkon said. It was the first time he'd spoken during this meeting, which was the first time he'd been invited to sit with the leaders while they strategized.

"True," their father said, casting a curious look at his son. "And that is why we keep the friendship, but not the trust. Solveig—what are your thoughts, my sun?"

She had been quiet as well, but she had been paying close attention. Paris was where her destiny lay. Knowing as well that this was a test, the leaders of their people listening to hear if she herself could lead, she spoke clearly and with conviction. "The man Magni brought us was twice a traitor. To his people, and to the Franks. He cannot be trusted. I agree with my mother's wisdom, and with my father's. We should press on and see this wall, and then we should make a plan to breach it."

"And if we can't breach it?"

"Magni," Solveig's father answered, "A walled city is not so different from a castle. The wall obstructs the people within more than those without. They put all their faith in the stone, and leave other defenses weak. Again and again, we've seen this."

Leif leaned in. "And yet, we should be wary. It's been many years since we've failed, but best we not believe we are invulnerable. Let us see Paris and know the real truth with our own eyes. We push on and take Rouen again. Then we'll establish a strong encampment for a base and make our plan."

~oOo~

That night, they set up only the barest camp, enough to feed and regroup, to guard and to rest, because they meant to move up the river with the next daybreak. A watch was set, and some raiders went to the river to fish while others tended the fire and set up mead and fresh water, or found the place where they would lay their heads.

People slept in groups in a camp like this, for safety and warmth, and made what comfort they could. While her mother and brother fished, Solveig and her father set up their sleeping area, behind a fallen log thick with lush moss.

Every world she'd walked in that wasn't her own was familiar and yet strange to her. The grass and trees, the hills and valleys, the streams and seas were all like those at home, and yet they were not. The leaves and colors were different. The blossoms were almost what she knew but not quite. And the smells—each world had its own scent. This one, here deep in the shadow of its trees, had a kind of tang to it, like the rich spices that came from the merchant ships. Solveig stood tall, tipped her head back in the dappled sun of late afternoon, and took a deep breath.

"Have you shaken off your foul temper?" her father asked, coming between her and the sun.

"I had no foul temper."

He gave the look he always gave when one of his children said something he thought beneath them in some way. "Solveig. You sailed apart from all of us. I know you quarreled with your mother before we left."

Of course he did. Her parents kept no one's confidence between them but their own. "It wasn't a quarrel."

That was true. Her mother had simply told her she wasn't good enough, and then Solveig had walked away, into the woods, where there were no eyes to see her and find her wanting.

Her father took hold of her arm and led her to the fallen log. She stood rigid there until he gave her an almost-gentle push, and she sat hard on the moss. He took his seat at her side. "Tell me what happened."

"You know. She told you, I'm sure."

"She told me her story. You know we have no secrets between us. And she was upset—she needed my comfort. Your mother loves you more than there are words to say it, Solveig. I don't understand this tension between you."

Solveig had many secrets, but she would tell them all to everyone the whole world over, she would expose her every weakness to everyone and stand for all their ridicule and judgment, before she would let her father know she had even one. His disappointment in her, his disillusionment, she couldn't bear. Not him.

So she found a lie that was close enough to truth that it might pass by him. "She talked to me about Magni. Everyone wants us to be together. No one thinks what we want."

"Do you say you don't want that?"

Better to avoid that question. "I don't know why you do. As long as I can remember, you've talk about it."

He grinned and hooked his arm around her. She couldn't help it; she leaned in and settled her head on his chest. So broad and strong. All her life, she'd tucked herself close to her father and known she was safe and loved. Even now, she knew it. "My little húsvættr, dropping over the eaves to hear things not meant for her ears. I want you to love with your whole heart, and I care not who that might be. Your mother feels the same. I think Leif and Olga feel as we do. It was only a lighthearted dream among friends, to see our children mated and our friendship sealed in such a way. To share

140

grandchildren. I think none of us has advanced the cause to you or to Magni, have we?"

That was true. No one had pushed them together. At least not overtly. She shook her head. His long beard brushed her brow.

"You avoided my question. I noticed. Do you want Magni?"

This conversation was her own fault. Deflecting from her true quarrel with her mother had brought her to yet another fraught topic. Afraid to speak the answer, Solveig closed her eyes and tried to calm herself.

Her father was still as well, and they sat and listened to the forest—the low rumble of their people, the song of late birds, the rustle of small animals moving in the brush.

A small rock rolled out nearby, and they both sat up straight and looked around, seeking friend or foe. A spotted grey creature, something like a heavy cat, trundled by. Otherwise, they were alone.

"I await an answer, Solveig. Whether you do or not is your choice, and Magni's. No one else. The life you choose should be the life you wish to live. I'll not force you in any direction. Nor will your mother. But you have twenty years. The time has come to choose a life. You will be my daughter always, but you must become your own woman as well."

That was what she wanted. To be her own woman. "How can I be my own woman if I'm Magni's woman?"

He gave her the look as if what she'd said was beneath her. "Would you say that your mother is my woman?"

She nodded.

"Would you say that she is more than merely that?"

Of course she was. "Mother is special. She's the God's-Eye."

Her father's brow tightened into deep furrows. "Be careful where you use that name. You know she doesn't like it. She accepts it, but she shouldn't have to hear it from her own children."

"I'm sorry. But it's true. She's a legend. I'm just…" Solveig stopped. They were too close to the worst thing.

"Her beloved daughter. And mine. A shieldmaiden in your own right. A woman on the cusp of your story. Solveig, it isn't your mother's eye that makes her a legend. It's her heart and her will. It's her strength and her spirit. With her love for me, and mine for her, she stands stronger. I am stronger because I'm her man. Our love doesn't diminish us. It lifts us up."

He put his fingers under her chin and lifted so they were eye to eye. "I know you want to step out of your mother's shadow. I understand. But you won't manage it on your own. We cannot live this life alone. You run away from the things that will give you all you want and more. The bonds of love aren't chains to hold you back. Love who you will, my sun. But love."

Her mother had accused her of running away as well. It seemed that everyone thought she was a coward. Solveig had stood up and taken two steps away before she realized that she had been about to prove them right. She froze. Behind her, her father stood, and she turned around and faced him.

He was smiling in the way she knew best of all. "You never did answer my question, but I think the answer lies in that. You want him. And you want yourself."

Her mouth would form no answer still, but he was right, and he knew it.

He pulled her into his arms. "Take what you want. Take all that you want."

~oOo~

With her father's words, and the echo of her mother's in Geitland, ringing in her mind, Solveig moved through the camp. She sought Magni without quite meaning to. It wasn't so simple as to have her parents' counsel and thus simply know what was right. And yet she wanted to see him.

She found him along the edge of the forest, in sight of the river, chopping wood. He'd stripped his chestpiece and tunic away, and she stopped before he saw her so she could watch him work.

He was a beautiful man; there had been no question of his appeal. Broad-shouldered and well muscled. His hips were slim and his legs strong. Like her father, his chest was hairless.

He'd washed, and wound his hair into a loose braid, as he always did when he worked like this. When he raided, he pulled only the front part back into braids, leaving the rest to fan over his back. At leisure, he wore his hair like his father did, loose and unadorned.

A tattoo spanned the top of his back, from shoulder to shoulder; she hadn't seen it before. Its ink was dark, as if newly etched. Perhaps after the last raid. It was an image of two birds, ravens, she thought, like Odin's, and they seemed to fly as his muscles surged with each blow of the axe. Solveig felt every shift in his body in the very core of her own.

Wondering if he was still angry with her for the way she'd spoken to him in the Geitland forest, preparing herself as best she could for rejection, she went forward.

143

"You spoke well today. About Paris." She tensed as if he might turn his axe and cut her down.

She'd timed her words with his swings, so that she wouldn't startle him overmuch. But he didn't seem surprised at all. He must have been paying wide attention as he'd worked, keeping one eye out for trouble.

Had he known she'd stood there, among the trees, watching him? At the thought, Solveig felt her face grow hot.

He dropped the axe and picked up his tunic, using it to wipe his face. "You're speaking to me again?" As he asked, he brushed his tunic across his chest. Solveig couldn't stop her eyes from following that motion, over his glistening skin, his rolling muscles. It worried her, the way her body sometimes ignored her mind when he was near.

"You're the one who walked away. With another girl's flowers over your shoulders." No, no, no! That wasn't why she'd sought him out. Not to quarrel!

Why *had* she, then? Well, because she wanted their friendship. She missed him, the keeper of all her secrets. She wanted to make peace with him. She wanted...

Magni sighed, and the sound was frustration itself. "I don't wish to fight with you, Solveig. I've had enough of battle for the day." He yanked his tunic over his head and pulled it down over his torso. The linen clung to his work-dampened skin.

"Wait."

He stopped in mid-motion, bending to pick up the axe again. After a pause the length of a heartbeat, he picked it up and stood tall, holding the handle with a loose grip. He stared at her, waiting.

Solveig didn't know what to do or to say. Her heart thudded far harder than it ever did in battle.

He said nothing, but he didn't move to leave again. He simply stood where he was. He waited.

Her parents' words echoed in her mind.

Take what you want. Take all that you want.

Here on the earth, there are delights you're missing.

Our love doesn't diminish us. It lifts us up.

And Magni's words. *I will wait.*

She was not a coward. She was a shieldmaiden, born of legends, and she was brave and strong. Not a legend in her own right, not yet, but no wisp to be trampled underfoot. ·

Or perhaps she *was* a coward. There were things she wanted, but she had yet to fight to have them. She feared failure, and that was craven.

The bonds of love aren't chains to hold you back.

"What do you want, Solveig?"

Take what you want. Take all that you want.

"I don't want to be obscured by any man. I don't want to be pulled from my path."

He said nothing. His expression didn't change. He waited.

Our love doesn't diminish us. It lifts us up.

Squaring her shoulders, she went to him. This man whom she had loved all her life like a brother. This man whom she loved now as a man. Good and strong and beautiful. He would not hold her back. He never had.

She set her hands on his chest. "I want you to love me as a woman."

He flinched and grabbed her wrists in his free hand. She thought he might push her away, but he only held her and stared into her eyes. "I do. I love you for all that you are."

She wanted more than the words. Now that she'd taken this path, she needed to know its terrain. "I want you to show me. I want to feel it."

"What?"

Every part of her will was committed to the task of keeping her body from trembling. Never had she been more terrified. "I love you, Magni Leifsson. I trust you. If you would have me, then have me."

Something wonderful happened then. Magni's face changed. It softened, and a light entered his eyes and made them glitter.

He looked at her the way her father looked at her mother. A look of naked, consuming love.

She was trapped in that look, lost in his glittering eyes, but she heard the thump as he dropped the axe, and then his arms were around her, and his mouth was on hers. As he drew her tightly to his body, his tongue pushed between her lips, and it was like no other kiss they'd ever shared.

Solveig let go of fear and doubt. She let go of legacy. She wrapped her arms around Magni's neck and clung to love.

10

All the times Magni's hands had been on Solveig, hundreds of times throughout their lives, thousands, never had it been this. They were entwined now so tightly they'd almost become one.

While his tongue searched her mouth, memorizing its silky taste, he pushed his hands up her back until they were at her head, gripping braids stiff with sweat and blood from the earlier battle.

They were in Frankia. An enemy land. Though a watch was set and patrols ran the woods, he would keep the topmost part of his mind high and alert. But the rest of himself, he would devote to the woman in his arms, for as long as she would stay there. For whatever it was she wanted of him.

He knew everything about her, and yet he was surprised by the feel of her, the way her body locked with his just so, the way her breasts swelled against his chest, the sound of her breath, the skim of it across his cheek.

She began to learn their kiss, to settle into their sharing. Her hands wound into his hair. Her leg nudged between his. Her tongue found his and slicked along its edge. The full core of him, from that point, through his heart, and his belly, straight to his sex, thrummed and clenched. What did she think of the hard ridge digging into her thigh?

"Solveig," he gasped, turning his mouth so he could find breath and perhaps some sense. The part of him that had been tasked with keeping alert had already forgotten its mission. "Tell me what you want."

Her eyes were wide and clear with surprise, and with dawning comprehension, and she didn't answer at once. She only stared up at him, those wide eyes glittering above cheeks rosy-bright.

"Tell me," he prodded and set a light kiss at the corner of her perfect, sweet mouth.

"I want everything."

Her answer made him smile. "Everything? All the world? Right now?"

She returned his smile. "Show me, Magni."

"Tell me again."

She rose up on her toes and brushed her cheek over his beard. "I love you."

He'd known long that she did—longer than she herself. But the words filled him nonetheless. "And I love you."

A twig broke nearby, and they both turned toward the sound. Solveig's hand dropped from his hair to the pommel of her sword, and Magni let go to grab the axe from the ground.

Håvard and Torsten passed, on patrol. They only nodded in greeting, but their broad grins said more than enough regarding what they'd seen.

They walked on, and Magni and Solveig stood still and watched until they were out of sight.

The river glinted through the trees, long streaks of red glow. The day was dying. Magni wasn't sure what Solveig had been prepared to do, here in the woods, but they were too far from camp, and too close to the river, to be safe in the dark.

"We should return to camp." He picked up her hand.

She pulled it free. "No! I don't—I don't want to spend the night with my parents and Håkon. I want to know, Magni. I want to feel. I don't want to wait."

Neither did he. He'd been waiting all his life, and wouldn't have waited another second, but desire did nothing to change reality, and one of them had to think beyond their want. "It's not safe here. Not in the dark."

Her head swiveled as she studied the darkening woods. "Closer to camp, then. But still alone. I don't want to be…amidst everyone, either."

"Nor I." He held out his hand; perhaps if she chose to take it, she wouldn't be so quick to pull free. "If you truly want this, we'll find a place."

She set her hand in his. He closed his fingers around it and led her back to camp.

~oOo~

His father had shown little surprise but much interest when Magni had collected his roll, but he'd only warned them not to stray beyond sight of the fire.

They'd taken a torch and found a copse of small trees, the ground amidst them covered in soft moss. They were close enough to camp to see its glow and hear the unison whisper of many people quieting for night, but far enough to feel alone.

Solveig stood between two trees while Magni spread a fur over the moss. When he held out his hand to her, she looked over her shoulder, toward the camp.

Was it wrong to do this here? Outdoors, in a foreign land, where enemies might lurk in the shadows? It was. "We can wait, Solveig. Until we're home."

She faced him. "We don't share the same home."

"We might. Stay in Geitland with me, when we return."

In the way her expression blanked, Magni could see that she hadn't thought that far, hadn't considered what life would be when they were mated. She was hurrying along a path she didn't know, one she'd feared, and he'd just thrown up the first barricade.

"Or I will go to Karlsa with you. But we should wait."

"No." She entered the shelter of their little tree ring and came up so close that she nearly stepped on his feet. "No." Her hands pushed under his loose tunic and grazed his belly. Oh gods, how that felt. His muscles twitched wildly, and his sex grew again.

She noticed. Her eyes dropped to his belly and came back up. A smile flowered, blossoming in her cheeks. "My touch does that?"

He nodded. Magni had been a man in every respect since he'd had fourteen years. He'd held his heart for Solveig, but when she'd declared, on a wooded cliff above Karlsa, that she'd wed no one until she was a legend, he'd freed his body to know the pleasure it could find. Women found him comely, and he was the jarl's son, so he'd had no shortage of fair girls, and women, to warm him and teach him during the past five years.

Never was he gladder of that tutelage than now, when he knew he could show Solveig what she wanted to experience. It would be good for her, because he had been taught well.

More than that, he now also understood the limits of his experience. Inside his chest, his heart beat a feverish tempo. To couple with love—this was as new for him as it was for her. The way his body responded to her touch wasn't nervousness or even physical pleasure. It was love. Like a lightning-flash straight to his soul.

He yanked his tunic up and away, dropping it to the fur at his feet.

Her hands slid up higher, smoothing over the planes of his chest. While she explored the terrain of his body, he focused his attention on uncovering hers.

He unlaced her chestpiece, and she left off her caressing study to help him remove her clothes. Then she took over entirely, brushing his hands away, and he focused on his own clothing. Solveig shed each piece purposefully, without affect, as if she prepared to bed down for the night's sleep, though they would have stayed clothed on this night if they were truly bedding down.

At the thought, Magni remembered where they were, and he stopped and studied the darkness beyond their trees. If they were set upon in the midst...

Solveig stopped as well. "Something?" she whispered.

"No." He looked more deeply, but only saw black beyond the aura of their small torch, staked into the ground. "I worry."

"If they come on us, they'll follow the light. We'll have time to dress and run back if the camp is attacked, but they'll not find us here." She picked up the torch and upended it, dousing it in the dirt. Darkness swallowed them whole. He felt her hands on him again, sliding around his waist and up his back. "Please, Magni. Show me."

With his breeches loose on his hips, he picked up her bare body and laid her down on the fur. In his mind's fantasies, he'd seen her clearly when he first had her, watched pleasure paint her face, but he could do without the sense of sight. She filled all his others completely.

He found her mouth in the dark, and this time, she knew exactly what to do. She opened, and her tongue met his. She hooked her arms around him and shifted her body, lifting one leg, bending it at the knee and planting her foot alongside his hip. She'd moved so that her sex was against his, only the leather of his open breeches between them, and she ground her hips into him.

The chuckle he'd intended became a stuttering groan instead. He lifted his hips and broke their kiss, making some space while there was still time. "You move too fast. There's more than that joining to feel. It will be better if we spend some time before."

"I want to feel it."

"You will, I swear. Let me lead. I know the way."

She huffed. "How many?"

He understood, and wished that he didn't. "Is that a conversation for this moment, Solveig? Is it something you really wish to know?"

She didn't answer.

"I would it had been only you. From the start. When you gave me hope, there were no more."

Another huff; her breath breezed over his face. "That was only weeks ago."

"Indeed. There were years after I told you how I felt before you gave me hope." Wanting to restore the tone between them, Magni bent his head and brushed his nose over hers. "Can we speak of this later?"

He felt her nod, and he claimed her mouth again before she could think of more words that would turn this moment of love into a battle instead.

While he kissed her, with his higher mind, Magni strategized. They couldn't indulge in languorous lovemaking, not here in the Frankish woods. Clearly, and as usual, her nervousness had become combativeness; best to cover her mouth until her body could distract her. So he would keep his mouth on hers and hold off tasting her for a more peaceful time. Tonight, their first time, should be beautiful and momentous, but perhaps not all-consuming.

He would use his hands to show her all the points of her body that could feel pleasure, until she was ready to feel him inside her. Eager as she was, she wasn't ready yet. He'd had maidens before, and they'd all felt pain at first, some more acutely than others. Sometimes, there was blood. Something inside would tear, he knew that. It would help if her need for him were great when he entered her.

When he brought his hand up and cupped her breast, his higher mind went quiet and his dreams came to life. She gasped in his mouth and arched her back, without any fear at all. He closed his fingers around the point of her nipple, and it went hard. Her arms clamped tightly around him, and the leg she'd planted at his hip hooked over his back. Gods!

Then one hand swept down his back, into his breeches, and clutched his arse. Nothing about the hot, writhing woman in his arms seemed naïve.

Was she a maiden? Could this be all instinct?

She was a grown woman and had been for years. She'd made no promise to him—even now, she'd made no promise. If she'd lain with men, she was in her right to do so. An unmarried woman who bore a child might be a source of talk, but otherwise a woman was as free to find pleasure as a man was. But the thought made Magni boil with jealousy. If she wasn't a maiden, she'd let him think otherwise. She'd led him to think so—to believe that no one had had her before him.

He broke away, lifting his head and letting go of her breast to prop himself up on that arm.

"Magni?" He couldn't see her face, but her voice gasped and shook.

No. He'd have known if she'd been with others. As she knew of him. There would have been talk. All their world thought them promised to each other from the cradle.

But he'd expected shyness and hesitation from her. Why? She'd never been shy with him. On this night, she'd been the one pushing them toward this. He hadn't seduced her, she'd seduced him. Was that because she trusted him, or because she knew what they would do?

"I won't hurt you," he said, as an answer where one was wanting, and because there would be something to be learned in any response she had.

Her hand came up and stroked his beard. "I know it will hurt. All the girls talk and talk. But I'm not afraid."

She was a maid, of course. He'd been unfair to think she'd lied, and to be jealous, when he'd been free with his body. "I love you."

"I love you as well." He could hear the smile in her voice. "Will you touch me again like you were?"

"I'll touch you everywhere," he said, and brought his mouth and hand back where they belonged.

She responded to his every touch as if lightning surged from his fingertips. He disentangled himself from her legs and leaned on his hip so that her body was open to his explorations, and though he couldn't see, he memorized every inch of her silky flesh within reach. Every inch but those few between her thighs. She quivered and gasped, making the soft mounds of her breasts tremble against him, and she finally tore her mouth from his and sucked in air until her lungs were full.

"Magni!" It was a shout and a whisper, both. A command and a plea. "Please!"

His mouth free, he dipped his head and captured a hard pearl of nipple between his teeth. He didn't bite—tonight would be only gentle love—but she jerked and flung her limbs around, then slapped her hands to his head and held him where he was. He finally let his hand travel lower, past her belly and down, until soft curls brushed over his fingers.

"Oh," she gasped, almost without sound. "Magni."

As he suckled her, he pushed his fingers between her legs, through her folds. She was as wet as ever he'd felt, and hotter than he could believe. His finger skimmed over the bead at her center, and her hips came up off the fur and hung there, as if she floated.

"More, more, more."

Long before he'd known for himself, before his sex had felt its first need, a boy he knew had told him that rutting to release was like scratching an itch. He'd said you could even do it with your hands. The boy had been older, and Magni, with only nine or so years then, had no cause to disbelieve him, but it had seemed bizarre.

Now, he had his own experience to know Erik's description hadn't been so far off—and yet miles away as well. He smiled as he flicked his finger back and forth over the node of Solveig's most intense pleasure, letting his fingernail graze it just lightly every now and then, as if he meant to ease an itch. Her body heaved with each sweep of his finger.

He lost his rhythm when she sat up. "Solveig?"

She grabbed his hand and slammed it back where it had been. "Don't stop. But I…I touch myself, but I…this…it's…I thought I knew…"

They spoke in whispers. Laughing just as quietly, he sat up as well. "I know. Nothing we can do to ourselves is its equal."

He slipped behind her and pulled her back to recline on his chest. Then he tucked his face against her neck, biting gently into her soft flesh. He caught a breast with one hand and slid the other between her legs, to find her itch again.

She completed almost at once, digging her hands into this thighs, clamping the leather, and some skin, in her fists. Her body went rigid, and her feet scrabbled on the fur, but she didn't cry out. Her juices flowed over his hand. She released wildly, for an eternity, and almost completely without sound.

He stopped exciting her body, but he didn't move otherwise. He held her, keeping his hands in place, while she returned to calm.

"I know why my parents do this so much," she murmured at last, and Magni chuckled.

Of course. She'd seen coupling all her life, just as he had. There was little she didn't know except the feel of it. No wonder she wasn't shy. He'd known few shy girls, in truth. It wasn't a common trait among their people, who lived in close proximity with each other, with few walls between them, all their lives. He couldn't say why he'd expected Solveig to exhibit it.

Except, perhaps, that he wanted her to be his alone. His treasure, not to be shared.

"Would you have more? Would you have me, even if it might hurt?" As wet as she was, there was no better time.

She nodded on his chest and moved to lie down again, but Magni had a better idea. He caught her around the waist and lifted. Sensing what he was trying to do, she helped, and turned around so she sat on his legs, facing him. His sex had escaped his breeches and stood up between them like a spear, so pronounced that it made itself known even in the dark.

"Do you want me to touch you?" Her hand wrapped around him, and he was nearly undone.

He closed his hand around hers. "No. I'll not last long that way. Touch me like that another time. Now, sit down on me. Fill yourself with me, and stop when you wish. If you wish."

She rose up on her knees and scooted closer. His hand still held hers around his shaft, and they held him together as she sank onto him.

"Ah, gods," he grunted as her body enveloped him and held him tighter than any fist could.

Her sex had not yet met their hands when he felt the fragile membrane that proved beyond doubt that no one had yet gone where he was. His tip pushed against it, and she gasped and flinched upward.

"That's it?"

He nodded, then remembered that she couldn't see him. "Yes. The pain comes when it breaks."

"There is pain now. It burns."

"Your sheath is tight. I think it's the stretch."

"Yes. That's what it feels like. You don't quite fit." She laughed. "Does that make you proud?"

In truth, in ordinary circumstances he was proud of his size. Boys compared with each other, and he had nothing to be ashamed of. But just now, he worried about her pain. He liked her humor, however. It spoke of her ease and, in turn, eased him. "It is a mighty sword, at that."

She slapped his belly. "Well, then. Let's see if its blade strikes true." She pulled her hand from him, knocking his hand free as she did, and sat down fully.

The sensation was so explosive and profound that Magni went stiff and solid as iron, from head to toe. Not even sound would move through him. The lack of sight had heightened all his remained senses, especially touch, and he could feel every pulse and twitch inside her. Hot and soft, firm and wet, throbbing around him like all of life converging on the point of their joining.

Solveig was quiet as well. Her hands dug into his shoulders, and he could feel the shiver of tension in them. He fought to take a breath deep enough to allow him to speak.

"Solveig?" His voice grated like the keel of a ship over sand.

"Hurts." A stunted gasp.

The word shook him from his reverie. "I'm sorry. Lift up. I don't need—"

"No!" She forgot to whisper. "I do need. I need you to feel what I just felt. What you gave me."

"There's no need to be in pain for that. You can touch me with your hands."

She flexed, and they both groaned, for their own reasons. "I want this."

He grabbed her hips and held her still. "I don't want it if it hurts you. Don't do that to me."

His body wanted it, no matter how she felt or what his mind said, and he'd mustered all his will to stop her. When she flexed again, his will slipped. He groaned and tried to speak but could form no words.

"It hurts less each time I move," she said, and he decided to believe her and give in to them both. He released her hips and wrapped his arms around her, finding her mouth in the dark.

He let her move as she would, and he could feel her searching, seeking an ease to her pain and, perhaps, a path to her pleasure. For his part, every flex and roll and sway drew him higher. He held off as long as he could, hoping that her pain would end and pleasure begin, but soon, too soon, he was rocking with her rhythm, clutching her bottom, chasing his release.

When he needed more breath, he broke away and let his head fall to her shoulder. Her mouth was at his ear when he heard it—a tiny gasp, striking a different, higher note. He knew that sound; already it was familiar. He'd heard it when he'd used his hand.

She'd found pleasure.

Claiming fresh restraint, he rolled, laying her on the fur again, and took over. With his every thrust, Solveig struck that gasping note. He slid his hand under her, lifting her hips, and drove a bit harder, and her gasping refrain became a name: his.

"Magni…Magni…Magni!"

"Yes," he answered, gritting out the word. "With me. Are you there with me?"

She didn't answer, but her hands twisted in his hair and pulled, her sheath clenched around him, and he let himself go, withdrawing from her at the last possible moment and spending over her belly.

He collapsed atop her, and they lay gasping and damp together. When he could, he found his tunic—he thought it was his tunic—in the dark and wiped them both clean.

"How do you feel?" he asked.

Solveig purred and rolled to tuck herself at his side. "I tingle and thrum."

Apt words for his own feeling, as well. "We should dress before we sleep, love."

"Love," she sighed and said no more. It seemed they would sleep bare in these Frankish woods tonight.

Keeping as still as he could, Magni felt around the edge of the fur for his cloak. He spread it over them, folded Solveig in his arms, and closed his eyes.

~oOo~

Magni woke with a sense of doom, and flipped his eyes open at once, reaching for his axe. It wasn't there.

Vali held it, cocked in his hand. He stood over them, snarling.

Solveig slept on, snoring lightly, as if they weren't in enemy territory with an Úlfhéðinn father looming over them like a furious mountain.

Her father tossed the axe, and its blade sank into the ground quite near Magni's head. He hadn't missed. If he'd meant him harm, Magni would have had an axe between his eyes.

"If you'd gotten her killed, cavorting in the Frankish woods like fools, I'd have had your skin for a cloak and your skull for a helm. Dawn breaks soon. We strike camp and sail on."

He turned and stomped off toward the camp. Magni watched him go, trying to settle his heart.

"Solveig." He nudged her shoulder. "Wake up." She moaned and tucked her nose under his cloak. He shook her harder. "Where do you think you are, love? We must wake and go. We're in Frankia, remember?"

That brought her eyes up. "Trouble?" She sat up, and Magni was momentarily distracted by the sight of her. Even with her braids matted and mussed, still dyed in places by the bloody battle of the day before, she was magnificent. The blushy tips of her breasts peeked over his sagging cloak, and he briefly considered pushing her back to the fur.

Then he remember Vali.

He answered her question. "With your father. Not with the Franks. Though I'd rather face them, I think."

"My father?"

Magni nodded. "He woke me. Displeased that I had you here. To say it lightly."

Her laugh surprised him—and offended him a bit. An angry berserker was nothing to laugh at, he thought, as the man who'd spent the night with that berserker's treasured daughter.

"He threw an axe at my head. I don't think he was joking."

"You'd be dead if he meant you harm. He's not angry about this. He all but threw me at you."

"What do you mean?"

"Only that our parents will be pleased that we are mated." She stood, and again, he took in the view, until he saw that blood smeared her thighs. She didn't notice, however, and stepped into her breeches without any appearance of discomfort.

His silence seemed to pique her, and she turned, holding her tunic, her chest still bare. "We *are* mated, yes?"

He rose to his feet and drew her into his arms, savoring the touch of their bare chests together. "Yes, my love. I would wed you as soon as we return home."

"To Geitland." Her tone was not agreement. It was recollection—that hesitation she'd shown the night before, realizing that she hadn't seen far enough, was back.

"Or to Karlsa. I told you, Solveig. We'll decide together where to make our home."

"But you're Leif's only heir. You'll be Jarl of Geitland someday."

"If I wish. There are others who could lead. You'll be Jarl of Karlsa. Would you cede your father's seat to your brother?"

She frowned and pulled away. "I…I don't know. I didn't think."

Magni knew this, what was happening in her mind, and he knew how to stop it. He caught her arm and drew her back. "Solveig. Stop. All that matters now is that we love, and will be wed, and that we will decide together what we'll do when the time is right. We both would have our fathers live on forever if we could. We needn't hurry toward their deaths by planning for what would follow. Until we must make a choice like this, let us leave it aside. For now, we can live in both places—Karlsa when we wish, and Geitland when we wish."

Her eyes sailed back and forth between his, and he felt as if she were examining his every thought. When she had what she needed from that study, she nodded.

"Yes? You will marry me?" He wanted the word.

"Yes."

11

Solveig leaned against the wale and watched Frankia go by. They were approaching the next town, the farthest inland they'd traveled during their previous raid—or ever before. Beyond this place, the next place of note, according to the hide map they carried, was Paris. A city of gold and splendor, it was said.

The banks of this river were quiet and uninhabited. They'd seen no one, not even a fisherman, since they'd struck their camp. It seemed that the town they'd next approach might be as poorly defended as the one at the mouth of the river had been. The damage they'd inflicted earlier in the season had crippled the Franks badly.

Behind her, raiders at oar grunted and pulled in time, and Solveig let herself be lulled, not to dullness but to calm.

A shadow moved over her, and she looked up at Magni, who smiled and sat behind her, framing her in his legs and arms. She tensed at that, the possessiveness of it, and he cocked his eyebrow at her, but then she relaxed. By the time they'd left the woods that morning, the whole camp had quite clearly known how they'd spent night before; they'd all leered and japed at them as if no one had ever rutted in the woods before, so there was no point in discretion.

Besides, she liked the way it felt, to have him wish to touch her this way. To be touched this way. She leaned back against his chest and allowed herself to feel the ease of their connection.

She and Magni had touched each other with affection all their lives, but now, all was different between them. Even something as simple as his hand on her shoulder was different. With each touch, she felt a claiming. And she felt it as something that was right. Her father had told her that love wouldn't diminish her, and here, now, in Magni's arms, she could believe that it might be true. If she were careful and stayed out of his shadow.

Solveig knew her own body well, not only as a warrior but as a woman. She'd explored it fully and found all its points of pleasure—or so she'd believed. Yet what she and Magni had done was entirely new to her. She'd asked him to show her what she'd been missing, and he certainly had. But last night was more than the delights of the flesh. There had seemed to be something hovering around them in their circle of trees, like an aura. Something that couldn't be contained in their bodies.

What she'd asked of him had been more than their flesh. She'd asked him to show her love, and he had.

She'd sailed with him and his father this time because she wanted to be near him, and because it had seemed right—like Brenna God's Eye and Vali Storm-Wolf, they were mated, in the eyes of their people as much as between themselves. It frightened her, the thought that already she was part of a whole rather than whole unto herself, but she remembered her father's words. She made him speak them again and again, ceaselessly, in her memory.

Love doesn't diminish us. It lifts us up.

She'd been right that her father wasn't angry about their joining. The first faces they'd seen had been her parents, and they'd both simply smiled as if nothing new or momentous had happened. Just the next step on a path they'd plotted long ago.

Her father had asked, as they'd laded the ships, if she was well, but he'd been content with her assurance that she was. Then he'd warned her to keep her head about her in Frankia, day and night. And that had been that.

Magni's head bent to hers, and she felt his beard, and then his lips, on her neck. Her body leaned toward that touch before her mind could think. There was something in this new bonding that she needed. Something she'd never felt before, though she'd loved him longer than only the past night. Perhaps she'd loved him like this for years.

"We should be looking out," she murmured, turning her face so that his beard brushed her cheek. A bit of the black she used to mark herself for battle colored the golden fur on his cheek.

"I am. How do you feel?"

It was their first moment of something like privacy, here in a ship with a hundred of their clanspeople, since they'd left the woods.

She felt swollen in body and soul, but delightfully so, an ache she wanted never to lose, a pain she craved. "Well. You?"

"Brilliant."

"Our names are on everyone's tongue this morning."

He laughed. "You wanted your story told."

For Solveig, that thought brought worry, not humor, and she tensed, pulling away from his embrace.

Before she could challenge his jesting words, a whistling split the air between them, and Magni flew back, slamming into the nearest oarsman, who grunted and fell over.

"SHIELDS!" she shouted even before her eyes had found the arrow rising up from the oarsman's side. As she grabbed her shield from the wale, another arrow sank into the ship, a scant inch from her hand. "SHIELDS!"

Leif picked up the call, his greater voice booming over the river, and she heard the thunder of hundreds of shields locking over the skeids.

"Magni!" With her shield over her head, under a wooden canopy as all the raiders locked their shields together, Solveig dropped to Magni's side. He had his hand on his face, and blood rushed through his fingers.

"I'm well, I'm well," he protested, but she yanked his hand away to see for herself. A long gash sliced his cheek from nose to ear, over his cheekbone, just above the edge of his beard. Blood gushed, but the wound, when she pressed it, didn't go all the way to bone. The arrow had only grazed him.

Relief exploded through her chest, and she slammed her mouth over his. He flinched and then grabbed her head with his bloody hands and held her to him. Quick and hard was their kiss, while arrows beat like mallets over their heads. The Franks had been ready to defend this place after all.

It was time to fight.

"Archers up! They're shooting from both sides!" Leif roared. He worked his way to the stern and then stood tall, exposed.

"Father!" Magni pushed Solveig back and followed his father. Solveig started, too, but then Leif threw up his shield, and she saw where he was looking, what he was doing. She went to the side and saw her father in his ship. They were conferring. The thunder of arrows was too loud for her to understand what was said.

Leif and Magni then dropped low, and her father dropped out of sight as well.

"Pull to port! To the bank!" Leif shouted.

As the oarsmen settled back at their posts, Solveig saw the other ships turning to port as well, and she understood. They couldn't fight both sides at once. If they split up, they would be too few in both places. But if they chose one side and moved the field out of range of the other, then they might need only fight one side. A bloody victory on one bank might be a victory on both.

Her father and Magni's had found great use in the stories Christians told about them. They called raiders *heathens* and *barbarians*—words that meant something other than human. Something bigger and wilder and more terrifying. They had made them monsters.

Often, the stories preceded their raids, traveling to parts of the world they'd not yet gone themselves. When they arrived, the people simply offered up treasure and begged them to go away.

Solveig had heard many times that the raids of Geitland and Karlsa were not so terrible as the raids of other jarls. Her father and Leif had made rules that other jarls did not— against taking many slaves, or harming children, or oldsters, or women who didn't fight—so they were not so *barbarian* as others. But they reaped the benefits of the stories.

And they went wild in battle, to add verses of their own.

For this battle, they would have an audience of Franks across the river, and they should see that the raiders were every bit as terrible as they'd been told. Solveig grinned and filled her lungs with air that reeked of Frankish fear. As the skeid landed at the bank, she bent her head, dropped her shield to its proper place before her chest, and drew her sword.

Battle rage. It rose up from the deepest part of her, the part that still throbbed from the night before. It pulsed through her, making her heart thump heavily, filling her sinews with fire and need. She forgot she was a daughter. She forgot she was now a lover. She forgot she was a woman. She was only her sword and her shield, her hunger and her fire.

When the roar went up, hundreds of northern voices shouting their shared craving for victory, Solveig added her own and then leapt from the ship and ran up onto the shore.

The Frankish archers broke at once, running for better range, and the raiders chased them down, slashing at their backs and legs to bring them to the ground. Solveig moved forward, everything around her a blur, only her target focused. She could sense the full fight, but it didn't need her focus, only her sense.

She knew her mother and father fought together at some distance to her left. She could hear their shouts. She knew Leif fought ahead, and Håkon behind.

She knew Magni fought at her side, so close she caught spatters of the Frankish blood he spilled. Normally, she worked to put herself a bit apart from others; she fought better with room to move her feet and control the contest, but this time, she stayed near and found that they moved in step with each other, becoming one force against the Franks, turning their backs to each other, closing off that point of attack for their foes.

Aware of it without thinking about it, Solveig moved with Magni, charging, feinting, turning. His shield came between her and a blow; later, she blocked one for him. When a Frank spun between them, they attacked. When another flanked, they changed places.

Frankish bodies fell and fell, and they climbed over and found more. An armored fist caught her in the ear as she pulled her blade through another soldier's neck, and Magni was there to catch her fall. She shook the stars from her sight and slammed the side of her shield into the offending Frank's belly, putting all her force into the charge. He folded over her shield, vomiting on its red eye, and she slashed her blade across his neck, cleaving his head. It sat on her shield like dinner on a tray. She tossed it away and sought another fight.

There was none. All the Franks were dead or fled. Solveig stood, panting, on the blood-mudded earth, her shield up and her dripping sword still poised for a fight.

A light touch grazed her cheek, and she spun, lifting her sword to swing. Magni threw up his shield in defense. "Solveig!"

She blinked and held her breath, forcing it to slow. As the battle receded from her bones, she let her sword rest at her side. Magni's face and beard shone and dripped with blood, and his chestpiece was soaked with it.

"Are you hurt?"

"No more than before." He swiped at the open wound on his cheek. His grin made it gape. "But I shall at last have a scar."

She laughed, and once she started, she couldn't stop. Magni soon joined her, and they stood on a hill above the Franks' great river and laughed until they ached.

Leif came up to them, his face a mask as bloody as his son's. "Enough. We aren't at leisure yet." He nodded toward the river.

Solveig and Magni sobered and turned to look. Soldiers were still arrayed across the water.

She scanned their own bank and tried to understand how many raiders they'd lost in this fight. If they'd lost any, it was only a few.

Her father and mother and brother were blood-soaked but apparently well, walking toward them now. To Leif, her father said, "They stand ready. Shall we cross and fight?"

Leif nodded, and then cut it short. "Hold." He swiveled his head, searching their party. Raiders were already killing the wounded soldiers and scavenging from bodies. "LINE UP!" he shouted in a burst.

Solveig didn't understand, but she obeyed, as did they all, forming two lines across the grassy hill above the river. Just below that short rise, their four longships waited, sails furled.

Seeming to understand what Leif had in mind, Solveig's father slammed his axes together. Her mother lifted her shield and beat the God's-Eye Blade on it. Håkon drummed his shield with his sword as well, and the beat rolled over them all.

As she kept time on her own shield, and Magni and Leif did the same, Solveig understood. Hundreds of thunderclaps struck at once with each beat. Across the river, the line of soldiers began to waver.

Her father and mother, and Leif, all took a step forward exactly together. The rest of them followed. And then hundreds of raiders stepped as one, marching toward the river, toward their great ships, bringing Thor's thunder with them with every step.

By the time the raiders reached the water, the hill on the far bank was empty. The soldiers had fled.

~oOo~

Solveig and Magni stood on a high hill with their parents and her brother. No one spoke. Every voice was silenced by the view before them.

172

Paris.

Her mind would not agree with her eyes. What she saw could not possibly be real.

How many people lived in a place so large? Thousands and thousands, certainly. Karlsa claimed almost two thousand souls, and it was a tiny fraction of this. Geitland was four times as large as Karlsa, and *it* was a tiny fraction of this.

Tens of thousands? Hundreds of thousands? Could there *be* so many people in one place?

It wasn't a city. It was a world unto itself.

The world of her home was small, she knew that. Karlsa was prosperous, because a generation of raiders had brought great wealth home from faraway lands every year, but it was very far north, with winters that lasted all but a few weeks of each year and blew with murderous harshness in their darkest days. Only the heartiest folk called it home.

Geitland, much farther south and nearer those faraway lands, was the biggest world she'd known. To her, it had always been an immense place. Even Mercuria, in Anglia, with its many towns and castle lands, had seemed smaller to her in her single visit there, because people weren't as crowded together in Mercuria as they were in Geitland.

But this—the city itself seemed larger than the entire holding of Karlsa, all the way to its borders. That couldn't be true, but Solveig's confused mind wouldn't let go of the notion. This one city was bigger than her whole world.

The traitor, Amaury, had spoken true, though incompletely. The city was well defended, enclosed by not one wall, not two walls, but three, one inside another, each one many times the height of any man, and each taller than the one before it.

Even the river was tremendously defended—an enormous stone bridge, like a castle itself, spanned the water. There would be no way to burn it down, and to pass under it would mean more than a rain of arrows. She'd heard stories of boulders and—worse—boiling oil being dumped from walls onto raiders below. Certainly Franks so frightened of defeat that they'd built *three* walls would be provisioned with such weapons.

But at the center, right in the middle of the river, was its god house—and, it seemed, its castle and king. Protected by that mighty bridge, and then by the third stone wall that seemed miles high.

If they went by river and under that bridge, only one wall blocked their way. The tallest wall—too high to scale. But there was a gate, and gates could be broken, no matter how well fortified. There was no other possible path that Solveig saw: they must sail to that island and breach their great gate.

"We are not enough," Magni muttered at her side. "We are not even five hundred."

"Not every person in Paris is a soldier," Solveig countered. She wanted to fight; she needed it. This was Paris. *Paris.* Her destiny. She knew it. She would raid Paris with Magni at her side. They would win this great city, and then she could return home and wed him. After they'd taken Paris, and she had shown her worth.

"We know the Frankish soldiers. They are no match for us." Håkon's voice was a growl.

Rarely, of late, did she and her brother agree. He'd been distant and petulant with her for years now. But he seemed to want Paris as much as she did.

"I believe Magni is right," her mother said. "Even if only a portion of the people of this place are soldiers, they will be far more than we."

"We need an army," Leif agreed. "Perhaps Magni was right to consider Gunnar and Tollak in this."

"We can't turn back again!" Håkon protested, expressing the words and the emotion that Solveig herself felt.

Solveig's father dropped a controlling hand on Håkon's shoulder. "What we do now will echo through the ages, Håkon. We cannot be rash. Let us return to camp. We should speak with the party about this before we make our decision."

~oOo~

The decision was made for them, while the argument among the party was in full flower. Many raiders, still stinging from the early end of their previous voyage to Frankia, wanted to press on and fight now, arguing that the odds didn't matter. If they died, they would die bathed in the glory and honor of their great ambition to take such a city. A grand jewel in the Christian crown.

Others wanted to win the city and agreed that returning in greater force was the better choice. The season was aging, and a year to prepare for a real war would make them all the stronger the following summer. Greater strength would mean success, and greater honor for it.

The aging season, the others argued, was a reason to stay and fight, not turn and wait.

Solveig sat on a water barrel and watched as her people threatened to come to blows and find their answer that way.

Then a horn blew, announcing riders approaching. The note and pattern of the blow told them that it wasn't a fighting force, but a peace party.

Magni turned to her, and Solveig met his eyes. They shared the same wary confusion. The raiders hadn't struck Paris yet. They weren't even finished staking their camp.

All the raiders felt it; they stood and took hold of their weapons, but they didn't advance from the center of camp. Leif and her father did, and the rest hung back, ready but unsure for what.

Magni stood at her side. Her mother came to her other. "It's not a parley," she said. "They pull a cart."

Solveig tipped her head to the side so that her father's broad body wasn't blocking her view, and she saw what her mother had seen: Four Franks, in sparkling regal garb, rode toward them, three on matching white horses trimmed with gold, and one driving another white horse pulling a cart. On that cart were four chests. Four.

It wasn't a parley. It was the result of a parley. A ransom.

Magni laughed. His newly-stitched cheek pulled and made the expression awkward, but it didn't lose its mirth. "Treasure already? My father's gambit at the river worked better than we thought."

Solveig couldn't believe it. "They'll not even fight?"

"Our story keeps their eyes open in the long night, it seems," her mother said. She sounded angry, not pleased, and Solveig turned to her.

She stared at the cart the way she stared at an enemy. The God's-Eye stare. Of course. She wanted revenge for Ylva's death.

She'd been quiet during the argument, as Solveig had, and she'd supported Magni as they'd looked out over Paris, but she'd wanted the fight, and she was disgusted that the Franks would give in so easily.

Honor or treasure was the choice before them now. Fight, or take the Frankish gold and go home to fight the next year.

Solveig wasn't surprised when they took the chests and set their swords aside.

Nor was she pleased.

Her destiny waited, yet she came no closer.

~oOo~

The voyage home was smooth, despite a new bite of chill in the air as they moved northward. Within a few weeks, the sea would be treacherous and deadly cold.

They'd raided twice this season and brought good treasure home each time, but as the coast of Geitland emerged from the horizon, Solveig felt bitter and restless. Even Magni's arms around her couldn't calm that sharp ache. Still she was no one of note. Only Valisdottir.

And now, Magni's woman.

"LEIF! TO PORT!"

Solveig didn't see who'd shouted, but she looked to her left as Leif came over. A small boat approached from the shore, coming much farther out than was prudent for such a vessel. Two men rowed while another stood and waved a white flag.

"DROP SAILS!" Leif shouted, and Magni leapt up to help bring the sail down. Solveig turned and saw the other skeids doing the same

Her blade was in its scabbard at her side, and she pulled it free. Around her, she could feel people make themselves ready for trouble. Blades sung out of their scabbards. An archer collected her bow from near Solveig's feet.

The little boat pulled abreast of their skeid. The other skeids floated near, waiting. Tension wrapped around them all like dense fog, lying on the surface of the sea.

"What news?" Leif asked, looming over the fisherman's boat.

The man with the flag answered. "There is trouble, Jarl! Geitland is overtaken!" As the rumble of shock and anger rolled through the skeid, the man continued, "And Karlsa, too! Tollak Finnsson claims himself king over all! He lies in wait for you!

12

The raiding party turned and followed the little boat, away from home.

They were exiles. Homeless. And their family was not whole.

Brenna sat against the side of the ship and wrapped her arms around her knees. She'd left three children at home, in Frida's care: Agnar, Tova, and Hella. Hella had only nine years. Now their home had been overrun, Vali's seat stolen from him, and their children were...where? Dead?

She'd only just tamed the feral, vicious grief of Ylva's passing. Nothing in her life had weakened her like the sight of her daughter, broken and bleeding, dying in her father's arms.

If she were to lose three more? She'd withstood many torments and hardships in her life, but that, she would not survive. Not even the strong shoulder of Vali's love would hold her up.

Her husband stalked the full length of the skeid like a caged beast, his fists clenched and his face twisted with rage. There was little room for his pacing, yet all the others around him made way.

Brenna's mind reached back and plucked up the memory of Åke's defeat, when Leif and Vali had overtaken the jarldom. She'd argued that his wives and children should have been killed, even the babes, because a cleaved head could not plot, and someday those children would be men who might seek vengeance in their father's name. Vali had argued that if they killed all who might someday be an enemy, they'd have no friends. He and Leif had let the women and children go free.

All these years, a small voice inside her had wondered which of them had been right. Would Åke's heirs take their vengeance when they were old enough, or would Vali and Leif's mercy be remembered?

Those children were young men now, a few years more than Solveig. Ripe for vengeance. But it hadn't been they who'd stolen Brenna's home and torn her from her children. It had been Jarl Finn's heir, Tollak. An alliance decades old, one that had helped build the Mercurian settlement, was now broken.

Had he killed her children? She could only believe that he would. Had they suffered? She could only hope that they had not.

Though Vali and Leif had both made changes to the ways of their people, Tollak kept the old ways. His raids were wild and brutal, and slaves were his most important treasure. At home, it seemed to be his way to rule his people, rather than to lead them. Dofrar, his holding, abutted the northern border of Geitland, and the boundary was clear when one moved from the most northern Geitland village to the most southern hamlet of Dofrar. Geitland's people and their homes were markedly healthier than Dofrar's.

Jarl Finn had been a mighty warrior in his youth and a fierce leader with harshness of his own, but he'd been fair. Tollak Finnsson was not his father—whom, it was said, he'd killed in his sleep.

But the jarls had kept a friendship, seeing the interest in moving commerce and travel through their holdings. The people of Dofrar had access to Geitland's better trading and busier port, and the people of Geitland, Halsgrof, and Karlsa could move over land, through Dofrar, when sea travel was impossible. And occasionally, they came together to make a vast raiding party.

Had he killed her children? Had they suffered?

"Brenna."

She looked up. The warp of rage had left her husband's face, leaving sorrow and worry in its place. He crouched before her and held out his hand. "We strike land soon. They've led us to Krysevik. Let us find out what we can and make our plan. We will find our children. And then I will burn Dofrar to the ground, from east to west and south to north. I will rend Tollak into pieces with my teeth and feed him to my wolves. This will be answered, and we will win. There will be a reckoning, I swear it."

~oOo~

"Olga!" Leif vaulted over the side of his ship and ran through the water. Brenna stood and watched as he swept his wife high off the ground and clamped her to his chest. Olga, at least, was safe.

She scanned the cluster of people in this small village who'd come to see such great ships land on their scanty shore.

Vali saw them first. "There! There!"

Before Brenna could see what he'd seen, he grabbed her by the waist and jumped from the ship with her. They landed hard in the water. When Brenna had her feet again, Hella, her dark sprite, was splashing through the waves toward them. The water was too deep, and Brenna ran forward to the shallows, but Hella was swept by the tide before she could get to her.

"Careful, little mouse!" Vali laughed and lifted their youngest child high over his head. She was so much smaller than the rest of their children, so much more delicate. But she giggled as water dripped onto her father's face from her sodden dress.

Tova ran up as well, and Brenna caught her in her arms. Her children were alive. "My love! Are you well?"

"Yes, Mamma. We ran in the night, when they came. Frida hid us with Åsa, and then Elof came for us, and we came here."

Åsa was a völva, a witch and a seer, who lived in deep in the Wood of Verðandi. She'd kept their family safe on a few occasions. Elof...the name was common enough, but she wasn't sure she knew him.

"They burned the hall, Father." At Agnar's stoic remark, Brenna sought our her son. He stood at the edge of the water, perfectly erect, perfectly still, perfectly serious. He wore a sword on his back. It must have been borrowed; with only thirteen years, he didn't have a sword of his own yet, nor an arm ring. Waiting for both dragged at his patience, but Brenna was stalwart on the matter.

Many would have said that a boy with thirteen years was a boy no longer, but Brenna did not agree. She'd been on her own at that age, and she'd been terrified and too young to take care of herself well. She'd given herself into slavery so that she could have food and shelter.

Her children were children until they were old enough to face a harsh world and stare it down. Like his older siblings, Agnar could wait until his fourteenth year to begin training and his sixteenth to raid.

Ylva's dying face filled her mind's sight, and she pulled Agnar into her arms, clutching him and Tova as tightly as she could. Even sixteen years was yet too young to face death.

"Come." Vali was at her side. Hella, in his arms, leaned down and tugged on Brenna's braids, as she'd done since she was small. "We need answers." He nodded, indicating something or someone up ahead, and Brenna looked that way.

Ulv. Åke's son. He stood with his arm around a woman Brenna seemed to know but could not quite place.

Turid. She was Turid. Åke's youngest wife, near Ulv's age. The mother of his youngest sons, those very sons she'd once thought should be killed. Elof was the eldest of Turid's sons. Brenna had once been their slave.

It had been Åke's great ambition to unite all of Scandinavia under his colors, and he'd made his first and final attempt on the backs of Brenna and Vali, and Leif and Olga, and their friends and families.

Now, Tollak Finnson seemed to have the same goal, and Åke's sons sought to stop him.

The story seemed to have made a circle, and yet Brenna could not follow its path. "That's Åke's wife."

"Yes," Vali agreed. "As I said, we need answers."

~oOo~

They'd been led to a small fishing village, and Brenna estimated that they were no more than fifty miles from the Geitland border.

Krysevik, the jarldom to the south and west, reached far overland, to the opposite coast. It mirrored Geitland in that way, spanning the land from coast to coast, with but with one large community, at the seat of the jarl. Jarl Blakkr's seat, as rich as Geitland, was located on the opposite coast. This accounted for the passive peace between their lands. They were too far distant to bump shoulders, and there was little that either wanted or needed from the other. What they wanted came not from each other but from the wide world.

Years before, while Leif's jarldom was yet new, Blakkr had turned his back when one of his far-flung chieftains attempted to overtake Geitland, and he'd turned his back again when Leif had meted justice to the failed raiders. Since then, the jarls had continued to ignore each other.

Brenna doubted that Blakkr offered them sanctuary now. They were nowhere close to the town of Krysevik. Hundreds of miles away. If he'd had word of Tollak's move, he hadn't had it for long.

As soon as they'd all been ashore, they'd talked with Ulv and Turid—and with her sons. Åke's sons, who were helping to save them. They now knew the extent of Tollak Finnsson's perfidy. And of Vali's wisdom in saving Turid and her sons long years before.

Tollak had claimed all the land from Karlsa to Geitland and named himself King of Geitland, which he now called the territory that had two weeks ago comprised four jarldoms.

He'd allied with Gunnar Ivarsson to take Geitland and Karlsa, and then he'd killed Gunnar, Jarl of Halsgrof, to claim it all for himself. Tollak sat in Leif's seat, and all his warriors—those of Dofrar and Halsgrof both, an army of elite raiders—now lay in wait in Geitland, meaning to burn the returning raiders before they could dock.

The skeids had no good defense against an attack of fire from their own shores. They were weary and depleted from the raid. The risk of losing Geitland for good was great.

Ulv had been on watch when Tollak and Gunnar had attacked. He'd gone to Olga first and gotten her to the caves in the woods before going back to fight as well as he could on his lame leg. They'd been so obviously outnumbered, and so weakened without their best fighters, that he'd called a quick retreat—and saved as many as he could of Geitland's people, who were here in the village now.

It wasn't many. A hundred or so. Brenna hoped that the farmers and merchants and craftsmen who'd been left behind were safe and well enough under a new—and temporary—jarl.

As Tova had reported, Frida, Karlsa's healer and a dear friend, had saved Brenna and Vali's children. And Åke's sons had traveled far north, at great risk, to find and save them.

Turid had taught them that Vali was a great man and a good jarl who had spared them when few would have.

Brenna now sat between Vali and Håkon before the fire at the center of this village. Again and again, her eyes sought out her children, needing assurance that she hadn't dreamed their safety.

Oili, the völva of the village Brenna had been born in, had foreseen that she would bear many children, that she and Vali would fill their home with daughters and sons until it was complete. Together, they'd had seven children, from their first, Thorvaldr, born and died on the same day, in Estland, to Hella. Hella's birth had been difficult, and Brenna hadn't been seeded again in the nine years since. Their family, it seemed, had been completed.

But it wasn't. Without Thorvaldr and Ylva, there would always be lack.

The empty space felt smaller when her surviving children were near. On this night, when she'd been so sure that she'd lost three more children, and they'd all lost their home, she nonetheless felt a near completeness. Vali at her side. Five of her children around her. The friends she held dearest close and safe. Tollak hadn't taken everything.

185

Hella sat on Vali's lap, and Tova sat before Brenna's feet. Agnar and Håkon sat together, talking quietly. Solveig…Solveig was finally moving from the circle of her family and making one of her own. She sat with Magni. Leif's son had hooked his arm over her thigh, and their hands were interlaced. When Solveig leaned on Magni's arm, and he kissed her head, Brenna felt a warm peace.

Her beautiful, tempestuous, searching child. All her life, from the time she could put her own feet on the ground and straighten her legs to stand, Solveig had wanted to do and be *everything*. She held herself to impossible standards, and she fled when she failed to reach a height only gods might touch.

Brenna knew well that Solveig measured herself against her and found herself wanting. No amount of talk, neither soft words nor harsh, could seem to shake Solveig's conviction that she was called to walk in her mother's footprints.

Neither could she see that she *was* following the same path, and well. She was a powerful warrior. In Frankia, when they'd charged the bank, she'd fought with all the will and strength of any shieldmaiden of legend, and she'd amassed a mountain of kills.

She'd seemed determined, all these years, to deny herself a life until she had a story. Brenna's heart calmed to see her in love and at peace with Magni. There were no two better matched in all the world. She was tempest, and he was ease.

She could think of some who were matched as well—their parents, for instance—but none better. She was surprised, and gladdened, to see her daughter finally understand that.

When Leif came to her and Vali, he was still holding Olga's hand. Brenna hadn't seen them parted since her friend had splashed onto the shore. She understood the need. After the consuming fear and uncertainty she'd felt, wondering if her children lived, she couldn't bear to have them away from her.

As he crouched before them now, though, he finally released her, and, with a smile at her friends, she went to Magni and Solveig and sat with them. Olga understood that Leif wanted to talk with them in privacy.

Vali set Hella on her feet and pushed her and Tova toward the cluster that was Olga, Solveig and Magni. Brenna kept her eyes on them as they went.

"To Geitland at dawn," Vali said when the children were clear. "We destroy this usurper and all who fought with him to take our homes."

Brenna was stunned when Leif shook his head. "He stands fifteen hundred men at Geitland, Vali. More than three times our number. Elof has word that many of my people would not pledge to him, and he cut them down like dogs. Women and men, farmers and craftsmen. He sits in that chair and waits for us. We cannot best him. Not as we are. Chests of gold are no weapons.

"You would have us cower here, like village mice? Shall I take up the nets and learn to fish? No!" Vali pounded his fist into his thigh.

Brenna set her hand on her husband's leg. Her own lust for battle had dwindled as she'd aged, and as she'd nurtured her children. In the midst of the fight, she felt charged and powerful as ever, but in the aftermath, she'd grown weary. After losing Ylva, and the fear that Agnar, Tova, and Hella had been killed, she was exhausted. She wanted to lose no more children before her own death. If Leif had another way, she would hear it. "Vali. Let him speak."

Leif turned his attention to her. "It carries its own risks. But hear me out. We sail on. To Mercuria. And we ask our friends for aid. Leofric has united much of Anglia under his banner and amassed a mighty army." He locked eyes again with Vali. "With that force behind us, we will *bury* Tollak. He will be but a speck of dust at our feet. And then you and I will claim two larger holdings, and no land shall come between us. And when we achieve Valhalla, Magni and Solveig will unite it all. And only *then* will there be a kingdom in our land."

"It's too late in the season. We won't make it back before winter." Brenna knew then that Vali's interest was caught; he was considering particular points of the plan rather than the plan itself. He'd already accepted its worth.

"You mean for us to stay the winter in Mercuria," Brenna said, grasping the whole of the plan. "To sail when the weather breaks again.

Leif nodded. "The winter here will be harsh in the condition we're in. We have gold but nowhere to spend it. Our supplies are depleted by the journey to Frankia. Those who got away did so with only what they could carry. We go to a warmer world, spend the winter with our friends and with our families in Norshire. When summer comes again, we will be strong and rested and well prepared." A vicious sneer distorted Leif's face. She'd never seen such a look on him before. "I want a force that will fill the harbor. I want Tollak to piss his boots when we sail in."

~oOo~

The decision was quickly made and agreed among all the raiders. They would sail to Mercuria, with all due haste, and spend the winter amassing a force that would destroy Tollak and, for years to come, discourage any others from the folly of stealing from Jarl Leif or Jarl Vali.

The village was too small to accommodate the refugees from Geitland and Karlsa, and certainly had no room for the hundreds of shocked and weary raiders that had landed on their shore. The people of Geitland had staked a camp at the edge of the village, and the raiders expanded it.

The skeids could, barely, make room for any of the refugees who wished to join them. About half of them did, most thinking to settle in Norshire and make a new start.

There were many risks to Leif's plan. Sailing so late in the season was dangerous, especially a voyage so long. The seas and skies were most tempestuous on the cusp of a season, when warm and cold battled for primacy in the clouds. There would be children on this voyage, and women and men who weren't trained in sailing. If they panicked during a storm, they could endanger everyone on board.

But Leif was right. It was their best option, and likely the only one that would restore their homes to them. So the dangers were worthwhile.

They would take two days to make any repairs the skeids needed after Frankia, and to restock their provisions as well as they could. Two days. And then they would sail to their salvation, or to their deaths.

Vali settled onto the fur behind Brenna and hooked his brawny arm around her waist. He smelled of mead; he and Leif and Ulv had been talking long into the night. "I thought you'd be sleeping, my love."

She lifted his hand and pressed her lips to his knuckles. "Thinking. Vali, do you tire of the blood?"

He pulled gently, and she turned onto her back and looked up at him. The fire still burned at the center of the village, and a few torches were yet lit. The light reached to their camp and made a soft glow over his face.

He brushed his fingertips across her cheek. "The fight, you mean?" At her nod, he answered, "No. Do you?"

Surprise had sharpened his question to a point. Brenna was surprised herself, and yet she was not. Her relish of battle had waned since Solveig's birth, sheering off in imperceptible layers until she'd begun to feel the difference. With Ylva's death, a chunk had fallen away. "I would like our children to know peace."

"They know peace, Brenna. They have always known peace, and love, and comfort. Until now, the home we made has been in peace. We seek the fight. It doesn't find us."

"Until now."

"Tollak will pay."

"What if...if we'd been able to stay in Estland..." Long ago, she and Vali had planned to settle in Estland and farm. She'd been happy, thinking of building a home with Vali and raising their family in that tiny village, among friends.

"Brenna, what is this? We're not farmers. We didn't raise farmers. We're warriors. As are our children." He calmed suddenly and pulled her close, turning onto his back and tucking her head to his chest. "This is Ylva, isn't it? Ah, my love. She is in Valhalla. She is well. Her death was good."

"No death so young is good."

Vali didn't answer, but a light tremor passed through his arms. Brenna knew he grappled with his own grief; she understood that his image of their daughter now holding their firstborn son sustained him. Her mourning was, in that way at least, selfish. She wanted Ylva with them, here, in this world. But when she pined for her, she dimmed Vali's sight of their children at peace and with the gods.

"Forgive me. Today has shaken me."

He kissed her head. "This world is to be passed through, shieldmaiden. It is a waypoint on the journey. We meet our family on the way, but we are always only traveling here. It is beyond this world that we will know peace and eternity. Only there will our family be complete."

She propped herself on his chest and looked down on his face. So beloved. The years of their life had left their marks, forming lines and creases, greying his hair and beard, but he was as fiercely handsome as ever he'd been. His love for her blazed from his eyes as hot as ever it had. He would always be the most beautiful thing in her life. "I love you, Vali Storm-Wolf."

"And I you, shieldmaiden." A smirk pulled up a corner of his mouth. "The children are very near tonight. Do they sleep?"

She looked around. Hella and Tova were cuddled together a few feet away, both of them snoring softly, sleeping the untroubled sleep of innocent childhood. Agnar lay against a log, perfectly still. Håkon had gone off on his own. And Solveig slept with Magni.

"They sleep." She lay back and began unfastening her breeches.

Vali rolled to his side and worked the lacings on her chestpiece. Brenna shimmied out of her breeches and began to open his.

When he spread her legs and pushed into her, they both groaned on a whisper. Brenna hooked her legs and arms around her man. After twenty years as parents, they had learned well how to couple in quiet.

But their love burned hot and wild as ever.

PART THREE

WOMAN

13

Their people had settled Norshire, and forged a friendship with a Saxon king, more than ten years before. Magni and Solveig had only been to Mercuria once, five years before. Magni remembered the pretty village their people had made, as well as the king's grand castle—which Astrid, his family's dear friend and the king's wife, claimed as her home.

He also remembered the long voyage and the toll it had taken on his mother, who was much stronger on land than on the sea.

This voyage, undertaken in more challenging circumstances, with fewer resources, by people already fatigued, had taken a harder toll on her. For days, she had been too weak to stand. And yet she'd managed to tend to the others on their ship who had taken ill as well, even if she'd been too weak to do more than tell healthier people how to tend to them.

The changing weather had caught them in its grip twice. The first storm had tossed them about but had done little damage. The second storm, however, had claimed the mast of the second Geitland skeid, and taken a dozen people into the sea with it. They'd managed to claim only three of those souls back.

For two days, the remaining skeids had taken their turns pulling the disabled longship through the sea. It slowed their progress terribly, and if another storm had spun from the skies, they would likely have taken heavy losses.

When the land of Anglia rose up from a misty horizon, a chorus of weary voices cheered. Their voyage was not yet over—Mercuria was farther south, and cliffs faced the sea for long stretches of the coastline—but they knew that, at least, they would not be swallowed whole by Ægir, the drunken jötunn of the sea.

Magni went to his mother. Solveig sat beside her, helping her take water. He'd asked her to watch over his mother when she'd first collapsed, and since then, Solveig had hardly left her side. She would kill him before she'd admit it, but her nature was soft behind the shield of her strength.

Crouching down, he took the skin from her so he could help. "Mother, we'll be ashore soon."

She offered him a wan smile and pushed the water away. "That is good. I'll be glad for the world to be still again. Magni, you fret too much about me. I'm only tired. Others are far more ill than I. Check on little Jari."

Her body had rejected food and most water for days, and she had few reserves to spare. Now, her cheekbones seemed to slash the sides of her face, and her dark eyes had sunk deep. She was more than tired.

"I'll go," Solveig said and stood. "Sit with your mother. You've barely rested for days."

Magni looked over his shoulder. His father stood aft, helping untie the towing rope and release the disabled ship. The three intact ships had brought their sails down. It was time to go to oar, and the fourth ship could run on its own power again.

"No, stay with her. I need to row, but I'll check on the boy before I do." He squeezed his mother's hand. "Soon we'll be ashore."

She nodded and let her eyes close.

The Norshire harbor was too small to accommodate four skeids. They came ashore instead on an expanse of reedy sand. Atop a high hill, a dense wood rose up alongside the shore, dark and foreboding. Magni stared into its shadows and reminded himself that here, they were not raiders. They were among friends. There'd be no danger for them in this land.

Magni's father picked his mother up and carried her to the shore, cradled in his arms. He, too, had worried deeply for her health.

Many of their large party were too sick, or hurt, or weary to travel far immediately. The day was ripe, and the castle was hours away, so they began to stake a camp.

As Magni helped unlade the ships, his father came down from the camp and hailed him. "There is a small village nearby. Vali and I are going there to find horses, and we'll ride to the castle. I want you to help Brenna here. Our people need rest and sustenance."

Solveig jumped from the skeid and stood beside Magni. "We can hunt. The wood there must have game."

His father nodded. "Deer, boar, and small game, yes. Nothing like our beasts, but enough. And there is fresh water—a stream that runs to the sea—a mile into the wood."

"We'll take enough game to make our people strong, Father," Magni answered.

"Keep watch of your mother as well." His father rested his hand on Magni's shoulder. "See to it that she eats first."

"She won't," Solveig countered. "She won't until the children and the sick do."

They all three knew that Magni's mother would set herself aside. But Magni grasped his father's arm. "I'll make sure of it. And I'll see that she rests well. I'll take care of her."

~oOo~

"Must we compete in all things?" Magni grabbed the stag by its antlers and heaved it onto his back.

Solveig glared at him. "You keep a count as well."

While their fathers traveled to the castle to announce their arrival to the king, Magni and Solveig had formed a party and gone into the wood to hunt food and collect water. They'd sent raiders who remembered the land for the water.

"But I don't get angry when you surpass me."

All their lives, they'd competed with each other. Or, rather, they'd measured themselves against each other. When they'd been young, Magni, the younger of them, hadn't vied with Solveig so much as chased after her. But then he'd grown into a man, and the times of their births hadn't mattered so much. Solveig had become decidedly competitive. She hadn't liked him growing bigger and stronger than she.

But he was a man, and she was a woman. He could hardly be blamed for the truths of their bodies.

Solveig didn't agree. In the brief time since they'd been mated, she seemed particularly protective of the advantages that she did have—her greater skill with a bow, for instance.

He dropped the body of the stag onto the litter, which carried the carcasses of that stag, a young boar, and assorted smaller creatures. It wasn't enough, but some in their party had lumbered loudly through the wood, scaring much of the game away. Magni stared at the mound of dead animals and considered sending the clumsy hunters back with the litter, to let the more skilled trackers move farther into the trees.

"You haven't surpassed me," Solveig grumbled, distracting him. "I've got more kills."

He turned to her and took her hand. "Your badger and five squirrels to my boar and stag. I think a boar should count for a few squirrels. And the stag for even more."

"Smaller targets take more skill."

"Larger game feeds more people. That is why we hunt, yes?"

Her eyes narrowed dangerously, and Magni knew she had no rebuttal. He smiled and brought her close. "You're the better shot between us. I feel no threat to admit it. I'm going to send the litter back. You and I and Frode can go on—in quiet—and find more game. I doubt we'll take another large beast, after all this tromping around, but we might take more small ones, if we keep keen eyes. Small beasts are your specialty."

"You jape at me." But her expression softened, and a smile emerged from her stormy look.

"Only because you're so fierce when there is no fight. Will you hunt with me so that we may feed our people?"

He hadn't meant to hector her, but she was immediately chastened. Her cheeks even flushed pink with a kiss of shame.

He replaced that kiss with one of his own. "Come. If you've tallied more kills than I when we return to camp, I'll celebrate your victory tonight, between your thighs."

She smiled. "And should you somehow win?"

"The same. Pleasuring you is the greatest prize I can imagine."

~oOo~

They ate well that night, and the party settled for rest with bellies full enough, and throats slaked enough, for comfort. Their fathers didn't return, but they'd expected to be away the full night.

The next morning, near dawn, Magni woke as Solveig slipped from his arms. The air was heavy with moisture; a fog lay over the ground, and over the people sleeping there, one so thick that he wicked water from his face with a flick of his hand.

"Solveig?"

She tied the laces on her breeches and left her tunic loose over them. "My mother is about," she whispered, pulling a boot on. "I'm going to help her revive the fire."

Magni looked over at his own mother. She'd rallied a little during the evening, and she seemed still comfortably at rest, but he leaned close and watched to be certain that she breathed. She did, and he let loose a breath of his own.

"Solveig, hold."

She had her boots on and had picked up a fur to wrap over her shoulders. Her braids had loosened during the night, probably while they'd coupled, and long, loose tendrils framed her face.

He wasn't ready to give her up for the day. It was at night, when they shared furs, and in the morning before they'd shed them, that Solveig felt most his. She dropped her shield, she set aside the burden of the greatness she felt she must achieve, she forgot that she was a shieldmaiden and the daughter of legends. In the quiet, when their bodies were bare, she was only Solveig, and only his.

But once she was in the sight of others, she held him at the end of her arm. Even when he embraced her, he could feel the difference. When the sun was up, her mind whirled and questioned every touch.

He lost her every day and reclaimed her every night.

Now, still on the ground while she stood above him, waiting for him to explain why she shouldn't go help her mother, he simply lifted his hands.

She considered him, her hands on her hips. "There are things to be done."

"It's not yet full light. The camp is quiet. Stay with me for a moment longer."

"I'm only going to the fire. Not even out of sight."

He held his hands up and said no more. Finally, she relented and came back down, nestling into the circle of his arms.

"This is foolish," she muttered, but she relaxed against him and let her fingers play in his loose hair.

"Shhh. Be mine for a while longer." Magni tucked her close and rolled onto her, settling his legs between hers. She didn't protest, not then, and not when he pushed his hand under her tunic and found the pillow of her breast.

"Åh," she breathed as her nipple tautened under his fingers. "Magni…"

"Tell me what you want of me, shieldmaiden," he murmured, flicking his tongue lightly over her parted lips.

She pushed him back. "My father calls my mother 'shieldmaiden'."

"So she is. And so are you. Would you have me not?" It wasn't an unusual word, and it was apt.

A frown creased her brow. "I don't know."

"There are many other things I might call you." He pushed her tunic up and exposed her bare chest. "Beautiful." A kiss between her breasts. "Fierce." Another kiss to the base of her throat. "Lover." Just above her nipple. "Warrior." Her nipple. He swirled his tongue around its hard point until her back arched. "Friend." His lips found her other nipple. "Mine."

"You confuse me," she moaned. "Your touch, your words. I cannot think when I'm so close to you."

"Good. You think too much. Always have you thought too much. Let your mind be quiet, Solveig. Trust me. Love me. Feel." He pushed his hand into her breeches. "Tell me what you want of me."

"Don't swallow me whole," she pleaded and pulled his mouth to her own.

~oOo~

The sun was not yet at the top of the sky when their fathers returned, and with a larger party. The king and queen rode with them—and following them came carts and horses to help the visitors move to the castle.

Astrid, the queen, was one of their own people, a dear friend to his parents and to Solveig's as well. He'd heard the stories of Estland and of the early years of his father's leadership in Geitland many times. But Astrid had left Geitland when he was quite young, and he'd seen her only a few times since then. He had no strong memory of her or affection for her.

He enjoyed seeing his parents' joy at their reunion with her, however. Since they'd returned home to find it stolen, his father and Solveig's parents had been somber in their calmest moments, and burning with black rage otherwise. The arduous journey, exacerbating their losses, had only made their mood bleaker, and their temper coiled around them all.

It was good to see them all smiling again.

It would be a long winter away from home, but if they could return in the summer refreshed and restored, with the power of Mercuria at their backs, then Magni felt sure that they would unseat the usurper Tollak and restore order to their world.

"I wonder what winter is like here," Solveig mused, coming to stand at his side. She must have been thinking similar thoughts in her whirlwind mind.

He took her hand and laced their fingers. Before he could answer, Astrid did. Magni hadn't thought they were in earshot, but she turned and smiled, and stepped their way. She wore an elegant dress in a heavy fabric, but some kind of a leather chestpiece, too soft to be armor, over it. As she walked toward them, the skirt parted down the center, and he saw that she also wore breeches and leather boots.

Solveig seemed particularly interested in her clothing, and stared at her legs even as she stood before them.

"Grey," she answered, to Solveig's musing. "And wet. The green dies away, and rains come often. The people here think it's cold, but it's not. And there's not much snow or ice. We keep the castle bright and cheerful and feast often, to hold the drear away. And the warm returns more quickly and lingers longer than it does in the North."

She made their words, but they sounded strange. She'd developed an accent that Magni had never heard before.

With a glance at their joined hands, she held out her own to them both. "Come. We have horses for you to ride, and we've set the castle abuzz preparing to feast your arrival. It's a great boon to have you here!"

~oOo~

Magni had spent time in this castle before, but his mind seemed to have discarded the memories as too fantastic. Though he'd been raiding four years, and they'd defeated other kings, they'd never overrun any of their castles, and he'd never been inside any other.

He couldn't understand why anyone would build such a thing. King Leofric's castle was enormous, and nearly every space they moved through seemed empty, or nearly so, but for the furnishings and collections. All the rooms, even corridors, were accented with things set on posts or hanging from the walls. Weapons, fabrics, images framed in gold, figures carved from stone—they all seemed to have no purpose but to be seen. The furniture was massive and heavy, gleaming dark wood and burnished metals. The walls, floor, ceilings were of stone. Despite the fabrics on the walls and draped from the ceiling, every room was filled with chill and echo.

Walking beside him, Solveig seemed captivated. She, too, had been here before, but the memories hadn't etched themselves into her mind, either. As they walked past a room that opened wide onto the vast corridor, she broke from their group and went to stand before an image hanging on the wall. It showed a man, draped in colored silks, with a gold circle around his head. Another man, more plainly attired, kissed his cheek.

"Is this their god?" she asked, reaching out to brush her finger over the surface, tracing the golden circle. When she took her hand back, she rubbed her thumb over her fingertips. "It feels like gold."

Magni touched as well. The surface of the gleaming circle around the man's head was slick and cool, like metal.

He snatched his hand back, feeling guilty, when Astrid's husband, Leofric, King of Mercuria, walked up to them. "Do you like it?" Leofric spoke their language fluently. Magni, conversely, knew only a few words of the Anglian tongue. Talking with anyone here other than Astrid, Leofric, or their children was nearly impossible. Among them all, his father had the best grasp of the language of this place; Magni tried to stay close enough to his father that he didn't feel entirely lost.

"Is it your god?" Solveig asked the king, boldly confident. There were ways of address that the people here observed, but Leofric didn't behave as if he cared whether the 'Northmen' observed them.

"It is His Son," the king answered. "Our Christ, who is also the Lord as well."

Magni dashed a glance at Solveig, who looked as confused as he. Leofric laughed. "Astrid didn't understand it either. It isn't meant to be understood. It is something to be known without understanding. To be accepted."

Solveig snorted. "Knowing without understanding is for fools and children."

The king smiled at her. "You women of the North are ferocious creatures, all of you. May I ask—do you have proof of all the feats of all your gods? Do you *know*, or do you believe?"

She blinked at him and snapped her mouth shut. Then an idea seemed to occur to her, and she put her hands on her hips. "Our gods come down and let us see them. They walk among us whenever they wish. They speak with us and feast and fight with us. So yes, we *know*."

Turning back to the image on the wall, Leofric said, "That is who that man is. God coming to us. He walked among us for many years. He grew from a babe to a man, and He lived as one of us all the while. He knew us—our weaknesses and our pettiness, as well as our strengths and our goodness. Then, He allowed us to kill Him so that we might see ourselves as we truly are, and so we might see the depths of His love for us in that sacrifice, and He washed us of our sins."

"You killed your god? And yet you live?" Magni asked, not knowing if he was impressed or contemptuous.

Solveig had no such conflict. She laughed. "Your god is weak to let betrayal live on. There is no honor in that! That's what you worship?"

"There is great honor in forgiveness, Solveig. To forgive a great wrong is to show great strength."

Letting a loud suck of her teeth suffice as a comment, Solveig said no more. But Magni's attention had come to rest on the other figure in the image. "Who is the man that kisses him?"

"That is Judas Iscariot, the man who turned Christ over to his enemies in exchange for thirty pieces of silver. The painting is called 'The Betrayal of Judas.'"

"And you honor such a worm with hangings on your walls? Christians are *fårskallar*." Solveig made a face like she'd tasted something foul and flicked her hand, batting away the very idea of Christianity.

"Forgive me. I don't understand that word. For-skall-ar?"

"It means idiots," Astrid answered, sweeping in with her youngest daughter, Æbbe, on her hip. "Or, more to the point, it means sheep-heads. Are you arguing with our friends, husband?"

Leofric took the girl from her mother. "No, my love. We are discussing the differences in our beliefs."

Astrid considered the small image and made a face not unlike that which had tightened Solveig's. "Judas. The betrayer. He killed himself after Christ was crucified."

Magni was growing bored with the talk of Christians and their god, but Solveig seemed truly disturbed, even angered by the image.

"A betrayer and a coward as well. And here he is kissing your god," she said. "Why make such a thing? Why not show him dead? Why show him at all?"

"Judas betrayed him with that kiss." Astrid took Solveig's arm and drew her across the room, to another image on another wall. Magni followed, and Astrid showed them a painting of a man hanging by a rope around his neck. "There is vengeance among Christians, too, Solveig. Judas is in Hell, which is very like our Helheim. He suffers for all eternity as a suicide and a traitor. There is a limit to even this God's forgiveness."

Solveig scoffed. "Do you follow this god now?" She knew Astrid even less well than Magni did, but the question of Astrid's beliefs was clearly important to her. Magni tried to understand why.

He was thinking so hard that he found himself squinting at her.

Astrid answered calmly. "I love our gods, Solveig. I know them. But the God of Mercuria, I know Him, too. You will see—when we visit Norshire soon. All the gods live there together." She hooked her arm around Solveig's. "Come. I came looking for you so that I could show you to your rooms. We feast tonight, but there is time to rest and refresh yourselves." She paused and looked Magni up and down. "One room or two for the both of you?"

"One," answered Magni.

"Two," answered Solveig at the same time.

Astrid looked sidelong at Magni, and then at Solveig. She shrugged. "Two rooms, then. And sleep where you will."

Magni held back as the women walked down the corridor. Two rooms, though they had slept together every night since that first. Again, Solveig made distance for no clear reason. Even when their hands were linked, she managed to put a castle between them.

The King of Mercuria stood waiting for him, his little girl falling asleep on his shoulder. "Fierce women make the best mates, young Magni Leifsson. They are worth the effort. This I can assure you."

An Anglian king telling him about the women of his own people. Feeling sore and intruded upon, Magni could only manage a terse nod.

14

"I'll have fresh clothes brought up—I'm not sure we'll have leathers that will fit you, but tunics, at least, and I'll send someone to clean your leathers while you wash."

As Astrid spoke, Solveig wandered around the room. So much space for only herself, and so soft everywhere. When she'd come with her parents to Mercuria before, several years earlier, she and Håkon had shared a chamber connected to her parents' chamber. She didn't remember it being so full of cushions and draperies.

She'd believed that the softness these people created in their world made them soft as well. She believed it yet. To be standing here, homeless, surrounded by Anglian sumptuousness, and to be seeking their aid because her people weren't strong enough on their own…Solveig clenched her fists. She wanted to be away, alone, but she knew not where she could run in this place.

Magni had been hurt that she'd wanted a room of her own; she'd seen it clearly, and she'd felt it keenly. But her head roiled with fractious, restless thoughts. She felt angry and resentful and overwhelmed and in awe, and none of it yet made sense to her. Magni told her she thought too much, but if she was thinking too much now, it was because none of her thoughts would be still. She had that inexplicable need to push away, from everything, that drove her into the forests of home. Here, in this place that wasn't her home, she had nowhere to run.

She turned and considered Astrid—a good friend to her parents, but a woman she didn't know well. The stories said that she'd been a great shieldmaiden. They also told that she'd been captured by the Mercurian king, that she'd been horribly tortured, but that she had tamed the man and the land and become its queen. Solveig could see the truth in the stories simply by looking at her. She carried herself in a familiar way, and her expression, though kind, had an edge Solveig recognized—as if between her flesh and her bone was a layer forged of steel.

Scars, pale and soft with age, marked her face, throat, and chest. Scars both of battle and of brutality.

And yet she'd forgiven the king and married his son. She'd given him four children. Solveig felt the same restlessness to think of that as she'd felt to look on the paintings of the Christian betrayer. All this forgiveness was bewildering. Betrayal should be met with vengeance. If Astrid was the warrior she was professed to be, why would she give up revenge for forgiveness?

She studied Astrid's scars, and the queen didn't seem to mind her scrutiny. After a while, Solveig's attention widened. Astrid's scarred body was covered by beautiful fabrics— lustrous silks in a rich blues that seemed melded to her body in some places and flowed away like water in others. Her gown was trimmed with silvery threads that glittered, and there were small, iridescent gemstones strung on the threads.

For all her contempt for the softness of the Anglian world, Solveig had some gentler interests herself. She enjoyed beautiful clothes and baubles, and she attempted, when she wasn't raiding, to make herself as pretty as she could—not to attract men, but because it made her feel a different kind of strength. From the time she was tiny, her father would return from raids with a leather pouch just for her, filled with shiny things. When the trading ships came to Karlsa, she'd asked for silks and jewels. Of late, she'd bought those things for herself.

She reached out now without meaning to do so, wanting to touch the gemstones glinting on Astrid's sleeve. When she saw what her hand intended, she dropped it at once, abashed.

But Astrid saw and moved close, offering her arm. "The Keeper of the Wardrobe learned long ago to make gowns I like. They move freely, so I might fight in them if ever I need to. Other women of the land have taken to wearing a like style. Since you'll be here for the winter, I'll take you to him, and we'll have him make some for you, if you'd like."

Solveig petted Astrid's sleek arm and let her fingers play over the shimmering threads at her wrist.

"Solveig? Would you like gowns like mine? We'll have leathers made as well. This is your home until summer, so I want you to be comfortable."

This was not their home. They were exiles. Homeless. Until they could reclaim land that had been stolen from them, they were refugees in this strange place. Solveig had never before felt so untethered. She met the queen's eyes. "Will you fight with us in the summer?"

Astrid's eyes shone with conviction. "We'll discuss the matter soon enough. But whatever Leofric decides about the kingdom, I'll answer for myself: I will fight with you. You asked me before if I follow the Christian god. What I believe about gods has grown complicated. But I think you were really asking who I am. I am Astrid of the North, and I will fight with my people."

Her voice rang with the passion of a warrior, and Solveig's cacophonous mind began to settle. She nodded, and let her hand fall away from Astrid's silken arm. "May I…" she asked, and then stopped, surprised that she'd spoken.

"Yes?"

What had she meant to say? She brushed her thumb over her fingertips, still feeling traces of the silk and silver. "May I...is there a gown I might wear tonight?"

Once that thought found its place, Solveig felt it keenly. She wanted to put away the leathers she'd worn for weeks, that she'd fought in, bled in, and sailed in. She wanted to strip to her skin and bathe completely, and she wanted to wear something beautiful. In this place, where she was helpless, she wanted not to think of a battle she was too weak to win.

In this place, so removed from the world she knew, so far from the gods who favored her parents and sat waiting for her to be worthy, she wanted to be beautiful.

She wanted Magni to think her beautiful.

The Queen of Mercuria smiled. "Come. You're taller than I, and your bosom is a bit ampler, but I think we can find something in my wardrobe. After, I'll send up a girl to help you bathe and dress. The gowns can be difficult without assistance, until they are familiar."

~oOo~

The gown she'd selected was green, the rich green of deep, still water. A green she'd never seen before in cloth. Tiny clear crystals sparkled across her chest and swept in swirling patterns over the skirt. Astrid told her that it was a winter dress, one she'd worn for a feast during their holiday that was like *jul*, but Solveig didn't care. It laced at the back and fit perfectly. There was a silken underdress in gold, and that had been too snug, so she wore another in black. The skirt didn't skim the ground as it would have on Astrid, and it wasn't split the way many of Astrid's gowns were, but Solveig liked the tiny black shoes with ribbons that wrapped around her ankles, and she liked that they peeked out where she could see them with each step.

The 'girl' who had helped her was actually a woman, considerably older than Solveig. Audie was sweet and did more than help her wash and dress. She also did her hair, twisting it into loose coils and pinning it with jewels. She knew some of Solveig's words, and they managed to have something like a conversation. Solveig liked her very much.

There was a long glass in the room, and Solveig didn't recognize herself. It was as if she were in disguise as a fine lady of this strange place. She felt beautiful.

And she felt strong in these clothes. In silken shoes and sparkling jewels, her blade and shield hung on the wall, she felt an exhilarating power move through her.

Audie helped her find her way to the hall, where they would dine. Magni stood in the foreroom with their families and friends. He, too, had washed and dressed. He wore fresh, dark leathers that shone. His golden hair gleamed. He'd tied part of it back as he often did for battle; it was a look she preferred. Solveig's belly twitched, and her sex clenched. He stood there like Thor himself at the door to Valhalla's great hall.

Not all of the people who'd sailed to Mercuria were invited to feast in the hall. Only the leaders and their families, and their close advisors. The rest were feasting, but at a fire in the camp they'd set up on the castle grounds.

Their parents, and Solveig's siblings, and a few others, stood in the foreroom. Everyone was washed and dressed for a celebration. The men wore clean and polished leathers, like Magni. Of the women, however, only she had chosen such an elaborate costume of the women of this world. Her mother and Olga both wore much simpler gowns, as did Tova and Hella.

She'd wanted to be different from her normal self, but now, confronted by that difference, some of the power Solveig had felt in these clothes evaporated.

Then Magni came to her. She hadn't seen him since they'd stood in the room and argued with the king about his god. He'd been upset with her when they'd parted, though he hadn't expressed it outright.

Now, a smile spreading across his handsome face, he crossed the room. "You are like Freya, come to walk among us in grace and beauty."

She smiled; she'd thought him like a god as well.

He set his hand on her waist. There was possession in that touch, and it made Solveig's mind clamor, but she stilled the noise and met his eyes.

"You are no long angry?"

"I wasn't angry, Solveig. I'm perplexed. But we can speak of it later." He took her hand and led her to the wide doorway, where two guards in matching armor stood.

A man who'd been standing with their parents went to the door, and Solveig realized that he was Bjarke, one of their own, who'd helped to settle Norshire, and who was now a nobleman of this world. He had a woman on his arm; Solveig remembered her, as well—his wife. They were from Karlsa.

"As some of you know," Bjarke said, "this world has its own rituals. They are different from ours, but no less important here. There will be music, and the room will stand as we pass. There is a table arranged for us. It would be best to come into the hall in a queue, with Leif and Olga and Vali and Brenna just behind me, their children following, and the rest after."

Solveig remembered some of this from her previous visit to Mercuria. She remembered the hall, and a feast among people in elaborate clothing. She remembered strange music and dancing. She remembered people staring. Many people staring.

Behind Solveig, Ulv sneered and limped back, as if he meant to walk away. "I want none of their spectacle. This world is made of fools and sheep."

"And warriors as well," Magni rejoined. "Warriors whose strong arms we need."

"Astrid would want you with us, Ulv," Leif said. "I want you with us. I owe Olga's life to you."

"We all owe you," Solveig's mother added. "And Turid, and her sons. You saved our children. You saved us the devastation of an ambush in Geitland. You gave us the chance to prepare our revenge. This feast is a celebration of that chance." She came to him and set her hand on his arm. "This winter, we will get to know who it is we ask to fight with us. We will see them in their rituals as much as in anything else."

Ulv considered Solveig's mother for several seconds. Finally, he nodded. They all arrayed themselves according to Bjarke's instructions and walked into the hall.

~oOo~

As before, after the meal, there was dancing. Music had played while they ate as well, and Solveig didn't like it. It was played by scratching tight strings with sticks, or plucking at them, and it made the back of her neck tense. There were also small pipes and drums, more like the instruments of home, and she liked those better, but the strings seemed to be what Mercurians liked best.

But after the meal, servants came and cleared the tables and then moved them aside. Leofric led his wife down from their platform to the center of the room. A heavy drumbeat that Solveig recognized started up, and the king and queen held out their free hands toward Solveig's parents, and Leif and Olga, and all of their party. Bjarke and his wife, and the other Norshire settlers who were present at the feast rose as well.

Magni offered his hand, and Solveig took it. They joined their people in the middle of the room, making a circle. This was music and dancing that she knew.

The others watched as their people moved in their circle to the rhythm of the drum. A pipe joined in, adding a lighter, more complex rhythm—strange, but not unpleasant. She turned to face out and caught Magni's hand and her father's again, then, at the right moment, turned inward again. Her silky skirts swirled around her legs.

The small shoes made her feet feel odd on the stone floor. Almost as if she wore no shoes at all. She slipped on her next turn, only slightly, but Magni broke free from Bjarke's wife's grip and set his hand at the small of Solveig's back, steadying her. A needless gesture, but sweet. Feeling light and at ease, she smiled at him, and picked up the dance again.

After a while, they opened the circle, and people of Mercuria danced in the northern way. They knew the steps as well as Solveig or anyone she'd grown up with, as if dances like this were as much a part of their lives as the strange music that had played during the meal. Solveig found herself smiling, and then laughing, as she danced.

But then the music changed again, to a strange, stringed tune, and the ring of dancers broke up and formed into something she didn't understand. Solveig let go of Magni and her father, and she stepped back, toward the side of the hall. She didn't know this music, or this way of moving. Feeling her displacement keenly, she turned away, searching for something she had no hope of finding, or even defining, in this world.

Magni followed her; she felt his fingers catch her own before he was abreast of her. "Don't run, Solveig. Not from me."

She turned to face him, letting him keep her hand. "There's nowhere to run. Where would I go?"

Without a word, he led her from the hall. The two guards, stationed at either side of the wide portal, didn't acknowledge them at all. They seemed not even to blink.

With some distance from the strange music and the crowd of people, Solveig calmed again. In the comparative quiet and privacy, Magni took hold of her other hand. They faced each other, their hands linked between them.

"Wed me here," he said.

Solveig felt her jaw unhinge and drop. While her stunned mind tried to find its sense again, before she could remember language and find words to say, he went on.

"You say you want your story told first. Solveig, your story was being told before you were born. You are the child of the God's-Eye and the Storm-Wolf. You were born on the solstice with the kiss of the Sun on your shoulder. You are a great shieldmaiden, your mother's mirror, and you scale the mountains of bodies of enemies you've slaughtered. You are destined to mate with me, son of Leif, and together will we someday forge a unified land. Do you not hear the tellings? Do you not listen? Your story is told, everything you do adds to it, and it will be told long after you are in Valhalla. You are a legend already."

Still her mind could make no words. Everything he'd said was true. Of course she'd heard the stories. It was those very stories that carved so deeply into her heart and soul, that made her feel that she was so much less than she should be.

Magni, of all people, should know that. He should look into her, as he so often did, and know it. Instead, he held up the thing that made her weakest and told her to feel strong.

Perhaps he didn't know her at all. And he wanted to wed? In this strange place, while they were exiled from their home?

Shaking her head, she broke free and turned away, trying to walk rather than run.

Walk where? To the room she'd been given, she supposed. If she could find it again.

She'd gotten far down the wide corridor before Magni caught her arm and turned her back. She hadn't heard him come up behind her.

"Solveig."

They were before the room she thought of as the Judas room, where she'd argued with the king earlier in the day. It seemed fitting, as she churned with betrayal and confusion. Again, she tore her arm free of Magni's grip, but rather than run, she stepped into the dark room. She had found her words.

"I know the stories! I hear them all the time, in whispers and in songs. Told around fires and slurred by mead. I am the child of legends. I'll be wife to a jarl—perhaps a king. I'm my mother's mirror. I'm my father's sun. I'm your woman. What am I to *me*? Who am *I*? I will never be as great as Brenna God's-Eye. I can only be her reflection. I'll never be as strong as Vali Storm-Wolf. I can only mate well and expand his holding. I'll never be wise and good as Jarl Leif or Magni Leifsson." In a burst of fury, she ripped the shoulder from her luxurious gown and bared the mark she'd been born with—a deep pink, but pale, in the shape of a rayed sun. "Sunna herself favored me, and yet I am nothing but the pale reflection of the greatness around me."

There was sadness in Magni's eyes, and frustration, and something else—pity, she thought. When he stepped to her, she shoved him back. "I don't want your pity!"

"And you don't have it!" He came close again, pulling her torn gown up over her shoulder. "Solveig, I don't pity you. You pity yourself, and too much!"

Furious now, she swung her fist. He caught it before the punch could land, and his hand tightened painfully. He didn't let her go. Instead, his other arm swept around her waist, almost as if they would dance like the Mercurians, and then he marched her backward until she hit the stone wall. The painting of Judas kissing the Christian god hung a few inches away.

"You *do* pity yourself. You're so consumed by what you haven't achieved that you are blind to all that you *have*. You run and hide because you don't want the eyes of others on you, but they are not judging you. They're *admiring* you. They watch not to observe your failures but to bear witness to your victories. Why will you not see what is so plainly true? People say you are your mother's mirror because you are so much *like* her! They see the same light of greatness in you. They say you are your father's sun because they see his great love for you and they see you giving that light to the world. Solveig! How can you be so magnificent and so petty all at once?"

Again, Solveig lost her sense of words. She could only gape at Magni's face—red and furious, scowling at her like never he had before. Petty? He'd called her *petty*?

Her mind crashed and stormed. All she could muster was an inarticulate shout. With that, she broke from his hold, shoved him away, and ran.

This time, he let her go.

~oOo~

After only a few wrong turns, she found the room she'd been given, and she slammed herself inside.

But there was no peace to be found here. In the forest at home, she could be one with this world and all the others. With her hands in the dirt, her back against a tree, surrounded by the senses of life, she could find her center, her place.

This room was made for decadent comfort, but nowhere in it was truth. No number of lovely hangings and sumptuous fabrics could conceal the fact that hewn stone blocked all connection to life of the earth and the sky. The windows were covered with glass, so no air could pass through.

There was no peace here, and her mind wouldn't settle.

Petty? She was not petty. All her life, Magni had been her touchstone. Someone who would understand her always. Someone who would be calm when she stormed. Someone who never judged her, never found her wanting.

But here, now, he was like all the others, and Solveig was adrift in this stone tomb that these people called a castle.

No. Without Magni's understanding, she was lost.

She tore open the door and fled the room that was not hers.

~oOo~

He wasn't in the hall, where the dancing continued. Solveig stood at the vast door and watched. Her brothers and sisters, and her mother and father, all seemed at ease, the children playing with the princes and princesses, and the adults talking together, their postures relaxed.

She resented it, how easily they had all set aside the outrage in their homeland, but there was no room in her mind for that feeling to gain much purchase. Magni wasn't there, and that was her chief concern.

Was he in his room, then? She didn't know where that would be, but the room she'd been given was one in a long row of rooms. The rest of her family was meant to settle close by. Perhaps Magni and his parents were near as well. She returned to that part of the castle.

There were many doors, all of them identical, and all of them closed. But just as she was weighing the choice to knock on them all or to give up and go back to her own room, Audie came into the corridor from a door at the end.

"Oh, hello." She dipped down, which was a gesture of respect among some of these people. "You need help?"

She'd asked the question in Solveig's own words, though they sounded strange. Remembering that Audie could understand some of her language, she asked, "I seek the room of Magni."

"Magni. Your man?" She augmented the question with a sweep of her hands over her covered head. Solveig understood her to be trying to describe long hair.

"Yes. Magni."

Audie grinned and waved her near. Solveig went to her, and the sweet servant pointed to a door not far from the one from which she'd entered the corridor. "I know not he there," she said, each word coming deliberately.

Solveig nodded. If he wasn't, she would wait for him. "Thank you."

Bobbing again, Audie went off down the corridor. She knocked on Solveig's parents' door, and then went in.

Alone, Solveig, knocked on the door Audie had pointed her to.

Magni answered. He'd shed the outer trappings of his clothing and wore only breeches and a loose tunic. He'd untied his hair, and it fell forward over his shoulders.

Inside her skin, her muscles fluttered with uncertainty. Since he'd first touched her as a man touching a woman, Solveig had felt shaken so hard that soon she would shatter.

If he was surprised to see her, he didn't show it. Nor did he speak.

She hadn't considered what she would say or do when she faced him again. She'd only known that he *must* understand her.

"I'm not petty," were the petty words that came out. "You don't understand."

He didn't answer, but he stepped back, and she went into his room.

The door closed with a heavy thump. When Magni still didn't speak, Solveig spun on her heel, feeling vulnerable, as if she must protect her back. He stood against the planked oak of the door and folded his arms across his chest, but he said nothing. His expression was opaque to her. Not blank, but closed.

"You don't understand," she said again, to break the silence.

He said nothing. His eyes would not stray from hers. He simply regarded her, inscrutably.

Her heart throbbed out of rhythm, but she squared her shoulders and took a breath. "If I am admired, it is for nothing I have done. If you're right, and I'm a legend already, it's for the things my parents have done, and things people

222

believe I will someday do, not for what I have done. I try to be the woman that people see. Every day, I try. But it's a mark I cannot reach. You say I am petty, but that's unfair. I'm not petty. Nor am I magnificent. I'm *ordinary*. I am made up of stories, but they are not made up of me."

His expression still enigmatic, he unfolded his arms and took a step in her direction. She took the same step backward. They both stopped, no closer to each other than before.

"Please don't be angry with me, Magni. If you don't understand me, then I will have no one who does."

He held up his hands, palms facing out, to her. "Count the scars, Solveig. Each one is a secret I vowed to keep for you. Each one is something only I know about you. I've kept every one of them. I understand you. My very flesh is a map of you. When I say that you are magnificent, I say it with the full knowledge of you—all the things you wish the world to see, and all the things you hope no one ever will. I see you. I feel you. I understand you. I love you. You are magnificent."

His palms were crossed with faint lines. She turned her own hands over and stared down at them. They looked like his. Most of those scars were his oaths to her. Magni had never had many secrets. Solveig had always been the one who hid her truths away.

"I don't know who I am," she whispered, to herself as much as to him.

His hands covered hers; he'd closed the space between them. "I can only tell you the woman I know, and swear to you that I will not block your way while you seek to know yourself. I want only to join you on the journey. At your side."

"How can you be so sure of me?"

He held a palm before her again. "I need only look at my own hands."

"Magni," she whispered. There was nothing else she could think to say, nothing else she wanted to say. She was calmed. Always, he could find the way to settle her mind.

Because he did know her. Better than even she knew herself.

She pulled his open hand to her, bent her head, and kissed a palm that showed his lifelong love and loyalty. "Magni," she said again, breathing the word over his skin.

"Solveig." His free hand skimmed around her waist and drew her against him. The hand she held pulled free and cupped her face. His mouth came to hers, hot and fierce and yet gentle, claiming only as much as she gave freely. Solveig wound her arms around his neck, sighing at the cool silk of his hair and the hot satin of his mouth.

His room was much like the one she'd been given. Rich fabrics covering stone walls, a stone floor. Heavy furniture. A low fire in a massive stone nook. It was no nearer the true world than the one she'd fled not long before. But she wasn't alone here. Things made sense here. *She* made sense here. She wasn't alone here. Because she was with him.

As Magni groaned and deepened their kiss, Solveig let herself be consumed.

The hand at her back tugged at the lacing of her gown, and she felt it go loose around her bust and waist. His hand left her cheek and pulled on the part of the gown she'd torn earlier, dragging it down her arm.

His tongue receded from her mouth. His lips grazed hers as he murmured, "Stay with me."

There was nowhere else she could be. Magni could always quiet her mind. Even his presence, sitting beside her, holding her hand. Sometimes even simply that. This, with him, was where things truly made sense, in her mind and in the world. Always it had been so. She belonged with him.

"Yes, always," she gasped and dropped her hands to clutch handfuls of his tunic. She pulled upward, and he broke away, grinning, and helped her rid him of the linen. He helped her out of her gown and underdress until she stood in nothing but her little shoes with the ribbon ties.

Surprising her as she tried to lean in for a new kiss, Magni turned her around. Behind her, he skimmed his callused hands over her shoulders and down her arms. She felt his breath and beard on her neck, and his lips followed the path a hand had forged. He paused to favor the mark of the sun, swirling his tongue over that place until her skin tingled and fluttered.

His hands hooked around her hips, and he dropped slowly to his knees, trailing tiny kisses, velveted by his beard, down her back. Her body burning with the sparks of sensation his touch caused, Solveig could only close her eyes and tighten her fists and try to keep still while every muscle inside her danced wildly.

Always before, they'd coupled out of doors, in only imaginary privacy. Never before had they been entirely alone, with the luxury of warmth and quiet and time. Never before had he *adored* her in this lavish, timeless way.

From his knees, he untied the ribbons of her shoes and unwound them from her ankles. She stepped out of them, one at a time, her knees shaking. He pushed them out of her way, and she was entirely bare. Entirely vulnerable. Entirely safe.

He stood, brushing his body along hers all the way. Before she could turn and face him again, he swept her into his arms and carried her to a bed heaped with soft coverings. He laid her down and shed his clothes. His sex bounced and stretched, and Solveig nearly reached out as if that part of him could take her hand on its own.

They had coupled often since that first night; only on the skeids had they passed any night without it. Solveig was still a novice at this kind of physical pleasure, and she still found his body mysterious in its delights. The way his sex could be hard and stiff as a sword and yet feel soft in her hands. The way his body skimmed along hers, and how her senses all rushed to the points of their connection. The way that, when he filled her, she felt full everywhere, not only at the join of their bodies. Even her mind seemed to wrap around him as he thrust into her.

Often, the recollection of his body in hers, on hers, around hers would overrun her during the day, when she was fully clothed and at work, and she would have to stop, clutching her belly, while her body relived the memory.

To have someone so familiar, so loved, become someone so new and exciting as well—Solveig felt it as a boon. A destiny.

When he joined her on the bed, sliding along her body to rest at her side, at first he only looked down at her with eyes wild with passion, in a face calm with love. "Wed me."

Even now, calm and awash with love and desire, Solveig couldn't give him that—it wasn't fear or self-doubt that stopped her. She couldn't say yes because it was wrong. This time, though, she felt no worry to deny him, because it wasn't a denial at all. "Not here. Not in this place. It's not home. I don't want to wed you in a foreign place."

He smiled, and she breathed out her relief. "When we are home, then. Among our people."

"Yes. Yes. I want to be your wife, Magni."

He took her mouth, shifting his body over hers. Solveig opened her legs, and her heart, and let him claim her whole.

15

Leif stood before the Christian god house and looked down the hill. The settlement town of Norshire had grown in the few years since he'd last visited Mercuria. Indeed, in each visit over the course of the past ten years or more, since they'd first made their friendship with Leofric's father and founded this town, Leif had seen a changed Norshire. Their people's new life in a strange place had rooted and blossomed, growing ever greater.

The town bustled along the lane that meandered down the steep hill to the little harbor, and the morning rang with the sound of work. Leif had come to know that sound as the cycling rumble and clang of prosperity. People had needs and the resources to meet them, so people had work and thus the resources to meet their own needs. Smiths, seamstresses, cobblers, farmers, bakers—everyone had something to do, and they moved along the lanes and through the structures of the town with purpose. When they took their leisure, they did so together, congregating at the town circle or in places called *taverns*, which were, as well as Leif could imagine, somewhat like great halls—in function, at least.

The buildings here were a unique blend of the northern style and the Anglian style, and over the years, the blending had become more subtle. No longer did two ways of being jostle together; now each way seemed to influence the other and become a thing of itself.

Even this god house was different from all the other god houses Leif had seen in Christian lands. The front doors of this one were ornately carved in a familiar way, and the crosses embedded in the pattern, at the center of each door, hardly seemed crosses at all.

Astrid had said that all gods live in Norshire, and Leif could see that it might be true. This was a place of joining. The people who'd settled here were different. They spoke both languages, and their knowledge of the Anglian words had twisted their tongues around the words with which they'd been born. Their dress was different, too—like their buildings, they made their clothes from both places and thus unique to them. Here on Mercurian soil, the people of Norshire had made a world that balanced on the seam between two others.

"I have horses ready for us. I thought you'd want to ride into the fields. It will be a good harvest this year." Bjarke, who'd once been a raider and was now the Duke of Norshire, stood between Leif and Vali and clapped his hands on their backs.

Vali, as entranced by the town before them as Leif had been, offered a distracted nod in response.

Bjarke was one of Vali's own clansmen and had been a close advisor. When Vali didn't seem ready to move, Bjarke nudged him. "Vali?"

The great man turned his head. "This is the life Brenna wanted in Estland. You've made it here."

Surprised, Leif cocked his head and considered his friend. This wasn't the first time they'd visited Norshire and remarked on its success. It wasn't the first time they'd compared that success to the failure at Estland. Memories of Estland were fraught for Leif; they'd all lost much there, and he'd been blamed for too long before he'd been understood and forgiven. And yet, he'd met Olga there and found his heart's ease.

With Vali and Bjarke, he didn't like to speak of it. Memories of their condemnation still burned, even these long years after the wounds had healed. But what was in Vali's voice and eyes now wasn't condemnation. Or perhaps it was—but not toward Leif.

"Vali." Leif took a step closer. "What's on your mind?"

Vali sighed heavily and dropped his head. The thick hank of his greying braid fell over his shoulder like a serpent. He took another deep breath before he spoke. "What if we were to stay?"

Such words coming from Vali Storm-Wolf stunned Leif so much that he took a step back. Bjarke did as well, and the shock on his face must have been a mirror of Leif's own.

"You would give up Karlsa? Have me give up Geitland? Let Tollak win and claim himself *king*?"

Vali didn't lift his head. Staring down at his boots, he sighed again. The great Storm-Wolf carried a burden of defeat on his sagging shoulders, and Leif and Bjarke exchanged a wary glance.

Leif had known Vali more than twenty years and had counted him a dear friend for nearly all that time. He knew him for the man he was—brave and mighty, and yet only a man. Not a god. Not invulnerable. Not immortal. A great man, though not without flaws. One of the best of them all.

Never in all the years of their friendship had Leif ever seen defeat lying on his friend's shoulders. Through losses and injuries that would have killed nearly any other, Vali Storm-Wolf had stood tall and broad-shouldered and conquered them all.

This was Brenna. She'd once asked Vali to become a farmer in Estland, and he had agreed. Now, reeling from the death of their daughter and the danger to their youngest children while they'd been in Frankia, Brenna God's-Eye had again asked her husband to put up his axes and shrug off his wolf.

Leif didn't need to ask Vali to confirm it; he could see it plainly, and he knew the conflict in himself. Olga wanted him to stop raiding as well. Over the past few years, it had become a constant refrain of their partings. But he would not sit down until he could step down. When Magni was ready to take his place, then he would put up his sword. Not before.

Magni and Solveig—even if any honor could have been found in a surrender to exile, for their children, Leif and Vali could not allow Tollak to win. As they had aged, their power had been less about their legends and more about their legacy. They must regain Geitland and Karlsa for their heirs. They had made them warriors. They could not at this late date make them farmers instead.

And there was no need that they should. They would prevail when they returned to their home. They would have their own power and that of Mercuria, and they would not be denied.

Norshire hadn't always been a place entirely of peace, and it might not always be. Their warriors, those who had settled, and those who'd sailed to their aid, including Leif and Vali, had fought on the side of Mercuria twice in the past, helping Leofric and Astrid to conquer their enemies and expand their kingdom. It was one reason that they'd known they could count on Mercuria's aid now. There was more than friendship between them. There was also debt.

Vali had lifted his head, but he hadn't spoken more. He looked out, to the sea beyond the harbor.

Another glance at Bjarke told Leif that the duke was still shocked at Vali's dejection. Leif stepped around him and faced Vali. He set his hands on his friend's shoulders and waited for his eyes to focus on him.

"Brenna has taken a hard loss. You both have. If she wants a quieter life for your youngest children, and you want to give her this, I understand. Olga would like a quieter life as well. Perhaps we might join you, and we can sit down in our old age. But we cannot leave Tollak to cement his role as king. There are others, thousands of others, who are our people and didn't get away. We cannot abandon them. And there are our children who would take our place someday. We cannot simply surrender their legacy. We must claim it back."

Vali nodded at once. Leif understood that his friend had already known all the reasons they could not now stay. He agreed; he wanted to fight. Vali Storm-Wolf would never be happy sitting down while others fought his battles. But he loved his wife above all else in the world, and she had been weakened by these terrible losses. He would give over everything to restore her.

"We have to fight, Vali. Brenna will understand that. In her heart, she knows as well as we do. In her heart, she agrees. She is a warrior, and she understands."

Again, Vali nodded, and the defeat fell from his shoulders. He stood straight and breathed deep and clear.

~oOo~

Leofric sat at the head of the dark table in his solar. Leif sat facing him. Between them were arrayed the most powerful of their people: Vali. Brenna. Bjarke. Ulv. Astrid. Dunstan, a duke of Mercuria and Leofric's closest friend. And Magni and Solveig, there to learn.

The first time Leif had sat at this table, he'd faced Leofric's father, and suspicion had made him feel as taut as the skin over a drum. But enemies had become friends at that meeting.

"Eight hundred miles," Leofric said, not for the first time. He shifted his glance from Leif to Dunstan, then back to Leif.

"From west to east, or from north to south, Mercuria spans two hundred miles. And claims the greatest portion of Anglia."

They all used northern words. Though Leif and Vali were fluent in the Anglian tongue, Brenna had no ear for languages, and the others knew little of it either.

"The North is no small island such as this," Magni replied. "It is a great land."

Leif shot his son a glance but didn't censure him. He liked to see such fire and confidence, and knew that it wouldn't be arrogance in Magni's heart.

The king nodded. "To any man, his home is great. But we will need a new strategy to fight at one time on two fields so far flung, each from the other."

Vali leaned in. "Astrid. Tollak has claimed all the land from Geitland to Karlsa as one holding. Remember how we brought Åke down."

The queen nodded and turned to her husband. "Long ago, another jarl sought to do what Tollak has done. We defeated him—we reclaimed the smaller holding and then went for the greater." She turned back to Vali. "But we, too, did what Tollak did—we attacked when Åke's raiders were away. We know he has a force comprised of all the best raiders of Halsgrof and Dofrar waiting for us."

"In Geitland," Vali countered. "Not in Karlsa—if he waits for us in Geitland, in Karlsa and elsewhere he will have only a small guard. If we land far north and fight our way south, we can claim the land as we go. Until he sends his force to meet us where we are. Then we will reclaim it all and soak the earth with his blood."

"Eight hundred miles." This time, it was Dunstan saying those words.

"Eight hundred miles, yes," Brenna answered, irritation biting on the ends of her words. "Are Mercurian men too weak for such a journey? Perhaps you should arm your women, then."

Astrid barked a laugh at that, and it broke the tension of the meeting. "I have tried to encourage women to fight, Brenna. But this god wants women to keep the home, and his priests countermand me. Only a scant few have sought to take up a sword, and they only to protect their own world. It is not so easy to make shieldmaidens where never have they been before."

Leif cut through these incidental remarks and faced the king. "Will you fight with us or no, Leofric?"

"The people of the North stood with us while we fought fractious neighbors and increased the realm. The people of the North were with us when we repelled the Danes. You taught us the northern ways of fighting and made us stronger. You gave me my wife, and thus my heirs. We owed you a debt once, and repaid it with unity. You have stood with us in all the years since and never called for aid before now. Of course we will fight with you."

When the king finished, before any other could answer, Dunstan jumped in. "Your Majesty, you speak honorably and true. But if I may…" When Leofric nodded, Dunstan continued, "It could be a long war, made over such a distance. A long voyage, and a long war. Long away from our home with our army—our best soldiers. It would leave us vulnerable, Sire. There are yet those who would unseat you if they could." He looked down the table at Leif. "Exactly as you have been unseated, when you were turned toward other battle."

Leif ignored Dunstan and kept his attention on the king. "Will you fight with us or no?"

Leofric gripped his wife's hand. "We will fight with you." Shifting his glance to his friend, he added, "Dunstan, you will lead here, in our stead. We will stand a force of protection and defense, and during the winter we will meet with our neighbors and ensure the security of our borders."

Dunstan paled with affront, but his words were measured and respectful. "Always have I fought at your side, Your Majesty."

"Yes. Always you have been my true friend, and I trust you with our greatest treasures: our children, and the realm itself."

Dunstan seemed as if there was more he would say, but he simply nodded. "I am yours to command, Sire."

"I shall stay in Mercuria as well," offered Ulv.

Leif looked down the table, surprised. Ulv had been suspicious and resistant among the Mercurians and even with the people of Norshire. "Ulv?"

Ulv patted his leg. "I'm no good to you as I am. And the winter here is…easier." He seemed ashamed to admit it. "Turid would like to stay, and I would like to make a family before I am too old to enjoy it."

Sitting beside him, Bjark grinned and tugged on Ulv's greying braid. "It's too late for that, old man." Ulv punched him on the shoulder, and the people at the table laughed.

Taking up the seriousness in Ulv's decision, Leif waited for the table to quiet. "You want this?"

Ulv leveled a look at him. "Turid wants it. I want her happy. And I'm useless in the north."

"Not useless. You've been at my side for years. I trust you in my stead."

"And Geitland was lost on my watch." Leif opened his mouth to argue that point; he blamed Ulv not at all. He'd kept Olga safe. But Ulv stopped him with a raised hand. "I'm staying, Leif."

Hearing in his tone that there was no argument to sway his friend, Leif finally nodded. He'd grown to rely on Ulv to keep Geitland well while he was away and to look after Olga. He had no one in Geitland he trusted so much besides his son, who sailed with him. But he wouldn't attempt to force his will on his friend.

"It is decided," Leofric pronounced. "This winter, we will prepare for a great fight in the north. My friends, you will win back your homes, or we will die in the glorious attempt."

~oOo~

They spent the better part of the afternoon discussing logistics for both the fight and the preparation. When they finally set aside their maps and their arguments, Leif realized that they'd been working by torchlight for some time. The world beyond the glass windows had gone grey with twilight.

As they dispersed to prepare to share a meal in the king's private quarters, Leif sent Bjarke out with Magni and Solveig to share the news with the rest of their people, who were camped on the castle grounds.

One point of their discussion had been the sheltering of their people. A full winter spent in tents would be an untenable hardship, particularly when their leaders slept on silks. It had been decided that huts would be erected on the outskirts of Norshire.

Leif worried that the winter would cool the raiders' fire for vengeance and victory. Especially if they had homes built here and time to make them comfortable. He'd have preferred longhouses, which could shelter them all in warm familiarity but not give any one of them too much sense of ownership. But longhouses would have little use for the people of Norshire after the raiders left.

Already he'd lost Ulv, and even Vali had wavered. It would behoove Leif to be sure that his people kept their losses in mind and remembered the cause they had to fight.

Shedding those thoughts, he opened the door to the suite of rooms he shared with Olga. He'd left her that morning still lying abed. She'd been weakened by the voyage, and the night before they'd been with their friends until well past midnight, so she'd been wan and exhausted in the morning, giving him some concern despite her protestations of health. He was glad to see her looking fresh and herself this evening, sitting by the fire.

She wore a gown he'd never seen before, one more in the style of Mercuria than in their own. It was silk in a red so dark it was nearly brown, and the fabric shimmered like something brought down from the night sky.

Her spectacular dark hair, with its single, wide sweep of white, was coiled so that it lay on her back, caught up in a net that sparkled with garnets. The people of this place, the leaders at least, enjoyed the display of their wealth. They dressed to exhibit that more than anything else. It was better to be rich in Mercuria, it seemed, than it was to be strong.

But he loved the sight of his beautiful wife draped in finery worthy of her.

She smiled when she saw him and held out her hands.

He went to her and clasped her hands in his, crouching before her. "My love, you are beautiful. You glow. Are you feeling better?"

"I am, but I think I might feel ill often for a while yet."

She was smiling that warm, somehow mysterious smile, but her words gave him worry.

"Is there something wrong?" He put his hand on her forehead—cool and smooth.

She shook her head and took his hand in hers, setting it on her belly instead. She covered his hand with both of hers, and her smile grew.

"There is nothing wrong," she murmured.

Leif stared at their hands on her belly, feeling cool silk against his rough palm, and tried to focus the sudden onslaught of thoughts in his head. Magni had nineteen years. Never had they tried to prevent Olga bearing another child, and they had enjoyed each other very much, and very often, for all of their years together. Could she now, after all this time, when he approached fifty years of life and she had more than forty— could she now be carrying another child?

No—it was impossible. But they had thought Magni impossible as well.

He lifted his eyes and met Olga's, watching him with that same smile. "I haven't bled for three months. I thought it meant my time of bleeding was at its end. But I've been ill and weak, and there are other signs that made me wonder. Still, after all these years, it seemed more likely that age was the cause, age and sadness for missing you, and anxiety when we were overrun, and the difficult voyage. So much has happened in so short a time. But today, when the seamstresses were adjusting this gown for my frame, we all saw the truth. You and I will have another child, Leif. One who will be born before the summer comes."

Too much in awe, too consumed by love, to do anything else, Leif wrapped his arms around his wife and laid his head on her lap.

There they remained, before a low, cheerful fire, in a quiet room not their own. Leif closed his eyes as Olga combed her fingers through his hair.

A child. A sign of favor from the gods. They would reclaim their home, and it would again be filled with the innocent joy of their child.

The world kept its balance.

16

Magni rested a gleaming new sword on his hand, testing its balance. All around him rang the song of smiths at work, beating hot steel into blades and armor.

He wasn't interested in a new sword for himself. He wielded Sinnesfrid, a sword handed down to him by his mother, from his father, in the way of their people. It was a mighty blade, and his father had become a great jarl wielding it.

Magni would pass Sinnesfrid to Solveig on their wedding, and through her to his own child someday, but until then, he would wield no other. He was here at the smithy, testing new blades, because his father wanted him involved in all the matters of preparation for the war they meant to make when summer came again. This would be different from a raid. Never before had Magni faced a fight like the one they meant to wage: Long and pitched. On home soil. Against their own people.

His father had fought in this way before, as had Vali, and Brenna. Many of the older raiders had. But Magni, Solveig, Håkon, and the others of their generation had not. To prepare for it so far from home—it made Magni feel fragmented. Things were done differently here. War was made differently here. Even the smiths did not do things quite as he'd known them to be done. And they made great heaps of metal armor, mail and plate both.

Nearby, his father grumbled as one of the apprentices helped him into a plated chestpiece. As long as Magni had been aware, his father had worn boiled leather armor with metal woven into it. He'd been surprised to see him considering plate for the coming war—until his father had explained that it was intended as a concession to his mother, who was carrying another child. It was said that Leif Olavsson led with his heart, and he had the heavy scars on his chest to show that it was true. Magni's mother wanted him to protect himself so that their new child would know his father as well as Magni did.

Magni would have a sibling, one who might well be little older than his own children. The thought both gladdened and unsettled him. Above all else, however, he was relieved to know that his mother's recent weakness had such a benign cause.

Pushing the apprentice away with a huff, Magni's father drew his sword from its scabbard and stepped to the back of the smithy, in a clear space where he might brandish his weapon. Magni flipped the new blade and caught it by its grip. He watched his father try to learn to move under heavy plate.

He was slow and awkward, and he quickly gave up the attempt. "No. I am too old to learn to fight under such constraint, and too skeptical of its benefit. Better to be nimble and evade the blow than to be slow and withstand it. Boy!" He beckoned the smith's apprentice over again. "Rid me of this useless burden." When the boy only blinked, Magni's father said different words, in a different tongue. Then the apprentice helped him out of the armor.

The smith who'd fashioned the useless burden in question showed deep concern. He came to Magni's father and spoke. Magni's father shook his head and then clasped the man's shoulder and gave it a shake. Unable to understand most of the Anglian words they'd exchanged, Magni could only interpret the gestures. He thought his father had reassured the smith that he didn't hold him to blame for the armor.

"Mother won't be pleased," Magni said on a chuckle as his father came up. When he sheathed his own sword and held out his hand, Magni handed the new blade over to him, and his father hefted it as he had done.

"I will speak with your mother. I'm more likely to return to her if I can fight. Plate might keep my heart safe, but it will get my head cleaved when I am to slow to evade a strike." He caught the blade by its grip. "What do you think of these Saxon swords?"

"They are lighter, and the hilt feels narrow. The king says they are quicker than our heavier blades, and tire the arm less."

"And what do you think of that?"

"I think Saxon arms must tire quickly."

His father laughed. "I've fought Saxons, and I've fought with them. They rely on their minds too much and on their hearts too little, I think. But they are not so weak as you might think. They fight well—only not like us."

"They had to sneak to best you." Magni knew well the story of the failed raid, when they'd lost Astrid and been driven back, burned and beaten. Brenna was among the warriors who carried the scars of fire, and Vali had come closer to death then than ever else.

"It's true. But long have we been true friends and allies. We've each learned from the other and been made stronger. They'll be a great help to us when we reclaim Geitland." He handed the sword back to Magni, who replaced it on its rack. "Now, let us meet up with the others and see how the people here celebrate their jul."

~oOo~

It was a strange thing to walk through a light world so near the winter solstice. Winter nights were long in Mercuria, but they were hardly endless. Each day, even on the solstice itself, had hours of true daylight.

Not beaming sun, however. Clouds covered the sky most days, and only a glow noted where the sun was—but that glow hovered much higher in the sky than it did in their world.

Mercurians huddled up in heavy cloaks and layered clothing, but the air was no more than cool on Magni's skin—more like dawning summer than full, deep winter. A cloak was all he needed, and some days, even that weighed too heavily.

There had been much rain as well, and the sodden earth sucked at their boots as they walked through Norshire.

Magni liked this town. It felt a bit like home and yet was different in ways that interested him. Here, many of the residents still spoke his tongue, though with the unusual accent like Astrid's and Bjarke's. He'd come to define it as Saxon sounds on northern words.

Their buildings here were more like those he knew than elsewhere in Mercuria, though not quite. And people dressed and even worked in ways more like home.

But, for the larger part, the settlers seemed to have given up the Æsir and turned to the Christian god. The god house rang its bell in this place as in all the others of Mercuria, and the people left their homes and went to kneel.

They did not celebrate the solstice in Mercuria. This land of the Christian god celebrated something called *ahdfent*, as he understood the word. What it had meant was weeks of dour quiet, when the Saxons did little but pray to their god and starve themselves. The displaced raiders had worked mostly alone in Norshire, working on lighter preparations for the sail home and the war they would make. They'd repaired the disabled skeid and refurbished the other three, which had taken damage in the storms as well.

But on this day, the Christian people came back to life, and a feast was planned in the castle, welcoming not only the landed, noble people but the common people as well, those near enough to make a journey to the castle. Others would set feasts in their towns, supplied by bounty from the king.

Bjarke had explained that this feast was much like a jul feast, with ample food and drink, and more than ample merrymaking. As Magni walked with his father toward the stables, squelching through the mudded road, he could see it—dark greenery had seemed, of a sudden, to sprout all over, in sprays on doors and garlands swinging from eaves and spanning the road. Some of the trees were even festooned with figures made of wood and straw, in the fashion of home, where they left tokens to entice the forest spirits to return and bring the warm with them. Their beliefs were different, yet their symbols were much the same. He found it fascinating.

They'd come to the god house, the *church*. The priest stood at the top of its steps, about to close the doors. Magni saw, carved into those doors, two birds, like ravens, rendered in a pattern much like his own tattoo. His birds were Huginn and Muninn—Odin's ravens, who flew around the world and brought the Allfather news of his realm.

He wondered how the Christian god felt about the greatest Norse god's spies standing at his door.

"Would you join us?" the priest asked. Magni had learned enough of the Saxon tongue to understand that much. Feeling a gentle draw to know more about these Christians, he might have said yes. But he turned to his father, who was shaking his head.

"We thank you. But our gods live elsewhere."

The priest inclined his head and stepped into the church. When the doors closed, Magni stared at the ravens, one carved into each door, facing each other. Each beak touched a cross, and arms of each cross spanned over the birds. They seemed almost intertwined with each other.

"Do you not wonder?" he asked his father. "What it is they do in there?"

"Astrid has told me. They kneel. The priest speaks in a strange tongue. He tells them what they should do and how they should be. They take a bit of bread and wine and think they eat of the god himself. They kneel again."

"They eat their own god? Why? Should they not be mighty giants if they feed on a god? But they are smaller than we, so he must not be so potent. Why do they think this god so great?"

"That, she has not said." He chuckled and clenched the back of Magni's neck in his hand. "You ask many questions with no answers. Come. We need not understand the Christians to call them our friends. Let us leave them to their kneeling and see how Brenna and Solveig do."

~oOo~

Solveig and her mother were in a pen adjoining the stable, among a small group of horsemen and stable boys, who seemed not so beholden to this world's god and toiled on this day like any other.

They'd been working with the Mercurian battle steeds, preparing them for a sea voyage. Mercuria had never fought a battle beyond Anglian shores, and their horses didn't know how to stand onboard a ship.

Mercuria had only one ship sufficient for a sea voyage like the one they would take, and that ship, Leofric had commissioned specifically to carry his queen to the north to visit. It was not a warship and only armed enough for self-defense. Vali and Håkon had gone with Leofric and Dunstan that morning to a large harbor town in the south, to check on the progress of shipbuilding. They would need at least four ships to carry their warriors, weapons, and steeds. Meanwhile, Brenna and her daughter helped the horsemen train their steeds to withstand the sea and be strong when they touched land again.

Solveig and her mother shared a powerful affinity for animals. Magni had heard Brenna say on several occasions that she preferred animals to people. Solveig hadn't used the same words, not in his hearing, but he thought she felt the same. Animals were uncomplicated, and never disloyal. When they were devoted, they remained so forever, and they asked nothing in return but kindness. They didn't judge.

Magni went to stand at the fence and watch his woman work. In the few months of their time in Mercuria, she had well and truly become his woman, leaving behind the shackles of her uncertainty. Magni thought it was easier for her here, because few knew the legend of her parents, and she could simply be Solveig, a woman from the North.

He'd seen that right away, from the moment she'd walked into a castle room dressed like a princess, in glittering gown and sparkling hair. Here, she was not the God's-Eye's daughter. Here, she could be the woman she wished to be.

It was why he'd wanted to wed her here. He'd seen her in that first dress, the night they'd arrived, and known. In Mercuria, she was free.

Soon, she'd felt it, too, although he doubted that she fully understood the change—she yet believed that she would not be complete until she had achieved her greatness. Still, she'd been happy in these months, and they'd grown as close as any husband and wife might be. She wanted to wed at home, and he understood, so he hadn't pressed. He had enough as they were. They were truly mated, and he could wait for the rituals.

Now, in the paddock, she was dressed in leather and braids, muddy to her knees, with streaks and spatters of brown, drying to grey, on her face and in her hair. She was glorious.

They'd constructed a rocking platform, to mimic the motion of the sea. The horses—this one, at least, a big, muscular black that looked much like the horses of home—hated it. The black grunted and whined as the handlers forced him onto the unstable base. One of the men lifted his hand, holding a crop, and Brenna caught his arm and said something sharp, shaking her head and giving him a glare that, at home, would have made any man quake. Even this man, who didn't know the legend of her strange eye, was cowed. He tucked the crop into his boot and stepped back. The other men and boys worked more gently to get the horse up.

Solveig held the black's lead, stroking his nose, trying to calm him. When they got all four of his immense hooves onto the platform, he danced and whinnied and yanked at his lead. Solveig stood firm, barely moving against his strong pull, letting him have enough head that he wouldn't panic more, but not so much that either of them would be hurt.

Finally, he understood that if he were still, the base would also be, and he calmed. As he felt more secure, he let his head fall, pressing his nose into Solveig's chest. She leaned in, as if they were dear friends embracing. The horse heaved a great sigh, blowing the air through flapping lips, and, with that sign of his ease, Brenna stepped onto the platform, shifting the balance off.

The black threw up his head, nearly knocking Solveig back, and looked wildly around, trying to shift his feet and understand why he was moving when his feet were on something solid.

Solveig stood firm, a steadying presence, centering the horse's attention while Brenna moved around the platform, shifting the balance until the horse could accept the motion and adjust his footing.

Magni watched, enchanted. It was at times like this, when she wasn't focused on, or even aware of, being seen, that the magnificent woman she truly was shone most clearly. Here in Mercuria, that woman had blossomed. He hoped she would take that flower with her when they returned home, and that it wouldn't wither and die.

"You carry your heart in your eyes," Magni's father said, leaning on the fence beside him. "No one could look on you and doubt your love for her. You chose well, my son, and so did she. She is like that black beast, and you are for her as she is for him—she a wild spirit, and you a strong base to help her keep her feet through her storms."

Unwilling to tear his eyes away from Solveig, Magni simply nodded.

~oOo~

Solveig laughed and leaned forward, nudging her heels into her horse's flanks, and the black steed leapt out ahead, picking up the gallop as if he'd been waiting their whole ride for just that moment. Great clods of muddy earth flew up in a wake behind them.

"You don't know where you're going!" Magni shouted at the black's receding hindquarters.

After weeks of rain and chilly drear, the sun had broken through the clouds and hinted that it pulled summer along in its wake. Night was yet much longer than day; there would be weeks before they could call the season changed, and prepare to depart for war, but this day offered a reminder of what summer would be.

The castle had woken to blue sky and bright sun, and spirits were high everywhere. From the royal family all the way down to the lowliest servants, everyone smiled and stepped with a bounce. Even the horses felt the renewal in the air.

That morning, before they'd risen from their bed, Magni had suggested that they give the day over to leisure, and Solveig had readily agreed. When they'd met their family and friends, they'd all, even single-minded Vali, had had the same idea. Solveig's parents were off at play with their younger children and the royal family. Håkon had gone to Norshire to visit with a girl who'd caught his fancy. Magni's parents were staying close to the castle; his mother was large with child now, and his father hovered and fretted and growled like a bear.

Magni had suggested a ride in the forest. He'd been out hunting with the men a few weeks earlier, and they'd stopped to rest and warm themselves in a tidy little hut tucked deep into the trees. Not a hut, truly. Too well appointed to be a hut. The king's hunting lodge, in fact. Sitting with his father, and Vali, and Håkon, and the king, and the king's friend, Dunstan, drinking and laughing, making desultory comments about the coming war, Magni had seen beyond all those men and pictured Solveig, stretched out, long and lithe, on a fur by the stone fireplace.

When he'd woken in a sunbeam that morning, his first thought had been of that—a day away, to ride and laugh and rut in a place removed from everything and everyone but each other. He'd told her as much, trailing a finger down her silken bare arm, and hungry joy had fired her eyes.

But she didn't know where it was, he himself only barely remembered the way, and she now tore through the dense forest on that wild monster of a stallion. Her hair and cloak flew back like banners, and her laugh resounded.

Gods, what a woman he had.

He kicked his own horse into a gallop and gave her chase.

Remembering a narrow side trail that cut across a bend in the main path, Magni turned his horse onto it and nudged the bay gelding forward. In the thick of the summer, he could tell, this path would be nigh impossible to clear at such speed, but the diminished foliage of winter gave him sufficient room. He landed on the main path mere seconds before Solveig arrived in the same place. She reined her black to a stop.

"You cheat! Always you cheat!" Her color was high, a rosy glow over her fair face, and her smile bright, ruining the outrage in her accusation.

He laughed. "Always you accuse me of cheating when I win. I never agreed to race. If I had—is not a strategy that wins the best strategy, by its very winning?"

Her only response to that was a contemptuous noise. Magni brought his horse to hers until they were side by side, facing opposite directions. He leaned over and caught the neckline of her tunic, tugging her toward him. When they were close enough, he brushed his beard over her cheek. "We are not far now—just a little back the way we came, there is a trail. Will you join me, so I can claim my prize?"

She sighed and turned her head, touching her lips to his. "I thought you weren't racing. How can you have won a prize to claim?"

"I won on the day you said you would be mine. Every day with you beside me is a prize."

Her laughter trilled over his lips. "You should be a skald, bending words so prettily."

"Not I." He covered her mouth and kissed her deeply, savoring the taste of her happiness. Her horse shifted, snorting with impatience, and broke their connection, but Magni still had hold of her tunic, and he didn't go far. He smiled into Solveig's eyes, alight now with arousal. "My destiny lies elsewhere—to live a story with you, not merely to tell it."

17

Solveig swung down from the horse she'd come to claim as her own, a large black stallion with a single white mark, one not so different from her own sun, on his forehead. She called him Aggi. When she landed on the ground—less muddy here, where it was covered with the deadfall of old leaves and pine needles—Aggi swung his head back and pushed at her hip.

She laughed and dug into a pocket of her cloak. "One day, I'll not have sweets for you. Will you be so docile and devoted then?" She held out her hand, and Aggi picked the slices of dried apple from her palm.

"Docile? That beast?" Magni walked up beside her, leading his bay.

Solveig only smiled. She enjoyed that Aggi was reserved and suspicious of everyone but her. When she'd first seen him in the Norshire stable, months earlier, even their most experienced horseman had called him unrideable. They'd been reluctant to cut him to make him more manageable, because he was such a fine physical specimen for breeding.

And he was certainly that—deep black, even in bright sun, with a thick, lush mane. His broad, muscular frame rolled and surged under his gleaming coat.

It took three men to bring him from his stall for grooming and care. When they turned him out to run loose, it took hours and several more men to bring him back in. Aggi was not a horse who easily tolerated constraints or expectations.

Something had drawn her at once to the stall where he paced and snorted and yelled, kicking relentlessly at the walls. While her mother and father had spoken with the horseman, she'd gone to stand at the stall door and watch him, and found herself talking to him. He'd turned to watch her, his eyes and ears signaling his wariness. Eventually, he'd walked over and nudged her arm.

After some time spent talking with him and stroking his face, laughing as he lipped at her arms, Solveig had noticed that the stable was quiet. Thinking her parents had gone on without her, she turned and found them, and the horseman, staring.

That was how she came to have a black stallion of her own. Word of her taming of their wild beast had come to the king, and he'd bought the horse and presented him to her for a gift.

Solveig hadn't known how to train a horse, but her mother and the head horseman, Cenhelm, had been teaching her. Cenhelm was a good man, if sometimes overly, in Solveig's mind and her mother's, forceful with his charges. He was teaching her, and Aggi, well.

Aggi trusted only her, but he was willing to be led by others, as long as he associated them with Solveig. She liked that very much, to have a majestic creature like this know her at such a depth that only she was worthy of his trust.

Standing before this humble little cottage in the Mercurian forest, Solveig gave her horse an affectionate bump and smiled at the man beside her. "He's docile for me, and that's all that matters."

Magni swept his free hand around her waist and drew her body to his. "It's a feeling I know myself."

She leaned back from the kiss he'd meant to take and cocked an eyebrow at him. "Do you imply that you've tamed me?"

He wiggled his eyebrows as a riposte. "If the saddle fits."

He was teasing, and she took it as such, but there was also perhaps some truth in it, she knew. Shaping her face into a mask of broad outrage, she shoved on his shoulder. "Öhm! What kind of prize do you think your arrogance will win you, Magni Leifsson?"

Laughing, he let her go and took Aggi's reins from her. "Go into the cabin. I'll put up the horses, and then I'll show you."

~oOo~

The cabin wasn't large, but it was comfortable. Once they had a fire crackling and the light meal they'd brought —bread and cheese and wine—spread over a humble plank table, it was cozy as well. There were chests against the walls, filled with furs and linens, and hunting supplies, and cookware. Magni spread out a large covering made of furs, and they sat on the floor before the fire and enjoyed their meal. When he finished eating, he stretched his long frame out and propped himself on his elbow to stare at the fire.

Solveig finished her wine and leaned back against a heavy chair, sighing with satisfaction. Much to her surprise, she had become fond of Mercuria over these months. She enjoyed the castle, and the people in it, and its fineries and rituals. She liked Norshire and its remnants of home. Her family, even as they prepared for war, seemed more at ease here, in this place they didn't lead.

And she herself felt comfortable and settled in a way that was new. Every day, they worked toward their return home. Every day, they discussed the coming war and made their preparations. But she would miss this foreign place and the sense of belonging she'd discovered here.

"You've gone somber," Magni said, reaching for her and pulling her close.

She shook her head. "Not somber. Pensive."

"What thoughts fill this beautiful head?" He pressed his lips to her temple.

Only Magni could hear such thoughts and be trusted with them. So she asked the question that had taken form. "Would you think to stay here?"

He sat up and faced her, unvarnished shock making his face slack. Solveig dropped her head, abashed. "I don't fear the fight."

His hand came under her chin and lifted. "Of course you don't. I'm only surprised. I thought you'd want to go home and find your story there. I thought you wanted to wed there."

"I do." Searching for the words, she let her frustration out on a breath and lifted her head from his hand. "I do. This is not my place. I want to win back Karlsa and Geitland, and I want our fathers to take back their seats. I want to be there with my family. Only..."

How to say it? How to *know* it?

"You feel right with yourself here, like never before. There is no legend looming here, making a shadow over you."

Now Solveig gaped in shock. "Yes." Her eyes began to sting, and she blinked before that sting might become tears. "Yes."

With a gentle smile, Magni tucked her close again. "You think I don't know that? You think I don't see it?"

"I'm only coming to see it myself," she muttered. His way of knowing her made her love for him all the deeper, yet it was disconcerting to have herself explained by another.

"If you wish to stay in Mercuria, I will stay with you."

"But you're your father's only heir." Håkon could take her father's place. He wanted it badly in any case. But there was no one but Magni to take Leif's seat.

"Ah, but I am not. My mother gives birth to another child soon."

"He will be very old by the time that child could take his seat."

"True, but my father is strong and hearty. And he above all others would understand my choice."

Solveig considered this shocking development. They could stay. Did Magni really want that? Did *she* really want that? What would they be here? What would they do?

Before the questions could clamor together and cloud her mind, Solveig sat up again. "Do you want to stay? Answer me true, Magni." A blade of urgency had sliced across her words.

He took her hand and squeezed it. "I'd answer you no other way. I want to go home. I want to honor my father's great leadership by taking his place when it's time and continuing his legacy. But I would happily stay with you. You, Solveig, are my true home. Do you want to stay?"

Turning to the fire, Solveig watched the flames dance and let their patterns and rhythm focus her mind. Did she want to stay? Did she want to give up the life, the story, the legacy she'd been born to? Did she want to give up her family? Her mother? Her father?

Tears threatened again, and she blinked them away, but not before one escaped and hurried down her cheek. Pulling her hand free of Magni's, she swiped it away.

"No," she breathed. She tried again, finding conviction for the word and its purpose. "No. I don't want to stay. I want you to honor your father. I want to honor mine. I want to go home and find my place there." Finally, she looked back at Magni. "Only…I want to take this feeling I've found…I want to bring it home with me."

He brushed his fingertips over her cheek, across the wet trail of one renegade tear. "Then do. You are the same woman here that you are at home. All that has changed is what you feel. So clutch that feeling. Wrap it around you and keep it close. Carry it with you always, until it is as much a part of you as your shield and your sword."

"What if I can't?"

He leaned close, touching his forehead to hers. "Then I will carry it for you and keep it safe so it's not lost. But we *will* bring it home with us."

"Magni," she whispered, grabbing at his shoulders. His name broke apart on a sob.

He closed her tightly in his arms, covering her face and mouth and neck with kisses. "I love you, Solveig. Always am I at your side."

Words failed her, so she could only nod. He was her true home as well.

His lip found hers and claimed them fully. As his tongue pushed in and filled her mouth, Solveig clutched her arms around his torso and twisted her fingers into his tunic. They'd both shed their outer layers when they'd settled before the fire and were wearing only breeches and tunics. Solveig enjoyed dressing like the noblewomen here, and she had, by now, a sizable wardrobe of elegant gowns, many of them split to accommodate breeches underneath, but when she worked, or rode, she dressed as she always had—in leathers and boots, without the finery.

When Magni pushed forward, taking her down to the fur, Solveig moaned and arched up. Yes, oh yes, what she wanted more than anything right now was to be one with him, to have their physical connection reflect the hold of their hearts. She could feel his sex, an iron rod against her thigh, and she lifted her hips to grind against him. He groaned and flexed, driving himself against her body.

They tore at each other, frantically searching for laces to undo, pushing, pulling, rending their clothes away. Solveig heard the rough rip of fabric and didn't care. They rolled and grunted, arched and moaned, flexed and gasped, all but rutting while they rid themselves of everything between them.

When they were both bare and breathless, Magni grabbed her leg as if he meant already to enter her, but Solveig, seized by a sudden need, kicked away and shoved hard on his chest, pushing until he rolled to his back. He stared up at her, flushed and gasping, and she smiled.

She knew him, too. And she knew the things he liked best. With his perfect, steady, self-sacrificing love wafting around her, she wanted to give him something in return, to make him feel her love for him in his very pores.

Pulling her hair to one shoulder, she leaned over him. She kissed his mouth and then ducked away before he could deepen it. She nipped at his beard, nuzzling along his jaw. She sucked at the slender lobe of his perfectly-shaped ear. She drew her tongue lightly down his throat, across shoulder. She took tiny bites across his chest.

Beneath her, he groaned and huffed, his chest heaving with each erratic breath. He coiled the fall of her hair around his hand and held on, but she resisted each attempt to direct her or hold her in place. She meant to be slow and purposeful, so that he had no doubt of her devotion. His sex bounced and strained with her every touch, but she didn't hurry toward it.

She tasted all of his chest, working her way, with tiny kisses, gentle nips, and languid licks, across the carved terrain of his muscular body.

"Solveig," he groaned as she made her way down his belly. "Please. I must have you."

"You shall. All of me is yours to take."

Finally, she arrived at her true destination, and paused, hovering a scant inch over his throbbing sex, already glistening with his need. His hips lifted, pushing up to her, but she raised her head out of his way.

She had, a few times, given him pleasure in this way, but she yet had much to learn. He enjoyed it, perhaps more than anything else they did, and she was discovering ways to make him enjoy it even more.

Wrapping one hand around him, she dipped her head and pressed a soft kiss to the tip of him, licking the salty tang from her lips.

"Solveig!" Now it was a grunt, and his fist in her hair pulled sharply.

She drew his tip and a bit more into her mouth and then stopped there, sucking lightly. Magni made a feral noise and began to thrust his hips with the tempo of her mouth, driving himself in. She opened her eyes and looked up his body; his eyes were closed, and his brow was drawn tight in concentration.

His arousal excited hers to a pitch so fierce it wouldn't be denied, and without thinking, she shifted between his legs so that she could reach down and find the part of herself that ached for him. Ah, yes. Her eyes fluttered shut.

Everything moved in perfect rhythm: her mouth suckling, his hips flexing, his hand pulling her hair, her own hand between her legs, their breaths mingling loudly above them. Completion began to swirl in her sinews, and she moaned and hurried her hand and her mouth both.

And then he went still and lifted his head and shoulders from the fur. She opened her eyes and saw him staring down at her with eyes blazing with fire and need. In a heartbeat, she understood—he'd never seen her touch herself. In the next heartbeat, she knew that he liked it. She shifted her legs so that he could see better, and she sucked him deeper into her mouth at the same time.

He roared. Like a bear. The sound echoed off the stone fireplace. And then Solveig found herself spun—he'd grabbed her and hefted her and flung her, all before she could quite understand that he'd moved.

He'd turned her on top of him so that her legs were at his head. Not just her legs—her sex. He clamped his arms around her waist and buried his face between her thighs. No longer could she touch herself, but no longer did she need to. His tongue was on her, flicking over that perfect, tiny, wondrous part of her, and she was still at his sex as well. She basked briefly in stunned elation, feeling his bearded face and astonishing mouth on her, then took him back into her mouth.

Never had she shared pleasure in such a way or even thought it possible. For all the rutting she'd been witness to in her life, for all the ways she and Magni enjoyed each other, this was completely new, and completely wonderful. He had pleasured her with his mouth many times, and she had pleasured him a few, but both together? A song should have been made of it.

The completion that had begun to move in her picked up power and speed and drew all her attention to her own core. She intended to bring him to release with her mouth, but each suck and flick he made held her in thrall. Soon, she could only hold onto him, with his length pressed to her cheek, and give herself over to brilliant release.

Loud, ugly sounds came from her mouth, and she buried her head and bit down to block their path. When her finish crashed through her, like a wave over rocks, she screamed against her closed mouth and tasted blood.

Just as it ended, Magni again flipped her, this time to her back, making her gasp out a burst of air, and then he was over her, facing her, between her legs, his long hair making a drape around their faces. Never had he been like this, forceful to the point of roughness. It was new, and exciting, and she felt entirely and fantastically overwhelmed.

As he had earlier—so very much earlier, it seemed—he grabbed her leg, pulling it up to his hip. He shoved into her at once, dipping his head at the same time to suck a breast into his mouth.

"Magni!" she cried as he drove refreshed sensation all through her. Her release hadn't yet stopped pulsing, and already he was sending new sparks of ecstasy into her blood and bone. Grunting wildly with every thrust, he pounded his body into hers, making his sex reach the deepest part of her. His mouth sucked hard at her breast, forcing brilliant stars of need to shower over her skin and through her belly. All she could do was hold on. She clutched at his back and did exactly that.

She completed again, digging her fingers into his back, crying with the force of the pleasure, wanting it never to end and unsure how she could survive much more. Then, without losing his rhythm, he grabbed at one of her hands, dragging it from his back, and pressed it to the fur, holding it like a shackle. He finally let go of her breast, and he stared down at her, his expression wild and frantic.

Following instinct, Solveig wrapped her legs around him and lifted, bring her hips up and thrusting to counter and deepen the savage force of his thrusts. The depth was almost past pleasure, almost pain, but she looked up into those beloved eyes and saw the feeling feed his fire, and she quickened her pace, driving just as hard as he, taking them even farther. She saw his release happen, breaking over his face. He roared again and threw himself backward, out of her, so quickly that she cried out, too.

He hovered over her on shaking arms, his complexion gone red, and spent in a hot spray over her chest and belly and legs.

Collapsing at her side, he sucked in great gusts of air. Solveig rolled to face him, breathless and nearly senseless. When she could see and think more clearly, she noticed that his beard around his mouth was red. With blood.

"You're hurt." She touched her fingers gently to his mouth, seeking a wound.

He caught her fingers and kissed them. "Not there, no. The blood on my beard came from your mouth.

She was hurt? She hadn't felt it. When she checked her own mouth and found no pain but the abrasion of their passion, he laughed and rolled to his back, canting up his leg so his knee pointed to the ceiling.

Solveig looked down his body, saw his softening sex lying on his thigh, and the gleam of his seed on them both—and then she saw that his thigh bled freely from a wound near its top.

She'd bitten him. Viciously. She looked at her hand and saw that she'd wiped blood from her mouth.

"Forgive me," she whispered, embarrassed. "I didn't know."

Magni laughed and pulled her close. "I cannot think of a better way to earn a wound. You've given me all my best scars, my love. And this one, I will keep most fondly."

Solveig settled against his chest. He lifted her hand and kissed her fingers. "You are carved into my body, Solveig."

"And you are carved into my heart," she whispered against his skin.

18

Three of the castle's bitch hounds had whelped in the past few weeks, and the grounds teemed with puppies. Astrid's children and Brenna's youngest two demanded daily to see the pups, and they'd begun a routine of coming down to the kennels together. Brenna enjoyed the break in each day—and she, too, was happy to spend time with the pups.

Mercurian dogs were smaller and sleeker than the dogs of home, but pups were pups, whatever the breed—heartrendingly sweet.

Astrid's two youngest, Eadric and Æbbe, had only five and three years, and they were easily excited and overly rough with the pups. While Astrid caught Eadric back from snatching one off its mother's teat, Brenna dived for Æbbe, who'd picked another pup by its tail. She shrieked and kicked, flailing in Brenna's arms.

No novice in matters of tempestuous toddlers, Brenna clamped her arms around the girl and carried her outside the whelping kennel. Over the months they'd lived in the castle, she and Astrid, with children so close in age, had become closer than ever before. An obscure rivalry that had subtly tinted their friendship in the past was gone, and they'd taken to mothering their children as if they shared them.

"PUPPIES! MINE!" Æbbe screamed from her twisted, reddening face. "MINE!"

Brenna held her close, ignoring the battery of little feet and hands, and put her mouth to the child's ear. "Do you like the puppies?" she whispered. Brenna hadn't bothered learning the Mercurian tongue; she'd long ago resigned herself to the truth that new languages were nearly beyond her ability, but Astrid and Leofric's children had been taught both their parents' native tongues from birth.

She whispered the same words two more times before Æbbe settled enough to hear and respond. She nodded, gulping in noisy gasps of air. "Puppies," she whined.

"I like the puppies, too. But I don't wish to hurt them. Do you?"

Æbbe shook her head sharply, making pale blonde curls bounce. "Kiss puppies."

"I like to kiss them, too. I like to make them happy. Do you?"

A nod, and another sniff. Her eyes were dry; her wails had been entirely for show.

"They are only small and weak, so we must treat them gently. I would like to sit on the ground and let them climb onto me for a cuddle. Would you sit with me and be very quiet so they aren't afraid?"

At Æbbe's nod, Brenna carried her back into the kennel, where Tova and Hella, and Astrid's older two, Godric and Eira, sat on the ground all together, giggling under a writhing mound of love. Astrid sat aside with Eadric, whose arms were crossed and his face pinched in an age-old shape of young outrage.

Æbbe grunted and strained to get down, and Brenna tightened her hold. "We'll be gentle together, yes?"

"Yes. Down! Down!"

Brenna sat on the ground near the others and settled Æbbe on her lap. The girl stretched out her chubby arms and grunted with strain until one of the puppies, a small one the color of cream, bumbled over and sniffed at her hand, his little tail flipping. She grabbed at the pup, but Brenna took her hand. When Æbbe looked back at her, scowling, Brenna shook her head.

"Gentle. Always gentle." She took Æbbe's hand and stroked the pup's head. He flopped over and showed his belly, and Æbbe laughed and patted him.

Leaving Eadric to sit and pout, Astrid came over and crouched beside Brenna. She stroked her daughter's curls, but Æbbe was captivated by the pup and paid her mother no mind.

"The children will be sorry when we sail," Astrid mused. "They've enjoyed having friends so close in age."

Brenna watched them playing together. Her Tova and Astrid's Godric were quite close in age, mere months apart. Hella and Eira had less than two years separating them, and Eadric was just behind. And, of course, the hellion in her lap.

The hellion in question tried to lift the pup, grabbing at its ears, but gently, which didn't hurt the animal but was ineffective for her purpose. She gave a frustrated grunt. With a chuckle, Brenna picked up the pup herself, gave him a quick snuggle, grinning at the scent of his breath as he tried to nibble her nose, and set him on Æbbe's pudgy lap. Hella came over with two more puppies, one settled like a babe in each arm, and she sat before Brenna and Æbbe and put the puppies in Æbbe's reach.

The little girl slapped her hands together and giggled in the full, elated, unguarded way that only a small child could. Hella laughed as well, her blue eyes dancing. She smiled up at Brenna, and Brenna could see the pride her youngest had taken in making a little one happy. It was too early to say, Hella was yet quite young herself, but Brenna believed that her youngest would be no shieldmaiden. She was smaller and slighter than her siblings had been at the same age, and her interests lay nearer to the hearth than theirs. She was light and love and gentle care, without a fierce thought in her sable head.

How would Hella fare if they returned to a world torn asunder by the usurper?

Amidst the cheerful ring of children's laughter and puppies' squeaks, Brenna considered the future, as well as the present. The children *were* happy here. They had friends to play with, and comfortable rooms. They were learning the language and customs of this place, but had touchstones of their own in the ways of the settlers. Mercuria was a place of true peace.

The children had been happy at home as well, but their home had been taken from them, and no one could say what Tollak might have left of it.

"I think I would like to leave my youngest here when we sail," she said, answering Asrid's remark. "We don't know what kind of place we'll return to, or how hard fought our victory will be. And they would be safe here, away from the dangers of war. May they stay until we can be sure our home is safe and well again?"

Astrid and Leofric would fight with them, of course, and none of the children left behind would have a parent with them, but they would be together, tended to by the people of the castle, and overseen by Ulv and Turid, and by Dunstan, who had a wife and children as well. It would be better to leave them here.

"Of course they may," her friend answered at once. "Will Vali accept this plan?"

Brenna wasn't sure. He would be glad to have them safe, but Mercuria was a far distance from home, and it might be months, perhaps longer, before they would see the children again, even if Tollak were defeated swiftly. It hurt her heart to think of missing so much of their dwindling childhood, but if it meant they would be in comfort and away from the blood and stench and destruction of battle, she would sacrifice that time. Convincing Vali to do so, however, might take patience and care.

"I'll speak with him."

~oOo~

Later, when the governesses had taken the children up to the nursery, and Astrid had gone of to do the work of a queen, Brenna went in search of her husband. She wished to have the matter of the children settled so she could set it from her mind and resume her share of the preparations for war. The winter here had broken. They would wait a few more weeks, to be sure that northern seas had sloughed off their winter slush, but the time for their departure was nigh.

She found Vali in the castle yard, with Håkon and Agnar. Training. Agnar had fourteen years now, and their older children had all begun their training at that age. But Brenna's heart pounded to see her husband swing even a blunted sword at the youngest of their sons.

Losing Ylva had truly weakened her heart. Try though she might to see the world as she had, through the hardened eyes of a warrior, the thought of any more of her children taking up their brutal life dimmed her sight and made her tired.

Moreover, it unsettled her to see Agnar training now, particularly, when they were preparing for battle.

Agnar had taken up a sword when Tollak had seized Karlsa, and Old Orm, a wizened warrior who'd fought long years with them before he could no longer close his hand around his sword's grip, had told of the boy fighting with a valiant heart and an inexpert arm. Vali had since been eager to train him up quickly, arguing that he was too old to hide behind a servant's skirts when battle came to him, and they risked him harm to leave him untrained.

He was right, Brenna knew. She also knew that Agnar, desperate to be a warrior like his parents and older siblings, would take well to skills he'd been observing all his life, and then he would clamor to join them, young as he was. It worried her to see him leap headlong toward danger and death.

Age and loss had changed her, certainly.

Still, she didn't intervene as her man and their boys sparred in the cool sun of an early summer afternoon. Instead, she found a discreet place to tuck back and watch. Ensconced in a dark corner, beside a mysterious dark door, she leaned against the wall and watched.

For more that twenty years, among her favorite sights was that of her man wielding a weapon. He'd shed his tunic on this day of new warmth and was sparring the way he fought—bare-chested. The people of the castle had long since given up being scandalized by his bare skin and paid their group only enough mind to keep themselves beyond the fray.

His body had earned more scars over the years, but it had not lost its firm, contoured breadth or its power and agility. His muscles flexed and rolled as he swung and feinted, pausing to instruct and critique.

After a while, he stepped back and directed Håkon and Agnar to spar. Håkon was aggressive at once, dangerously so, charging at his younger brother, swinging with such force that Agnar tripped backward and tumbled to the ground, dropping his sword and cowering behind his shield.

Vali let it happen, but his eyes never wavered. Brenna knew he was in control. He held out his hand for Agnar, who ignored it and regained his feet and his sword on his own. Then Vali turned to Håkon and brandished his own dulled sword. He meant to spar with Håkon himself.

Brenna smiled, understanding her husband's intent. He would explain the moves of a strong defense to Agnar, while at the same time humbling Håkon for attacking his newling brother with such force.

It played out as she'd expected, Vali calling out his moves to Agnar while driving Håkon back until he, too, was left to cower behind his shield.

Håkon. He'd been a gleeful, happy child, but as he'd become a man, he'd grown quarrelsome and discontented. She and Vali had spoken of it often, and their minds had met on why Håkon was as he was, but not how, or whether, they could change it.

Håkon resented his older sister. Solveig had, or would have, the things he wanted, and he would not be satisfied with less. They were much alike, although much apart as well. Like two sides of a coin. Both were driven by expectation. Solveig strove to be worthy of the things she had, and Håkon believed the things he had should be worthy of him. Neither could seem to be satisfied.

And yet, here in Mercuria, Solveig was changed. Brenna thought it was for Solveig here as it had been for herself in Estland, those long years before. A place where few knew what was said of you was a place where you could discover what there truly was of you.

Brenna had brought that new self-awareness with her when she'd left Estland. It had gotten her through the hardest trial of her life, because she'd known her place and her people, she'd felt their presence in her heart even from a world away, and she'd had the hope that came with a great love. Because she'd had Vali.

She hoped that Magni was the same anchor for Solveig, and that her daughter would return to their world stronger and more content.

Håkon, however—his path yet seemed dark and difficult.

"Brenna!" Vali called. "Join us!"

Discovered in her dim nook, Brenna came forward. She had developed reservations about raising warriors, it was true. But she could hardly ask her children to turn from the path of their choosing simply because it eased her heart. That was precisely what her mother had tried to do to her, and it had driven her to leave her home and go out into the world alone.

If her children were warriors, her best care of them was to help them be the greatest warriors they could be.

Agnar desperately wanted to raid, and he was old enough now to train. Not to fight in this battle, no. But he would be a mighty warrior someday, and if he found his death in battle, it would be a death he had chosen.

As Ylva had chosen her death.

Vali had spoken that truth to Brenna many times in the months since their daughter's death, but now it finally sank into her heart, not only to give her ease but to be believed. Ylva's death had been a good one, full of honor and story. All she had wanted was to be a great warrior, and she had achieved her dream.

With a lighter heart, Brenna stepped out into the sun and went to her men. She would not hold Agnar back. When he was ready, he could fight.

~oOo~

At the door to the room she shared with Vali, Brenna was obstructed from entering by a cluster of servant girls carrying a large tub through the threshold. She stepped out of their way, and they all bobbed clumsily, trying to bow at her and muscle the heavy tub into the corridor.

"'Scuse, ma'am," one of them muttered, keeping her eyes averted.

Brenna answered with a curt nod and went into the room.

Vali stood before the fire, wiping his bare body with a thick cloth. She smiled. No wonder the little birds had seemed so scattered. In their own world, her man's size, in all regards, was impressive. In this smaller world, it was unearthly. And these people seemed shamed by their bodies, a shame Vali didn't share, nor any of their people.

"You frightened the servant girls again."

He rumbled a low chuckle and picked up a carved comb. "They frighten easily. And they needn't hover, but they will not leave unless I shout—and then they shake if I do."

"I don't think they have leave to go, when they are to serve you. You put them in a dilemma."

He sighed heavily. "They are slaves who call themselves free. This world is strange. I miss home." Sitting on a hard, tall-backed chair, he tossed the cloth over his legs and began to work through the long, thick hank of his hair, freed from its braids for washing.

Brenna took the comb from his hand. She stood behind him and began to work it through strands that had gone iron grey. His wet locks felt cool and silky on her fingers, and she took her time and savored this intimacy between them. She combed his hair, feeling him relax and settle into the pleasure she gave.

But there was something on her mind, and eventually, it would no longer be denied. It wasn't her way to prevaricate, so she simply said, "I would like to leave the children behind, when we go."

He jerked his head around, staring up at her over his shoulder. "Brenna?"

"We can return for them when we know our world is as it should be."

Vali said nothing, but she could see his shock and resistance in the blaze of his eyes.

"We don't know what we'll go back to, Vali. We don't know what Tollak has wrought in our absence. Nearly a year has gone by. We've prepared well, but so might he have." Feeling too much emotion surging into her throat, she stopped and grabbed hold of her composure before she continued. To speak of this meant to put her worries and, yes, her fears into the world. "There might be nothing left of home but the land itself. And we are expecting, at least, a long war of many battles. Tova and Hella are so young. Why take them into uncertainty when they are safe here, when they have comfort, and friends?"

He turned fully, wrapping his hand around hers and taking the comb. "We will be away from them for very long, should we leave them. Months. Longer. Never have we been so long away from our children, my love."

She nodded, struggling to speak. When she tried, the words only croaked. "But they will be *safe*."

When he pulled her onto his lap, she came willingly, gladly, and curled against his chest. "Is this Ylva?" he asked, quietly.

"No. I've found my peace with that. But she was a shieldmaiden, who died in battle. She chose her death. I want all our children to live at least so long to have that boon."

272

"A year away from our youngest."

"Perhaps not so long as that."

"Brenna, don't tell yourself stories."

He was right; it would likely be a year. Even a swiftly won war of such magnitude might take all the summer, and then the chance to return for them would be lost until the season renewed. "Yes, a year."

She felt his beard on her cheek and his lips at her temple. "My heart aches to think of it."

"And mine. But Vali, they will be safe."

"Tova and Hella will stay, then. And Agnar?"

In the yard earlier, she'd known the truth of her youngest son, who was no longer a boy. And yet, "He's not trained enough to fight the war we face."

"No. But he has skill in his marrow. More patience and keenness than Håkon had at the same age. I would like him with us. To stand back and see what is the life he yearns for."

She would have had him stay, but she knew Vali's wisdom, and that Agnar would be thrilled to be allowed to join, even in support. "Yes. Agnar should sail with us. But the girls stay, and we will come for them when our world is right again."

Her man closed her in his arms and tucked his head in the crook of her shoulder. "We will make an offering to the gods so that it may be quickly so."

19

Magni felt Solveig's arms snake around his waist, and he looked down and watched her hands link together on his belly. The fresh morning sun streaming through the window made the fine, pale hairs on her arms sparkle.

"The night has come and gone," she whispered. "Did you never sleep?"

He shook his head. While the night had yet been full, he'd unwound from her, leaving her sleeping quietly, and he'd stood at the window since, and now the sun had well risen. "There's been no word for hours."

"You know it takes long to bring a child forth." She slipped around him and insinuated herself between him and the window. Magni smiled. With her hair loose and wild from their coupling before sleep, and her face soft and rosy with rest, wearing a flowing shift that barely caught the edges of her shoulders, she was the picture of innocence. New sun gleaming around her like the golden circle around the head of the Christian god's son made her seem embraced by Sunna, who, it was said, had kissed her shoulder and filled her with light and might on the day of her birth.

"I know. But I cannot help my concern. My mother is so small, and she has been so weak all these months. Perhaps she is too old to bring this babe."

"Women older than she have brought babes. It is not so unusual. Frida's mother had new children when she was grey and stooped. Frida has a grandchild older than her youngest brothers."

"Frida—your healer?"

"In Karlsa, yes. The one who saved Agnar and the girls. She stayed behind, in Krysevik, because her daughter was ready to bring a second child."

Magni remembered the woman, but hadn't realized that she'd stayed behind. Though he didn't know Frida well, the thought of her now made his stomach feel sour. Soon, he and his father would leave the rest of their family behind. His mother and this new child would not sail home with them.

"The babe might have a year of life before he will know our father. My mother will be alone with the babe."

Solveig laid her head on his chest and lifted his arms so they encircled her. That move woke him to her presence in a fuller way, and he tightened the embrace and bent his head to press a kiss on her crown, lingering there to let the silken feel and clean scent of her hair soothe him.

"She won't be alone," she spoke against his bare chest, her lips and breath caressing him. "She has made great friends with Elfleda. My mother and father are glad to have her with Tova and Hella, too. She will keep our family together and well, and we will restore our home to us all."

Magni wasn't precisely sure when it had happened, but over the course of the past weeks and months, Solveig had stopped speaking of their 'homes' and 'families' and begun using the singular terms. Karlsa and Geitland were no closer in space than before, but she had stopped seeing them as distinct and separate. Better yet, she'd stopped thinking of their families as distinct. Their families had been close all their lives, but now, with their mating, they were one. Magni had known that as long as he'd loved Solveig, but for her to see it as well—it meant that she saw herself as part of that whole.

Again he hoped that her sense of belonging would stay with her when they were home.

Magni wondered what it must be like to feel such a burden of expectation and legacy that one could not find one's fit in one's own home. He had been raised in his father's shadow, and he was expected to take Jarl Leif's place someday and continue his legacy of egalitarian prosperity and compassionate strength. He was expected to be a strong and brave warrior of repute and honor. But none of the stories of his father made him more than a man. They told of the brave and good and strong and fair and loving man that he truly was. To be like his father was an expectation that Magni, born of the man himself, and of a woman just as fine, could reach.

Solveig's parents were both said to be superhuman, favored of Odin himself. Unless she could feel the workings of the gods in her own body, how could she ever believe she could meet the demands of such a legacy? He'd always known the cause of her turmoil and guardedness, of course. With him she'd been open about it, and he could perceive it with his own senses. But knowing it was true was far from knowing how it felt, how it weighed on the soul.

He'd told her that he would carry the peace she'd found here, so that she could keep it when they returned to the world where her parents were legends. He hoped with his whole heart that it would be true.

He lifted her chin and kissed her lips. "We should dress. I want to check on her."

Her hands came up and petted his bearded cheeks. "Would you like me to go with you, or would you rather I stay back?"

"I want you always at my side."

"And that is where I will be."

~oOo~

The corridor was quiet. Even just outside the door to his parents' chamber, Magni could hear nothing from within. He knocked on the door.

It opened after a few seconds, and Elfleda, the old woman who led the castle servants and served as a healer and midwife, peered through the crack. She spoke the northern tongue. "Your mother is yet at her work. I will ask your father to come out to you."

With the door open, he could hear the sounds of people moving and working within. He thought he heard the murmuring rumble of his father's voice, spoken to soothe. But he couldn't hear his mother at all. He looked over Elfleda's head but saw nothing but a bit of the fireplace, the edge of a chair, and the open door beyond, where their bedchamber was.

"Is she well?" he asked, clutching Solveig's hand in a fresh burst of worry.

"She is hard at work. I will speak to your father." With that, the old woman closed the door in his face.

He turned to Solveig. "She didn't say she was well."

"She didn't say she wasn't, either. Come." She pulled him across the corridor, where there was a nook in the stone wall, with a tall, colorful window and a velvet bench against it. With an affectionate shove, she made him sit. And then she knelt before him and took both his hands. The position she'd taken, so clearly signaling her focus and devotion to him, sent a charge of love through him.

"I remember when Mother brought Hella forth. She was in the birthing bed for three days. In the last day, her screams filled the air all through Karlsa. My mother, the great God's-Eye, screamed and screamed. No one had ever heard such a thing. I thought my father would go mad. Finally, Hella came, and she was blue. She was silent, as if my mother had spent all of her screams as well. Father grabbed her and ran out into the sun. I remember seeing him go, the way the life cord dangled and caught around his leg. We all followed after him. He went out into the sun, and he put his mouth on her little still face, and he gave her his breath. I could see her color change, and her little feet move, and then she cried. It was a tiny, frail sound, and then it got louder, and then she yelled, and the whole town cheered." She smiled brightly.

The story gave him as much worry as comfort, but he trusted that Solveig meant it for comfort. He squeezed her hands. "And your mother?"

Solveig's soft smile faded away. "She was weak and ill for days after, it's true. When Father returned to her, she was insensible, and another woman with a babe at the breast took Hella as well until Mother could do so. But she was well and strong again. Father told me later than Hella had been born bottom first and face up, still curled up in her sac. Frida had never delivered a child in that way. If Mother could survive that and bring a healthy babe from it, you have little to worry for Olga."

"She is not a shieldmaiden like your mother. She is small and fragile."

"Small, but not fragile. Not a shieldmaiden, but a warrior nonetheless." Her hands left his and lifted to his face, cupping his cheeks. "She has an iron will and a mighty heart. She survived horrors and lived to love and thrive. She leads at your father's side. She made you. She will be well and strong and raise up this child as she raised you to be the wonder you are."

Sitting in this nook, buffeted by worry for his mother, Magni realized that the tables had turned between him and Solveig. She was comforting him, being strong for him. She had cut to the meat of his stress and known that simple platitudes would not have eased his heart, but a real story, that showed the dangers and fears as well as the happy outcome, would.

So often, he thought of himself as the mast of her ship, standing steady while the storms raged in her mind. But she was the same for him.

The door to his parents' rooms opened, and his father was there, exhausted and stressed. Magni stood up so quickly he nearly knocked Solveig back. She moved with him, though, and stood up gracefully.

"Father! Is she well?"

He didn't like the sigh that was his father's first answer. "It is a hard birth. The babe isn't coming down…I don't understand what the women try to explain, and Olga…at least she hasn't sent me from the room as she did with you, but she doesn't speak or make any sound." He gave his head a hard shake. "She is tired, my son, and her work continues. But she is working."

The same words Elfleda used. Magni cast a glance at Solveig and wondered how he would feel to have her suffer in this way to bring him a child.

It was the lot of husbands in this work, he supposed. To be entirely powerless.

"Is there anything I can do?"

His father gave him a weary lift at one corner of his mouth, what might have been an attempt at a smile. "No. There is nothing we men can do in birth except worry and wait."

He managed a truer smile for Solveig, and stroked her hair—still loose—with paternal affection. "I will bring news when I have it," he said and went back into the room.

Magni took a few steps in that direction, not thinking that he would follow into the room, but unhappy to be separated by the door between them.

"You're right, Solveig. It's my mother who made me. My father, too, I hear enough how like him I am to believe it, but it's my mother who taught me how to be the man I am. She's the most gentle person I know. The most forgiving, the most compassionate. Everything around her calms, as if she lays down ease in her wake. I know I'm a worthy warrior as well, and I know I have my father's mind and sense of rightness, but the things in me that I'm most proud of are those that are like her."

She hooked her arms around his neck and curled her fingers in his hair. "I think it's your mother in you that makes you able to love me, even when I'm not worthy of it."

"Always you are worthy."

"I have no need for you to salve my ego. I know I must learn to love you better, as you deserve. I know that I think too much of my own struggles, and that my struggles are bigger in my mind than they ought to be. Was it not you who called me petty, after all?"

"An intemperate word said rashly. As you made clear not long after." Their argument that night, however, had sparked an important change between them. He hadn't felt a distance from her in all the months since. "You are worthy, Solveig. Of love. Of admiration. Of all the things you want, for all the things you are."

She closed the minute distance between them and rose up on her toes, brushing her lips over his. "With you, I feel that it's true."

His mother had been laboring with the child for more than a full day, and, knowing that the going was difficult, Magni was afraid to wander far from the room. He settled in that little nook with Solveig, and they waited. After a while, Vali and Brenna came, and stayed. And Astrid, at midday. Leofric checked in regularly, and he sent up chairs and a table and a spread of food and drink, and the wide corridor became crowded.

Occasionally, the door across the way would open, and a servant would come out, or go in, and everyone waiting would go quiet and stare. But the servants only curtseyed at their queen and went about their way. Astrid left them to their work and didn't ask them for information, explaining that it was best to know the outcome, not the process. Brenna nodded in agreement, so Magni left it alone.

Finally, in the afternoon, they heard the cry of a babe—one cry, faint through the thick door and the wide expanse of the room between them, and then silence again. Everyone stood and stared at the door. At long last, it opened again, and it was his father, looking weary beyond measure. He held a bundle of cloth in his arms. Remembering the stories of Vali running out into the world with his first child and with his last, both of them still, the first dead and the last at its door, Magni held his breath.

Then the bundle moved, and his father smiled. He met Magni's eyes. "Your mother is well, but tired, and she has dropped off to sleep. You have a sister, Magni."

As their friends, their family, cheered, he went to his father. The babe was small and pink, with the dark hair of their mother, already a thick thatch of it on her wee head. Magni laid his hand on that soft puff, sticking up at ends around a tiny, pinched face. It was the softest thing he'd ever touched in his life.

She opened her eyes and scowled up at him, and he had the clear impression of being scolded for disturbing her rest. He laughed and took back his hand, and her expression cleared as her eyes fluttered shut again. "She is beautiful."

He hadn't taken his eyes off the babe, but he sensed his father nodding. "We will call her Disa."

Disa. Spirited one. "It's a good name." Magni turned and found Solveig, standing beside him, watching him. He held out his hand; she came to him at once, and he embraced her completely, tucking her as close as he could manage. "Someday," he whispered against her ear, "I would like to hold a babe that we made together."

He felt her nod against his head, and her arms tighten around his waist, and he saw their future.

~oOo~

"To exclude those who wish to fight for their homeland will cause strife here and cost us good fighters in the war, Vali." Leofric leaned in, his eyes intent on Vali's.

Magni, staying quiet in this debate, trying to understand all the dimensions of disagreement, turned to see Vali's reaction.

The big man crossed his burly arms over his chest. "They are loyal to Tollak and Gunnar. We cannot risk betrayal in our midst."

"*Were* loyal to Tollak and Gunnar," Leofric countered. "More than ten years have they been on Mercurian soil, building lives, fighting alongside us. They *are* us, more now than they are of the land of their birth. They fight for us."

"To say what you do is to say that *our* settlers are no longer loyal to their homeland, either. Do you mean to claim them as your subjects?"

"Since Norshire was founded, they have been subjects of this realm. Our alliance—our true and deep *friendship*—silences your point. They are loyal to all of us, because we are loyal to each other. Yes?"

Vali glared, but he didn't let a pause grow before he nodded. "True friends. Yes. Can we say that of all in Norshire?"

Mere days before they would depart for war, a problem that had been raised months ago and set aside had presented itself again. A Norshire settler had withdrawn his name from the rolls of warriors. The man was from Dofrar, and had been a raider sworn to Tollak's father, before he'd set his sword and shield aside for a plow. He'd claimed an ill child as the reason for pulling from the fight, but when three others from Dofrar had also removed their names, the situation had taken on a cloud of suspicion.

Vali wanted all of the settlers who'd come from Halsgrof and Dofrar, the holdings of Gunnar and Tollak, scrubbed from the rolls—seeming to forget that both he and his wife had been born in Halsgrof.

It would mean a loss of more than a hundred fighters, and discontent in Norshire, among those who'd been forced to stay behind. Now the leaders sat in Leofric's solar, which had become their war room, seeking a solution that settled their suspicions and kept their force strong.

It was often said about Magni's father that he was a good man and a great jarl. About Vali, the reverse was said—that he was a great man and a good jarl. Perhaps this was a cause for the depth and steadiness of their long friendship and alliance. They magnified each other's strengths and dulled each other's weaknesses.

One of Vali's weaknesses was trust. He gave it carefully, and once given, he held it precious. But when it was broken, it was nearly impossible to win back. Now, with so much lost and so much more at risk, he'd drawn a hard line. To him, anyone who'd ever sworn to Tollak and Gunnar, or to their fathers, was suspect. He'd allowed the others to set his concerns aside early on, but with these few men pulling out, he was adamant against the rest.

"These men weren't sworn to a traitor, Vali," Magni's father said. "To hold them accountable for actions that happened a decade after they left the North and settled a world away would be like holding Brenna accountable for Åke's betrayals."

Vali's eyes narrowed at his friend. "I held *you* accountable."

"Yes," Magni's father agreed. "You did. Unfairly, which is my meaning here."

"If there were a way to determine their fealty now…" Magni offered, thinking as he spoke. "At home, we would ask for a renewal of their vows on their arm rings."

Leofric shook his head. "I'm sorry. Your raiders from the North—of course, if you should wish such a swearing, we will assist your rituals. But those who've settled here—I cannot have them sworn to a leader so far away. They are subjects of this realm, and I must have their allegiance." He faced Vali steadily. "You understand, Vali. You must."

Again, Vali agreed with a nod, but this time, he let the moment linger before he did.

"Not all the men of Norshire wear arm rings, in any case," Astrid offered. "Many have set them aside."

Brenna leaned in, putting her elbows on the table. "But they might be reminded, at least, of the solemnity of that promise.

A renewal of vows is a good idea. But more than that—there are a few boys who have become young men while we've been here, Agnar among them. To witness these young men taking their first vows, that will stir up their fire to see home restored and to remind them that Tollak and Gunnar broke a solemn promise."

"You would let Agnar take his arm ring? With fourteen years?" Vali's stormy opposition was eased by his surprise at Brenna's suggestion.

"We've already decided that he should travel with us. Though he will not fight, still he will face danger. It's right to honor him for the risk he takes. And Jarl Vali's son making his first vows will resonate through the entire war party."

When Vali's conflict still pulsed around the room, it was Bjarke who spoke. "Vali. There were betrayers within Karlsa and Geitland both. People who helped from within, for reasons known only to them. There is no way to be sure we have the perfect loyalty of every single fighter, because people are complicated and few are paragons. All we can do is give them something to fight for and be prepared at our back and flank as well as what comes head on."

At last, he let the tension leave his body. "Very well. As I am again alone in my thinking on this, I will defer to the group."

~oOo~

They performed the arm ring ritual in the center of Norshire, on the day of their departure. They were sailing from Eldham, a large trading town in the south of Mercuria, and normally they would have bid their farewells there on the docks, but the town was too far distant for Olga to travel, only two weeks after delivering Disa, so they had decided that Norshire would suffice.

The occasion of the six boys becoming men, the youngest son of Jarl Vali Storm-Wolf and Brenna God's-Eye among them, was solemn, and Magni saw that all of the fighters and their families were wholly moved. Agnar was the last to swear, to his father, and upon the bestowal of his arm ring, his mother handed him a small sword—not a battle sword, but one with which he could defend himself. The weapon of a warrior in training.

Agnar beamed brightly and held his new sword aloft, and the solemnity broke as everyone in the town circle, more than a thousand voices, cheered together.

Then Leofric, Vali, and Magni's father all asked the raiders to vow together to serve their goals in the coming war. The fighters did so with one voice.

And then it was time to bid their families farewell and begin the trek to their ships.

These new men would not be feted with a feast. Instead, they would celebrate their coming of age by sailing off to war.

In the tradition that had developed over his years of raiding with his father, Magni went to his mother first, and his father held back. She was still pale from the hard work of bringing Disa into the world, and she was manifestly sad on this day, but she was stronger than she'd been in long months, and her smile when he went to her was real and full of love and pride.

His sister napped comfortably, slung across their mother's chest. Magni peeked in and brushed her tiny bump of a nose with his fingertip. "I wonder who she'll be when I see her again," he mused softly.

"Not half who she'll be when she has her brother and father to love her and make her strong and brave." His mother grasped his hand. "I am more proud of you than I could ever say, my mighty one."

He folded mother and sister into his arms and held them close. When he felt tears welling in his throat, he didn't let them fall. "We will reclaim our home and bring you back to it, Mother."

"All I need is you and your father to come back to us."

"We shall." He kissed her cheek and stepped back. She knew that the promise he made on every parting was an empty one, sincerely though it was meant. When warriors parted from their families, it might always be their final farewell, and his mother knew it as well as he.

When his father went to her, Magni saw her brave face falter, and he couldn't watch that. He turned and searched for Solveig.

He found her walking away from her young sisters. She'd left her parents alone with them, just as he had his family. They met in the space between their parents' sorrowful partings, and Magni grabbed her and held on.

PART FOUR
LEGEND

20

Fury and despair warred in Solveig's soul, making her chest thump and her stomach boil. Magni stood just behind her, his chest a shield at her back and his arms light but strong on her shoulders.

She stood like a stone as the skeids pulled into the Karlsa harbor. All the ships were nearly silent as they came through the grey water toward a forlorn shore.

They'd embarked on this journey at the earliest likely opportunity, and this far north, winter hadn't yet entirely retracted her claws. The wind was brisk, and swaths of snow, the lingering remnants of once-deep drifts, streaked over the land.

Her neck creaking with tension, Solveig turned to see her father and mother in the next skeid, standing at the prow, much like she and Magni were. Her father seemed to sense her attention and met her eyes across the morning mist. His expression didn't change, and he didn't look away.

Understanding that he felt everything she felt and more, drawing strength from that, Solveig turned back to the sight before them.

The white talons of winter made stark contrast against the jagged spears of burnt wood stuck up in clusters, the charred bones of buildings that had been homes and shops and a great hall. As far as Solveig could see, no building had been spared.

The docks were gone as well, only the pylons yet standing, like gapped teeth, in the lapping shallows.

Karlsa was gone. Her home was gone.

"I'm sorry, Solveig," Magni murmured at her ear.

So much emotion battled for dominance inside her that none could rise. She roiled and stormed, and was entirely numb. "We can't assume there is no guard here," she said.

If he was surprised by the cool pragmatism in her voice, he didn't show it. With a squeeze of her shoulders and a kiss at her ear, he let her go, and she bent and took up her shield and sword.

Karlsa had a good shoreline, gentle and wide, so the oarsmen of the four skeids piloted them all the way in, until they hit the soft bed. The Mercurian ships dropped anchor at a distance, where their deeper ships were yet afloat.

As soon as her skeid ran aground, without waiting for another sign, Solveig grabbed the wale and vaulted into the water.

Icy seawater sliced into her legs, all the way to the tops of her thighs. She was glad of it, of that knowable discomfort, like a pinpoint of focus within her chaos. The world resounded all around her with the roaring splash of raiders leaping into the water. But no human voice rang out. Everyone was stunned to silence.

They were not raiders, not here. This was their home. And it was gone.

They stalked up to the scorched earth that had once been home. Ready for a fight, she converged with her parents and brother, all moving toward each other without any signal but the draw of their shared blood.

Her father moved into the lead. Despite the bite of cold in the air, he'd stripped off his tunic and furs, and stormed up the berm bare-chested, with his axes held at a cant and his shoulders wide and rounded with readiness. Solveig and Håkon stepped in behind him, and their mother came up abreast of them.

Agnar was with them on this journey, but he wasn't walking with them now. Without looking back to check, Solveig knew that her mother's brief delay in joining them had been to keep Agnar back. He hadn't been trained yet enough to fight, certainly not enough to lead.

This was Karlsa, their own homeland, so the other leaders—Leif and Magni, Astrid and Leofric—gave Vali's family primacy. But Solveig could sense Magni's nearness, and his concern for her. She didn't need to look back to know he was close; she could feel him at her flank and just behind.

As they neared what had been the town circle, just before the serrated black fangs that remained of the great hall's scorched walls, her father stopped and held his arms up, halting the fighters. "We are not alone," he said, the words clear and carrying, but not shouted.

Solveig stepped to his side to see what he saw, and he nodded to direct her attention. In the midst of charred earth and blackened bones, there was a grouping of burnt wood and ash that had once been a small fire—a campfire—and had burned many times in the same place, as one would if a camp had been made and a fire kept for a span of time.

Since the ruin of Karlsa, someone had made camp here. A guard, under orders from Tollak. There was no other reasonable possibility.

Then Solveig saw that the faint swirl of ash coming from that round sear wasn't an effect of the wind that gusted around them. It came from the dead fire. Because it wasn't yet

293

entirely dead. Buried somewhere in the ash were embers yet hot.

The guard had seen the ships approaching and had scattered before the coming fighters could detect them.

"Did they flee, or do they hide?" Little was left of the town that might shield an ambush, but they were close enough to the wood that the guards who'd made the fire might be sheltered in the trees, watching them come onto the land. Watching them right now. The destruction of the town had cleared the sightlines.

Her father answered her question with one of his own. "What would you do?"

Unless it was an army—and why would it be?—the guard was drastically outnumbered. Ridiculously so. But Solveig couldn't imagine running. "Lie in wait."

"And I."

A light laugh escaped her lips, surprising her; she found nothing here amusing. "No, you would not. You would stand on the berm and take them on."

"That would be my impulse, yes. If I followed it, I would be reckless, and I would put more than myself at risk. As Úlfhéðinn, it is my nature to stand and fight no matter the enemy I face. But as jarl, I must consider the people I lead before I think of any else. It is a constant battle I wage inside my chest, whenever I wield my weapons—between the hunger in my heart and the wisdom in my mind." He leveled his look. "What is the wiser course for those who were here?"

He was teaching her, Solveig understood. Sharing his wisdom about the work of leadership. It was the way he'd always given her lessons—by musing aloud, asking her opinion, and dissecting what she'd offered.

Her mother had taught her to fight by facing her with a sword. Her father taught her to lead by bringing her to his side while he led.

She thought now about the question he'd posed. What would the wiser course have been for the guards that had been here? If it were a small force, and they'd seen the horizon fill with half a score of ships, they should have fled. But what if they'd been under orders to hold the position? Would Tollak have left a large force so far north, in a town he'd burned to the ground, when he couldn't have known how strong a force Jarls Vali and Leif would bring back? Or if they would return at all, after so long away?

Before her nascent answer could form legs in her mind, the song of an arrow provided the true answer. It struck the earth at Håkon's feet.

Only that single arrow. Everyone stared at it, their shields up, but nothing else came. Solveig understood that arrow to mean one of two things: a warning, or a misfire. In either event, it served as notice.

She saw that her father would shout before he did so; his chest filled with air and expanded. "THE WOOD!"

He ran forward, unshielded, and the fighters took up his roar and charged with him.

~oOo~

"Let me see." Solveig's mother took her by the chin and turned her head. With a narrow look, she studied the wound across Solveig's forehead.

To Solveig, her mother's eyes were simply that—her mother's eyes. She'd been looking into them from the day of her birth, and there was nothing at all she found strange in them. Of course she recognized that they were not matched as was every other pair she'd ever seen, but she'd never bothered much with the question of why Brenna God's-Eye's right eye was so different. It either carried the power of the Allfather or it did not; in either case, she was Solveig's mother, and her eyes were her eyes.

But she knew the look that chilled the hearts of others, and she could see why it might. Especially now, while those mismatched eyes glowed out from a face streaked with blood and earth. To any who hadn't been raised at the breast of the woman who bore them, they might indeed be terrifying.

"I'm well, Mother." Solveig pulled from her mother's grasp. And she was—she'd been hit with the pommel of a sword, and her head ached, but it was the only wound she'd taken.

"I'm glad. But be it so, you do need to have it closed. Go to Gudmund."

The battle healer would have time to stitch the wound; he hadn't had much to do. Few had taken wounds in this battle, and even fewer had been significantly injured. After three weeks of fighting, they'd suffered fewer than a dozen losses among them, and they'd wiped out every force of Tollak's fighters they'd encountered. All the way through Karlsa and most of the way through Halsgrof they'd moved, like a scourge.

Not like a scourge. Tollak and Gunnar had been the scourge, burning their way from north to south. The town of Halsgrof, while still intact and inhabited, had fared scarcely better than Karlsa. Half of it was burned, and only half of its people remained alive.

The people they'd met there, freed from the oppression of a large resident force loyal to Tollak, had described the devastation they'd survived. Though he'd allied with Gunnar, and it had been Gunnar's men who'd destroyed Karlsa, when Tollak had turned on his ally, the same fate had been dealt to

Halsgrof. They'd stopped short of total destruction only because the battle had been more even—Gunnar's men had fought for him against Tollak's men, an alliance turning on itself.

Because Leif and Solveig's father had been raiding in Frankia with the strongest of their people, Karlsa had been left with only a bare force for its defense. The same was the case in Geitland. They'd had no hope of staving off the attack.

Now, those raiders, and the army of Mercuria, camped on the southern edge of Halsgrof. They'd liberated the town, killing every enemy they'd found.

It was strange to camp in one's own home. Here in Halsgrof, the sense of displacement wasn't as acute as it had been that first night, after they'd slaughtered the tiny force of guards in Karlsa and made camp near the ruin that had been their great hall, their actual home. Solveig had sat up all through that night, cocooned in Magni's arms, and felt the loss of her whole life storming inside her.

After three weeks, weeks of battle and victory, the blade of that pain had dulled. And yet the unreality of making a temporary shelter in the world of her birth—making it because she no longer had a home in her homeland—rasped at her heart.

Her mother handed her a strip of clean linen. Solveig took it and pressed it to her forehead.

"You fought well today, daughter. Your grace and power with a sword is matched by few among us, man or woman."

Her mother had never been one to offer praise where it wasn't warranted, and she had never been so lavish with it for Solveig before. Few remarks would have had such an impact.

More grace and power than most others, men or women—these were words with which people spoke of the God's-Eye.

Knowing her mother wouldn't expect or appreciate gratitude for an assessment she considered only truthful, Solveig quashed the strong urge to thank her. Instead, she nodded and said another truthful thing. "I seek only to be worthy to stand beside you on the field."

"I would not have allowed you on the field unless you were, Solveig. Always have you been worthy. Now, you are also great." She squeezed Solveig's arm. "Go to the healer."

She walked away. Solveig stared after her, stunned. Before her mother could leave earshot, she called out, "Mother!"

Her mother turned, cocking the brow over her legendary eye.

"I love you," Solveig said, suddenly desperate to have those words said between them. Though the feeling had never been in question, in either direction, it had been too long since the words had been said.

"And I love you. My child with a heart as bright and hot as the sun." A smile lifted her cheeks as she pointed across the camp. "The healer. Now."

~oOo~

"It will be a good scar. Not as good as mine, of course, but good." Magni pressed his lips to Solveig's temple, just at the edge of the tender spot.

"Yes, yes," she teased. "Your scar is most impressive." The track left by an arrow across his cheek had long been fully healed. The stitching hadn't been so carefully done on his face as on hers, so the scar Magni carried pulled at his cheek a bit and drew his smile to one side. She found it charming. Alluring, even—and she was likewise charmed by his pride in it.

A check of her reflection in a water barrel had shown a tidy row of tiny stitches. She might not scar at all. It was Magni who had the obsession with scars, however—well, Magni and most men she knew.

For her part, she didn't need to be marked to remember her fights. She took pride in all the blows she'd ducked, not the ones that had landed.

She took Magni's hand and returned her attention to her brothers, who were sparring. Håkon was aggressive with Agnar whenever they sparred, consistently driving his younger brother back, swinging his sword as if he meant harm, though he swung with the flat side forward, in the way their seasoned raiders trained. He said he did it to sharpen Agnar's reflexes, but not even their mother was so severe in her training methods. Solveig liked to keep watch; she didn't quite trust Håkon not to hurt Agnar—she didn't quite trust him not to intend to, though she couldn't say why he might.

Right before her eyes, while she was focused on the clash of her brothers' shields and swords—Håkon's the heavy, potent steel of a raider, and Agnar's the smaller, more brittle iron of a novice—their mother appeared, swinging the God's-Eye Blade up and blocking Håkon's next swing.

She cut in between them, swinging at Håkon, driving him back, forcing his shield up to block her blows. Then she turned to Agnar, and Solveig could see her explaining something to him, but she couldn't hear the words.

When their mother stepped behind Agnar and gestured at Håkon to come in again, Solveig felt a rush of powerful sentiment flow through her. She remembered an afternoon in Karlsa, when she'd been training with her mother. Training and failing and feeling desolate. She remembered her father stepping behind her, as her mother had just done for Agnar, and showing her the steps, as if battle were a dance. Which, in a way, it was.

On that afternoon, her father had closed her up in his arms, holding her and making her body move as it should. In the vivid memory, she could still feel the overwhelming sense of being caught between two lovers moving together. Never in her life had she felt more connected to her family, her world, or herself than on that afternoon.

Her mother hadn't embraced Agnar as wholly as her father had held Solveig on that long-ago day, and she faced another son, not a lover, so the effect before Solveig now wasn't exact. But the memory rang out, and her heart ached with love for her family. She knew right then that she wasn't homeless. She'd never been homeless. She had always belonged. She'd always been part of the people who'd made her. Always had she been worthy.

"Solveig?" Magni asked, worry tilting his voice.

She swiped at the new wet streak on her cheek and shook her head. "I'm well." Letting her attention fall from the family of her childhood to the family of her womanhood, she faced Magni. "I'm very well. I'm home. I love you, Magni Leifsson."

His face shone as a bright smile canted up the side of his face. "And I you, Solveig."

"Solveig Valisdottir," she corrected. And kissed him.

~oOo~

Through Karlsa, and through Halsgrof, they'd moved, over land, cutting through every defense they encountered. Only in the town of Halsgrof had they found anything like a real fight. The talk in the evening among the leaders had turned toward the idea that the war would occur in Geitland itself, and a discussion of how they might preserve as much as they could of the town and its people while fighting a war in its center.

In addition to the Mercurian battle horses they'd sailed with, they'd amassed a herd of workhorses. Grateful people, cheered by the return of Vali Storm-Wolf, Brenna God's-Eye, and Leif Olavsson, with a strong army at their backs, had offered up anything they had that might be of use, and that had included all the horses they could spare. Leif and Solveig's father had paid them with gold, despite the refusal of many to accept it.

Solveig rode into the territory of Dofrar, Tollak Finnsson's ancestral holding, with Magni and Håkon at her sides. Her parents, and Leif, and Astrid rode abreast before them. Leofric rode beside Magni, just behind his wife. Solveig liked that; in Mercuria it was clear that men preceded women in virtually all things. Even a warrior queen like Astrid hadn't been able to make women fully equal. But here in her world, her husband, a king in his own world, rode behind his wife and followed her lead in strategy as well.

Within an hour of crossing into Dofrar, Solveig could sense a change in the atmosphere. Dofrar had been poorer than the other holdings always, and since Tollak had taken the jarl's seat, the countryside had been left to flounder. Thus there had always been a different feel in the holding. But now, it was eerily empty and quiet. Even in the calm of a warm summer morning, overcast but not gloomy, the heavy quiet was unsettling. No livestock, no wildlife, no birdsong.

"It's like this world has died," Håkon muttered.

Their father pulled up his horse and twisted in the saddle. "But it hasn't. The leaves are green, the grass is lush, the breeze is fresh. Fields are fallow, but the soil isn't dead. Only untended." His eyes shifted to Solveig. "What does such a silence say to us?"

She considered that. A world that was friendly to wildlife was quiet only when animals were wary. They were wary around predators, or when they watched for predators. They left when a place had become inhospitable, either through lack of resources or surfeit of dangers. There was no lack of resources here, not for wildlife.

"People were here. Hunters. Either they cleaned out the game, or the game fled." Her father watched her, showing no expression. Waiting. Solveig thought more. "Many people. Recently." The next thought occurred to her, as she looked around at the few humble buildings of a single, isolated farm. Many people had not made a permanent residence here. But there were signs, as she scanned her surroundings, of habitation—the grass had been flatted in wide sections. Rocks and logs were clustered in regular groups. The signs had been purposefully obscured, but they were there. "A camp. An army?"

Her father smiled. "I agree. Leif? Brenna? Astrid?" All nodded.

"But why have they retreated, then? Before the fight?" Håkon scowled, looking around.

"Why would they, Håkon?" their mother asked.

"Because they're sniveling cowards," he growled.

Solveig didn't think that was the answer. "They haven't. They know we're coming, and they've moved to a more advantageous location."

Again, her father smiled, and his attention homed in on her. "Where would that be?"

She looked around. From this vantage, a vast, grassy valley with only a few copses of trees, she could see far. And she could also understand exactly why Tollak's army had moved back. "They were on our way to meet us. They got word that we were close—one of their people in Halsgrof must have escaped—and they moved out of this wide clearing. Too much visibility here." Where they themselves now stood, their whole army, clustered in the open.

"We need to move," Magni muttered, scanning the horizon all around them. "There—that hill. Look."

They all looked. A break in the overcast sky had let a fissure of bright sun move over the grassy plain, and in that roll of light, Solveig saw. A track, faint but wide, in the grass at a distance. Tollak's army had crossed that field. They were behind the hill.

"This is our battlefield," Solveig's mother declared. "We fight here, perhaps for everything."

"We are known now," Leif said, staring off at the hill that rose against the horizon. "In our whole dimension. If we're right, and they await us over that hill, then they have scouts who see us all. That's to their advantage."

"We fight with the righteous power of vengeance," Astrid asserted. "There is no power stronger in our world but love, and we fight for that as well. That's to *our* advantage."

The hill in question was off to the southwest, not directly before them. Solveig considered that. "They meant to flank us. If we come at them straight on, we shift our field from defense to attack. That's to our advantage as well."

Leif turned his horse to face their army. "An army awaits us beyond that hill!" he called out to their fighters. "We fight here and reclaim our lands, or we die here and achieve Valhalla! In either outcome, tonight we will be home!"

~oOo~

Acting solely on their suppositions, before they'd had sight of any one of Tollak's fighters, they sped across the wide valley. If they'd been wrong, they might have risked everything. Galloping at the fore on Aggi, with her family at her sides, Solveig felt the responsibility keenly. She had been instrumental in making the call.

But as they neared, they saw men running from the top of the hill down the far side. Scouts. Watchers. They'd been right.

If Solveig's parents were truly favored of the gods, then they would not crest that hill and find an unbeatable horde on its other side. They would find victory.

As her father, her mother, Magni's father, and their friend Astrid hit the base of the hill, her father dropped the reins of his steed, pulled both his axes free, and raised them over his head. "ATTACK!"

His army echoed his roar, and the thunder of their charge redoubled. The earth shook and the air split.

They crested the hill.

On the other side was a much smaller valley. A glen. Filled with fighters, their front rows locked into a shield wall.

An army as large as they had been led to expect. At least fifteen hundred warriors.

But the force that had sailed from Mercuria was half again as large.

As arrows flew from the rows behind the shield wall, Solveig watched her father kick his horse into a jump, still brandishing his axes and using the power of his legs alone to guide the steed. It leapt over the full height and breadth of the shield wall and landed behind it, crushing several archers and breaking the wall. When the rest of the true army of

Karlsa and Geitland engaged, the enemy force was porous, and combat was one-to-one.

Solveig pulled Aggi back and swung off while he turned, tucking her body and landing on her feet, then allowing herself to roll with her momentum before leaping to her feet again.

A shieldmaiden with a red hand painted over her face ran for her, screaming, her axe raised over her head in both hands, as if she meant to cleave firewood. Solveig easily blocked her and slashed her sword across the woman's waist. She was already fighting her next opponent when the shieldmaiden's entrails splashed across her boots.

Lost in battle rage, Solveig fought. She gave herself over to the dance, let her body sense and know and react, hacking and slashing and stabbing, blocking and feinting and ducking, while the world around her crashed against her ears. She could sense Magni nearby and hear his grunts and shouts. She knew where her father was. Her mother. Her brother. Tendrils of consciousness fed out from her mind and knew they were well and strong. The rest of her she let loose and let fight, felling foes and climbing over their bodies for the next one.

There was no fear in her, not anywhere. This was where she belonged, and if she ended here, it would be right. A death in battle was the greatest end their people aspired to.

She sensed Magni moving closer, and knew he meant to defend her. But to do so, he would confine her, so she danced away, moving back and around.

Then she caught sight of something that made her feet stutter and her eyes blink. Agnar. Agnar had left the safe rear, with the wagons and supplies, and had made his way over the hill and into the scrum.

He had no armor, no leather. He carried his own small sword, and his training shield, bare wood without his family's colors. He had only fourteen years, and had been only a few months in training.

But he was spattered with blood clearly not his own, and his sword dripped with gore.

In the flash of a moment it took Solveig to see her brother and understand his purpose, Agnar was beset by two foes at once, and the boy who'd been driven down by his older brother again and again fought them both without hesitation.

But he was not fully trained, and there was no heart stout enough and no innate skill powerful enough to compensate for lack of experience when outnumbered and facing a larger, more experienced foe.

Solveig cut down an attacker almost as an afterthought, not bothering to be sure of a killing blow, and ran to her youngest brother. Her mother could not lose another child.

Before she could get to him, Agnar was driven to the ground by a powerful strike that he'd managed to block. The force of the blow against that weak shield knocked him off his feet and cracked his shield in twain. He cast it away and held his sword with both hands as the next blow came, just managing to block it but almost losing the sword to the effort.

Agnar was going to die.

"NO!" Solveig called, slashing down a fighter who'd leapt into her path. But she'd heard an echo as she'd yelled—not an echo. Another voice in the same timbre, shouting the same word at the same time. Solveig spun, pulling her sword through a body she barely noticed, and saw her mother throw herself between Agnar and the blow meant to kill him.

The sword meant for the son went through the mother instead. It had been a stabbing blow rather than a slash, driven from above; Solveig saw the blade go into her mother's neck and come out through her back, tenting the mail chestpiece she'd worn for the past few years.

"NO!" Solveig screamed again and was finally there. As the fighter drew his sword out and her mother fell, Solveig swung her blade in a great arc and separated the man's arm from his body. Without a pause, she caught her arc on the follow-through and shoved the blade through his belly, jerking her hilt sharply to the side when she felt the grate of his spine against her steel. She felt bone sever, and the man who'd killed her mother fell to the ground, gurgling.

Some part of her senses noted the blinding light as another fissure in the clouds opened and sun streamed onto the battlefield, but Solveig's mind wasn't on the weather. She went for the other man who'd attacked her brother, driving her sword again and again, barely seeing him but knowing the dance, hacking again and again and again, even after he was on the ground and silent but for the sound of her blade on his body.

Behind her, she heard her mother's name. "BRENNA! BRENNA!"

It was her father's voice, so full of anguish that Solveig felt it like a blade through her heart, and she knew what she had to do. She stood guard at her mother's body while her mighty father fell to the ground beside the woman he loved, and she determined that she would fight off any and all who might disturb him in his grief.

21

He knew when she'd been struck; he'd felt it like a blade through his own heart, the pain so keen and consuming that it nearly stopped the swing of his arm as he cut through the chest of one of the betrayer's men. As soon as the body dropped from his axe, Vali spun, seeking his wife.

They never fought far from each other, but Brenna never wanted him too close, either. She insisted that he hemmed her in.

He found her at once, with the same sense that knew she'd been injured, and what he saw made him stand tall and still as a tree in the midst of a battlefield, losing all sense of the action around him.

She was down, lying on her back over a mound of men. Agnar (Was that Agnar? It was. How—) sat splayed behind her. And Solveig fought over her, her sword blurring with speed as she slashed and hacked at a foe.

Brenna was down. *Brenna was down.* The distinct beat inside his own heart that was her presence there fluttered unsteadily.

Movement at his flank; he swung an axe and felt it hit meaty flesh, but he didn't turn to see. He pulled his axe through and ran for his wife.

"BRENNA! BRENNA!"

As he landed on his knees at her side, he sensed Agnar scrambling, and diverted his attention to his son, long enough to see Leofric grab the boy by his arms and drag him back, out of the fray. Above him, he knew Solveig fought, and he let her.

Brenna yet breathed. Her eyes were on his. Those wonderful, beloved eyes.

The sword had cut deeply into her neck, just above the line of the mail he'd insisted she wear, and thick, bright red blood— heart's blood—pumped out like a river washing over her chest.

"No, no, no, no." He caught her up in his arms and settled her at his chest. Hot blood drenched his arm as well; the sword had run her through.

The wound was mortal. Her life spilt out over his hands. "NO! NO!" he shouted. "NO!"

"Vali," she gasped. The word burbled wetly on her tongue, and a stream of blood flowed from her lips. "Vali."

"I'm here, shieldmaiden. My love."

"Ag—Agnar…"

"Safe. He's safe."

He felt her body shift as his assurance gave her ease; it seemed she'd been clinging to life to be sure of their son's safety. Like a blow from Thor's hammer itself, Vali understood: Brenna had saved their son. She'd sacrificed herself to save her child.

As soon as she knew Agnar was well, Vali felt her death move forward. Her features slackened, and her skin paled.

As if remembering an old dream, he knew that the battle raged on around them, but he felt no sense of urgency for it. Within this moment, his final embrace of the woman he'd loved since he was a boy, nothing else in all the nine worlds mattered.

A spray of blood rained over them both. The fresh gout from above struck Brenna's face, but she didn't react at all, not even to close her eyes. Vali brushed the gore from her cheeks and eyelashes.

"My love, don't go." He would never be ready to live without her.

She smiled—faint and soft, but true and deep nonetheless. "Good...death. Yes?"

Though his heart shattered, he didn't beg her again to stay; he knew that she could not, and he wouldn't give her guilt in her last moments. He gave her the ease that he could. Touching his head to hers, he said, "Yes, my love. The most valiant death of the warrior mother. Saving our son, saving our home. You will be with Ylva and Thorvaldr soon. And your mother and father. All the gods and all the worthy dead of all the history of all the world will feast in joy to have you with them. And Thorvaldr will know his mother's arms at last."

She nodded. The movement of her head made the blood run faster, and her eyes flared as she struggled to take her last breaths. Vali put his hand over her neck, trying to staunch the flow as much as he could, but the force of the blood pressed on his palm, and he knew she was at her end.

"I love you, Brenna. All my life have I loved you. Wait for me at the doors of Valhalla, shieldmaiden. We will be together again."

Seeming suddenly to rally, Brenna managed to lift her hand. She laid it on his cheek. "Love..." she gasped, a word Vali felt more than heard. "He waits." Her eyes shifted from his and looked up at the sky. "The sun..."

Just as he'd known when she'd taken the wound, Vali knew the moment that her spirit left.

He drew his wife's body tightly to his chest. He turned his face up to the sky, into the blazing sun, and howled.

~oOo~

He knew not how long he stayed there, clutching his wife, kneeling in the blood-frothed earth while the battle churned around them. It could not have been more than a few moments; when the world began again to push at his senses, little had changed. The battle was yet fully engaged. His wife's blood still ran warm, though the forceful pulse was now merely seepage. Their daughter yet fought above him, clearing the space for her mother's death and his own grief.

Solveig. At her last breath, Brenna's eyes had turned to the sun. But her last words hadn't been about the orb in the sky, Vali realized. They'd been about their daughter. He looked up and saw that Solveig fought with Magni, just before him, and they were nearly overwhelmed. Comers charged at them from all over the battlefield.

Their enemies had seen the God's-Eye down and the Storm-Wolf lost to grief. They were running in to be part of the story of the death of legends. And they would take Solveig down.

His wife had laid down her life for their son.

He would not allow their daughter to lay down her life for her father. Solveig had a story yet to be told.

Vali set Brenna gently on the ground. He grabbed his axes and leapt to his feet.

As he shoved his body into the fray, he fought recklessly, swinging his axes wildly, indiscriminately. He knew what he was doing, and he knew that he would leave grief in his wake. But his story was finished. It had ended with Brenna's final breath. He'd lived long and accomplished much, and his legend had been made—a legend that had been about his love for Brenna above all else.

The world he and Brenna had built was gone. Solveig would build the next one, and there, she would find the story she strove so hard to tell.

But he was Vali Storm-Wolf, and he would not go down easily. He would fight, and if any could kill him, then he would welcome it. So he took on all comers, pulling their attention from his daughter and the man she'd chosen to stand at her side. He sensed his friends joining, too—Leif and Astrid and Leofric and the others—drawn to him, to defend him, and he was glad. His greatest achievement, after winning the love of Brenna and fathering their children, was the depth of his friendships. A man who could earn the love and loyalty of such good and great people had lived a life worth living.

Still surrounded by Tollak's men, Vali barely felt the wounds they dealt him as he dropped them two by two. He'd taken grievous wounds in battle more than once and had survived; the one who killed him would need more than a lucky blow to bring him down.

He was pulling his axes through two chests at once, his arms spread wide as he sliced through boiled leather and loosed guts onto the ground, when he finally took the blow he'd sought. A spear, into his bare chest and straight through. He felt it nick his heart.

His eyes focused ahead, and he saw the one who wielded the spear. She hadn't thrown it; she'd driven it into his chest and still held it, gripped in both hands. Her eyes were wide with shock—and, too, with regret.

A shieldmaiden. Vali smiled. He was glad it was a shieldmaiden, and a young one at that. She would likely die for this, but her story would be made on this day. The girl who'd felled the Storm-Wolf. There would be a seat for her in Valhalla.

She pulled the spear back, and Vali fell to the earth.

~oOo~

He lay face-down in the mud, and the fight went on around him. He was not struck again, nor trod upon. The wound to his heart must have been small; he could feel his life leaving, but slowly, meandering out of his body.

He must have drifted away for a while, into blackness. When next he knew anything, a knowing faint as a mist, the world was quiet, and he was being turned over. He felt no pain. The sun warmed his cold face and blazed red against his eyelids.

"Father? Father!" Håkon's voice. The light of the sun dimmed, and Vali felt his son's long hair on his cheek. "He breathes!"

Vali's head jostled and lifted, and he felt himself resting at an angle. Håkon had set his head on his legs. Remembering the day he'd held Ylva like this, on a battlefield far away, Vali felt his waning heart cramp and bleed.

Brenna. Brenna was gone. Brenna had left the world here, in this place. Vali forced his eyes open and blinked against the glare of the sun.

But Brenna was there, looming over him. The sun circled her head and made a shadow of her face, but it was Brenna. His beautiful, fierce, magnificent wife. She was here. He lifted his hand to her, and she caught it in her own.

"Father, I'm here."

Not Brenna. Solveig. Remembering his purpose, Vali blinked again and made his mind clear. "Solveig. My sun." The words sounded strange and distant.

"I'm here." She squeezed his hand. "Don't go. Pappa, please."

She hadn't called him Pappa since she was young enough to set on his knee.

"This end…is good. I want it. My life stops with hers." Each breath he took to speak was harder than the one before it.

"No!" Solveig dropped her head to his, crashing their foreheads together. "No, Pappa, please," she whispered against his cheek. "I'm not ready."

With effort, he turned his head, finding her soft skin with his lips. "You are, my sun." The world began to dim around the edges, and his heartbeat slowed in his ears, but he had more to say. He scraped up the dregs of his life and his will. "You are ready. Build our world again. Love your man. Make your story."

He felt her head shaking. Even now, she rejected what was so obviously true. Vali found the strength to lift his arm, and he hooked his hand over his daughter's neck. "Yes, Solveig. Your story…is your own to tell. Every day…you make a verse, and…and…always…you've made us proud."

The world darkened and went suddenly quiet. Vali's arm dropped from his daughter; he could feel life leaving his limbs. "Brenna…I need Brenna…" He wanted to hold her one last time in this world, but his arms wouldn't lift again.

"I will bring her," a voice said, one he knew well, could feel in his heart, but could not place. A friend, though, he knew that and was grateful.

"Father." That voice, he knew, and the hand that squeezed his shoulder.

"Håkon," he gasped, struggling to make his eyes see. "Håkon…" He had more words to say, important words, final wisdom for his errant son, who felt such a chill in his sister's long shadow. And Agnar, where was Agnar? It wasn't his fault; he needed to know that.

Tova and Hella, where were they?

But Vali's mind pulled away, out of his bones, and seemed to float, and no words would come from a body that had no breath left to power speech.

He felt Solveig let go of his hand, and he tried to catch her, to keep her, but she moved away. But then Brenna was at his side, her head lying on his chest. He knew that perfect weight as well as he knew his own soul. Someone lifted his arms, and Vali held his woman again.

Brenna. My love.

~oOo~

He stood on a field mounded with bodies. At his feet, his daughter and son knelt. And Leif, his dear friend. They wept, but Vali knew not why.

He turned into the bright sun and saw, at the top of the hill, his wife. Tall and proud and beautiful, dressed for battle in the boiled leathers she'd worn when first they were mated. Her golden hair gleamed in its battle braids, and her right eye was marked with black. Her shield and sheathed sword rested on her back. She was young, at her strongest peak of life.

Beside her stood a man, cloaked in black. Taller even than Vali himself, the man towered over Brenna. His long white hair flew back loosely in the wind, and Vali saw the leather strap over his right eye.

Had Odin himself come to claim the soul of the God's-Eye?

The man in black gestured with one hand, a sharp, underhand wave toward Vali, and two hulking wolves suddenly appeared from behind his cloak and charged down the hill toward him. Geri and Freki, coming for him.

Vali Storm-Wolf was of the Úlfhéðnar, trained as one of the most elite of all warriors, sworn to serve the Allfather himself. They took the wolf as their symbol. So he felt no trepidation as Odin's own wolves bounded toward him. Instead, he went to meet them.

His boots did not sink into the blood-drenched earth as he walked. Nothing impeded his progress at all. He wasn't floating, but all the world around him had become immaterial.

The wolves reached him, turned, and took places on either side of him, and Vali understood. Odin had sent his wolves as escort. The Allfather had come to claim him, too.

He would not be separated from Brenna, not ever again, for all eternity.

Vali left the field, and the world, and climbed to join his wife.

22

"Father? Father! Do you have words for me? FATHER!" Håkon shouted into Vali's still face. "FATHER!"

"Håkon!" Solveig shoved him back. "Enough! He is gone. They are both gone. Do you not see?"

Magni could hear the tears in her throat, and he could see them on her face, making clear streaks through the blood of battle, but her voice was strong and steady. He wiped his own cheeks and crouched beside his love, where she knelt beside her parents. His father crouched nearby, staring at his hands, covered in Brenna's blood. He'd carried her from the place of her death and laid her in Vali's arms.

Mother and father, both dead on the same day, on the same field. Magni could not fathom the depth of Solveig's loss.

"I am here," he said at her side.

"I know." She didn't turn to him, but her words wrapped around him. "Thank you."

A growl tore the air, and Håkon leapt up, leaving his father's head to drop to the ground with a slack bounce. Håkon vaulted over the bodies of his parents, and Magni turned in his crouch to see the reason.

Leofric and Astrid approached. Astrid ushered Agnar along with them, her hand on his shoulder. The face of the boy—clearly a boy and not a man in this moment—showed the waxy, wild-eyed rigor of shock and grief.

"YOU KILLED THEM!" Håkon shouted and drew his sword at his unarmed brother. Astrid jumped between them, her axe drawn, and blocked Håkon's blow.

He had struck to kill. His own brother.

"HÅKON!" Solveig had stood, and her voice carried across the field. She held her own sword, prepared to fight, and she strode toward her brothers. Magni stood and followed her, ready to defend her, though he didn't think she'd need his help.

Håkon whirled to face his sister. "As much as if he'd wielded the weapons, he killed them," he snarled. "He had no place on this field, and they are dead because he could not fight for himself."

Magni shifted his attention to Agnar and knew that the boy believed it was true.

"No, Håkon," Solveig said in a tone meant to settle the storm. "Mother and Father were warriors. They died in battle, as we all hope to do. There is no fault here."

The battle had been hard fought but decisively won. Dead lay everywhere, and the triumphant warriors combed the bodies, seeking their friendly casualties and finishing the wounded enemies. The quiet after so much chaos seemed to fill the air with a strange rumble.

"It's not true simply because you say it is, sister." Håkon shoved his sword into its sheath and stalked away, toward the hill. At the same time, Agnar broke free of Leofric's paternal grip and ran. He ran away from Håkon, away from his sister, from his parents' bodies, from the field of their victory and of their loss.

"Agnar!" Solveig ran after him. Following the instinct to protect her that rode him always, Magni started to follow, but his father's hand held him back.

"Leave them. There is no danger, and they need the moment." He gave Magni's arm a tug. "Let us see to Vali and Brenna. We will carry them back to Halsgrof and release them in the harbor, where our ships are waiting. That is the land of both their births, and it's fitting they should be sent off together from the place they first met."

His eyes still on Solveig and her brother, Magni heard his father and agreed, but he couldn't yet tear himself away. Solveig had caught up to Agnar. Like all Vali and Brenna's children but Hella, Agnar was impressively tall. He'd not yet filled out into a man's breadth, but he met his older sister eye to eye in height.

Solveig clutched her brother's shoulders and spoke to him with evident earnest feeling. Agnar shook his head and tried to twist away, but Solveig held on and drew him back to face her.

Magni could sense, without hearing, what Solveig said. Agnar's shoulders collapsed, and his body shook with weeping. Solveig drew him into her arms. At the sight of her strength for her brother, Magni felt able to turn away and follow his father.

His father gathered Brenna up and draped her over his arms. Astrid picked up her hands and set them on her chest so that they wouldn't dangle. Then Magni and Leofric bent to the work of carrying Vali's huge body through the field, over the hill, and to the wagons.

Before they could lift him, a heavy shadow fell. Magni looked up and saw at least a dozen warriors, bloody and weary, but ready to carry their friend, their leader, and their hero to his rest.

Working together, they settled him carefully on their shoulders and began the long walk.

~oOo~

"Solveig."

Magni said her name before he got too close so he didn't startle her and find himself on the end of her blade. She'd been quiet and tense since the camp had been staked and the work done for the night. With the dawn, they would ride back to Halsgrof and send her parents to the next world.

She was about to mount her horse, the Mercurian stallion she'd named Aggi. But the night was dark, with only a slim curve of moon. He laid his hand on her arm. "Don't go."

Her head sagged forward.

Since they'd left the battlefield, she hadn't wept. Her shoulders had stayed straight and strong, and she'd taken her parents' place in the leaders' discussions. Now that place was hers. As well as he knew her, he could only guess at the weight of the responsibility she bore, or how it might chafe. She'd been inscrutable since she'd led Agnar off the battlefield and stood with him at the side of the wagon that carried the bodies of their parents.

She'd kept her attention on the work of the camp, the plan for her parents' burial, the plan beyond that to take the ships from Halsgrof to Geitland and meet Tollak there, now that the bulk of his army had been destroyed. She'd focused on Agnar. She had not allowed herself a moment of quiet, and Magni was sure that when she did, she would crumble.

He therefore was sure that she meant to ride into the dark woods to do it, and he could not let her go alone.

"Magni, please."

"It's not safe, my love."

She cast a glance over her shoulder at him. "We killed every fighter within miles of this place. There is no risk."

"Håkon has not returned." No one had sighted him since he'd stormed away from the field.

"He's my brother. He would never harm me."

Magni would have agreed, once. "He's Agnar's brother as well."

She spun, and Aggi shied a little, tossing his head and making his bridle jingle like a bell. "That was passion and grief, not malice. He is my *brother*."

Knowing better than to press the point, Magni raised his hand and brushed his fingertips across her cheek. She'd washed, and her hair was only loosely braided, a single plait over her head and down the length of her spine. Wisps had slipped free and caressed her face—and, now, his fingers.

"You shouldn't be alone."

"I need to be alone, Magni. Please. I need it."

He disagreed; Solveig got lost in her mind when she isolated herself. But he would not force himself on her. Full of worry and sorrow, he nodded and stepped back. She swung up onto Aggi's bare back and rode away from the camp, toward the woods.

Always she ran to the woods.

~oOo~

Magni sat alone at the fire. The night was old, and the rest of the camp slept, but for the warriors on watch or patrol. Hours had passed, and Solveig had not yet returned. Nor had Håkon. He would not, could not rest until she was safely back.

So he sat alone at the fire, his sword unsheathed, and waited for her.

The camp had been quiet long before it slept. Their victory had come at a heavy price, but no death weighed so much as the two whose bodies lay side by side in a wagon. Their sagas were full of stories of the God's-Eye and the Storm-Wolf: their great honor, their fierce valor, their godly strength, and their fiery passion for each other, for their children, and for their people. To lose them was a blow almost greater than the worth of the victory over Tollak—who had been defeated well and truly, though he might not yet know it.

The whole camp mourned the loss of their legends. And yet, that evening, Magni had heard the story of the battle told around the fire. Of the God's-Eye's sacrifice for her son. Of the Storm-Wolf's wild grief and the otherworldly power of his final fight, dropping a hundred foes before a spear split his already broken heart.

And of Solveig, their daughter, standing on a mountain of kills, fighting off an army to shield her father as he bid his farewell to her mother.

They said that she'd fought with such strength and brave fury, such a fiery heart, that the gods had taken notice, and Sunna had torn open the clouds, shining her light down over her, so all of Asgard could see.

Solveig Sunheart. The name had caught the instant it had first been uttered, and had spread from mouth to mouth around the camp.

A few told of Magni, too, and said her true love fought at her side, but the story they told was about her, not him. And that was as it should be. He had been there, beside her, and always he would be, but he had no need to be told in this story. His story would come later, and he felt no impatience for it.

While she had run away to her forest solitude, Solveig had become the legend she'd always felt the burden to be. Warriors who had seen Solveig fight told those who had not; later, any man or woman who'd been on that field, no matter what their eyes had seen, would tell the story of the deaths of Brenna and Vali as if they'd been right beside them. It was the alchemy of stories: facts and hopes and dreams, blended together to make truths.

Lost in those thoughts, Magni almost didn't hear the footsteps approaching in the dark. He leapt up, his sword in hand. But it was Solveig's face that the guttering firelight showed before him.

He sheathed his sword with a sigh of relief. "You are well. Thank the gods."

She simply stood there. The light was too dim for him to discern her expression, but he felt tension emanating from her. "Solveig?"

"I don't…" The words were little more than a gasp, and pitched higher than her normal voice. Like a plea. "Magni…I…"

She wasn't well at all; of course she wasn't. She was in grief, and, this time, fleeing into the wood hadn't eased her. She'd finally found the limits of solitude.

But she wasn't alone; never had she been. "I'm here, Solveig." He held out his hand, and she took it, and her hand trembled against his palm. When he tugged and brought her to him, she sagged against him.

325

He held her and brought her down to sit with him, and her body softened entirely, as if she'd run out of her own strength. He tucked her as close as he could and offered her his.

And finally, she wept.

~oOo~

When the greatest among their people went to Valhalla, their tradition was to send them to sea and burn the ship. The body would be dressed in the dead's finest garments, and the ship would be filled with their most treasured possessions, the things that would be of best use and value in the next life. Women and girls would fill the space that was left with greens and flowers, if the season were right.

A favored slave was often sacrificed and sent along with their master, but Vali and Brenna had not kept slaves in all the time of Magni's knowing.

As Solveig ordered the rituals arranged for her parents' leave-taking, it became clear that the lack of human sacrifice would not be the only shift in tradition.

Most of their possessions had been lost when Tollak overtook, and then destroyed, Karlsa, so her mother and father had no finery to be garbed in. But Magni doubted that Solveig would have chosen fine clothes for them even had all their belongings and treasures been spared.

She prepared them for death as if for battle. She washed them both herself, alone and apart, braiding her father's hair, and her mother's, in the way that was their custom. Then she had them dressed in leathers, her father bare-chested, and his headed wolf pelt over his head and shoulders, in the way of the Úlfhéðnar. She dressed her mother in one of her own chestpieces, which had been modeled on that which her mother had worn in her youth. She blacked her mother's right eye in the way she'd done for battle: the soft skin around the eye in solid black, and thick rays drawn from it, over her forehead, temple, and cheek.

She did not cover her mother in mail; she'd told Magni that mail hadn't protected her in this life and could not be trusted to do so in the next.

While she took tender care of her parents, Magni, his father, Astrid, and the others emptied one of the Karlsa skeids and built a double bier over the center rowing benches. A ship was burned only with the greatest of their dead; a ship was their people's greatest asset, and to offer it up spoke better of the dead inside it than any word might.

As the night before, the camp was quiet while they did this solemn work. Those who weren't needed on the ship prepared the rituals for their other, more humble dead: three score warriors lost on that one field. Those dead were sent off first, buried in the ground with their weapons and shields.

When her parents were dressed and the ship's bier was ready, Solveig, dressed in a plain linen gown that must have been offered to her by a woman here in Halsgrof, with her hair loose and flowing in golden waves down her back, carried her mother's sword—gleaming and clean—and laid it on her chest, folding pale, dead hands over the hilt.

Next, she crossed her father's mighty axes on his chest. When both mother and father were fully prepared, Solveig called Agnar over. He came reluctantly, his head and shoulders low, pushed forward by Astrid's insistent hands. Solveig tried to get him to see them and bid them farewell, but his grief and guilt held his head down until Solveig freed him to skitter back to the side.

He wasn't a warrior yet. No matter how badly he'd wanted to be, it was clear that Agnar hadn't grown enough in his heart to fight with them.

Between the two litters on which her parents would be carried to their bier, Solveig stood alone, a hand on each one. She bowed her head and was still. Though the posture she held now wasn't much different in appearance from Agnar's defeated stoop, it could not have been more different in meaning. Solveig bore her legacy, and she understood its responsibility. All her life, she'd been clamoring to find her role, her fit. Now, she had a wide gap to fill. Her story had come at a precious price.

She wasn't defeated; she was only sad.

The night before, she'd let him carry her to their sleeping pallet, and she'd wept until her body had nothing more to offer up. He'd held her through the night, but she'd never spoken of her grief. She hadn't needed to; thick strands of it had wound around him as he'd held her.

When she'd woken, she'd been pale and puffy-eyed, but calm and stoic, and she'd gone about the business of her parents' end with steady purpose. She would be jarl now, and she stepped into the role at once.

Magni knew the deep chasm of her pain, and he knew what she needed to climb from it, so he made sure to be in arm's reach, but not closer. She would come to him when she needed him, and when she could afford to feel weakness and seek comfort.

Fighting the urge to go to her now, Magni waited. He stood beside his father, at the head of all their army and all of the surviving citizens of Halsgrof, and he let her have her private grief before an audience of fellow mourners.

She lifted her head and turned to face them. With a single, stoic nod, she indicated her readiness to proceed.

Magni handed her her mother's shield. He and his father, and the other strongest of the men, lifted the litters and carried them, with reverence and care, to the shore and the ship that would be their funeral pyre.

Solveig walked ahead of them all, pulling Agnar to her side. She carried her mother's shield before her and walked down to the end of the pier.

Håkon had not yet returned. They would send his parents off without him. And without Tova and Hella, safe in Mercuria, innocent of their loss.

The litters were laid side by side. Solveig stepped into the ship and settled her mother's shield in its place at the head of the bier. Before she climbed back onto the pier, she bent and pressed her lips to her father's forehead, and then her mother's. She let her head rest in the space between theirs.

As her final act of tenderness, she linked their hands together.

Agnar, his expression dark with pain, remained on the pier. When Solveig moved to the side of the ship, ready to return to his side and Magni's, her brother walked away, back to the shore. Solveig watched him go, and so did Magni. They both saw Astrid catch him and keep him close.

Knowing that she would welcome his touch now, Magni went to Solveig and helped her from the ship. He wrapped her tightly up and felt her take his strength.

"Stay with me," she murmured.

"Always."

The Halsgrof seer said his words and splashed heavy gouts of oil over the bier. The ship was unmoored and set loose onto the sea.

When the ship was well enough away, Magni heard the sing of bowstring behind them, and a flaming arrow arced over their heads. Then another. Both landed true, and their fire caught in the oil at once. His father and Astrid had fired the ship.

Solveig turned in his embrace so that she stood before him, at the end of the pier, and they watched the ship burn and take her parents away from her in the smoke that rose to Asgard.

~oOo~

Most of their force had been on foot from Karlsa to Halsgrof and even beyond, fighting every pocket of resistance they met; only minimal crews had sailed the ships from Karlsa and awaited them in the deeps just beyond Halsgrof until summoned to the port. They had attempted to cover every angle from which Tollak might attack and to dominate every conflict they engaged. They'd been entirely successful.

In Halsgrof, the ships came in, and that had decidedly ended the battle for that town and for the holding.

They'd intended the same strategy all the way to Geitland, until the battle in northern Dofrar that had wiped out the main of Tollak's force. And taken Vali and Brenna from them.

From Halsgrof, their full force, all that survived of it, boarded three skeids and six Mercurian ships and set their course for Geitland. They no longer needed to fight a ground war. It was over and Tollak's army was destroyed, but Tollak himself still sat in Magni's father's seat, and there was vengeance to make. Jarl Leif Olavsson wanted to fill Geitland Harbor, and the usurper to see his death coming.

~oOo~

When they'd arrived at Karlsa, they'd been greeted by destruction and desolation, with nothing left of the town they'd known. When they'd arrived at Halsgrof, they'd found the calamitous marks of Tollak's scourge on that town as well, though enough had been left to call a town.

Arriving at Geitland, Magni felt a dizzying sense of unreality. For weeks, they'd moved through a world still reeling from a violent shift in power. But Geitland, his home, looked exactly the same as ever it had.

The harbor was empty, and shore was quiet, and that was unusual on a summer afternoon, but otherwise, the ships might have been simply returning from a raid—and not one of any especial repute.

It wasn't until the skeids drew up to the piers, and he saw Tollak Finnsson's shields hanging on the great hall instead of his father's, that the two worlds of past and present settled properly in Magni's mind.

There was no one—no one—on the shore or the berm to meet them, in either friendliness or hostility. In fact, though the town was intact and nearly as it had always been, it seemed to have been emptied of its citizens.

"Be wary," Magni's father said, scanning the shore. "Shields ready!" he called to the rest of the ship.

But there was no volley of arrows, no sudden charge of warriors from the flank.

"Did he run?"

"If he did, we don't stop until we find him. We will have his head for his treachery and destruction. Even if he is dead, I will cleave his skull from his spine before I call this finished."

Magni had never heard such rage thunder over his father's tongue. He turned and saw Solveig staring at the great hall,

331

her head tipped in the posture she affected before every battle, her expression stony and fixed. The wide swath of black she painted across her temples and eyes made them seem to glow. She held her shield before her, and she rested her hand on the pommel of her sword.

He had no need to ask if she was ready.

They climbed onto the pier and walked to the great hall. *Their* great hall. Astrid made her way forward and displaced Magni, taking up the position at his father's side, leading them. He didn't fight her for it; once, His father and Astrid had been a team leading their people. Still they were great friends.

A goat trotted across their path, bleating. Nothing else but the warriors stirred.

Magni's father and Astrid reached the hall and tore open the doors.

A stench rolled from the open doorway and forced the first rows of them back, coughing and retching. Magni was the first to regain his equilibrium; he went to the door, holding his breath as much as he could and taking air through his mouth when he needed.

"Gods," he muttered at the sight of the hall.

His father stood at his shoulder. "The gods have forsaken this place."

"Not this place, Father. Not our home. That *man* is forsaken. Because this is not his place."

Tollak. Sitting on Magni's father's seat. On either side of the hall, men and women hung from the rafters by their necks. Their faces were bloated and purple, and their tongues stuck out fatly. Men and women in common clothes. Not warriors. No one of power. Simple citizens. People. *Their* people, of

Geitland. Their neighbors and friends, who'd been unable to run on the night Ulv had saved Magni's mother.

The stench was their rotting flesh and the leavings of their bodies' deaths.

He recognized the man nearest him. Erik, who had been a friend in their childhood and who'd grown into no great man. Magni had heard that Erik had aided Tollak in their first attacks. He didn't mourn that death, but he was unsettled to see him rot nonetheless.

In the center of the hall, a man had been spitted over the fire. His blackened corpse hovered over dead coal and ash.

Geitland had seemed ghostly because it was peopled with ghosts.

Sitting above this place of evil death, in the seat of Magni's father, was Tollak Finnsson.

He'd cut his own throat; the dagger sat in his lap, his hand still loose around it. The blood glistened wetly over his chest; he'd not been dead long. How long had he lived alone among the horrors of his own making?

Suddenly, Magni was jostled, and Solveig pushed past him, past his father. Unsheathing her sword, she strode by the dangling bodies and through the slurry of their deaths and stalked up the platform, straight to the body of the usurper. Grabbing him by only his hair, she yanked him from the chair. His body fell forward, landing on a slant down the two steps of the platform. She descended those steps and raised her sword over her head, gripped in both hands. With a shout that was her battle cry, she slammed her sword down and took Tollak's head off. It rolled away, stopping under the dangling feet of a hanged woman.

She brought the sword down again, and again, and again. Her shrieks continued, each one ending in a grunt as she struck, but their tone changed. No longer was each one a battle cry. Instead, Magni heard despair and grief canting the rage sideways.

He went to her, shaking off his father's hand as it shot out to restrain him. This was not the time to leave her alone. No one knew her better, and he knew what she needed.

Tollak was in pieces; his thickening, reeking viscera scummed the floor.

Standing behind her, Magni timed his move so that she wouldn't harm him or herself, and he grabbed her arms, stopping their arc. She fought at first, but it was a fight of instinct, not awareness, and he held on.

When she was quiet, panting in his arms, he put his mouth to her ear and said, "I'm here."

Her sword fell from her hands. Her knees buckled, and Magni followed her to the floor, holding her, loving her.

23

Leif took a drink from a horn cup and leaned on the table, toward Solveig. "Tomorrow is the seventh day, Solveig."

With a curt bounce of her head, she let him know what he already knew: that she had not lost track of the days and was well aware of what tomorrow meant. The seventh day following the death of her parents. Seven days seemed not nearly enough time. She still woke with the feeling they were alive. She still thought to ask her father's advice. Inside her, they weren't yet gone.

But in the custom of their people, seven days was the limit of mourning. A new jarl of Karlsa would be named tomorrow.

There was little of Karlsa left to lead; a total of perhaps five hundred souls, including those in the countryside. Most of them were homeless. Or, at least, unsheltered. Solveig supposed that they all had a home in the land itself.

"Your father meant you to claim his seat on his death."

Another sharp nod. All her life, she'd known that. "And I shall claim it. Should I be challenged for it, I will fight to win it. What there is to claim or to win."

Magni grabbed her hand and squeezed. "You'll rebuild—*we* will rebuild. I'll be with you every step." She felt his hearty assurance and steadfast love in the warmth of his skin over hers, and it made a respite of calm in her heart.

Leif smiled at them both. "You know that anything you need of Geitland you shall have. Including my son."

Solveig answered his smile with a grateful one of her own and gave Magni's hand an affectionate pulse. "Thank you. But there is rebuilding to be done here as well."

A wave of her free hand toward the rest of the dim hall demonstrated her meaning. The hall was usable again, but Geitland had hardly been spared the plague of Tollak's power-fueled madness.

It had taken a full day with everyone working to remove all traces of the usurper's corruption of the great hall. Leif and Magni and Astrid had led the effort with jaws clamped shut with anger. Everyone worked in near silence; it seemed as though the world had gone mute when Solveig's parents had left it.

She had lost herself in the work as well, driving her body as hard as she could. She'd discovered that she needed both busyness and solitude to keep her emotions contained now. True solitude, running out into the wild as she'd done all her life, hadn't given her the strength it always had. Not this time. This time, her mind spun and shrieked when she was truly alone.

But she didn't want to be in company, either. She had no need or desire or ability to talk, not about the things that churned her heart. She could barely tolerate the condolences and stories people offered her. But when there were things to be done, then she could focus and be strong. Her mind quieted when there was work.

And it quieted when Magni held her.

She'd tried to talk to him, that first night, to speak the chaos in her mind. When the dark forest and Aggi's sturdy companionship had failed to settle her, she'd gone to Magni to ask for help, to seek the certain steadiness of his arms, but words had failed her utterly. There were no words that could describe the noise, the pain, inside her.

He hadn't needed any. He'd known, and he'd offered her his arms, and his chest, holding her close all night without demanding any explanation from her. In the days since, he'd been a constant presence at her side, just close enough so that she knew always that he was there for her when she needed him. And at night, he held her while she cried.

He waited for her. Always had he waited. She wished she'd understood earlier the importance of that. She wished she knew how to make up for her tardiness, how to be worthy of his patience.

But she did understand now, and she would spend the rest of her life loving him the way he deserved to be loved. Whether she was worthy or not, she would treasure the gift of him.

After the hall had been cleaned and the bodies were buried or burned—Tollak's was left in the forest to rot, and his head was piked at the harbor—a völva had come and cleansed the space of any ill lingerings.

After that, the fighters had left a force on guard in town and ridden out into the countryside, seeking those who'd been displaced. As they encountered people, they'd learned the hard news about the harsh year of Tollak's reign. Terror and deprivation and death. A generation's worth of bounty and prosperity stolen from them all.

While they'd been resting in Mercuria, feasting and planning and growing strong, Tollak had been sucking the marrow from the people of Geitland. Leif had rebuilding to do, too, despite the buildings still standing.

To Solveig's knowledge, there hadn't been tension between the jarls, no signs that a betrayal might have been coming. She knew the rumors about the death of Jarl Finn, but they had been only whisperings, she'd thought.

It seemed that those whisperings had been true, and Tollak had killed his own father. In his sleep. The act of a coward. Had it been the patricide or the cowardice which had driven him mad? Guilt, perhaps?

She tried to imagine Tollak in the seven days' mourning for his father, honoring the man he'd murdered, accepting condolences and remembrances from the people of Dofrar, then claiming the seat for his own as if stepping into his rightful place. Layer upon layer of deceit. Had he felt the burden of leadership, the responsibility of following a beloved jarl? Had it been that yoke which had broken him?

Leif broke into her thoughts. "We'll find whatever is left of our treasure"—it was said that Tollak had buried Leif's treasure all around Geitland, and Leif had trusted men and women out searching for it—"and we will raid for more, and Geitland will be strong again. So will Karlsa. But we have more to discuss than that. Our holdings have grown twofold, and we must decide how best to divide the claims of Halsgrof and Dofrar, which we've rightly won. I suggest we draw the new border between Geitland and Karlsa at the Ångermanälven"

That would more than double the size of her father's jarldom. Uncertainty about her fitness to take her father's place surged up and broke against the wall of her sorrow, and Solveig had to drop her head and clench her hands together to stave off the flood of emotion that nearly burst from her. Everyone sitting at the table around her was quiet, and she knew they waited, watching her.

When she was able, she let out the pressure with a sigh. "Perhaps it is better if it all remains one holding. All claimed by Geitland." She lifted her head and looked to Leif, whose face showed no condemnation or surprise. Only compassion in his eyes. Magni's eyes were so like his father's.

"You would give up the jarldom?" Astrid asked, and Solveig heard the bite of censure there.

"Solveig, no," Magni muttered at her side, as though he meant his words only for her. "Your father…"

He didn't finish, and there was no need that he would. Solveig knew. Her father's last words. *Build our world again. Make your story.* He wanted her to be jarl. She would dishonor him to turn her back on it.

She'd always known that someday she would take his seat. Only moments ago, in a reflex born of that long knowledge, she'd asserted her intention to do exactly that. But becoming jarl had been an abstraction, something that would happen far in the future, after her father passed on from this life in his wizened old age. Not now, when he'd been still mighty, and before she felt ready, before she'd understood who she was or would be.

It was better that he'd died strong, on the battlefield. It was the right death for a man like him, and a woman like her mother. Solveig knew that. They'd died together; they'd passed through the doors of Valhalla together. The gods had so loved them and their love for each other that they hadn't torn them asunder. It was good and right.

But it hurt. Bitter, empty pain sliced through Solveig with her every breath. Never again would her father brush his long beard over her face when he held her. Never again would she feel the crushing affection of his strong arms or hear the steady beat of his great heart against her ear. Never again would she see the small smile on her mother's lips that meant Solveig had pleased her. Never again would she feel her mother's fingers in her hair, settling a stray hair into a braid.

Never again would she see them look at each other in the ways that had shown Solveig the kind of love to want. The kind of love she now had with Magni.

Seven days was not long enough to mourn her parents. Seven years would not be long enough.

Leif reached across the table and tugged on her arm until she unwound her fingers and offered him her hand. He held it lightly, offering paternal encouragement. "Now is not the time to forge a kingdom, Solveig. The people who've survived these months in the clutches of a man who'd thought himself king will not tolerate another, not even me. You and Magni are to be wed, and that will bring us together in the way it should be done. When my time is over, and Magni takes my seat, that is the time to unify our people."

She sighed again and gathered up her focus and her fortitude. Leif was right. Her moment of weakness had been exactly that, a moment, and weakness. She nodded and locked eyes again with her father's friend. "Yes. I will claim my father's seat, and strive to do him honor in his stead."

~oOo~

Though the hall had been cleaned and cleansed, Leif did not yet sleep in the jarl's quarters. Magni had told Solveig that the thought of Tollak in residence there, in the space where he'd loved his wife and they'd raised their son, upset his father tremendously and made his loneliness for Olga and their new daughter all the more acute. So the hall went dark and still in the late nights. Leif slept alone in a small hut, and Solveig and Magni took up the one next to it.

Agnar, who'd always been a solitary boy and now wanted more distance than ever before, had taken a pallet and slept in the stable. Solveig hoped that the rituals tomorrow would mean a fresh start for him.

She'd never lived in such a space before. She'd grown up in Karlsa's hall, living in company with her parents and siblings. She'd spent many nights out of doors or under the cover of tents. And she'd spent months in the opulence of Leofric's massive castle.

This little space, not a longhouse but one built for a small family without ranging generations or livestock to shelter, was just a room. It had a fire pit in the center, and a cozy nook for eating and working, and a comfortable bed.

Magni knew the couple who'd kept this house before, an apprentice tanner and his new wife, but Solveig hadn't recognized their names. She'd only known the people of importance in Geitland, and a few of the servants who'd served in the hall. But she could feel the love and hope this couple had felt as they'd begun a life together.

They hadn't escaped Geitland or sailed to Mercuria with them, and they hadn't survived Tollak's reign. The woman had been one of the bodies strung up in the hall, and her husband had not been found. Or he might have been the man spitted over the fire.

Their house was warm and bright and cozy, and so very sad.

The night before the seventh day, after talking long with Leif and Astrid about the plans for her claiming of the expanded jarldom of Karlsa, Solveig approached the little house. The windows were open, and the light within glowed warmly. Magni was there already. He'd gone out to the near countryside that afternoon to help with the planting of a few quick-growing crops. They only had scant weeks left before the summer was over, and the coming winter would be difficult. Tollak had fought rebellion throughout his claim and had responded harshly to each uprising, burning crops and farmsteads as far as he could reach. To feed the remaining of their people through the winter would require careful rationing—and whatever they could grow in the time they had left.

Word was stretching across the land that Tollak was gone and Leif was in his rightful seat. Every day, more people, those

341

who'd been able to flee the reach of the usurper, returned to Geitland. Most of them were women and children, and oldsters. Mouths to feed. But each who returned showed renewed hope that the greatness of their world would return.

Magni sat on the bed, his boots off and his chest bare. His elbows rested on his knees, and his hands dangled loosely between them. His head was down. In the flash of a second after she'd opened the door but before he'd looked up and seen her, Solveig was struck by the understanding that he, too, sought solitude to feel weakness.

She'd never considered that; but then, she'd never sought him out in his solitude. Always it was Magni intervening in her times alone, and almost always, he was right to do so. He knew when she truly needed to be alone, and he knew when she was simply running away.

He was always there, where she needed him, whether she'd understood that or not, and it hadn't occurred to her that he might also have need.

These were the times she must become better at. It wasn't enough that he knew her. He needed to know that she knew him as well. She needed to show him that she understood.

He put on a smile and began to stand, but she crossed the room in time to stop him. With her hands on his broad shoulders, she kept him sitting. "You're weary."

Taking her hands from his shoulders, he put them together and kissed them. "Yes. The work is hard, and everywhere there are signs of what we left our people to suffer."

"We couldn't have beaten him last year. If we'd lost, we'd have left our people to suffer endlessly."

"I know. And yet we didn't suffer, while they did."

"And thus we returned and tore him down." His laments were familiar to her; she'd had all the same thoughts and regrets. It was easier to ease his mind than her own, and in easing his, she found her way as well. She set her fingers under his chin, feeling the softness of his beard, and lifted his head. "We did what was right, and the people know it. They stopped us from entering Geitland harbor, remember, when we were too few and too spent to defeat him."

A smile broke across his handsome face, and he pulled her to stand between his legs. "It feels good to lean on you."

"You should do it more often. I lean on you too much." She combed her fingers through the loose silk of his hair.

"No, you don't. You lean when you need it. As do I."

And she leaned so much more. "Am I so much weaker than you?"

She didn't mean it as a complaint or a challenge, not quite, but Magni put his smile away and gave her hips a shake. "No. But your burden is heavier. People see me and think, 'There goes Magni. What a fine man he is. What a good jarl he'll make someday.'"

"You are, and you will."

He nodded. "I believe that. I know my worth. But it's a man's worth. People see you and think, 'There goes the eldest daughter of the Storm-Wolf and the God's-Eye. How much brighter will their stars shine, shared in one body?' They named you for the sun itself, Solveig. That's how bright you are expected to shine."

She could feel the burden he spoke of in the words he used to describe it, and her grief in the loss of her parents clamped an angry fist around her throat.

"You *do* shine that brightly," he went on. "You are every bit worthy of your lineage, and to have the honor of loving you and being your strength when you need to lean—you make me stronger, Solveig Sunheart."

The sound of that name bit like a lash, and she flinched from it, but he didn't let her go. It was what she'd wanted all her life—to be more than simply her father's daughter. To find her own story. Now she had it. She'd heard the stories about her parents' deaths and her fight to protect them. She couldn't even say where fact and story were seamed together to make this new truth; she had imperfect and incomplete memories of that day. Except for her emotions. She remembered every single emotion of that day in vivid detail and had relived them every day since.

She had made her name. Her parents' deaths had made her into a legend. Tomorrow, she would become the jarl they had intended her to be. What would happen next in her life would carve her figure into their world.

But in her heart, the one that people now thought of as full of the sun, she would always and only be Valisdottir. The name she'd had since the day of her birth. A day of midnight sun.

The name she'd struggled under almost as long.

Into the silence left by her anguished thoughts, Magni whispered, "We'll build Karlsa up again, and I will stay with you there. You will have your home again."

With those words, the man before her swept away her painful thoughts. "I'm home now, Magni." She laid her hand on his chest, over his heart. "This is my home. *You* are."

"Solveig," he murmured as she bent to kiss him.

When his arms closed around her and he brought her down to the bed in this tiny cottage that had once been filled with the hope of new love, Solveig felt weight fall from her shoulders as if she'd dropped a fur away after coming home from the cold outside.

He truly was her home. Where she fit, who she was, what waited ahead of her, it all made sense to her when seen through the glowing windows of his eyes.

They fumbled together toward nakedness. Their writhing stoked their fire as they opened, removed, and discarded their clothes, until at last they were skin to skin. Magni's hot, heavy, strong body warmed hers at every point of contact and all the way through. His hair caressed her chest and shoulders as he sought a breast, and she cried out when he found his prize and drew it into his mouth, sending a hot spike of lightning through her body, deep into her core, making her pulse and surge. As he suckled, his fingers wandered lightly, tantalizingly over her skin, raising bumps everywhere, until he'd rendered her body his completely, beyond her control.

The roughsoft scratch of his beard coaxed her skin to tighten as his molten mouth drew harder and harder. Whether she pulsed in time with his rhythm or he could feel her and followed her pulse, she didn't know, but as always, they were one, and his hands and mouth and body on hers made her forget anything else. The wide world and all its delights and horrors, its pains and pleasures, all its joys and sorrows, friendships and betrayals, wars and loves—all of it disappeared, and they were alone in the warm glow of this bed and those candles and nothing else at all.

Desperate for more, for everything, she sought some thread of control; she flexed and writhed, trying to bring the hot steel of him from her side and settle it between her legs. But he countered her every move, keeping her pinned beneath him as he drove her to madness with his sucking mouth and traipsing fingers.

But those fingers wouldn't delve where she most wanted them. They stayed gentle and teasing, over her arm, her hip, her belly. Making her quiver and gasp. And need. Gods, how she needed.

She tried to push his shoulders, to make him turn over. He enjoyed when she rode him, and she needed him inside her. But he wouldn't budge. He had dominated her utterly.

Then he bit her nipple, just lightly, without pain, and the blast of hot pleasure stopped her body and brain completely. She arched sharply, hearing the squeal she'd released into the air and not caring, and then sagged, limp, into the mattress.

Magni chuckled and flicked his tongue over the nipple he'd been abusing so beautifully. "Let me do as I wish, Solveig. Just breathe and feel."

When she gave herself up to him, he rewarded her with what she needed. His fingers found her core and slid with tender firmness over the pinpoint of her slick ache. So frenzied had he made her already that she released almost at once, flailing under his determined caress, which didn't ease until she could only spasm and grunt.

Then he slid his body downward, grazing hers all the way, and lapped at the juice of her pleasure as if he could take sustenance from it. Each time his tongue hit the top of her folds and touched that bead of bliss, Solveig cried out, on the precipice of another dive toward ecstasy while ripples from the first still fluttered through her relaxed limbs.

Then that wondrous touch was gone, and she whimpered but could not stir her limbs to seek it, or even convince her eyelids to rise.

"Open your eyes, shieldmaiden."

To his command, her lids responded, and she saw him looming above her, his hair swinging at the sides of his face, the ends dancing over her chest. He'd settled between her legs, and, instinctively, she raised them, folding them at his hips. Gazing into her eyes, he flexed and slid into her. A strong, steady thrust that seated him deeply at once.

"Yes, oh yes," she moaned and wrapped her hands around him, bringing her arms up his back and hooking her hands over his shoulders. "Love me, Magni."

He flexed backward. "All my life," he answered and pushed into her again.

He never took his eyes from hers, or she from his, even in the extremity of their shared release. When it was over, they lay panting and tangled together. Then, as always, Magni tended to her, wetting a cloth and wiping her clean. When he settled again in bed with her, he turned to his side and cradled her in the curve of his body.

Solveig fell asleep that night, for the first time since her parents' death, feeling worthy of the future that began the next day, when she would step into their legacy. Magni would give her the strength she needed in those times when her own would not be enough.

He always had.

~oOo~

In the Geitland great hall the next afternoon, Solveig sat between Magni and his father for the sjaund. The first community gathering in the reclaimed hall was the ritual to end the mourning of her parents' death and name her jarl of Karlsa.

It was a ritual that by all markers of their customs should have occurred in Karlsa, before the empty seat of Jarl Vali Storm-Wolf. But there was no hall in Karlsa, and no seat in it, empty or otherwise.

It would be Solveig's responsibility to remake her homeland in an image that honored her father and reflected herself. Her first task as jarl would be to form the world she would lead.

In the meantime, she would claim her title in the hall of her parents' dearest friends.

Everyone in Geitland filled the hall. They'd sacrificed a beautiful white stag and a great boar, and there would be meat and mead and bread enough for everyone.

When the servants had poured mead into every cup, Leif stood and raised his high. His expression showed his own grief, but his voice carried through the hall, strong and assured. "We come together today to honor our most valiant dead, Vali Storm-Wolf and Brenna God's-Eye. Though they were not of Geitland, they were always of us, and it is right that we pay them this tribute." His head dropped, and the hall waited in silence. When he brought his eyes up again, his expression had changed; he'd set aside his own sadness, at least for this public moment. Now, he seemed simply intent. "We were honored by their presence in our world. For years, we basked in their light. The gods were good to give them to us for so long, but they have called them home together. Drink now in celebration of their places at the great table of the Allfather!"

The hall erupted in a communal roar, and everyone drank. Solveig did as well, though the mead seemed to go sour in the salt of the unshed tears filling her throat. They drank and roared again, once for each of her parents, and then Leif raised his free hand and quieted the crowd.

"We also come together to begin our next journey, and it means to be a difficult one. Here in Geitland, we have great work do. We've reclaimed our home, but next we must reclaim our prosperity." He paused to let that roar fade out, and that mead get swallowed. He glanced at Solveig and offered her an encouraging, proud smile before he addressed the hall again. "And our friends in Karlsa must begin anew, with a new jarl to guide them. Today, we name that jarl."

Another roar, but it stunted and died oddly, as if a great hand had choked the throat of the hall. The people standing at and around tables began to shift as someone who warranted space, from respect or from wariness, moved through them.

Håkon stepped before the jarl's table. A week he'd been gone, and he looked as though he'd spent every second of it at war. He was filthy. His hair was matted, and his leathers were stiff with mud and blood. But he stood straight and strong and seemed unharmed.

He drew his sword and held it upright, before his face. Looking directly at Leif past that blade, he said, "I am Håkon Valisson. I challenge my sister, Solveig, now called Sunheart, to single combat. To the victor goes the seat of Karlsa."

He hoped to kill her, and he hadn't even looked her way. Solveig, still standing, set her cup down. "Håkon, no."

Finally, he gave her his attention, a mere shift of his eyes. "Do you refuse? Do you concede the jarldom?"

"Father meant me to have it," she said, not knowing if it was the right answer or an answer at all.

Håkon's ugly smirk told her that it he thought it the wrong answer. "And I think he was misguided. If you are afraid to fight me and lose, then I will spare your life. Only step away and allow me to finish the sjaund."

They both knew that she was a better fighter than he. He'd never bested her in any spar, and he'd never matched her kills in battle. "I won't lose, Håkon. I don't wish to fight you because I will kill you."

He laughed. "You speak as if you care, sister. Then step down. I am the firstborn son. It should be mine."

349

"You're not firstborn, Håkon, son or no. Thorvaldr was first. I am the eldest living. And Father named me his heir. I won't step down. Please don't make me fight you."

Her brother, with whom she'd shared many happy adventures in childhood, walked to the jarl's table. Standing against it, directly in front of her, he dropped his blade and pointed it at her chest. A low thunder of protest waved through the room, and Leif and Magni both threw their arms before her, between the point of her brother's blade and her heart.

The blade struck his target anyway, though it didn't touch her skin.

"Håkon, this is madness," Magni growled.

Håkon ignored his friend and kept his focus on her. "Fight me or step aside, Solveig. I challenge you."

Solveig dropped her head. Her brother demanded that she kill him or be killed by him. She didn't understand how this had happened, what had gone wrong in Håkon's mind to make this happen. What had she missed?

Whatever she'd missed, whatever chance there might have been to shift their story to a different path, there was only one answer she could give him now. She lifted her head and met his eyes. "I accept."

"I will be your champion, Solveig," Magni said at once. "I will fight him in your stead."

Her pierced heart broke at the love in his eyes as he made his offer. She forged a smile for him and set her hand on his strong arm. "No, Magni. I will fight my brother."

This was her destiny, her story, and she would tell it, no matter the anguish in the verse.

350

~oOo~

The sun had taken up its midafternoon position in the summer sky. In the wide circle before the hall, where, a year ago, an age ago, Solveig had watched a girl drape a garland over Magni's shoulders, Solveig faced her brother. The troubles that had vexed and consumed her mind the summer before seemed so silly and trivial now. So petty.

Holding her sword, which had been forged in Estland and given to her mother by her father as part of their wedding ritual, and her shield, which bore the mark of the God's-Eye, Solveig waited. She was dressed for battle; she'd even blacked the mask across her eyes.

Håkon was dressed as he'd been when he'd stormed into the hall. He held the sword that their father had presented to him on the eve of his first raid, and his shield bore the God's-Eye as well.

Behind him, Harald, a friend of their father, stood with fresh weapons and a new shield at the ready. She was glad that Harald had agreed to stand with Håkon today, and she bore him no ill will.

Behind her, Solveig knew, Magni stood with the same array. This fight was meant to go to the death, and they would choose their weapons as they needed them.

Could she kill her brother? She would have to. But could she?

When Leif called the fight to begin, Solveig hadn't found the answer. Håkon charged at once, meeting her on her side of the circle. He shouted and swung as if he meant to cleave her head with the first blow.

Solveig threw up her shield and blocked it. She came in with a low swipe at his legs, hoping to incapacitate him, but he jumped sidewise and evaded her blow. He came back again at once, going for her midsection this time, and she only barely got her shield in his way. He was trying to kill her. Without any qualms at all.

She was better than he—faster, more graceful, more intuitive, more experienced. But he was bigger and stronger, and he felt fury in his belly, when Solveig felt only sorrow. As they fought, she knew the truth. She couldn't kill her brother. It would break her mother's heart. In Valhalla, she would know, she would see, and it would break her heart. And Solveig's own.

Her only chance to win, then, was to mangle him so badly that he couldn't fight. It would be a humiliation for him, she knew, to be left alive and defeated, but better that than to add another body to the burial mound that had become of her family.

She began to attack with that strategy in mind, going for his limbs. When she opened his arm, he laughed, thinking she'd missed, and charged in again. She feinted and caught the tip of his blade along her side. A wound opened and washed hot blood, but it wasn't mortal, and the pain was nothing but noise in the background.

A strike to his thigh opened a gash and hobbled him briefly, but he steadied himself on the next blow, aimed again at her head. With her blade, she blocked it, and the side of his blade glanced over her cheek. She felt the skin gape and then ignored it.

He surprised her by tossing his sword away. When he picked up an axe, she spent a flash of thought to consider if she should change weapons, too. But this was her sword, given to her father by his friends, passed to her mother as they married, and kept safe for their child. Their legacy.

When he came for her again, he charged right at her upraised shield and buried his axe in it, as if he'd aimed for the shield itself. He roared and yanked back. His superior strength bested her, and she understood too late that he'd done precisely what he'd meant to do: he'd snatched her shield out of her hand.

He heaved it far away, into the crowd, unconcerned where the heavy oak might land.

There was another shield behind her, and she could sense Magni pick it up for her. But it was plain, unpainted. No longer would she have her mother's eye protecting her.

"Solveig!" Magni called in shock when she stepped into the center, away from the shield he'd offered. She ignored him; Håkon had turned back with a new weapon, and he'd made a critical error.

He still bore his shield, but he'd selected a spear. It made no sense; those two weapons didn't complement each other in combat such as this. She didn't wait to see if he had another plan she couldn't fathom. Instead, she charged and shifted, coming in at his side, forcing him to turn. When she had him facing the blaze of the lowering sun, she took advantage of that single flash of blindness and brought her blade down on his shield arm.

Håkon shouted, and his shield dropped to the ground. His hand was still wrapped around its grip.

Blood spouted from the stump she'd made, and Solveig hoped she'd put an end to this horror. But her brother roared and muscled his spear forward. She ducked easily and brought her blade down again, cleaving the spear in twain. Then, because she needed it to be over, she stepped close to the brother she loved and buried her blade in his side, aiming so that she would miss the parts inside him that would bring his death.

He fell gasping to the ground, blood pulsing from his arm and running from his side. He tried to rise and failed. Tried again and failed.

"Kill me," he grated at her. "End it."

"I love you, Håkon. We have had enough death in our family. I will not kill you."

The crowd was silent. Solveig could hear the lap of the incoming tide on the shoreline. She stayed beside her brother, not knowing whether to help him or to walk away. Her sword dangled at her side, dripping his blood. The pains of her wounds began to scurry out and make noise. Her head clamored.

His face a mask of sadness and determination, Leif stepped in and pulled her to the middle of the circle, leaving Håkon alone on the ground. "This contest is decided. Karlsa has a new jarl. Solveig Sunheart!"

The crowd cheered its approval. Into the cacophony, Solveig thought she heard a shout of outrage. She turned toward that sound and saw Magni seeming to fly toward her. Continuing her turn, she saw Håkon's blade strike Magni's shoulder.

Her brother had stood and collected the sword he'd discarded. Then he'd lunged at her. From behind. After the challenge had been decided. Magni had leapt into his way.

Håkon was no better than Tollak. A coward and a traitor.

Or perhaps he was simply a man who wished to die, and had trusted his sister to do it.

That understanding passed through her mind in a heartbeat, and she raised her sword to finish the fight as she should have in the first place. But another roar, this one higher-pitched, split the air and Agnar charged in. He carried no weapon, and even Håkon was too surprised to deflect the blows that Agnar brought with him. The younger brother punched and kicked the older, bellowing with rage. Håkon managed to take a step back, then lifted his sword as if he intended to use it.

Solveig blocked that treacherous blow with such force that Håkon lost the sword. It spun from his remaining hand and dropped to the ground.

Leif grabbed Agnar, lifting the raging boy off the ground and carrying him to safety.

Solveig brought her sword up. She stepped over Magni, who was hurt but not badly, and stalked to her brother. "I love you, brother. Always I will. And now I will give you your wish. I hope the gods find you worthy of Valhalla."

She brought her sword up in both hands and took his head from his body.

He made no attempt to evade the blow.

When his body fell, Solveig went down as well. She dropped her sword and sagged to her knees, and the grief she'd held in private for seven days, allowing only Magni to know, burst from her heart and soul. She knotted her fists in her brother's filthy, bloody leathers and screamed.

Strong arms enfolded her, and she heard the voice she loved best in all this world at her ear.

"I am here," Magni murmured, his voice strained by his own pain. "I am here."

24

The day after Solveig was named jarl of Karlsa, after Håkon was buried and left to the judgment of the gods, Astrid and Leofric laded their ships with their Mercurian army and sailed home.

Their intention, and Magni and his father's fervent hope, was to send Olga and the children back immediately on their fastest ship, in the narrowing slice of time left before winter churned the sea and made the voyage too dangerous. If they missed that chance, it would be summer before he saw his mother and sister again, before his father was with his wife and newborn daughter again.

It was a distant hope, requiring a perfect alignment of fortune, and yet Magni watched the shoreline every day from the moment the Mercurians left their shores, long before they could possibly have reached home, much less returned.

His father did the same. Often, they stood side by side on the berm and stared out at the sea. But neither could indulge entirely in the distraction. His father had his jarldom to make strong again. And Magni had Solveig to support.

Since the day of the sjaund, she'd been closed in a way heretofore unknown to him. Like rock—strong and erect, but rigid and cold. It was as though she'd blown all the expressible emotion from her lungs while she'd knelt at her brother's body, and then her chest had gone to stone. Not even he could break through that crust.

They hadn't coupled since the night before she'd killed her brother. Their physical wounds had been minor, only gashes to be closed, but the hurt in Solveig's heart and mind was severe. Too severe to accept comfort. Every night, they slept together, every night he pulled her into his arms and she lay with him as if she wished to be there, but she wanted nothing else. She even turned from a simple kiss.

He'd held her in the town circle while she'd keened and rocked. When she'd gone quiet, he'd helped her to her feet and taken her to the healer, where they'd both been tended to. They he'd led her to the little hut that they'd borrowed. She'd sought his arms that night; she'd clung to him for hours, until the dawn.

She'd risen then and had turned to stone.

He understood it, of course. The losses she'd taken in a single week would have hobbled nearly anyone. He knew that she, especially, would fear the destruction in her grief, if she let it loose. Brave as she was in battle, she'd always feared her own feelings most of all. Only recently had she begun to embrace them as strengths to be celebrated rather than weaknesses to be quashed.

A grief so strong it buckled the knees and forced tears to fall in a flood—only someone who'd mastered the wisdom of emotion might be expected to recognize strength there. Solveig was merely a novice. So she'd turned to stone and locked her feelings away. Every one of them.

To anyone but him, she appeared strong and well. Each day, she worked with the rest of them to restore Geitland, and each afternoon, she sat with Magni and his father, and they worked out the plan for the return to Karlsa—how they would get there, what supplies they would carry with them, how they would feed the people who comprised the population of the enlarged jarldom of Karlsa.

His father had steadily maintained that they should wait out the winter in the more temperate climate of Geitland and begin rebuilding Karlsa when the sun returned. Solveig had steadily refused to consider it. Karlsa was her birthplace. It had been her father's jarldom for more than twenty years, and she dishonored him, she insisted, with every day that she allowed it to continue as a wasteland.

Magni would go with her wherever she went, but he agreed with his father. Even in the warm nurture of summer, the people of Karlsa would struggle at first; to make something from nothing was arduous work, and to make something from ruin was twice so. To ask them to take on the task in a far northern winter seemed harsh to the point of cruelty.

He'd said as much, in gentler words, and had been answered with a cold so sharp and dense it transcended stone to become glass.

Today, his father had said it in harsher words, calling her foolish and reckless—and, worse, selfish. Her crafted composure had shattered, and she'd fled the hall.

For the first time in a long time, Magni hadn't followed or tried to stop her.

Now, he stood on the berm and watched the empty sea. Ten days had passed since Astrid and Leofric's farewell. In the event of a normal voyage home, the time to prepare the people and ship to sail, and a normal voyage back, ten days was when hoping to see a ship on the horizon shifted from a fantasy to a possibility.

He needed his mother. He was a man with a full score years of age, but right now, he needed his mother. Her wisdom would show him the way to pull Solveig back from the edge she teetered on.

"You should go to her." His father stepped up beside him.

"I know. But I don't know what to tell her. Always, I've known how to talk to her, how to reach her. Since we were small. But in these days, she's too far away." He sighed and spoke his recent thoughts aloud. "I need Mother."

His father chuckled sadly. "And I, my son. It tears at my chest to be away from her like this." He looked down at his hands, open and facing up, and was quiet. When he spoke again, he seemed almost to have moved away, so distant was his voice. "I have a daughter I've barely held. If they don't return until next summer…"

A northerly breeze, nearly frigid with winter, spun up and whipped their hair, and his father shuddered. "My days of raiding are done. When Olga and Disa are home, I will do as your mother has long wished and stay home. You will lead Geitland's raids."

Magni's mouth sagged, and Solveig took a step back in his thoughts. His father had always said that he would raid as long as he held the seat of jarl, that no jarl should send others to fight battles he would not fight himself.

"Don't step down, Father. I'm not ready." Magni heard his words echoing those Solveig had cried at her dying father, and his heart twitched, remembering the sorrow of that day. Not quite yet three weeks had passed since. So much had changed.

His father pulled him close and sheltered his shoulders under a strong arm. "No, Magni. I'll not step down yet. There is too much work to be done. When Geitland is strong again, and Karlsa rebuilt, when you and Solveig are wed, when the stain of Tollak is cleansed completely, then we three shall sit and talk about unifying our world." His eyes bored into Magni's. "I would give up my jarldom to a *king*, Magni."

If he wasn't ready to be jarl, he certainly wasn't ready to be king. "Father…"

His father smiled and let him go. "Thoughts for another time. The future will hold its secrets. Only the seers can know what will be, and they speak to us in riddles. So make of each moment what you can. Find your woman. Ease her and make her see." He turned back to the sea. "And I will wait again for my love to come back to me."

~oOo~

On his way toward the wood to seek Solveig out, Magni was surprised to encounter her on the path out from the trees, and to find her not alone. Agnar walked with her, hand in hand. Magni was struck by how much alike they looked, both with long blond hair, both of a height. Agnar hadn't yet filled into his grown form, but he would likely be unusually tall and broad like his father, as Håkon had been. For now, though, he was not much broader than his sister, and from this distance, it was as if Solveig walked along with her own reflection.

The same had been true of Solveig and Brenna.

Like a typical boy, Agnar shed his sister's affectionate hold as soon as he saw Magni. Brother and sister exchanged words, and Agnar tolerated a kiss on the cheek, then strode out ahead, passing Magni with a nod.

He, too, had been stoic and controlled since his burst of rage and grief on the day Håkon had challenged Solveig and lost. But Agnar had always been one who watched quietly while others conversed.

Magni met Solveig and reached for her hands. She didn't pull away. "I was coming to find you."

"Is there trouble?"

"No. Except that which you carry with you."

Her chest swelled and sagged with a sigh, and then she stepped closer. For the first time in weeks, she'd moved to him of her own wish. "I'm sorry. The things I feel…they make me weary."

"I know. Rest on me." He tugged lightly on her hands, and she came all the way to him. He enfolded her in his arms and held her snug against his chest. The shattering of her shield that had driven her from the hall earlier had left her vulnerable and soft.

They stood on the path, in the dying summer sun, while a nascent winter breeze puffed around them.

Another chest-swelling sigh left Solveig on a hum. "You and Leif are right." She mumbled against his tunic. "We should stay the winter here. It's folly to think we could rebuild enough of the town before the snows set in to keep us fed and sheltered. Even a single longhouse would be a feat, and still we would have no stores of food but what we carried from here. All I could think of was restoring my father's legacy and doing him honor, showing him his faith in me wasn't misplaced. But it was. I'm a terrible jarl already."

Magni pushed her back and scowled into her upturned face. "Enough. You worry about dishonoring your father? You do so every time you doubt yourself. If we'd sailed to Karlsa and all starved, perhaps then you might be fittingly remembered as a weak jarl, unready to meet her role. But what you've done instead is heard wisdom from people you trust and heeded it, despite your own strong desire for another path. This sounds to me exactly how Vali led. My father has always said Vali Storm-Wolf was hot-blooded but too wise and mindful of his responsibilities to lead from his impulses."

Her eyes flooded, and tears rippled in their corners. "It hurts to hear him and my mother spoken of in the past. As people whose stories are ended."

He brought her close again, nesting her head under his chin. "I love you, Solveig Valisdottir." She accepted the new name people had given her and would carry it before her like the honor it was, but Magni knew that, now that it had been replaced, she cleaved in her heart to her father's name.

Leaning back again, she took his hand and held it with the palm up. Her fingertips grazed the white lines that laced his skin, all the scars from all the oaths they'd made in blood. To keep each other's secrets. To keep faith together.

"I love you so," she whispered and bent her head to kiss his palm. Mingled with the touch of her soft lips, he felt the wet of the tears she'd let fall.

~oOo~

The ship returned the very next day—not one of the Mercurian ships, but another as familiar and more beloved. His uncle's trading ship, which docked in Geitland harbor regularly.

Magni and his father, and Solveig and Agnar, hurried down the pier before the ship had been moored, and his father barely waited for the plank to come down before he ran up shouting, "Olga! Olga!"

Magni watched his big, mighty father lift his tiny, but no less mighty mother and the daughter she carried into his arms, and he felt a warm caress over his soul. He understood that love, how deep it delved, how far it reached.

It was a joyous but somber homecoming. Of course they'd learned of Vali and Brenna's deaths, and of Håkon's, before they'd left Mercuria, but it was now, when the family was as reunited as ever it could again be, that the loss fully flowered.

363

On the ship, Magni's uncle, Mihkel, stepped forward to the top of the gangway, each hand clasping a girl's: Tova and Hella. They stood as still as carvings, one fair and the other dark, one tall and the other small, their blue eyes wide and uncertain.

Solveig dropped to her knees on the pier and lifted her hands, a welcome and a plea. The girls shook loose of Mihkel and came down, weeping before they reached their sister, who held them close and stroked their heads.

"I'm here, I'm here," she crooned.

Someday, Magni would find the way to show Solveig this side of her: the way she was with her siblings, and with all people who needed her, how she was the strength they lacked, how she gave it to them until they could reflect it back. She felt small and selfish when she needed, but she never refused to give what she had when others had need.

His parents walked down the gangway together, hand in hand. His father had taken Disa and tucked her cozily on his chest, against his neck. Magni had a powerful feeling of familiarity, like he remembered the feel of his father's neck against his face. He couldn't possibly; in his earliest memories, he was a young boy running through Geitland after goatlings, not a swaddled babe. But the feeling remained, potent enough to squeeze his heart.

His mother stood before him, looking fresher than she usually did after a long sea voyage. She smiled up at him and raised her arms, and Magni dropped into her embrace, setting his forehead on her slim shoulder. "Mother."

"My boy. How I have missed you, *kullake*."

"And I you. But we are together again, and safe."

She pushed him back and gazed again into his eyes. "But not complete." She turned to Solveig, who'd stood again and had her sisters and Agnar close around her. Magni's mother reach her hand out. "Solveig, my heart."

Solveig nodded, blinking. Magni saw her pull more strength up over her shoulders like a mantle. Then she clasped his mother's hand. She said nothing, but when his mother drew her closer, she came, and she let herself be enclosed in maternal love. She set her forehead on a slim shoulder, and Magni's heart thumped.

~oOo~

They were wed four days later, at the edge of the wood. To keep safe as a legacy for their firstborn child, Magni presented Solveig with Sinnesfrid, the sword his father had given his mother upon their marriage, and that she had given to Magni when he began to raid. Solveig presented him with a newly forged sword, gleaming and glorious, the blade etched with the runes of the wolf, the raven, and the sun.

They observed all the rituals of their people, even racing through the dark toward their little hut, with the whole town at their heels, and throwing Solveig's bridal crown out to the raucous crowd, but the day's celebration and manifest joy was edged with solemnity as well. It marked as many endings as beginnings: the end of a long era of prosperity, the end of a summer, the end of legends. They faced a hard winter and then, in Karlsa particularly, a long summer building up a renewed world from the ashes of its ruin.

Everyone felt the shadow of the past and the loom of the future dimming the sun of Magni and Solveig's beginning.

But it was a beginning, and Magni would not let Solveig forget it.

He woke alone in his marriage bed while the night was dark. The candles had burned to stubs and guttered out; they'd fallen asleep in a sweaty tangle and hadn't dowsed them. Once the shield around her emotions had shattered, Solveig had been open to him again in bed and everywhere.

The hut was small, a single room, and Solveig wasn't in it. Gods, he hoped she hadn't gone off to the wood on their wedding night. That was a story that didn't need telling.

Magni stood and pulled his breeches on, grimacing at the stickiness across his belly and thighs. They'd fallen asleep without cleaning themselves as well. He pulled the lace snug but didn't tie it, and he went out to find his wife.

His wife. He grinned at the word. For long years, he'd wanted little more than what the day before had brought him: Solveig, mated to him before the gods.

She sat just outside the door, on a chair that Ingrid—the woman who'd lived here to start her married life, and whose life had ended dangling before Tollak in the hall—had perched on warm days while she'd spun her wool. The wheel was gone, but the chair had been left.

Solveig sat there, wrapped in a fur. Her loose hair waved over her shoulder and settled, in a curl, at the crook of her elbow.

The night was cold; his mother had returned not a moment too soon. Shivering, he took the few steps between them and crouched at Solveig's side. "Where are you, my love?"

A lopsided smile tipped her head toward his. "I am here. I heard a wolf and wanted to listen."

He kissed the temple she'd offered him. "Do you think it's your father?"

One shoulder lifted. "I don't know. I only know it made me miss him more sharply, and my mother, and I wanted to feel that. I don't know why."

Magni had never experienced such a loss, though he'd seen others grapple with it. He had a thought about why she would seek more pain, but he kept it to himself. His father and his mother, both, had taught him that sometimes wisdom meant keeping one's insights to oneself.

"I feel as if they're closer to me when I miss them more," she whispered.

And that was what he would have said. He brushed his hand over her back. "Would you like to be alone?"

She shook her head, and Magni leaned closer. They rested on each other like that and let the night continue to age.

Then he, too, heard the yip and howl of a wolf. It seemed nearby.

"I want to do them honor. I've wanted nothing in my life more than to be worthy of them."

He'd told her often how much he valued her, how worthy he believed her to be. He knew she believed that he spoke true, but that was not the same as believing that his word was fact. So he knew that there was no need, or value, in telling her, again, that she was worthy.

She hadn't spoken those words to hear that they were true. She'd spoken them to him, who kept her secrets, because he could be trusted with them. She'd spoken them to put her worries into form so that they could be contended with.

What she needed, what she'd always needed, and what he'd always been, was an ally.

So Magni didn't tell her again that she was worthy. Instead, he said, "I will help you. I am here."

EPILOGUE

SUNHEART

THE WOMAN SHE IS

Hella eased Solveig from her crouch and helped her to sink back onto the mattress. Even linens sodden from the effort of the work she'd just completed were a soothe to her now, as her child, her son, took his first gasp of the world's air and bellowed it out.

Frida set the child on her chest, and Solveig lifted her arms, which seemed made of iron, and held him close.

Magni leaned his head on her shoulder. Her two men, lying on her. "He is spectacular. This is the future we've made."

She kissed first the warm blond head of her husband, and then the slick, dark head of her son. Another pain struck her, but Frida had told her to expect it, so she pushed it away, as she'd been instructed, forcing it from her body as she'd done while her child had made his way into the world.

When it had passed, she relaxed and turned her head on the pillow to see through the open window and beyond this room in the jarl's quarters of Karlsa's great hall. The eerie glow of midnight sun warmed her eyes. Her child had been born at the solstice, as she herself had been.

"Magni," Hella murmured, in her low, kind voice, of a mature timbre already. "It's time for the life cord to be severed."

Knowing his role, Magni stood. Solveig felt him near her softening belly, felt movement around her, but she didn't look away from the window or turn her heart's attention from the warm, quiet boy lying on her chest. Magni was biting the life cord, severing the physical bond between mother and child, and releasing this tiny, precious boy into the world. It made her feel sad and lonely for her parents. A pain two years old surged up in her heart. Her eyes began to itch with the salt of tears, and she shut her lids to ward them away.

"What should we call him?" Magni asked, at her side again.

The boy stirred and fussed, and Frida said, "Hella, help Solveig put him to the breast. Remember how I showed you."

Hella had been apprenticed to Frida for a few months, since she'd had twelve years. Solveig's youngest sister had no thirst for battle; she preferred to soothe pain, not to cause it. Following her mentor's directive, she came to the other side of the bed and helped Solveig sit up more fully. Then she settled the boy at Solveig's bare breast. He stopped complaining at once and even seemed to smile.

When he latched to her, Solveig felt a bolt of sensation move from her breast to her womb and straight to her heart, so powerful she gasped and jumped. "Oh," she whispered. "Gods."

Frida nodded sagely. "That is the bond you feel, Solveig, forging between your hearts, stronger than the life cord Magni tore with his teeth. The bond between a mother and her child—none can sever it, not even with the sharpest blade or hottest fire."

As her son took his first meal and her sister and Frida tended to her needs below, and Magni sat enraptured at the bedside, Solveig studied the boy she'd made. He was beautiful and strong, with thick limbs and full cheeks. His hair was dark and thick, like her father and Magni's mother. What color his eyes were, she couldn't yet say; so far he'd barely opened them.

She hadn't considered what they might name their child; in fact, she'd actively prevented Magni from discussing it with her. After a year full of painful losses—her parents, her sister, her brother, her home—they'd spent nearly two years rebuilding. Karlsa was a town again, one that yet smelled of sawdust and tree sap but was beginning to thrive, and they were making plans to embark on their first new raid under her leadership the next summer. As always, they would raid with Geitland, now with Magni in the lead. Leif meant to make good on his promise to Olga to hang up his sword and raid no more.

They would sail back to Frankia, with a party enriched by the peoples of two lands which had once been four and would someday be one.

Paris had not yet been taken by any raiding party. The stories of the unbreachable circles of walls had grown into legend. Solveig knew now that her own legend had not waited her in Paris; it had grown in the soil of her birthplace. But Paris was the next great prize, so there they would go.

Not she—this boy would still be at her breast, so she would stay and nurture him while she led her people at home and Magni led them in Frankia.

She'd felt superstitious, planning so much for the future, and would not risk catching her child in that web. So she'd refused to plan for the child. Only in the past few weeks, when she'd grown so large she could barely walk in a straight line, had she allowed Magni to begin to feather a nest and her people to bring the gifts they so wanted to offer the babe.

Certainly, she'd had no intention of naming the child before he arrived.

But here he was. And he was perfect.

Magni brushed his fingertip over the silken skin of their son's arm. "I would like to call him Ingvar."

He wanted to give their son a name derived from the word *warrior*. She turned and looked at him, waiting until he brought his eyes from the child to her.

"And if he doesn't wish to fight?" She was determined that her children would find their own paths in love and in life. Even should she and Magni choose the right path for them, as her parents had for her, they would chafe against the chains of it, as she had for too long.

"One need not draw blood to be a warrior. One need only fight the battles they face with courage and heart."

"You speak like your mother."

He smiled and kissed her shoulder. "One of the greatest warriors I know. The other is *his* mother. He cannot help but bear a warrior's heart."

"Ingvar." She rolled it around in her mouth, tested its taste and shape and sound. "Ingvar Magnisson. It's a good name." She picked a tiny hand and pressed it to her lips.

~oOo~

A few weeks later, Solveig sat in the hall and smiled as Leif and Olga cooed over their grandson, who was nearly swallowed up in his grandfather's cradling arms. Disa, their daughter, toddled between her parents, trying to cover Ingvar in sloppy kisses.

Solveig felt Magni approach before he was there, and she shooed a cat and turned so she could lean against him as soon as he straddled the bench and sat at her back. He folded her up in his crossed arms and nosed the neckline of her underdress to the side so he could kiss the birthmark on her shoulder. "They love him already," he breathed over her skin.

"Of course they do. He's perfect."

"Father would speak with us about stepping down, if we're ready."

When Leif stepped down and made Magni jarl, their holdings would combine, and they would have far too much land under their control to be merely jarls. They would be king and queen of something new. She looked over her shoulder. "Are you ready?"

He barely hesitated before he shook his head. "My father still wants it. He only feels he *should* step down, since we'll be raiding with the next summer, and he'll not join us. But I'm happy to lead the raids for us all. I want more seasons of battle before I will feel ready to lead as a king." He kissed her shoulder again, this time letting his tongue out to trail along her skin, up her neck. "What do you think?"

"I don't want it, either. Karlsa is only beginning to stand tall again. I have work to do here, in my father's place. And I'm still learning as well."

"Then we'll stay in Karlsa and my father will stay in Geitland. He'll be glad."

"And Olga?"

"She has him home, away from the raids. She's already glad." His hands skimmed up from her waist and found her breasts. "He just fed, yes?"

"Yes," she purred. The intention in his voice excited her as much as the touch of his body. Ingvar had been born weeks ago, but they'd not coupled since before the birth. It was difficult with a babe between them always.

"He has my parents' complete attention. My sister's, too. We won't be missed." A hand dropped from her breast and settled between her legs, gathering up her hangerock until he could reach her body underneath. "Come with me, wife. I've missed you."

She nodded, and he leapt from the bench and pulled her back to their rooms. No one in the hall could have mistaken their intention. In fact, several horns of mead were lifted as they passed.

~oOo~

Tova swung her sword with a feral grunt. It struck Agnar's shield, and he turned the shield on an axis over his arm, trapping Tova's sword arm and forcing it to twist awkwardly. Then he stepped inward and tapped the blunted point of the practice sword against her chest.

"Now you are dead," he said and stepped back. He touched the point of the sword to the ground and affected to lean on it, as if bored.

In the past two years, Agnar had become a man. He'd filled out into a man's size and shape, and he had a woman he meant to wed. He'd shown himself to be a talented carpenter and carver, and he meant to be a great warrior as well.

He lived each day seeking to excel in all his endeavors. He lived to make his life worth the lives of their parents.

They never spoke of Håkon, but it was clear that Agnar had taken their brother's accusation to heart. Doing so hadn't stunted him, however. It had made him flourish.

Tova stomped a foot and turned to Solveig. "He's too big! I cannot fight him!"

Agnar laughed at his sister. "You mean to fight only children and dwarves?"

Solveig stood up and came into the training area. Ingvar napped comfortably, slung across her chest, and she didn't wish to raise her voice and disturb him. When she was close enough to Tova to speak quietly, she said, "Your brother is right. You must be prepared to fight men bigger than you. Sometimes much bigger. Imagine a shieldmaiden facing our father in battle." A cold finger strummed Solveig's spine; it was said that a young shieldmaiden had wielded the spear that had killed him. She wished she'd thought of another example.

"Father would have sliced her in twain." Tova said, growling with pride for him. She'd heard the stories, too, but she was too young to believe that her father might have been struck down by a single shieldmaiden. Solveig, however, knew that it hadn't been a spear that had killed her father. His heart had been dying before the spear had pierced it.

She took a calming breath. "That is my point. I would have you live to fine old age, Tova, so you must learn how to fight any opponent, no matter their size and their strength. You have strengths and skills and talents of your own. Use them."

Holding Ingvar close with one arm, she bent and picked up her sister's dropped shield. Tova used a battle shield in her training; she wanted the size and weight of it to become part of her bones.

It wasn't the shield of her father's time, with the mark of the God's-Eye. Solveig had chosen colors of her own: the same red that had been her father's color, but instead of a red eye on a field of sky blue, she'd chosen a red field bearing a simple, solid circle of gold at the center. The sun. She was Solveig Sunheart, after all. Jarl of Karlsa and daughter of legends.

She handed the shield back to her sister. When Tova had it, Solveig stepped behind her and pushed Tova's shoulder down and in.

"Always know the field around you. Front, back, and sides. Never expose your tender center. Protect yourself neck to thighs. Keep your shield facing your opponent, and brace it well."

"Those are Father's words," Agnar said. He'd come near. "I remember…" He trailed off. "You say them just the same."

She remembered. She would always remember. With her son sleeping against her body, Solveig found herself rocking in place, as she now often did, whether she held Ingvar or not. It wasn't much to begin a dance she'd been taught long ago, with her father's arms around her. She closed her eyes and began the steps. "Use your blade from the side. Put your blade where his is not. Step to the side and push in." She opened her eyes and sought Tova. "Follow me, sister. Do what I do. I learned from our mother and father, and they'll not lead you astray."

~oOo~

"I think his eyes are blue. Like yours." Magni peered into his son's face. "But…"

Solveig leaned in close and pulled the swaddling cloth down a bit. Ingvar's eyes shifted to her. He seemed irritated by all this staring his mother and father were engaged in. "But there are brown lines through the blue. Like my mother's, but both his eyes are the same."

Their son's eyes had been a dark blue, like Magni's, for weeks, but lately, as the summer finally gave over to winter, his eyes had changed. The blue had lightened to a color more like hers, and the dark had left traces behind.

"Not brown—dark gold," Magni corrected. "Like rays of the sun. And in the sunlight, his eyes seem green." Ingvar wrinkled up his face, effectively ending their study, and sought his fist to suck. Magni held him up to her. "He's hungry."

Solveig sighed and unfastened a brooch from her hangerock. "He is *always* hungry. We have cows who give less milk than I." But she smiled as she took her son and settled him to his meal. Nursing him was one of her favorite things in her life, no matter that it meant she spent half that life half undressed.

As he often did when their son fed, Magni simply crouched before them and watched. "You are so beautiful, Solveig. My heart aches with fullness for you and Ingvar."

Her heart ached, too. Always. For her losses, yes. She still mourned her parents, and Ylva and Håkon as well. No day yet had passed that she hadn't thought of them and hurt.

But every day, she ached with gladness and joy as well. She had Magni and Ingvar. She had Agnar and Tova and Hella, who were growing into their own lives and flourishing into their futures. She had Karlsa and the esteem of its people. Though the territory had nearly doubled, they were yet a small world—only ten score souls close enough to attend a thing when she called it, and only a few thousand souls more beyond that range. But they were hearty people of long winter, and they had survival pumping through their veins. Together they had built up what had been destroyed, and they had made it live again. Soon, they would thrive again.

And one day, she and Magni would unite their whole world under one shield.

She had made her story, and she would add verses through all her life. She was Solveig Sunheart, born of legends, with a saga of her own.

Wild love flared through her, and she reached out for Magni. He caught her hand and held it close. A frown creased his brow. "Are you well?"

379

"I am. Magni, thank you."

He cocked his head, and his frown eased into a curious tilt at the corner of his mouth. "For what?"

"For waiting."

The curious tilt became a smile, and he bent his head, resting his forehead on their linked hands.

"Always."

THE END

Susan Fanetti is a Midwestern native transplanted to Northern California, where she lives with her husband, youngest son, and assorted cats.

Susan's blog: www.susanfanetti.com

Susan's Facebook author page:
https://www.facebook.com/authorsusanfanetti
'Susan's FANetties' fan group:
https://www.facebook.com/groups/871235502925756/

Freak Circle Press Facebook page:
https://www.facebook.com/freakcirclepress
'The FCP Clubhouse' fan group:
https://www.facebook.com/groups/810728735692965 /

Instagram: https://www.instagram.com/susan_fanetti/

Twitter: @sfanetti

The Northwomen Sagas Pinterest Board:
https://www.pinterest.com/laughingwarrior/the-northwomen-sagas/